THE SHADES DRIPPED RED

ALSO BY PETER KURTZ

Black Jackknife: A Nick Montaigne Mystery

Debut novel in the Nick Montaigne detective series. Praised by *Publishers Weekly* and *Midwest Book Review*.

ISBN 978-1-7324789-0-9 (paperback)
ISBN 978-1-7324789-1-6 (ebook)

Evergreen Dreaming: Trail Tales of an Aging Hiker

An environmentally-aware memoir of backpacking adventures on the Appalachian and Continental Divide trails. Praised by *Publishers Weekly*.

ISBN 978-1-7324789-0-9 (paperback)
ISBN 978-1-7324789-1-6 (ebook)

Bluejackets in the Blubber Room: A Biography of the William Badger, *1828-1865*

A nonfictional biography of a 19th century trader, whaler, and Civil War storage ship. Acclaimed by Civil War and maritime historians.

ISBN 978-0-8173-1779-9 (hardcover)
ISBN 978-0-8173-8645-0 (ebook)

THE SHADES DRIPPED RED

A NICK MONTAIGNE MYSTERY

Peter Kurtz

Longitudes Press

Published by *Longitudes Press*, Cincinnati, Ohio

Library of Congress Cataloging-in-Publication Data:
Kurtz, Peter Scott
The shades dripped red: a Nick Montaigne mystery
p. cm.
1. Crime fiction 2. Detective fiction 3. Murder mystery 4. United States
5. Ohio 6. Kurtz, Peter
Library of Congress Control Number: 2023916474
First American Paperback Edition, 2023

ISBN-13: 978-1-7324789-4-7 (paperback)
ISBN-13: 978-1-7324789-5-4 (ebook)

Cover art by Alex Saskalidis, 187designz (Facebook: 187designz)

Back jacket photograph of author by Lynn Kurtz

This title issued as print-on-demand for reduced waste.

For Avi, Rory, and Isla with love

This is a work of fiction inspired by a true crime. Certain scenes or language may be disturbing to some readers. Names and places are products of the author's imagination or are used fictitiously, and any resemblance to locales or persons, living or dead, is entirely coincidental.

Prologue

Stillness settled on the neighborhood and the pink sheen of the early-spring sun faded into violet twilight and the wheel rubber crunched the chunky, walnut-sized gravel. The car slowly swiveled rightward into the school parking lot until it stopped in front of a green chain-link fence surrounding six forest-green tennis courts, their white lines now barely perceptible in the dying light. The car was the only one in the lot. Its engine grumbled like a large feline. The headlights switched off but the car continued to grumble.

The few tennis players from early in the day had canned their yellow balls, shoulder-holstered their rackets, and trickled homeward. Silence now replaced the earlier frenzy of hand-clapping, shouts, cheers, moans, and staccato announcements from the vicinity of the large six-lane running track and expansive athletic fields at the other, distant end of the school. Also now silent were the periodic and slightly ominous snaps of the starting guns, which had punctuated the leafy neighborhood like giant wet towels slapped against metal.

The car engine now became quiet, too.

In front of the car...beyond the tennis courts...beyond intervening Dahlia Lane...about a dozen forehand shots away...was Morning Glory Lane. The car was angled so a perpendicular line drawn from its front bumper would connect to a modest brick ranch house on Morning Glory. This particular house was in keeping with most other homes in the neighborhood of Turnham Green, one of a dozen upper-middle-class neighborhoods on the south side of the small city of Springbrook: three and four-bedroom homes on quarter-acre, manicured lots.

The address of the house on Morning Glory that the car now faced was one-fifty-seven. Had not several houses and a line of silver maple and red oak trees obscured things, the man in the car would have seen fleeting movements behind the lit kitchen window of 157 Morning Glory. With binoculars, he would have been able to make out the facial features of Donald and Irene Moore. They had just finished their evening meal and were cleaning up.

Police would later surmise they had eaten steak and corn-on-the-cob for dinner.

The door of the car opened and the man stepped onto the gravel. He pushed the door softly until it clicked shut, as if trying to harmonize with the crackles of the crickets in the trees facing him. He rested his right hand on the hooded frame of the side mirror. In his left hand he gripped the handle of a small black briefcase. His fingers opened and closed around the black plastic handle—like a donor in a blood bank might fist, then relax, in order to increase circulation. He tilted his head upward to penetrate the distance with his eyes. As he did so his eyes narrowed and his mouth opened slightly. The corners then curled into what might be called a grin.

It was a short walk from the tennis courts to 157 Morning Glory. There was only one route to take without crossing private property: exit the gravel lot, turn left on Forsythia Street, pass Dahlia on the left, then left on Morning Glory. Pass one house on the right, then…

The man walked. When he reached Morning Glory, before turning left, he saw the bright white glow of headlights about one-hundred yards ahead, at the end of Dahlia, a street that dead-ended at a small copse of woods. The glow then flicked off and the veil of darkness returned. The man sucked in a deep draught of air.

"Kind of you," he whispered throatily.

He turned left onto Morning Glory, a straight lane entirely dark but for the yellow glow of several houselights and lights from street lamps that hung over the curbs like carved, grotesque gargoyles. His eyes fixed on the second home on the right. As he walked, his head adjusted only slightly. As if his head turned on a swivel that had been dialed in to that one house. The only house that mattered. As if he had singular and pressing business there. Although he had remained in the shadows during his brief walk, sufficiently distant from the street lamps, his caution had been unnecessary, since he had seen no one. The only sounds that evening hour were two agitated dogs from the far end of the street, and the rat-a-tat of china from the first house on Morning Glory. He heard no sounds from that second house. The Moore home.

He paused at the end of a short, straight driveway that sliced through a dark-green lawn. Through the small kitchen window left of the front door, positioned just beneath a ruffled valance curtain with tassels that looked like splintered teardrops, he saw the head of a middle-aged woman. The head was tilted downward. It had compact, black hair. As it was now dark and the house's front light had not been switched on, the eyes would not be able to see him approaching.

He walked slowly but deliberately down the drive, wet from a sudden, late-afternoon shower, toward a curved walkway. He turned right at the walkway, glanced briefly at a round cluster of pachysandra ground cover, passed directly in front of the kitchen window while observing the still-lowered head, and stepped onto a small front porch that held several tastefully arranged pieces of redwood-stained furniture. He stood still in the shadows while facing the front door. Once more, he inhaled deeply. He breathed in the comforting aroma of fresh wood mulch and chopped fescue.

Hanging on a hook on the door was a small wooden sign. In pink and green pastel letters, surrounded by the tiny petals of cheerful flowers, read:

Spring into Spring!

The man—his lips clamped shut—cocked his head toward the street, just once. He started to lift his arm, then thought differently and took a step backward. He craned his neck to see if the head on the opposite side of the kitchen window was still lowered. It was. It was a head that, within a very short time, would look very different.

Content with the scene and with the purpose for which he had come, the man stepped forward and lifted his hand toward the front door of 157 Morning Glory.

PART ONE

Chapter One

"Remember, Sharon, I want to watch the evening news! Sharon? Sharon?"

Vern Wister, red-faced and cross-eyed and wearing his baggy evening sweater with the mallard ducks flying across a dime-sized cigar-juice stain on the front, was on his second "Vodka Vernon." He did not often watch television news, preferring to get the latest crime information through print media, but tonight he wanted to get "juiced" for what he hoped would be a juicy story about what had happened that day outside of nearby Conyers, Georgia.

He first heard about the murder-suicide on the radio while tidying up things at the downtown Atlanta office of MONTAIGNE-WISTER. Vern's senior partner Nick had entrusted him with grabbing the office reins and cleaning up old paperwork while he and longtime gal Annette "Annie" McBain were luxuriating in a long-awaited ski vacation out West. They had invited Vern and Sharon along, more out of politeness than anything else, but the married couple had never skied, both were considerably older and circulated in a much different social set, plus Vern knew how much Nick appreciated his "private time" with Annie, so they had declined Nick and Annie's gracious invitation. Despite his enthusiasm for being what Nick called "The Man" while he was absent, Vern seemed unable to allay periodic feelings that shifted in a murky zone halfway between gratitude and resentment.

Okay, yeah, it's nice to run things while Hefner is off playing with his snow bunny—and that leather sofa in the office anteroom has given me some damn good afternoon nap time. But shit, he treats me like his secretary sometimes.

Vern wanted action. Something to dangle in front of his boss. Maybe that thing over in Conyers could produce a case for Montaigne-Wister. There was still a motive to uncover. As Nick always told him, *there's something rotten in the state of Denmark.* Although Vern never could understand the connection to Denmark. And he was afraid to ask Nick.

His thigh-rub audible from his navy corduroys, he headed to the tilted, tomato-sauce-stained recliner; grabbed the remote, and collapsed in it with a moan. After the picture appeared, he pushed the MUTE button to stifle those *goddawful* commercials he hated so much. Once the talking heads appeared, he pushed the MUTE button for sound.

It was the top story—for once, in Vern's mind, actual *breaking* news.

"Okay, Sharon, here it is!" he yelled into an adjoining room. "Don't say anything for the next ten minutes!"

Male Anchor: *Metropolitan Atlanta is reeling today after a vicious murder and suicide in Conyers.*

Female Anchor: *That's right, Tom. Atlanta police are still baffled as to why an elderly man casually approached a visiting Chinese businessman, shot him in the head, then turned the gun on himself.*

(Vern belched, then shifted his hefty butt to the edge of the recliner seat.)

Male Anchor: *Here's KJOH reporter Ashley Cohen-Jones on what happened.*

(Vern turned up the volume.)

Cohen-Jones voiceover with images: *Police say at about 1:20 p.m. today a man at Imperial Incorporated in Conyers approached visiting Chinese businessman Xi Lao Bing, shot him in the back of the head, then shot himself in the temple. The murderer has been identified as sixty-eight-year-old Bertram Cabot Ramsey of Marietta. Imperial employees say he was lingering suspiciously outside the Imperial lunch room, then approached Bing and several Imperial executives from behind after they emerged. Authorities are still trying to determine why he targeted Bing.*

(The screen showed tall, dour-faced cop standing next to young, attractive, serious-looking woman holding microphone)

Cohen-Jones: *I'm standing with Police Lieutenant James Kwiatkowski of the Atlanta Police Department. Lieutenant, what do you think compelled Bertram Cabot Ramsey to murder Xi Lao Bing then kill himself?*

Kwiatkowski: *Thus far we have no clues as to the killer's motive and we're still investigating.*

Cohen-Jones: *Lieutenant, are you concerned about repercussions from China? After all, relations between China and the U.S nowadays are very tenuous.*

Kwiatkowski: *I, uh, can't speculate on what, uh, if any, difficulties this may present regarding international relations.*

Cohen-Jones: *Have any federal officials contacted you yet?*

Kwiatkowski: *Contacted me? No, not me, personally. Whether or not anyone else in the department has been contacted, I, uh, can't comment on that.*

Cohen-Jones: *Are police ready to classify this murder as a virus-related hate crime?*

Kwiatkowski: *That's a legal thing and I'm not going to get into that.*

(Vern snickered.)

Cohen-Jones: *Have police determined yet if Bertram Cabot Ramsey has any history of mental illness, or perhaps connections with the so-called "alt-right"?*

Kwiatkowski: *I'm sorry, I don't caveat that.*

Cohen-Jones: *One last question, sir. Bystanders at Imperial claim the killer muttered certain cryptic words. He supposedly said "Maraschino cherry" before shooting Bing. What do you think he meant by this?*

Kwiatkowski: *We believe the killer was mentally deranged. Therefore, we can only guess at what his twisted mind might have been thinking.*

Cohen-Jones, as she turned to camera and tilted her head: *That's the story so far here in Conyers. Back to you, Tom.*

Man Anchor: *Ashley, what exactly does the lieutenant mean when he says he doesn't "caveat" that?*

Cohen-Jones: *Tom, I have no clue, I'm guessing it's a military expression.*

Female Anchor: *Ashley, this is Leslie…have you been able to interview anyone at Imperial Incorporated to learn about Xi Lao Bing and why he may have been targeted by Ramsey?*

Cohen-Jones: *Yes, I've made efforts to speak with Imperial representatives. So far I've hit a brick wall, and I'm guessing they were advised to stay mum. My guess is that Bing was here on a sales visit, but I can't confirm that. As to why Ramsey targeted him, several Imperial employees—who have chosen to remain anonymous—insist that this must be a COVID-related hate crime.*

Male Anchor: *Oh-kay, thank you Ashley.* (He shuffled papers and turned to Leslie.) *Well, Leslie, it's been quite a day, indeed.*

Female Anchor: *And still so many unanswered questions.* (She shook her head and looked down at papers on desk.) *Stunning news, just horrible.*

Male Anchor: *Yes, indeed. Well, in other news, the COVID-19 death toll has reached a new milestone. The CDC reports that...*

Vern clicked off the TV. He gulped some more vodka then pushed back the recliner backrest until he was almost horizontal. Banging sounds came from the basement. *She must be doin' the laundry.* He revisited the news story in his mind.

Strange, sixty-eight-year-old. Why so much hate? Umm, pot roast, smells good. Yeah, Ruh...Ruh...From Marietta? Where Bristows live. What kinda gun, wonder. Imperial Inc? Wha' kinda products? (BANG BANG!) Does she have to make so much noise! Bet lotsa blood. Masks red too. Frickin' virus. Need shot. Don't wanna but gotta. (BANG!) Come on, Sharon! Umm...Sixty-eight years? Hell, older 'n me. Lotta hate there. And from Marietta. Nice area. Bertram...somethin'...Ruh...RAMSEY! Yeah. Did news say Ramsey has family? Kwiatkowski, what a turkey. Just tell enough, Kwiatkowski, don' overdo it. Spit and polish, soldier. HA! Ashley cute. Keep Nick on guard. What day is it? Tuesday. COVID hate crime. Poor Asians, U.S. scapegoat. Dumbshits everywhere. Wha' he say, 'international relations'? Hell, international incident! Somethin' else there. Lurch playin' cute. Visit tomorrow. Pat will have somethin'. Always does. Then call Nick. Yeah. Could be somethin'. Somethin' else there...

BANG!

***

Vern's lightly rusted Nissan Sentra reached Lee Avenue a little after 8:00 a.m. A man of habits, he would visit the office before heading to police headquarters. Then grab a morning paper and review the details of the previous day's Conyers fireworks. And what better place to review than in the dark, cloistered, mahogany-paneled office of Montaigne-Wister? *Gotta ease into the day. Too much commotion too early for a man like me isn't healthy. A hot cuppa breakfast blend and a fat, old-fashioned chunk of newsprint is on the agenda.*

He'd called Pat McCauley not long after the story aired. Pat was one of the few on the force who actually had a decent relationship with him and Nick. McCauley didn't scoff or find ulterior motives. A solid man, a family man, too, with kids nearly the same age as Vern's. In fact, Luke McCauley and Vern's boy Frankie had briefly played on the same select baseball team—until both got burned out playing forty-plus games each summer and went back to playing regular ball. *Nick had said it was a good decision. Yeah, baseball and wheels. No wonder Pat and Nick get on well.*

Vern sailed his Nissan into the Quick Stop Food Mart on Metro Parkway, filled the gas tank, snagged a sausage-and-cheese biscuit and copy of the *Atlanta Journal-Constitution*, then headed toward the downtown office of Montaigne-Wister. Once there he whipped up a carafe of Seattle's Best and plopped into Nick's swivel chair to plunge into the story. *Let's see if they screw this up like they did Richard Jewell.*

MURDER-SUICIDE IN CONYERS
Police baffled after man shoots Chinese businessman then self
By Dawn Knight
Journal-Constitution

Yeah, cops always "baffled." Least AJC didn't screw up the who-what-when-where-why. Congratulations.

He slowly sipped from his favorite mug—the one with a green "TULANE" that Frankie had given him—as his misaligned eye pupils scanned one column of the story then the next. In so doing he managed to pluck out a few more items of interest than what he'd gotten from Cohen-Jones the previous night. Ramsey was a widower and retired engineer. Lived alone, significant in view of the suicide. Avid hunter according to neighbors, so probably comfortable with firearms. Never mentioned China that anyone was aware. Bitched about COVID and facemasks, according to neighbors, but nothing too much, no raving, no anti-government diatribes. Only one problem with the law, a DUI which happened twenty-four years earlier. Nothing else.

And nothing on Xi Lao Bing, other than he was from Harban, China and was visiting Imperial for his manufacturing company, Kibitsu Consolidated of China. As with Cohen-Jones at KJOH, the paper casually mentioned "virus-related hate crime" while remaining safely non-committal.

Vern spun around in the chair while shaking his head, then waddle-walked to the carafe for a mug fill-up. *Somethin' rotten somewhere in Denmark.* He mulled over the paper's identification of Ramsey being a former engineer. *Wouldn't have worked for Imperial or they'd o' said. Maybe a competitor?* He poured another mug, spilling part of it onto the marble counter. *Dammit!* He tore off a paper towel and mopped the liquid, wiping also the rim of his mug, then shuffled over in his floppy corduroys to Nick's small collection of compact discs neatly stacked on a shiny walnut bureau. He fingered each disc, lined up according to the date Nick added them: *Chico Hamilton, Sonny Stitt, McCoy Tyner, Pharoah Sanders, Freddie Hubbard, The Car…The CARPENTERS? Annie musta snuck in that one.* He waddled back to Nick's swivel chair

and propped his white Reeboks on the desk. As he stared at
Nick's cherry humidor in front of him, he thought about the
paper's mention of Ramsey's DUI. Then about his own
alcohol-related traffic offenses. He mulled over what might
have brought on Ramsey's DUI. *Onset of a later problem?
I guess even engineers have problems like us ex-cops.
Monster at the bottom of every bottle. Wonder what his
story is.*

Vern glanced at the clock on the wall. *Shit, Pat's
waiting.* He shot up suddenly from the chair, banging his
right knee on the heavy desk and hurling a flurry of
expletives. On the way to the door he stopped suddenly,
rushed back to the desk, opened the lid of the cherry
humidor, and withdrew one of Nick's red-wrapped sticks of
cinnamon chewing gum.

***

The precinct was filled with people by the time Vern
arrived. He noticed that only a few were wearing
facemasks, and none of them cops. On the way to Pat
McCauley's office, located at the far end of a brightly lit
rectangular room filled with about thirty or so desks, he
passed the office of Lieutenant James "Lurch"
Kwiatkowski. Inside, one man sat alone, as if waiting for
the lieutenant. This man wore a pair of neatly pressed blue-
green slacks and a checkered shirt with the collar open. He
looked about thirty years old. He appeared very tall, well
over six feet, with neatly parted blond hair and a long face
that exhibited a blank expression. His legs were crossed
and both hands rested on one thigh. Vern noticed that
others in the room, mainly cops, allowed their eyes to
wander the stranger's direction, and glanced at him when
passing by Kwiatkowski's open door. They were the kind
of curious glances you might give a film star in a
restaurant, intended to be casual and cool, but were instead
awkward and intrusive. Vern had experienced this odd

precinct behavior a few times as a cop in Philadelphia. He knew the man was one of either two things: FBI or CIA. Probably the latter, judging from his clothes.

He came to McCauley's office, tapped lightly on the open door, and stepped inside. At a large desk covered with white papers, a nameplate reading DETECTIVE PATRICK A. MCCAULEY perfectly centered on the front edge, sat a genial-looking man in his late fifties. He had a boyish face; one might call it a "baby face," with a small, thick-lipped mouth and twinkling blue eyes. The only features which might give away his age were some small wrinkles at the corners of his eyes, and a head of fluffy, snow-white hair.

"Mister Wister, long time no see! Come in, come in!"

Vern sat in a rigid wooden chair in front of the desk.

"How's your boss James Bond doing?" McCauley asked with a mischievous smile.

"Ha!" responded Vern. "You wouldn't mean Nick, now, would you? He and his cougar girlfriend are out in Colorado skiing. His annual romp with the winter jet set."

"I'm not surprised, he looks like he might be a skier. And is he still driving that hot, turbo, green-and-black Porsche?"

"You're being too polite. Nick doesn't ever *drive*, he *thrusts*. And not just behind the wheel."

McCauley chuckled then leaned forward and asked in a conspiratorial tone, "And are you *borrowing* his rig while he's gone?"

"I sure am, I just did eighty miles an hour in a school zone. C'mon, Pat, you kiddin'? Nick probably monitors the odometer. Not my style, anyway."

"Yeah, didn't think so. What a character. Do me a favor. When he gets back, ask him to call me. I wanna ask about a Corvette Blue Flame Six. Dad has one in his garage collecting dust, and I need a mid-life crisis."

Vern laughed. "I hate to tell you, Pat, but mid-life is in your rear window, and there's no reverse gear."

"Wise-ass," McCauley dryly responded with a grin.

He stood up and walked to the door, closed it quietly, and returned to his desk.

"Okay, you're here to ask about that tragedy over in Conyers, right?" he asked rhetorically, his baby-face turning serious. "Vern, you know I can't tell you anything. I enjoy receiving a regular paycheck. Why don't you tell me what you know? Maybe I can safely lead you in the right direction. Safe for you, and me."

Vern smiled. "Pat, the only information I have is what television and print news have told me and everyone else. Ramsey was a widower, lived alone, ex-engineer. A DUI ages ago. No treatment for mental illness. And Bing…is that his last name, or first? I know the Chinese are different," he added, then paused with a concerned look. "Well…*Bing*, anyway…with Kibitsu Conglomerated in…"

"Uh, *Consolidated*, Vern," McCauley interrupted.

"Oh, yeah, okay…Kibitsu *Consolidated*…out of Harban, China."

McCauley closed his eyes and nodded. "Okay. Okay. I won't confirm or deny that. Emphasis on the latter. Anything else you need? Nice seeing you, then!" McCauley laughed.

Vern started to say something, then held up a fat finger, as if he suddenly remembered something. He stood and walked to the door and peered from the edge of the glass door window. "You seen him yet?" he asked.

McCauley joined him at the door and glanced toward Kwiatkowski's office. "Yeah, he's waiting for Lurch."

"They're dressing more and more casual these days," Vern said with a patronizing tone. "And lookin' younger, too."

"They like fresh blood fresh outta college. Naïve kids with psychology and criminal justice degrees who wanna see the world and show their patriotism. I tried steering Luke toward the Peace Corps, but peace is boring when your hormones are jumping."

Wister and McCauley took their seats again. "Anyway," continued McCauley, "that China connection has lotsa folks worried. Not surprising people like *him* (he nodded toward the suit in Kwiatkowski's office) are down here. Never know with China. It's a helluva tinderbox these days."

"So…so…" Vern started cautiously, before throwing any pretense of dignity out the window. "Pat, you gotta have some more. I'm hopin' to have a big birthday present for Nick when he gets back. This murder-suicide might lead somewhere for us. Talk to me, brother," Vern implored.

McCauley smiled, as if he understood Vern's dilemma but wanted to milk his anxiousness a bit longer.

"Okay, bud, but it's gonna cost you."

McCauley dropped his head as if in thought. Vern leaned forward.

"Well," McCauley continued, "I guess I can safely tell you without getting into trouble that…and I'm going to use the word 'press' here, but you know what I mean…the press *seems* to be playin' it like a hate crime. And the natter is—again, *off the record*—both the mayor *and* governor have talked to, uh, certain individuals. Probably precipitated by the Washington suits, including Skippy over there," he said sardonically, while nodding toward the fed in Kwiatkowski's office.

"So, as I don't have to tell you, the press is not getting much. There's a lotta worry by certain people about repercussions from Beijing. I know it sounds crazy, but that's the scoop. This Ramsey, who I think has no mental health history, and no criminal record—again, *off the record*—in the press's mind, he's clinically nuts and a paranoiac who blames China for starting the worldwide pandemic. So, Vern, what would you do with someone like this? What would you and Nicky investigate? I'm not telling you, remember, I'm asking you."

Vern began chewing one of his knuckles. "Well…um…we'd look into social media activities. Hoping for evidence of salvos left on Facebook…Asian, black, Jew, homophobia, misogyny…hates PETA…um, anything like that."

McCauley said nothing but continued with his baby-faced smile.

"Then, uh, if the powers can portray him as a sick loner who went off the deep end in crazy violent America, who's mad about the virus and not part of some anti-China plot, the easier it will be for Washington to deal with any anger. Right? They're concerned about Chinese-American trade relations. Probably don't want an international incident like what happened with North Korea and that kid from…where was it? Cincinnati, who was taken hostage, then died after being tortured. The flip side of that scene, you know. They're, um, scared to death of the United Nations gettin' involved, and politicians tryin' to score political points…"

Vern's voice trailed off. Pat continued smiling while offering nothing. The two men stared at each other for several seconds.

"Okay, anything else, Vern?"

"Yes. What do you think Ramsey meant by those last words of his? 'Maraschino cherry'?"

"Like Lurch said last night. 'Mentally deranged.' He said 'maraschino cherry,' Bing spun around, Ramsey shot him in the face. Anything else?"

"No, Pat. But I think we're in agreement…about what's going on here. Aren't we?"

"I can't answer that. Let's just say…I won't deny anything you've said."

Vern continued with his speculation. "To me, Ramsey sounds nuts. And he probably does to the majority of America, which is by now numb to random acts of gun violence…yeah, *used* to that stuff."

McCauley added, "'Remember, China has a totally different culture. They might perceive things differently.

And, so, the feds wanna make sure certain things don't happen. Trade relations are the order of the day. That's not an official Atlanta police position, that's *my* position. You, uh, know what I'm saying?"

Vern stared at McCauley. He knew Pat's hands were tied, but he'd been hoping for more than just a replay of what the television station and newspaper had reported. He didn't know what. But he had a veteran cop's clue that something more might be there, a motive other than pandemic-related *hate*, that might involve other people, and which might lead to a case for him and Nick.

He would soon get what he wanted.

He pulled out a large yellow-stained handkerchief and wiped it across his forehead, which was now several shades redder than normal. *Need a stiff drink.*

McCauley smiled. His shoulders and head began to softly shake, as if he was trying to stifle laughter, as if he knew exactly what Vern was thinking.

"Don't look so dejected, Vern buddy! I told you I might have a bone you and Nicky could chew on, didn't I?" He gave a self-satisfied chuckle. "But it's gonna cost ya!"

"Yeah? What's it gonna cost?" asked Vern disgustedly.

"Well, now, let's see," McCauley began in a teasing manner. "I want the keys to that lime-green Porsche. Just for a couple days. Before Nicky gets back. Deal?"

"You're *nuts*, McCauley!" he burst out while stuffing the handkerchief back in his corduroys. "First off, I can't *get* the keys, unless I wanna break into his apartment, which I ain't gonna do!"

"Calm down, calm down! I'm just *kidding*! You don't owe me anything."

Vern glared at him. "So what gives? You said you might have something. What bone is it that you have?"

"Well, it's just a tiny wishbone," McCauley began, "but maybe there's a little meat hanging on it. Never know, never know."

Vern leaned forward again, turning his good ear toward McCauley. "Okay, talk to me."

"Well…I guess I can spill this, since it has nothing to do with this case. But it turns out that Ramsey isn't exactly a total loner. He has family still. A daughter. She lives here in Atlanta. Name's Amber. I wouldn't be surprised if she popped into this precinct later today."

Vern lifted his eyebrows. "Well…better than nothing. A daughter, huh? Hmm."

"Yeah. But that's not the only thing."

"No? What else?"

"Well…this is separate from what happened in Conyers, so I'm safe. But…it seems that Ramsey also had a sister. A twin sister. And with Ramsey dead, the twins have been reunited. So to speak."

Vern relaxed his eyebrows.

"Reunited? I assume your playful circumcision means…"

"*Circumspection*," McCauley corrected.

"Huh? Oh. Yeah. Your playful circumspection…means she's dead, too. Okay, so *what*? My curiosity is aroused. How does that figure into things?"

"Well…tragedy must run in that family. The reason I say 'tragedy' is that both she—Ramsey's twin sister—and her husband were murdered. A double homicide. Way up there near Lake Erie or Lake Huron or wherever the hell Ohio is."

"Yeah? Really? Why? Who killed 'em?"

"Nobody knows. No one has yet solved the case."

Vern sat like a wax statue, his mouth open like whenever he and Sharon watched *Dateline NBC*.

"Okay, well…Nicky and I will jump on the internet and check out the fed LEEP database."

"I don't think so."

"Why?"

"The murders happened a while ago. Like, twenty-five years ago."

Chapter Two

By the time Vern finished his one-on-one with McCauley, the precinct was crammed with people. Cops were wisecracking at the coffee machine, interviews were being conducted, uniformed and plainclothes transients were shuffling down the narrow aisles. As he approached Kwiatkowski's office, he saw two extremely gaunt women wearing tight skirts and pump heels, their faces caked with colored cream, one with protruding cheekbones, mouth a frozen frown, tombstones in her eyes. He recognized these meth-addicted "lollipop girls" from occasional afternoon jaunts to "trick city," near the donut shop he liked to frequent. Scenes like this depressed him. They brought back disquieting memories of his days as a bunko cop in Philly, memories that his private investigative work had only partially displaced. He was glad to be soon exiting the grubby beehive he now found himself in.

As he shuffled passed Kwiatkowski's office, he saw Lurch leaning forward with his arms folded on his desk, his face displaying a scrunched sneer, as if he'd just uttered, "What the *hell* are you talking about?" The elegantly dressed government man calmly sat in the same position as earlier, his chair at a strategic angle to face Kwiatkowski, while also able to see anyone who might walk by or enter the office. His folded hands still rested on his crossed legs, his face was still resolutely blank. But he must have caught Vern approaching from over his shoulder, because he turned his head a few degrees in time to make brief eye contact with Vern, then follow his figure several feet down the aisle. Although this contact lasted mere seconds, in the days that followed Vern would remember it.

Just before turning the corner and heading for the opaque-glass exit door, Vern did a double-take. He saw a plain-Jane-ish woman about forty years, with caramel-colored hair that was swooped into a high ponytail, wearing wire-framed oval spectacles, a light-gray sweater, black slacks, and clutching a small gold purse. She seemed lost, as if searching for someone, turning her head in little jerks, as if trying to locate the correct desk nameplate. Vern noticed puffiness around her eyes, as if she'd been crying recently. He was almost positive this was Amber Ramsey. He was tempted to approach her to offer sympathy—and even took one step in her direction—then thought, *No, not the right time or place. Might be awkward. Poor thing.*

Vern's head was a tornado of thoughts and images on the drive back to the office. He replayed his conversation with Pat McCauley many times. His main thought, one that was beginning to gnaw on him, centered on McCauley's thunderbolt of the unsolved double-homicide of twenty-five years earlier. One of the reasons Vern, as well as his boss, had become private investigators was to jump into the dark well of seemingly unsolvable mysteries. Nick was a big reader, as was Annie, and when both were not working— Nick at Montaigne-Wister and Annie at her downtown travel agency—they were curled up with a good Hubert Selby or Ian Rankin novel (and when not, as Vern had so often embarrassingly discovered, curled up with each other in bed or on the couch…like the day early in their relationship when he almost caught them *in flagrante delicto* in the office after popping in with a surprise box of jelly donuts).

Vern on the other hand preferred the immediate titillation of television true-crime stories, like those he and Sharon viewed on *Dateline NBC*, *Unsolved Mysteries*, and *America's Most Wanted*. Vern's favorite true-crime documentary concerned the brutal serial killer who secretly enjoyed dressing up and taking photos of himself wearing garter belts, silk panties, stockings, and spiked heels. He was eventually caught, but only after he'd fashioned a web of lies while hiding behind a convenient image of q masculine, upstanding, patriotic and God-fearing Army major.

The other story that intrigued him were the assassination killings of three members of a Maryland family, including a quadriplegic boy, killed by a hired hit man to free up trust fund money. The case became a First Amendment cause cèlébre, going as high as the U.S. Supreme Court, only because the hit man had learned all his tricks from a book. And a book written by a middle-aged woman who lived in a trailer park and used the pen name "Rex Feral," no less. *Ain't America grand* were Vern's mordant thoughts. *Kill a family, have a book written that makes a million.* His captivation with this crime related not so much to the sordidness and violence, nor the identity of the author of the book, but by the psychology behind the motivations of the perpetrators. The kinky Army major was obviously a psychopath. A *sicko*. But how could any sane individual plan to kill, for monetary reasons, an entire family, including a disabled boy…and what kind of person would, also for monetary reasons, permit himself to be an *instrument* of death?

Vern was as yet unaware that he would soon be colliding with shocking similarities to both of these true-crime cases.

A *wishbone* to *chew on*. Those were McCauley's words. Well, Vern was already chewing away. He had a lawman's intuition this twenty-five-year-old cold case—this *wishbone*—might indeed have some meat for him and his partner. If there *was* meat, was it rotten yet, was it substantial enough to pursue, and if so, how could he and Nick access it? Maybe Nick would have some ideas. It might mean another road trip to Ohio, which wasn't exactly on Vern's bucket list. *I'll be damned if I'm heading back there. But hell, it's the only way. Hopefully whatever Peyton Place we have to shack up in has a better newspaper than that last Ohio town had. That rag was a joke. A decent steakhouse would be nice, too.*

***

The phone call couldn't have been more opportune. It came right as Vern was maneuvering onto I-85.

"Vern? Nick here. Have you burned down the office yet?"

"Nick! Hey, what's up, daddy-o! Say, how's Telluride? Man, have I got…"

"Yeah, can't talk long, Vern, we're getting' off the plane now. Cut the vacation short. Will tell you 'bout it. Anyway, headed to Annie's soon, then I'll swing by the office a few hours. Will see you there. Or maybe we can do Gilly's."

"Yeah, right, sure Nick. Let's do Gilly's."

"Superb. Say a late lunch, one-thirty or so?"

"See you then. And there. See you then-there. Ha! Man, have I got…Nick? You still there? Nick?"

Vern stuffed his cellphone into a pile of used tissues in the car console. Both hands on the wheel, he began slapping his thumbs against the rubber while accelerating. The timing was perfect. He could hit the office and maybe print out a few pages before meeting Nick at Gilly's. The egg salad sandwich Sharon made could stay in the office fridge. Gilly's was now on the agenda, and Vern's saliva glands went into overdrive as he thought of the veal parmesan he would soon be enjoying…with Nick, as always, picking up the tab. Vern wondered if Annie would be there, too. He enjoyed her company, she was "easy on the eyes," and she was a good buffer between him and Nick, who (depending on his mood) could be either genial or abrasive. The fact that he'd had to, for whatever reason, cut his winter vacation short might contribute to what Vern called "one of Nick's black moods." Annie would be a safeguard for any critical comments aimed at Vern. But another safeguard was Vern's recent talk with McCauley. Vern couldn't wait to fill in his boss.

As he approached the familiar glass door emblazoned with MONTAIGNE-WISTER, Vern noticed something that he hadn't seen before. Some of the letters of their firm name were obscured by something white, as if a giant bird had swooped by and splattered its droppings. He got closer and saw that it was white paint. Some vandal had deliberately sprayed over the middle letters so that only the letters "MON" and "STER" appeared. He stood in front of the door shaking his head. As a cop in Philly, Vern was accustomed to petty criminals and punks regularly spewing out the epithets "fuzz" and "pig," and earlier in his career he regularly heard "honky" from ghetto blacks. They came with the territory. But he'd since risen a little, and damned if he had to once again have to deal with such blatant disrespect. *But "monster" is a new one. Very clever.* He mulled over his and Nick's recent cases, recent scrapes that might have pushed some pissed-off punk toward this vandalism. The only thing he could come up with was that Atlanta kids were now starting to feel the effects of the COVID lockdown and needed to let off steam. At this he smiled. *Nothin' personal.*

He popped inside and, knowing that Nick would be arriving home earlier than expected, did some quick housecleaning. He threw away all the old newspapers he'd accumulated, tossed out any fridge food over a week old, dumped the cigar butts into the trash can and wiped the ashtrays clean, vacuumed the crumbs that had spilled onto the sofa and between the pillowed seats, rearranged Nick's *GQ* magazines according to their dates, and restocked the office humidor with fresh cinnamon gum. Unfortunately, he didn't have time to clean the paint off the door, but he hoped his boss would understand.

Then he logged into their shared PC to see if he could locate anything on the murders of Bertram Cabot Ramsey's sister and brother-in-law. McCauley had given him the names "Donald" and "Irene." Their last name was "Moore." Donald and Irene Ramsey Moore. It happened in Springbrook, Ohio. Twenty-five years earlier. Vern figured this would be around 1995. Double homicide. Unsolved.

Vern glanced at the computer clock. It was already ten after one. *Shit, only twenty minutes. Ten minutes to Gilly's. Gotta bolt in ten minutes.*

He punched the names into Google: *DONald and ELAINE MoOR SPRINgPorT*. He got a bunch of photos and recent obituaries but nothing else. Then he realized her name was "Irene," not Elaine, and the town was "Springbrook," not "Springport." He also managed to correct the spelling of "Moore."

He tried again.

DoNALD AnD...

"Caps Lock, you idiot, Caps Lock!"

He tried again.

DONALD AND IRENE MOORE SPRINGBROOK.

"Bingo-bango!"

Vern gazed with captivation at the search results. The first entry was a link to a Facebook page. Its heading read "Baffling Double Homicide – Donald and Irene Moore, an Engineer and…" The second link led to a Reddit feed. This heading read "Who Killed Donald and Irene Moore – 1995 – Reddit." They were the only two immediate results related to the homicides. All the others were unrelated.

Vern clicked on the Facebook link. It took him to a list of unsolved mysteries in Ohio, one of which contained the names Donald and Irene Moore. It was merely three curt sentences with a few basic facts. The only facts Vern hadn't already gleaned from McCauley were Irene's profession—nurse—and the exact date of the murders: April 15, 1995. Ten people had given the Facebook story thumbs-up "likes," and two had submitted comments. One comment simply said "Interesting fer (sic) sure!" The other comment was from a woman who said she had once worked with Irene at the local hospital.

Vern clicked the Reddit link. This led him to a page with the heading "Unresolved Mysteries." Similar to the Facebook page, the Reddit result was absent of any substantial facts concerning the murders. However, at the bottom of the page, in light blue letters, was a hyperlink address. Under the address were the words "Springbrook Daily News Journal Observer-Tribune." Someone had posted a link to a news article.

Vern checked the time: a quarter after one. *Five minutes!*

He clicked the link. His head swam as he stared in wonder at the result. It was a digital image of a black-and-white photocopy of the front-page story of the April 19, 1995 edition of the *Springbrook Daily News Journal Observer-Tribune*. The title, splashed across the top of the page in bold print, read:

POLICE MUM ABOUT SLAYINGS
Double Homicide Shocks Neighbors

In the middle of the page, next to the sub-heading, was a crude map that showed the location of the Moore home in relation to the main thoroughfares of the region. Next to this map was a larger graphic: a photograph of the murder scene: the front, outside of the Moore house. It was a plain-looking, brick, ranch-style house with a roof that had a slope almost flat. The front middle of the house had a small porch, but most of the porch seemed bathed in shadow. One small, three-paned window was centered above the porch. One large deciduous tree stood in the front yard about twenty feet in front of the porch. A white garage door and concrete driveway were on the left, the drive partially obscured by a white police cruiser that was parked on the side of the street. The police cruiser was in the foreground of the photo and seemed to dominate the scene. Obviously, the photographer wanted to convey the impression that something very bad had recently occurred behind the walls of this house.

The one word that might best describe the home in the photo was "modest." There was nothing fancy, nothing gaudy, nothing ornate, or even moderately decorative. It was an unaffected, pragmatic structure. Whoever lived here certainly believed in simplicity. But at the same time, the house had an oddly squat and flattened look, like a partially deflated air mattress. The tree in the front yard, and those few backyard trees whose tops rose above the house, had not yet bloomed. There were no people in the photo. Other than the jarring image of the police cruiser, the photo elicited a feeling of gray, late-winter blankness. "Deadness" might be more accurate.

Vern inhaled deeply. He felt frozen, glued to the story and photo that shone from the computer screen. After thirty seconds of mesmerizing scrutiny, he cleared his throat and began looking around absentmindedly. His mind eventually cleared, and he tapped the proper buttons to print out this single newspaper story. He then hurriedly grabbed the printout from the office print machine, quickly folded that day's copy of the *Atlanta Journal-Constitution* and stuffed it in the back pocket of his baggy corduroys, and whisked out the recently vandalized door.

***

By the time Vern wheeled his car into the parking lot of his and Nick's favorite Atlanta restaurant, the lunch crowd was dying out. Both men preferred it this way: less clatter and clutter, more apropos for discussion of serious business. No sign of Nick's rig in the lot, so Vern might have time to get a quick Vodka Vernon before his boss arrived. He locked his Nissan and lumbered across the parking lot, snarling "*Sonofa*—!" after his shoe sole caught a used, melted wad of bubblegum, then walked into the familiar tunnel with the dark-green canopy whose front had a large, scripted "Gilly's" splashed on it. Vern noticed Gilberto had recently added a humorously awkward, lost-in-translation slogan just below the name: "My Place is Your Home!"

He entered the dark interior and stomped past the large aquarium, past the line of portraits of autographed Atlanta celebrities and, without waiting to be seated, found a booth toward the rear of the main room. The Gerry Mulligan Quartet version of Rodgers and Hart's "My Funny Valentine" was playing. Within seconds a waiter appeared. He was wearing a baby-blue facemask over scruffy whiskers, hoop earrings in both earlobes, and his rolled-up sleeves revealed black tattoos on both forearms.

Who hired this guy? thought Vern. *Captain Kidd?*

"Yeah, I'll have a Vodka Vernon," Vern ordered before the waiter had a chance to speak.

"A…vodka…*what*, sir?"

"A Vodka Vernon," repeated Vern. "A martini with vodka instead of vermouth. Just tell Chet behind the bar, he knows what I drink."

"Yessir," the waiter replied blushingly.

Vern pulled the newspaper out of his pocket and laid it on the white tablecloth next to the butter knife. From his shirt pocket he pulled out the printout of the Moore murders news article and unfolded it, laying it on the table in front of him. His stomach fluttered as he tingled with anticipation while waiting for Nick to arrive. His boss always appreciated Vern's proactive approach to things, and Vern knew it. While he may not have Nick's investigative acumen, nor his coolness under pressure, Vern always created a solid base for their pending case constructions. He wondered what Nick's response would be to the Conyers tragedies, and he especially anticipated his reaction to what Vern had garnered from the McCauley meeting, his near bump-in with Amber Ramsey, and his plunging into the Reddit feed. It would be soon.

"Here you go, sir, one Vodka Vernon," the waiter mumbled behind his mask as he set down Vern's drink. "That's an interesting combin—"

"What the hell's *this*?" Vern barked. "An olive?"

"Uh, yessir. Chet must have forgot, so I took the liberty of—"

"I hate olives!" He tried to lift the olive from the glass but it kept bobbing away from his fingers.

"I'm so sorry, sir, here, let me get you a fresh drink," the waiter said as he nervously grabbed the glass from Vern. "Sorry sir, I'll have Chet fix another one, this time no olive."

"Yeah, thanks."

Vern had just started to read the news article when he felt a presence. He looked up toward the restaurant foyer and saw Nick. He looked like a statue, standing tall and straight, with his head tilted back and his chin in the air. He was wearing a light-gray, three-piece suit, the silver tie knot abnormally large, and his black hair was greased back even more than usual. At that moment he reminded Vern of an attorney who'd stepped onto the courthouse steps, had delivered a sententious statement to an eager crowd of reporters, and was anxious to reach a waiting limousine below. A cross between JFK Jr. and F. Lee Bailey.

The two made eye contact. Nick whirled slightly to respond to a waitress's comment, smiled and mouthed a few words, then walked toward the table.

"Good to be back in hot 'Lanta," said Nick dryly as he slid into the booth.

"Seriously? I thought you guys were having fun out there with the Kennedys, or Lindsay Vonn, or whoever skis out there these days."

"Vern, good to see'ya," Nick tossed in as an afterthought. "Well, yeah, we were having fun till my back gave out again. Thus the early departure."

"What, did you slam into a tree or something? Take a bad spill?"

"No, nothing like that. The skiing was all jake. Like a dream. And the town of Telluride is nice. It's in a box canyon, so we were snug as two bugs in a rug."

"What then? A rogue elk?"

"Let's just say the lodge rooms were very comfortable. Annie and I had a few late mornings. Guess I should have stretched more in light of all the…er…activity."

Vern's eyeballs enlarged as he stared penetratingly at Nick. Suddenly, the waiter arrived with Vern's new drink.

"I'm so sorry, sir," he began, his hand trembling as he set down the glass. "I'm new here and—"

"That's okay," muttered Vern peevishly.

"—I'd like to apologize and say—"

"Don't worry pal."

"—and say I truly—"

"Sure, no problem."

"—want to say if you need anything else—"

"How 'bout a drink for my friend here?" interjected an exasperated Vern.

"Glenlivet, please," Nick jumped in, "on the rocks."

"Certainly sir. I'll be right back. And let me just say—"

"It's okay, buddy, just get the drink," Vern cut him off.

Vern shook his head as the waiter skedaddled. "Sheesh, who the hell is Gilberto hiring these days? I need to plunk down bigger tips at the bar."

"What was *that* all about?" asked Nick. "Did he use vermouth instead of vodka?" Then Nick felt the urge for a familiar dig at his partner. "Vern, gin with vodka isn't a proper drink. You should at least add wine to make a Vesper."

"Look, I don't make fun of your Glen…whatevers," replied Vern testily.

The two investigators now properly reacquainted, they continued to make small talk. Nick discussed Annie and Telluride. Vern shared news about Sharon's recent diabetes diagnosis and son Frankie's efforts as a freshman at Tulane University. They ordered their food, Nick choosing trout meunière and rice pilaf, Vern selecting a club sandwich and Saratoga chips. Then they got down to business.

Nick reached across the table and picked up the *Atlanta Journal-Constitution*. He unfolded it and scanned the murder-suicide story for twenty seconds. Then he picked up the computer printout.

"Haven't had a chance to read that yet," said Vern. "What you think of the *AJC* piece?"

Nick's forehead creased in a look of concern. He continued to read the printout.

"Uh…I'm sorry…Vern…this is interesting." He looked up. "I'm sorry, what did you say?"

"I asked what you thought about the *AJC* article. About the Conyers murder-suicide."

"Already read it." He paused and returned his attention to the printout. "Yeah…I already read it online. Terrible."

Nick's forehead creased again as his eyes burned into the printout.

"This is fascinating," he said, as if talking to himself. "Fascinating."

"Really? Heck, I wanna read it too!"

"Sure…sure Vern. Hang on…I'm…almost done."

Vern adjusted his position in the booth as the waiter brought their food. Nick shook his head and handed the printout to Vern.

"Fascinating," he said again.

"You wanna tell me about it, Sherlock, so I don't have to read it?"

Nick pulled his plate closer to him. He placed his napkin neatly across his lap. He took a sip of his Glenlivet, adjusted his bulky tie knot, then picked up a lemon wedge and drizzled it across the fish. Then he cleared his throat and finally looked up at Vern, right as Sarah Vaughan's husky voice began diving deep into the chords of "Lullabye of Birdland."

"Fascinating. Okay…here's the story, Vern. This…" he halted and leaned over to double-check the names…"Donald and Irene Moore…could not have been more unobtrusive. A childless, middle-aged couple, forty-eight and forty-three years of age, I think—an engineer and a nurse—are gunned down for no apparent reason one Saturday night in their quiet suburban home in the normally peaceful town of Springbrook, Ohio. She was found in a separate room from her husband. Shot *once*, in the *back of the head*." He quickly glanced at Vern. "Remember that important detail.

"He—Donald Moore—is also shot once, in the back of the head. *But*…he's in the den, in a chair, at his computer." He placed a fluffy forkful of rice into his mouth and looked at Vern.

"Professional hits," said Vern.

"Yes. That's what it sounds like, on the surface. And that theory is bolstered by the fact that *nothing was stolen*. Also by the fact that none of the neighbors heard any loud noises on the night in question."

"Suppressor," said Vern, wiping a spot of mayonnaise from the corner of his mouth. "Definitely contract killings. Saw a few of those in Philadelphia."

"Well…you would think," replied Nick, drizzling more juice on his food. "But get this: relatives say the couple always locked their doors at night. But on *this* night the front door was *unlocked.* And police saw no sign of a break-in."

Vern's head bobbed up and down. "Yeah…yeah…that is weird. Hey waiter," he called, "another round o' drinks here please. And remember, no olive."

Vern turned to Nick. "Okay…okay, so…so we got clean hits on this couple, but the two are in separate rooms oblivious to what's gonna happen to them. So…so…someone had to either already be in the house, hidden, and snuck up on them…or it was someone they knew. Someone they allowed in the house. Like, a neighbor visiting. Or relative. Such as Bertram Cabot Ramsey."

"Right. That's what's so fascinating, and also frustrating. Someone hiding in the house is a long shot. But if it was a hit man—and it sounds like it was, based on the crime scene and absence of gunshot noise—why would the couple have let him in the front door? A hit man would have been a stranger, in which case they'd have never allowed him in, let alone turned their backs on him…*literally* turned their backs on him."

"You say 'him,' Nick. But it could have been more than one person."

"Possible but doubtful. Contract assassination killers usually work alone. First, they're loners by nature. Second, they like simplicity, and it's too messy to involve another personality in planning, much less execution. And third, they would have to share their 'wages,' quote unquote. No, I think it was one person. Probably male. Although I *have* heard of hit *women*. No double standard for murder."

"Interesting, Nick. Yeah, they might have let their guards down for a stranger who was female. Given her the run of the house, so to speak…like I do with Sharon. Hey! A hit woman posing as a realtor or interior designer!"

Nick smiled. The waiter placed their drinks on the table. Vern, feeling warm and rosy from the alcohol and the conversation, winked at him. The waiter's eyes squinted.

Montaigne raised his glass to eye level and peered intently at the liquid.

"There's also one other possibility. Though farfetched."

"Okay," began Vern. "And what might that be, Sherlock? Humor me."

"A murder-suicide."

"What?! But...but..." stuttered Vern, his forehead scrunching, "they would o' found the gun next to him!"

"Not necessarily. Supposing this...Donald...arranged something to make it *look* like murder. Eh? He engaged a confidante to carefully *remove* the suicide weapon. Maybe gave him or her a warped type of advance blood money to enter the house later. Hence the unlocked door."

Vern relaxed his forehead muscles and mouthed "Oh boy."

"But," Nick continued, "we'd have to check into things like insurance policies, death benefits, exclusionary periods...the condition of the Moore marriage. Not sure we should spin our wheels on all that. Like I said...farfetched.

"So you got this cold case tip from McCauley, is that what you said?"

"Yeah. He—oh, by the way, he wants you to call him. Something about a midlife crisis he's having—yeah, he gave it to me as a 'bone to chew on,' he said. Yeah, this Ramsey guy was an engineer and Irene Moore's twin brother." Vern stopped chewing suddenly. "Hey, come to think of it…didn't you say Donald Moore was an engineer?"

"Yes. Says in the article he was a design engineer for a company called Couch Industries."

"Wow. Two engineers. You think there's somehow a connection between Bertram Ramsey, Xi Lao Bing, and the Moore murders? And what's up with Ramsey's weird last words? He said 'maraschino cherry,' Bing spun around, first shot. Then second shot. End of story."

Nick shut one eye and tilted his head.

"Did you just say Bing 'spun around'?"

"Yeah, that's what McCauley said. 'Spun around.' Cops got it from the eyewitnesses."

Nick opened his mouth to say something but was interrupted by a short man wearing a dark suit whose black hair was pulled atop his head into a tight man bun. Maskless, he had a red face, prominent nose, and thick, dark eyebrows. He came out of nowhere and stood at the table, his hands on his hips, his head turning between Nick and Vern.

"NEE-ko! And-a Mistair-a Wistair! My two-a favorite private eyes-a!"

"Gilberto!" warmly exclaimed Nick.

"Hi Gilberto," said Vern somewhat less warmly.

"Where's-a my favorite lady, Annie, eh Nico?"

"She's putting away our things back at the place, Gilberto. But she says hi. We just returned from a ski trip to Telluride."

"Ahh. One-a my favorite places to-a ski! You-a, you-a do okay on-a dose black-a diamonds, Nico?"

"I did okay, Gilberto. So did Annie, thanks."

"How-a you two like-a my nephew, Enzo?" he asked in a lowered voice.

"Who? Enzo?" Nick asked.

"Yes. Heeza you wait-ah! Heeza takin' care o' you?"

Vern looked discomfited. Nick guffawed and said, "Oh, yeah, Gilberto, he's doing great. He deserves an increase."

"Ahh," Gilberto began, flipping his palms several times. "Maybe. Heeza new, leetle clumsy, but heeza good-a boy. But business rough-a dese days, dis-a virus…Madre di dio!" He shook his head resignedly. "Whadda you drinkin' Mistair-a Wistair?"

"Oh. It's…it's a vodka and gin, Gilberto."

"No olive, I-ah see."

"No. No olive."

Gilberto gave Vern a mock look of vexation. Then he spun on his heels and walked briskly away, flinging up his arm as if to say "La dolce vita!"

Nick and Vern smiled in unison. Vern shrugged.

"A good man," said Nick. "Did you know his place is our home? Anyway…yeah, connection. Vern, you could be right. Let me ask…did you see anyone else besides Pat when you visited the precinct?"

"Yeah, I was going to tell you. I saw a woman when I was leaving. She was just arriving. I think she may have been Bertram Ramsey's daughter. Amber Ramsey."

"Okay. That's good stuff. Anyone else?"

"Yeah. There was a guy sitting with Lurch. Real young, maybe early thirties. I've seen his type before. Pretty sure he was a fed. Pat and I guessed CIA. Pat says he's down here to push the story of virus-related hate crime. Said Lurch and them were contacted by the mayor and governor, worried about Chinese-American trade relations."

Nick remained silent for a full minute. He picked up his glass and drained the Glenlivet.

"This is *really* good stuff, Vern. Now…here's what I want you to do."

Vern finished his vodka.

"I want you to look into this fed. Try to attach a name. Might be difficult, Lurch is about as garrulous as a tree. But snoop around. I'm going to contact this Amber Ramsey. I'm very intrigued by this cold case in Ohio. However we're not taxpayer funded and can't make lemonade without lemons."

"Nick, I will. You know, he gave me a long stare when I walked past. I felt the presence of Big Brother. You think he's connected to that double homicide? He's too young. He was sucking on his mommy's tit in '95."

"Certainly, but he has a predecessor. And I'm not so sure he's CIA. The company Bing visited, Imperial Incorporated, deals with technical documentation, commercial and military. So I think 'our man in Atlanta' is probably NSA, which handles data and information. And those Morlocks were rooting around long before Edward Snowden and the Patriot Act were in the news."

"You got a point, Nick. Damn. So you think this is more than just a hate crime in Georgia…and we might have a crack at solving a twenty-five-year-old cold case in Ohio?"

"We have more than just a 'crack,' Vern. I think we have a chance at solving it, but it won't be easy. There are a lot of people to talk to and our necks will be on a guillotine. This is new territory…like that Appalachian Trail imbroglio a while back."

"Yeah, that was dirty business in more ways than one. Tromping through the mountains to find a psychopath who mutilates campers with jackknives. Ever clean the mud off your Italian shoes?"

"Nope. Bought a new pair."

"Wish I earned that kind o' bread," deadpanned Vern with a side glance at his boss. "Well, what exactly do you think we're dealing with *here*?"

Nick dropped a hundred-dollar bill on the bright white tablecloth, swung out his long legs, and stood erect, again resembling JFK Jr. by way of F. Lee Bailey.

"I think we're dealing with industrial espionage."

Chapter Three

Nick slipped a stick of cinnamon chewing gum in his mouth then checked his Rolex Submariner. It was still early afternoon, time enough to swing by Annie's and still squeeze in a possible meetup with Amber Ramsey. He debated making a trip out to Imperial Incorporated to examine the crime scene, although the Bing murder and Ramsey suicide had, since reading that printout of the cold case in Springbrook, Ohio, receded substantially in importance. In his mind, at least. Twenty-five years was a long time. It was a lifetime for a homicide investigation, and Montaigne knew that if a suspect hadn't been apprehended within a few months, chances are there would never be an arrest. Cops became desperate after so many blind alleys, then frustrated, then diverted by more immediate affairs. The public shifted between varying moods of morbid curiosity, fear, impatience, and anger at empty results, before eventually becoming absorbed by the mundane details of daily life and slipping back into diaper

changes, golf handicaps, and status concerns at the office.
Politicians, many of whom latched onto crime as an
election tactic, merely followed the capricious moods of
voters, and their "tough on crime" pronouncements—which
often translated into draconian punishment measures and
incursions on due process, and which sounded good on a
debate stage but actually *reduced* crime not a whit—had a
shelf life that mirrored public interest.

Blind alleys and cold indifference. Frozen indifference
after two-and-a-half decades, perhaps. This was what
Montaigne would be up against. But there was one dim,
blue light that burned within the darkness. As a young
university student, during those periodic moments when his
baseball ERA began to dip, Nick had briefly considered
journalism as a career. He liked to dig—probably why he
chose the profession he was now pursuing and rapidly
gaining recognition for—and he knew that the press not
only had its finger on the throbbing pulse of the public, but
it also had entrée into those shadowy corners of local
governments and law enforcement bureaus that the rest of
us were denied. Reporters remained curious long after John
and Jane Doe became jaded and bored. They also kept files.
Histories. In some cases, reaching back twenty-five years.
Even in sleepy boroughs like Springbrook, Ohio.

This was Nick's thought as he cruised down Peachtree
Street, clear and bright on this early March morning in
Atlanta, on his way to Annie's modish downtown
apartment. He'd contacted Amber Ramsey immediately
after leaving Gilly's—her phone number was public
record—and arranged to meet her at seven o'clock at her
home in Marietta. Nick was circumspect: he offered his
sincere condolences; he didn't mention the Moore murders;
he merely wanted to get a few biographical details about
Amber's father to assist with motive. He was pleasantly
surprised how accommodating she was over the phone, and
also how calm. But he was also aware that grieving family
members often tranquilized themselves immediately after a

tragedy. And someone blowing his brains out, preceded by cold-blooded murder, certainly qualified as a tragedy.

Traffic was forgiving, and Annie didn't live far from Gilly's, so Nick arrived at the parking garage in time to justify adjusting his car clock to Daylight Savings Time, slapping some Prada Luna Rossa Black on his skin, using the rear view mirror to reposition a few windblown hairs on his head, and once more glance over the April 19, 1995 news article on the Moore murders. That grainy photo of the flat-looking house, witness to a helter-skelter of mayhem only a few nights prior, and which—even as the news photographer clicked his camera—undoubtedly had telltale signs of blood and brain matter, enthralled him as much as it had Vern. *This article only hints at the drama that occurred within that house. God only knows what transpired. Did he plead? Was the woman entirely oblivious to what was in store?*

He made a mental snapshot of the article byline: *Martin Franes.*

Nick entered Annie's apartment building, rode the elevator to the eighth floor and, hands in pockets, gazed distractedly at his two-toned Forzieri shoes as he walked the long hall and mulled over his pending interview with Amber Ramsey.

Once arriving at Apartment 805, however, his thoughts shifted to his best babe…in Nick's world, "best" being the crucial modifier. She hadn't acted right on the flight home. Something was bothering her. Maybe he could find out and set things right. Montaigne hated conflicts and loose ends. He wanted everything sewed up tight. Neat and tidy. That included whatever crime drama he happened to be unraveling, and whatever interpersonal dramas he was immersed in.

He swiped the room key and stepped inside. Annie McBain was sitting on the bed. She looked like she'd just showered. He hair was up and she was wearing the pastel pink bathrobe Vern had bought her two Christmases ago.

Her smooth, chalky legs were crossed. She was reading a magazine. *Probably a glossy events magazine from Telluride*, thought Nick.

"Hi hon," he greeted her. She glanced up at him then returned to the magazine. "Hey, what's up? You haven't been acting right. Something I said? I hope you're not getting sick."

Annie shook her head. She flipped a page.

Nick removed his sport coat, laying it over a chair, then loosened his tie.

"Vern and I may be heading up to Ohio again. That murder-suicide in Conyers has given us some investigation possibilities. Not definite, yet, but…"

"Fine. Take your time up there."

Nick felt the sting. He sat on the bed next to her. He slipped his arm around her thin waist and leaned over and kissed her warm cheek. He stared at her as she continued flipping pages, pretending to be interested.

"Look Annette," he addressed her calmly and quietly, "if it's because we had to shorten our stay, I'm sorry. But what's the use of a ski vacation if one of us can't ski? You know the history of my back. And it was your idea, anyway, to stay inside that morning and…do it before I stretched. Hey, we had fun, though, didn't we? You seemed to really enjoy it, if I recall."

"That's not it. It's…it's…"

"It's what?"

She sighed and tossed the magazine across the room.

"It's a lot of little things. I don't know. Maybe it's this awful *virus*. The whole thing is depressing." She paused. "No, it's not that. I don't know. We don't *talk* anymore. Unless it's about one of your cases, or after sex, or…and you just called me 'Annette,' which you never do unless you're mad or we're drifting apart. It's like calling me 'Dearheart.' It's cold, lifeless. Patronizing."

"Babe, I'm sorry. You know—"

"And now you're going away again, for god knows how long. Nicky, I'm not getting any younger. I've got nine years on you. I've got a son who's in college. Sometimes I think our ages are incompatible, and I'm living with a man-child. I'd like some *permanence*. Some solidity. Assuming anyone in this world can ever get solid again."

Nick squeezed her waist tighter. He put his other hand on her exposed thigh and began massaging it gently, letting his fingers drift up under the pink robe flap.

"I thought you were happy with our arrangement?"

"*Arrangement!* I don't want an *arrangement!*" She began sobbing.

"It's okay, Annie. Sweetheart, it's okay." Her sobbing waned. She wiped her eyes with the back of her hand. Nick leaned and kissed the salty wetness on her cheeks.

"Look. I'll make a deal with you. When I get back from Ohio, we'll talk. I promise. I promise. I *promise*. Until then, give me some slack. *Candy lips.*"

Annie pushed her small, Mona-Lisa mouth into a weak, trembling smile. She looked up at him with watery green eyes. She dropped her head, then looked at him with a look of love, and smiled again.

"Oh-kay," she murmured.

He leaned over and planted a dainty kiss on the slightly recessive chin that he loved to nibble. Then he placed his lips on hers, and lingered there. He took her upper lip in his lips, then her lower lip, then her upper lip. Their lips kissed softly and tenderly for several minutes, making light smacking sounds, then the tips of their tongues began to caress and massage.

"I feel better now," she said after pulling away and rewarding him with another shy smile. "I feel stupid. I'm sorry. Anyway…so…what kind of case is this…up in Ohio?" Nick released his embrace, stood up, and walked over to the magazine, picking it up and placing it on Annie's dresser. He returned, sat down, and lifted his leg onto the bed.

"It's pretty intriguing. A double homicide, a middle-aged couple, occurring, get this, *twenty-five years* ago. Still unsolved. You're tempted to think, 'Okay, rural cops, Andy and Barney, no wonder it's unsolved,'…right? But some of these country bumpkins are really sharp. I'm looking forward to meeting them. Also the reporter who wrote the breaking piece. He writes well, and I get the impression he knows a lot, some of which might never have been made public. Not only that, but the byzantine corridors of the federal government could be a factor."

"Wow. Nicky, you be careful, honey. I don't just mean about this latest case. Will you promise me you'll use protection? Facemask, distancing…all of it?"

"Sure babe. I promise."

"I mean it. My college friend Cynthia is on her deathbed now because she didn't mask at a Mardi Gras party. This virus is no joke."

Annie stood up from the bed and walked to her makeup table. She slipped off the bathrobe and let if fall to the carpet and sat on the swivel chair, her luminous body reflected in the makeup table mirror. She let down her long black hair and began stroking it with a brush, turning her torso back and forth and sexily moving her tiny shoulders.

Nick turned and watched her for several seconds. He walked over and placed his hands on her bare shoulders. She appeared so vulnerable.

"We've got some time," he told her throatily. She stopped brushing. She smiled at him in the mirror. Without hesitation, she set the brush on the table, stood, and the two of them embraced, his arms and hands drifting over her naked back and buttocks, squeezing, caressing, assuring.

They then made tender and tentative love.

***

It was early evening when Nick got the call from Vern. He was getting ready to leave Annie's when Ronnie

Montrose's instrumental, guitar version of Gene Pitney's "Town Without Pity" rang out from his cellphone.

"Hey big guy, whaddaya got?"

"Hey Nick. Guess what? Got the name of that suit who met with Lurch. Name's Frank Hardy. And you're right, he's National Security Administration, not CIA."

"Wonderful. Frank Hardy? Why does that name sound familiar? It's probably a pseudonym. Good job. So, any news on who had his job in '95?"

"Not yet. But my brother-in-law—you know, the guy in Washington that I argued with over Christmas? Wears a purple Speedo at the beach? He does some kind of work with the NSA. I'm hoping I can claw something out of him. He owes me anyway, for helping clean out his ex-wife's apartment. She was a hoarder. God, you should o' seen that place. Like some—"

"Yeah, great Vern. I'm on my way to see Amber Ramsey. Wish me luck."

"You mean you haven't done that yet? Get with the program, son. Where are you anyway, Annie's? Never mind, don't answer. Anyway…ciao."

The sky was turning a mélange of violet, pink, and starfire orange when Nick reached Amber Ramsey's Marietta neighborhood, located just north of Larry Bell Park and the Cobb Aquatic Center. He found her house. It sat on a large lot near a curve in the road, a one-story red-brick and green-vinyl home with a two-car garage that faced a parking lot. It was in the kind of neighborhood where plastic shopping bags stayed snagged on tree branches for months at a time. *Not much money to play with*, thought Nick. He did not yet know whether Amber was single, married, or divorced.

He parked his lime-green machine in front of the forest-green garage doors, removed his cinnamon gum, and strolled to the faded green front door which, despite being March, still had a Christmas wreath hanging on it. *Faded paint…Christmas wreath…she must live alone.*

He rang the doorbell. Within five seconds the screen door opened. A woman about thirty-five or forty, conservatively dressed in a light-gray sweater and black pants, opened the door and invited him in. Her face was pale, wraithlike. Her reddish-brown hair was pulled back into a ponytail. Although not beautiful by those standards deemed so by advertisers and the film casting couch, she had gentle features and her own distinctive allure. Small mouth, sloping cheekbones to an understated chin, and a pair of gold wire spectacles that gave her a studious look and partially obscured age wrinkles at the corners of her large, brown eyes. Her most distinguishing feature was a rounded, slightly pronounced forehead. Everything below this tapered gently to her dainty mouth and chin, giving her a soft, mysterious, almost otherworldly look.

"Mr. Montaigne, I presume?"

"Yes…Amber?"

"Yes. Please come in. Sit wherever you like. It's a little messy, I apologize."

"Not messy at all, you should see *my* place."

They took seats opposite one another, Nick on the couch and Amber on the edge of a wooden rocker, her hands folded in her lap. Nick asked if he should wear a facemask, but she said it was okay.

"Oh, I'm sorry…would y'all like a drink?"

"Oh, no thank you. Normally I'd say 'yes,' but I know you're grieving, and I don't plan to stay too long."

"No, please stay as long as you'd like. I, uh, live alone, so there's no one to care for. No obligations. And I think the grieving is on the wane. Dad was really ill, and I'm happy he's at peace, and that he chose his own way."

"What was your father's illness? If you don't mind my asking."

"Not at all. He had stage 4 bullous myringitis. It had spread to his lower auricle."

"I'm so sorry."

"Why? He's dead now."

"Point taken."

"Anyway," Amber continued, "I'm not much of a griever."

"I'm the same way," said Nick. "I've been called 'cold' some times. But that's not true. I'm aware that, while grieving is an egoistic thing…those who died are at peace, after all…we grieve because we love. And that's a good thing. Right?"

"That's right. With Dad it's more the murder of that Chinese man that bothers me. And the way the media has portrayed him."

"And how is that?"

"They're saying it's a hate crime. That's absolutely ridiculous. My dad didn't have a racist bone in his body. And he was too smart to accuse, let alone *kill* someone because a disease started—*supposedly* started—in their country. I hate the way people are talking about him."

Amber's face had taken on a pinkish tone. Nick speculated her ire was helping to displace any grief. He remained silent.

"I don't know why he killed that man."

Nick debated how to phrase his next question. He didn't want to press too hard.

"Amber, what kind of work did your father do, if you don't mind my asking?"

"I don't mind. He was an engineer. All his life. He started up in Lima, Pennsylvania, a suburb of Philadelphia, where I was born. Then he transferred to a company here in Marietta, one of the largest in the nation, if not the world."

"Okay. Do you know if he ever came into contact with Imperial Incorporated, the company that Xi Lao Bing was visiting on business?"

"No, I don't know. He may have. You know, we had a typical father-daughter relationship. It got closer after Mom died, yeah, but he never talked work with me. No reason to, and I surely wasn't interested."

"Right. Totally understandable. How about…"

Nick paused. He wanted to permit some breathing space before jumping into what he was *really* curious about. And again, he didn't want to appear too eager.

"…How about your aunt and uncle's murders. Up in Ohio. How did those affect your dad? And, for that matter…how did they affect *you*?"

"Oh God," she gasped, shaking her head. "What a nightmare. I…I *loved* Aunt Irene. Uncle Don was nice, too. *Why?* Who could have done that to them? Oh yeah, Dad was really affected by that. He felt protective of Aunt Irene. Did you know they were twins?"

"No, I didn't."

"Yeah. I was only sixteen years old when it happened. In high school. Dad was really distraught. And he could not understand why there was no evidence, and why those awful police were stymied. Almost like they didn't *want* to find the killer. He even went up there…to Springbrook. Didn't do any good."

Nick shifted his body to get closer to Amber.

"So…who did he see in Springbrook? The cops, I'm sure. Anyone else?"

"Yes. There was a reporter. He was really good. Dad said he was a nice guy, too. He was as anxious to find the killer as Dad. Dad corresponded with him regularly, for a while. His name was 'Frame' or something."

"Was it maybe Martin *Franes*?"

"Gosh, it was a while ago. Possibly. How did you get that name?"

"It was the byline name on the original news article. Okay, you say 'for a while.' Why did they stop?"

"I don't know. Dad didn't say. But I do remember he fell into a funk…a depression…right about the time they stopped talking."

Nick paused again. He heard the ticking of a clock. Then he heard a car swish by. His mind drifted to the news photo of the Moore home. He was about to ask another question, but Amber spoke.

"I've always wondered if there was a connection between Dad and Uncle Don that I didn't know about. You know, something other than their being brothers-in-law. They were both engineers. Both of them were kind of quiet, didn't talk much. Then, when I heard about what he did…" she began, then started to sob. She quickly recovered.

"When I heard about that stuff in Conyers, I wondered if that Bing man had something to do with Uncle Don. Y'all think all of this is related?"

Nick nodded. "Yes, I do. It's really why I'm here. And again, thank you so much for meeting me, you've been through a lot these last few days. Do you have an idea what your dad meant by those last words of his?"

"I have no idea. He wasn't a fruit eater, especially cherries. He was more into vegetables…I'm sorry, I just can't help you."

"That's okay. Amber, are you familiar with the term 'industrial espionage'?"

She shook her head.

"Well, industrial espionage takes on several forms. But generally it involves stealing trade secrets from a rival company, or rival country. Sometimes it's for profit. Sometimes for more pernicious purposes. Like, gaining an edge on weaponry—manufacturing, chemical, biological—those areas.

"Sometimes a person is 'planted,' so to speak, within a company, and does the spying from the inside. This type of person is referred to as a 'mole.' At the opposite end are more laissez faire attempts at gathering secrets. A visitor might take photos or notes while making the rounds of a company. Someone like Bing, for instance. Now, I'm not saying this happened, please don't get me wrong. But it's a possibility.

"I realize this is all a bit much to digest. I don't expect you to understand it all. Even I don't understand some of the shenanigans that the military-industrial complex engages in. And I'm not sure I want to.

"But you're absolutely correct in suspecting a connection between your father, the mur—Conyers incident involving Bing, and your Uncle Don and Aunt Irene's murders. My partner and I would like to investigate. But—like I often tell my partner—" Nick began, then smiled, "we're not taxpayer funded. We need a client."

He sat back on the couch and waited for Amber's response to his suggestion.

"I see," she drawled. "Well…I don't know. I so much want to see my father's reputation salvaged. As much as it can be salvaged, anyway. This hate crime thing is disgusting. He was not that kind of a person. And my aunt and uncle's murders? Wow. If you could solve that, it would be enormous. It's been twenty-four or five years. *Nobody* has had any luck.

"But…I don't have much money. I don't think I could afford you."

Nick closed his eyes and nodded in sympathy. "I totally understand, Amber. Here's what I propose. If Vern and I—Vern's my partner—can establish a connection between Conyers and Springbrook...and if we do, if you would be willing to give us a retainer—that's just a little start-up money to cover expenses for our travel, room, board, et cetera—we can get started. Then, if we solve that double homicide, we charge you a reasonable private investigation fee for our efforts. If we don't solve it after a certain period of time, you don't owe us anything." He paused. "Does that sound reasonable?"

"Yes. That sounds more than reasonable."

As a punctuation mark, like a jazz percussionist's perfectly timed rim shot and a perfect capstone to their discussion, "Town Without Pity" suddenly blasted from Nick's cellphone. He reached inside his coat pocket with sweaty hands and withdrew it. It was Vern. Nick's heart began to palpitate ever so slightly. He hit the speaker button so Amber could hear.

"Vern. Hey. Nick here. I'm with Amber. What…what you got?"

Vern's beefy voice exploded from the speaker phone.

"Nick, you won't believe this! What a day! You and I are celebrating tonight, mister. You won't believe—"

"Right, okay Vern, I won't believe it, *what do you have?!*"

"Nick, you won't believe this! I knew something was up all along. That's why I met you at Gilly's. I'm so glad you came back—"

"Vern!" Nick uncharacteristically lifted his voice and interrupted him, as Amber Ramsey, overhearing everything, sat in suspenseful silence, her brown, doe eyes opening wider. "Please, tell me what you have!"

"Okay. Okay Nick. Here it is: that company in Conyers? The technical documentation firm? Where Bing was murdered the other day? Guess what? It was a tech doc contractor for *Couch Industries*…the company up in Ohio that Donald Moore worked for before he and his wife's skulls were cleaved."

Amber Ramsey's wide, otherworldly eyes opened even wider.

"But that's not all. I checked into that NSA punk who was in Kwiatkowski's office. My brother-in-law—you know, the one—"

"I know, Vern, he wears a Speedo. What about him? Frank Hardy was his name, right?"

"Right. Well, there are never any gaps, all these feds replace each other like guards. And guess who his boss was, his predecessor at the NSA."

"Who?"

"Bertram Cabot Ramsey."

Chapter Four

Springbrook, Ohio was founded in 1808 by a man named Ezekiel Eastabrook. Local historians differ as to the details of Eastabrook's origins, but most agree he was a Congregationalist from a family of mariners in Rhode Island who emigrated west to escape the sea and try his hand at farming. Somewhere in western Pennsylvania he met up with John Chapman—popularly known as Johnny Appleseed—and accompanied Chapman on his journeys westward, flinging seeds into the breeze while exchanging Bible passages with his older partner. The apocryphal story is that Chapman and Eastabrook—who reminded Chapman of his younger brother, Nathaniel—got into a vicious argument over the Holy Trinity, as well as Chapman's insistence on bringing pagan Shawnee Indians under the benevolent tent of Christianity, and they began hurling Macintosh apples at one another. This internecine warfare intensified until Chapman, the more devout and temperamental of the two, called Eastabrook a "blasphemous heretic," after which Eastabrook broke the friendship, obstinately pitching camp one evening under a large boulder, while Chapman soldiered onward. The boulder still sits on the edge of town and is referred to as "Eastabrook Rock." Historians also disagree on who won the apple battle, although Springbrook residents come down on the side of Eastabrook.

Eastabrook eventually built the first frame house in the area. Others moved in, attracted by the fertile farmland, good for corn, soybeans and, of course, apple trees. In the late nineteenth century a passenger railroad line was built just north of Springbrook, importing even more residents. The town was originally named after Eastabrook, but people kept spelling it "Easter Brook," so city fathers decided to make things simple, and because Easter occurs in the spring, the name became "Springbrook."

The town continued to grow throughout the twentieth century, spearheaded by the nearby train line. A 1931 directory lists ninety-nine industries and some eight thousand employees. The town reached its apex in the 1960s and early 1970s, with manufacturing firms catering to the lucrative "Rust Belt" steel industry springing up almost overnight, and established industries (like Donald Moore's company, Couch Industries) earning record profits. The south side of Springbrook (where the Moores lived in a neighborhood called Turnham Green) had a reputation for being clean, happy, conservative, and safe.

Unfortunately, with the nationwide displacement of manufacturing by Silicon Belt-originated technologies beginning in the 1980s, Springbrook entered a decline from which it hadn't recovered.

Despite the many changes and passage of time, Springbrook is most famous for—and still promoted it in its travel brochures—a 1953 visit by actor James Stewart. Stewart was evidently traveling on the train when he suffered a severe attack of food poisoning. He was carried off the train and admitted to Springbrook General Hospital (where Irene Moore much later worked as a nurse). Stewart quickly recovered, but he was so smitten by the friendliness of the town that he decided to stay over for three days, visiting Eastabrook Rock, eating at the premier dining establishment, Sharkey's, and playing golf with Mayor Hamilton while swapping World War II stories. Over time the legend of "Jimmy's Visit" had him staying four days, then five days, until it became a solid week—which was, like the town name, much easier for everyone.

At the time of Nick and Vern's visit, the town's population stood at 32,281. Their arrival coincided with scuttlebutt centering on the town's largest and oldest church, Central Congregational Church. Longtime Pastor Frederick Maugham had decided to retire, and church elders had selected a young, vibrant, university-educated man, Pastor Chip, as an interim minister, with hopes of offering him permanent employment. But Pastor Chip soon offended the staid sensibilities of much of the church. He not only wore blue jeans, but he had the audacity to deviate from biblical text and share personal anecdotes with the congregation. Additionally, unlike more traditional Pastor Fred, during sermons Chip actually left the pulpit and wandered up the center aisle while preaching. There were a few young parishioners who defended him by arguing, "Well, at least he doesn't walk up the side aisles." But they were outnumbered by the older puritans.

The clincher came when it was discovered that his wife—a shy, retiring woman whose social anxiety prevented her from mixing with the other ladies—had, years earlier, undergone electric shock therapy for depression.

Pastor Chip and his young family were soon unceremoniously packed off to rural Illinois, and a new interim minister was being advertised for.

This was the situation when Nick and Vern slowly tooled past the "Historic Uptown Springbrook" sign in Nick's lime-green vanity machine on their way to the

Comfort Inn to—they hoped—solve a brutal double homicide from twenty-five years earlier.

***

"What do you think is historic about this town, Nick?"

"I don't know. I didn't take time to read the Wikipedia article."

"Did you see that one historical marker, back before the city limits?"

"Which one?"

"The one that said 'Butterworth Station.' I wonder if that's where Mrs. Butterworth lived."

"What?"

"You know, Mrs. Butterworth. I wonder if back there is where she invented her pancake syrup."

Nick's jaw dropped. "Are you serious? That was an Underground Railroad station."

The investigators had a full plate. After checking in at the motel, Nick hoped to meet with local reporter Martin Franes, the guy Amber had said had helped her father years earlier—assuming he was still around. If anyone could summarize events between April 15, 1995 and the present, it would be this guy. Vern planned to feel out some of the neighbors—again, assuming they were still around. But before anything, they wanted to see 157 Morning Glory Lane: the house in which the Moores were killed.

The car entered city limits and turned right on Oak Avenue and went through several stop signs before arriving at the town square. On the corner of Oak and Church Street sat Central Congregational Church. An elderly woman and man stood at the foot of a series of concrete steps leading to two large, majestic, stained and carved wooden doors, the doors centered directly under a large white steeple. The twosome appeared to be in deep discussion. As Nick's car turned to wind around the town square, the woman and man did a synchronized double take, following the gleaming Porsche 911 GT2 RS as it cruised slowly around the square.

"Wow, that's an impressive church," remarked Vern.

"Yeah, a lot of these Midwestern towns have a church for their centerpiece. There's probably a gazebo nearby, too."

"You're right, Nick, there it is, on the green," said Vern as they passed the circular ivory-white structure surrounded by a dark-green yew hedge.

"Straight out of *Winesburg, Ohio*," wryly observed Nick.

The car picked up Oak again on the other side of the square, passed a bunch of small offices and retail businesses, then continued southward until it reached the residential zone, characterized by squat little brick houses, each with one steep set of concrete front steps framed by slightly crooked iron handrails, steep roofs with stained shingles, each roof equipped with squat black chimneys that protruded like fat, black cigar butts in an ashtray.

Then the Porsche turned left onto Chamomile Street. More stop signs, the yards and houses becoming larger, fewer cars parked along the curb. Then, directly ahead, a handsome, two-story brick edifice came into view. *SPRINGBROOK MIDDLE SCHOOL, Home of the Planters* read a sign way up on top of one of the brick walls. The car turned right onto Forsythia Street as the men's heads swiveled left toward a gravel parking lot graced by six tennis courts. It followed Forsythia down a small hill, passing Dahlia Lane on the left, then reached Morning Glory Lane.

"This is it," said Nick. "Just down a ways on the right."

Nick turned the wheel. His Porsche creeped down Morning Glory like a jungle tiger stalking prey. His heartbeat increased ever so slightly. He noticed that Vern had become quieter the closer they got.

Nick stopped the Porsche. They were directly in front of 157 Morning Glory. Both men gazed several seconds in silence at a plain, flat-looking brick ranch home with a tiny kitchen window poised above a dusky-looking porch area. They noticed a small section of the brick front was actually a slate-stone façade. The house had a forlorn appearance, as if all the tears of all those living and dead, who'd once known and loved Donald and Irene Moore, had doused their once-happy slice of quaint paradise. Vern unfolded the now-creased printout. He consulted it, yet again, as Nick leaned over and did the same. While the crimes had occurred two-and-a-half decades prior, it was if the house had been frozen in time. Except for the porch furniture, everything looked identical. Even the valence shades hanging behind the kitchen window looked the same.

"I wonder if the people who live here now know what happened," said Vern.

"Don't know," said Nick. "We may find out. I'd like to go inside."

"Now?" asked Vern, as if entering this private home was a kind of defilement.

"Sure, why not? I'm curious. Aren't you?"

"Well…well yeah. But shouldn't we—" he began to say. But Nick had already opened the driver's door.

As they walked down the short driveway, Nick heard a noise. Glancing at the house next door, he saw an elderly man standing on the other side of the front screen door, watching them. Nick pretended not to notice him and turned, continuing with Vern down the drive, then onto a small sidewalk curve, past a hairy crop of ground cover partially spilling over the sidewalk, and stepped onto a small, drab front porch typical of 1950s and 1960s brick ranch homes. The front door was on the right side of the porch.

Nick rang the doorbell. Vern nervously cleared his throat.

The door opened and a woman about sixty stood before them. She had salt-and-pepper hair. There was a small wart on the side of her nose. Other than that minor blemish, she was very pretty, with eyes that had a light twinkle. The eyes widened when she saw the two men.

"Hello? Can I help you gentlemen?" she cautiously inquired, carefully enunciating the words. Nick detected a foreign accent.

"Hello ma'am," Nick confidently addressed her. "We're sorry to bother you. My partner and I are private investigators and we just arrived in town." Nick pulled out his Georgia PI license from his coat pocket and displayed it. "It's our understanding some, uh, business occurred in your home many years ago…with a former owner…and we were wondering if we could ask you a few questions." He paused. "It's not about *you*, but about your *house layout*," he added, just to allay any concerns.

She smiled warmly. "Oh! About the Moore murders!"

"Yes! Exactly!" said Nick.

She opened the door and invited them in. Nick stepped inside and immediately began scanning the foyer. Vern followed shyly like a big skittish sheepdog.

"Oh, would you like us to wear facemasks?" asked Nick.

"No, that's fine, we can keep a distance. I applaud you for offering, though. Politeness seems to be a rare quality these 'me first' days."

"I agree. By the way, that's a beautiful oak in your front lawn," Nick gushed. "Probably a couple hundred years old by the looks of it."

"Oh, thank you. We call him 'Oakie.' Now…I'll bet you're here to discuss the crimes. Would you also like a tour?"

"A tour?" Nick asked in surprise. "Well, sure, if it's no inconvenience." She pooh-poohed him.

Nick placed her accent. *Northern English. Maybe Yorkshire.* The men introduced themselves. She introduced herself as "Beryl." She said her husband was at work, and she was retired.

"What an awful, awful thing," she said as she led them past a kitchen on the left and into a dining area straight ahead. "We didn't know the couple. We moved here about six years ago. There was a family who lived here after the Moores, and we bought the house from them. I don't know its history before the Moores, but I believe it was built in 1963. Lots of people were arriving in Springbrook then.

"Anyway, our realtor told us the gory details right at the start, in case we might be skittish about buying, but the entire tale *fascinated* us. Arthur and I *love* mysteries and crime stories!"

She halted at the dining table.

"Why are you gentlemen investigating, now? The Springbrook police gave up long ago."

"Well ma'am," began Vern, suddenly more courageous, "we're from Atlanta—that's in Georgia—and were hired by the Moores' niece. She lost her father recently, very tragically, and she and us think his death might be related to her aunt and uncle's deaths."

"Oh dear…I'm so sorry."

"Yeah, his death in—"

"His death was, indeed, tragic," Nick jumped in, as if to prevent Vern from revealing too much. "So, anyway, we're in town to poke around, and we just wanted to, well, take a peek at the scene of the crime, so to speak."

Beryl smiled. "Well, you've come to the right place! This is the dining room where Irene was shot." The threesome stood in a large white-carpeted dining area. At the far end of the room were a couch, piano, and television set.

"Arthur and I don't know exactly, but we think she was sitting about here," she pointed at the chair at the dining room table that was closest to the kitchen. "They say she was shot once in the back of the head. Thank God she didn't have to suffer." A few seconds of awkward silence followed.

She pointed toward the television area, explaining the master bedroom was in the back, and "a loo is at each end of the house." She led them the opposite direction through the kitchen sitting area, past a fireplace, and into the first of two bedrooms. This room had attractive wood-paneled walls and floor, a bed with large, fluffy pillows centered in the middle against the headboard, a dresser, night table, small wastebasket, and two generic-looking framed prints of flowers on one wall. That was it. The room's sparse furnishings suggested it was rarely used.

"And this is where Donald was shot. We call it the 'Red Room'…for obvious reasons. But the red is long gone. Thankfully." She glanced at Vern, as if checking to see if her gallows humor had registered with him. "Of course, the arrangement and decorations were much different when they lived here. For one, there was no bed. They used it as a hobby and computer room. We think he was sitting about here," she pointed to an area next to a tall, vertical window that faced out onto a handsome wooden deck. "At his computer, he would have had a charming view of this beautiful deck. Perhaps there were a few feeders out there for him to bird-watch, while he clicked around the Civil War Forum on AOL."

"Oh?" asked Nick. "Was he a Civil War buff?"

"According to Lee Chin across the street, yes. Lee knew him pretty well. You should talk to him, a very, very nice man. And his wife Jane is a lovely lady. They're Chinese-American."

Nick and Vern looked at each other.

"Yes, er, we'll have to do that," said Nick. "Any other neighbors still here who might have known them?"

"Well…definitely Manny Henderlong next door. He's been here forever. Unfortunately," she added with a look of disgust. "Then the Ropers on the other side, but only Regina is still around. Who else? Let's see, the Moores were here for eight years, so, doing the math…I think the Blacks, Whitney and Linda, across the street. They live next to the Chins. I…think that's about it. Although there may be others farther down Morning Glory, or on Forsythia or Dahlia."

"Thank you, Beryl, that's very helpful. By the way, you wouldn't happen to be from Yorkshire, would you?"

"Dear me! You're very close! We're from Cheshire, a village called Broadbottom, outside Manchester."

"Nick's pretty good with accents," interjected Vern. "He used to live in France."

Nick chuckled. "Vern's right, but I've also been a few other places. I'd love to visit Yorkshire someday. Especially the Brontë estate. I'm a big fan of Charlotte's *Jane Eyre*."

"Ah yes, we hold the Brontës in high regard. How about Emily's *Wuthering Heights*?"

"Not so much that book. A bit too turgid for me, although I did love the movie with Olivier and Merle Oberon. Merle was absolutely gorgeous. She looks very much like my girlfriend."

Beryl smiled. Then her face clouded.

"You sound…I'm sorry…did you say your name was Fontaine?"

"Montaigne. Nick Montaigne."

"Yes, I'm sorry dear. Montaigne. Well, Mr. Montaigne, you sound like you might know a few things. Are you familiar with the moor murders?" She looked at Vern. "Not Moore with a capital 'M' and an 'e' at the end. But 'moor' as in the windswept hills of north England. Arthur and I lived very close to where the bodies were found. Maybe it's why the murders here don't bother us as much as they might others."

"Myra Hindley," intoned Nick solemnly.

Beryl nodded her head while frowning. "Yes. Makes the crimes here look like a Sunday soirée. Anyway…the irony of going from the moors to the Moores has never been lost on us."

Nick nodded. Vern looked like a deer caught in headlights. Beryl led them out of the "Red Room" and back to the foyer. As they walked, Nick glanced into the kitchen, as if gauging distances, views, and positions.

"Beryl, you've been very helpful, we can't thank you enough."

"Oh, it's my pleasure dear. I will have to tell Arthur you were here, he would be absolutely chuffed to know. Not many people talk about the Moore murders any more. Occasionally we see children standing outside the house, pointing, sharing scary details and daring each other, as children are wont to do." She paused. "Where are you staying in town, if you don't mind my asking?"

"We're staying at the Comfort Inn, ma'am," said Vern.

"Oh dear. That's a shame. You can't find better accommodations? Well…why don't you stay here? Arthur wouldn't mind at all. We could have some great discussions, not only about the Moore murders, but about the Brontës and English literature, too!"

Nick swiveled his head toward Vern, who had a look of horror on his face.

"Why, that's so kind of you, Beryl! Vern and I are so appreciative. But are you sure we wouldn't be an imposition? It could be a few weeks before we, uh, wrap up the case."

"No! No imposition at all, dear! Like Donald and Irene, we have no children. It's a three-bedroom house, so one of you can kip in the Blue Room and the other can have the Red Room. I fix homegrown Mancunian cuisine, and you both look like healthy eaters." She looked at Vern. "Arthur says my beef brisket and blood pudding are to die for." She paused. "Sorry…it's an in-joke."

"Ha!" laughed Nick. "Well, we'll consider your kind offer, Beryl, thank you so much."

As Nick and Vern stepped onto the porch, Nick saw several boys hanging around his glittery green road machine. One of them was imitating a race car driver, shifting his hands back and forth as if turning a steering wheel. The other boys broke into laughter. Then Nick glanced at the bottom of the screen door. He saw a square of hinged, plastic flap, a small door such as a pet owner might have installed for the entry and exit of a small animal.

"Looks like you're a pet owner, Beryl. Cat or dog?"

"Oh, no. We don't have any pets. Actually, the Moores installed that little door for their poogle. Her name was 'Lisa.'"

"*Poogle*?" asked Nick. "Never heard of that."

"It's a cross between a miniature poodle and a beagle. Getting real popular these days, almost as much as the cavapoo. The beagle is both curious and loyal, and the poodle is the second smartest dog in the world. Our own British Isles border collie is first," Beryl added with pride.

"Anyway, the previous owners never changed the door, and Arthur and I have kept it, too. Just as a remembrance of Lisa, Donald, and Irene. A sort of memorial to them. God rest their souls."

"You mean they had a *dog*?" Vern asked in surprise. "Was it here at the time of the murders? Was it…shot…too?"

"Yes, they had a dog. You didn't know? Oh my. Yes, poor Lisa. She was in the house that night. But, fortunately, she was not shot. Maybe she cowered under one of the beds, who knows. The murders were on…a Saturday, I believe. And the police came on…Tuesday. So things weren't exactly tickety-boo for Lisa. She had no food or water for almost three days. The constable—I mean *sergeant*—said she seemed abnormally placid when they found her.

"She was the only witness to the murders. But dogs don't speak human." Her voice trailed off. "Do they."

Chapter Five

Even before the Porsche doors slammed shut, Vern pounced on Nick.

"Buster, there is no way I'm staying in that house!"

"Why not? Free room and board. Won't have to deal with noisy neighbors. That Red Room will give you a beautiful view of the outdoor deck…while you digest your blood pudding."

"Red Room, blood pudding, moor murders," Vern barked contemptuously. "I could tell that you liked her, but I thought she was ghoulish. Can't imagine what *Arthur* is like. I'll bet he's got a Frankenstein lab in the basement. Jeez! Glad I'm outta that place."

"You were a cop in Philadelphia. Why so squeamish?"

"Nick, I pounded a bunko beat, remember? And the few homicides I dealt with, well, those flimflammers deserved what they got. And I definitely never had to stay overnight in a haunted house. That place is creepy. So are the

English. I never cared for Sherlock Holmes, Jack the Ripper, all that," he attempted a Cockney accent, "'Cor blimey, guv-nuh! Found a bleedin' corpse in the bloody gah-den!'"

Nick laughed to himself. Vern's blood was up, a good sign.

"Okay, well, we can do Comfort Inn a few nights. Maybe you'll change your mind. Right now I wanna call that Franes guy at the paper, so get me that number. After lunch—maybe after you've calmed down—you can return to Morning Glory and try to talk to those neighbors she mentioned. Did you notice the guy next door—I think she said his name is Manny Henderlong—eyeballing us?"

"Yeah, I did. And it's interesting a Chinese-American couple lives across the street. We keep bumping into China." Vern paused. "I just heard another old Chinese was attacked in San Francisco because of this virus. What's the matter with people these days?"

"I'm not a sociologist," Nick answered, "but I would say xenophobia, tribalism, and poor leadership at the top. We need leaders who will nourish our humanity, not diminish it. Especially now.

"And speaking of nourishment, how about we try this place Sharkey's? In 'Historic *Uptown* Springbrook', though I'm at a loss as to what's so historic about it. Great steaks and walleye, supposedly."

The Porsche turned back onto Oak and went north toward "Historic Uptown Springbrook." Sharkey's was on the square. It had an outdoor canopy similar to Gilly's, but much smaller. The interior was extremely dark, each table equipped with one small electric candle. Vern made a favorable comment about the long bar, and Nick noted it resembled a speakeasy from an old film noir. The two men ordered lunch, Nick choosing the walleye platter and Vern opting for a Reuben with fries, and they discussed what they had scraped together about the cold case thus far.

Which, so far—at least until Nick could talk to reporter Martin Franes—wasn't much.

"What do you think, Vern?"

"About what? I like it. I like dark bars."

"No, about the case. Specifically, the house. Any thoughts about what exactly happened since our talk at Gilly's? Who might've done it?"

"Well…" Vern began, his crossed eyes squinting toward the large Guinness sign above the bar, "I'm pulled one way then another. Seems to me it's a professional killing. Has to be. Look, nobody heard any shots. Which means the killer used a suppressor. No sexual assault of Irene…that we're aware of, anyway. Definite hit man. Also, both were shot *once* in the back of the head. Clean and professional, no messiness. Yeah. *And no money was taken!* Murders for profit, you know, the killer woulda grabbed some cash, jewelry, dining room silver. But cops don't say that in the article. And they never found any fingerprints or curious DNA, at least that we're aware. Has to be hit killings. Question is…why? She was a nurse, he was an engineer. Why was a supposedly nice, upper-middle-class, suburban couple slaughtered in cold blood? It's crazy."

He stopped. The food was delivered. Vern complained that he didn't have enough fries.

"Yeah," said Nick, "those are all my thoughts, Vern. But here's something else."

"Wha'?" mumbled Vern while chomping his Reuben.

"Like we alluded to at Gilly's, how the hell did the killer gain entry?"

"Huh? Well…through the door…how else?"

"Right, through the door. There was no break-in. But if he truly was a hit man—and we can't leave out the possibility it may have been a hit *woman*—why did Irene or Donald allow him in the house? I mean, if it was a stranger, why would they open the door on a Saturday night and let this stranger walk inside their lovely home? It's not like the killer would have been dressed in a Terminix outfit to spray for bugs.

"Neighbors and relatives interviewed in the article said they always kept their doors locked, but the cops say the front door was *unlocked*. So the killer either had a key, or the Moores let him in without being concerned. If the killer had a key, how did he get it? If the killer didn't have a key, why would they allow a total stranger inside? They had to allow him in, based on where the bodies were found. There was no struggle at the door. Did someone claim he needed to use the phone because his car broke down?"

Vern digested Nick's words as he digested his meal. Mouth full, he nodded vigorously several times.

"Right. Right, Nick. I thought about that stuff. There's one other thing we left out, though. How does Donald's computer play into this?"

"Exactly. Great observation, Vern. And this is where it *really* gets complicated. First scenario: so, she's sitting or standing in the dining room, obviously with her back to the killer. BOOM. Gun goes off. Muffled, yeah. But still a sound. Then the killer walks out of the dining area, through the kitchen sitting area, opens the door to the den, and finds Donald in his chair at the computer. Donald never turns, and gun goes off. BOOM. Lisa running around barking or cowering under a bed somewhere.

"Why would she have her back to the killer? Why wouldn't Donald have left the den after the noise, or at least risen from his chair? It's gotta be the other way around.

"Second scenario: killer is in the den with Donald. Irene not worried because she either knows him or her, or Donald has introduced them. So she's playing solitaire at the table, doing a crossword puzzle, polishing silver…whatever. Maybe the TV's on, in killer's favor to quell any noise. Meanwhile, in the den, undoubtedly behind a closed door, killer has gun pointed at back of Donald's head and *is forcing him to get something, or destroy something, on the computer*. Killer gets what he/she needs from Donald.

BANG! Killer then waits briefly to see if Irene enters room. She doesn't. He then carefully opens the door, walks through kitchen area—gun tucked behind back—walks carefully and quietly toward Irene—who is sitting or standing and turned the other way doing her thing, maybe simultaneously watching *Seinfeld*—BANG!

"Two dirty deeds, done dirt cheap. Killer quietly exits house through unlocked front door, out into the dark night, maybe drives to Sharkey's for a gin and tonic…and escapes identification for twenty-five years."

As Nick was carefully relating his theory, the restaurant had slowly begun to fill with customers, most taking seats for lunch but a few at the bar. Springbrook folk were unused to seeing two strangers seated there for lunch, so a few heads had turned in their direction. Some ears had undoubtedly latched on to a few choice words: gun…Donald and Irene…BOOM…killer…BANG. But most Springbrook residents had become habituated to outsiders discussing their town's most infamous crime. In fact, over the past two-and-a-half decades, the Moore murders had become almost as reliable a piece of local folklore as Jimmy's Visit.

Vern smacked his lips and doused his final mouthful with a swig of Coke on the rocks.

"Ya know (chew)…ya know, Nick (swallow)…I like that second scenario. Makes very good sense. You analyzed that house situation very well." Vern sounded like a university professor complimenting a student on their essay.

"Thanks, Vern."

"You covered positioning and timing…straineous things like television noise—"

"You mean 'extraneous' things?"

"Right. Yeah, I like your logistics. But there's only one other question. What would the killer want out of Donald's computer? If he forced him to sit there before blowing his brains out, what could be so valuable to him? Or her? That's what I'm hoping to find out in the days ahead."

Nick checked his Submariner. "Which reminds me, we still need to check into the Comfort Inn, and I want to talk to Martin Franes, assuming he's still vertical and in Springbrook. And you need to make like a Mormon and ring doorbells on Morning Glory. Let's get going."

***

The Comfort Inn was on the south end of town near the interstate. Being a weekday, the parking lot was relatively empty but for a few trucks, and Nick's freshly waxed Porsche 911 stood out like a hippie at a Lawrence Welk concert. In fact, since arriving in Springbrook, he'd set a record for double-takes: eleven so far, not counting the boys on Morning Glory who'd taken an extended break from their COVID-era home schooling lessons. Counting turned heads was a minor hobby for Nick. He had a firm belief the planet was now experiencing a severe dearth of eccentrics, and he damn sure wanted to do his part to turn that around.

He'd dropped Vern off in Turnham Green by the middle school tennis courts, promising to pick him up in exactly three hours...Vern liked in-person cold calls over phone calls, and because of his everyman look, he usually got the goods. As Nick shifted into park at the motel, he fished out a stick o' cinnamon and popped it in his craw. He then grabbed his cell. He'd already placed the number for the *Springbrook Daily News Journal Observer-Tribune* in his cell contact list, so all he had to do was punch the name. Maybe he could get hold of Franes in time to arrange an evening meeting. Or maybe Franes would tell him to "get lost." Or maybe Franes was dead.

He tapped the link. The phone rang twice. Then a woman's voice.

"*Springbrook Daily News Journal Observer-Tribune*, may I help you?"

"Yes, you may. I'm calling in regards to an old newspaper article. I'd like to talk to the reporter who wrote the piece and ask him a few questions, if that's okay."

"Well, I'll need to know the reporter's name."

"His name is Martin Franes."

"Did you say 'Franes'? Like, F-R-A-N-E-S?"

"Yes, that's the name."

"Hmm. I don't think we have anyone here by that name. Are you sure his name is Franes?"

"Yes, I'm certain of it."

"Hmm. Well, when was this article written?"

"April 19, 1995."

Silence. Nick waited while softly chomping his gum.

"Gee, that was a long time ago. I've only been here a short while. Let me…hang on, let me get someone else to help you. If we lose connection, the person's name is Roy Turlock."

"Great, thanks."

Nick waited about two minutes. Then he heard a man's voice.

"Hello? This is Roy Turlock. Can I help you?"

"Yes, hello Mr. Turlock. I was trying to get Martin Franes, but maybe you can help me."

"I'll try. What gives?"

"My name is Nick Montaigne and I'm a private investigator. My partner and I are here from Georgia and we're investigating an old double homicide in Springbrook. Mr. Franes wrote the original news article describing the crime."

"Uh…oh...kay," Turlock answered hesitantly. "Can you tell me the name or names of the victims?"

"Donald and Irene Moore."

CLICK.

"Hello? Hello? Mr. Turlock?"

Did he hang up? thought Nick. *What the…!*

He checked his phone. It was blank. He sat in his car, stunned. An avalanche of thoughts crossed his mind. *Not like a trained journalist at all. Did Franes order him to keep quiet? Did his editor? Did the cops? Was he sick of questions about the Moores? Did his phone lose its charge?*

He sat without moving, in disbelief, for a few moments, his eyes following a heavy-set Hispanic housekeeper pushing an overloaded housekeeping cart along the sidewalk. He shook his head, looked at his phone, then riled himself, went to the motel lobby, and checked himself and Vern in. He got the keys to Rooms 115 and 117. He placed Vern's battered brown suitcase in Room 115, then rolled his turquoise Rimowa cabin case and polypropylene garment bag, containing his suits, into 117. He was tempted to call Vern to share his anger at being hung up on, then realized Vern might be in the middle of an interview, so he decided to call Annie. *Need to talk to her anyway.*

Sitting on the bed closest to the door, he was just about to touch Annie's name with his finger when "Town Without Pity" interrupted him. The number looked familiar. *Newspaper*. He answered.

"Hello?"

"Yes, hello? Yeah, this is Roy Turlock. Hey, I'm sorry I had to hang up on you. It's been a real bitch of a winter, I got shit comin' at me from all sides…you there?"

"Yeah, I'm here. This is Nick."

"Okay, yeah, sorry, so, you wanna talk Moore murders? Listen, I can't talk now. I'm in the damn hallway. Can't talk in the newsroom, 'specially about that shit. Can you meet me? Say, about seven o'clock?"

"Sure, sure. Where at?"

"Yeah, okay, cool, so you know where Springbrook Middle School is? Turnham Green neighborhood? Near the Moore house?"

"Yes I do. Just dropped my partner off near there."

"Cool. Okay, well, let's meet there at seven. Won't be any cars 'cept ours, evening time, no one plays tennis no more, and COVID killed the school anyway. Good, seeya there."

"Hey, great, thanks. Oh…wait…so, Martin Franes? Is he—"

"Look, I'll tell ya everything tonight. Gotta go. Seeya at seven. Bye."

Turlock hung up. It was maybe the quickest conversation to arrange a personal meeting that Nick had ever experienced. He looked forward to meeting Turlock. If he was in person anything like he was over the phone, the meet-up should be both productive and entertaining.

***

Vern thought the best thing was to do an up and back, knock off the houses in order. So he started at Morning Glory and Forsythia. The corner house, same side of the street as the former Moore home, was occupied by Regina Roper. *I think Beryl said she's the only one now living there.* Vern imagined a widow, stooping with corduroy face, large fleshy hump behind her neck, coiled white hair, maybe a ticking grandfather clock in the hallway, and lots of quilts and pillows and plastic flowers inside. *Hope there ain't no pharmaceutical smell.* He thought an elderly woman would be a good jumping off point. *Start the tour easy, gentle, with an old crone…maybe she'll give me cookies and milk.*

He approached the two-story house and walked up the driveway that connected to Forsythia, then down a long sidewalk parallel to Morning Glory. He stepped onto the colonnaded porch and rang the doorbell.

Answering was a woman who did not look like what Vern had pictured. She looked to be in her mid-seventies. Her medium-length hair was jet black, possibly dyed. Her face was thin, with a small mouth and prominent nose shaped like a shark fin. Her eyes were set close to the fin. She wore a white button-down shirt with a wide collar, black slacks, and was barefoot. She was lean and flat-chested. Had it not been for her long hair and eye makeup, from a distance she could have easily passed for a man.

"Yes? What do you want?" she asked peremptorily.

Vern introduced himself and got straight to the point.

"I'm a private investigator researching the murders of Donald and Irene Moore. I was told you lived here when they were around. Can I ask you some questions?"

She gave him a cold look.

"They already wasted my time twenty-odd years ago. But…if you *have* to…come in."

He stepped into the foyer. Vern glanced around. No grandfather clock. No quilts or flowers. No smell of baking cookies.

She led him into a large family room. They sat down.

"Shoot," she told him.

Over the course of the abrupt, ten-minute conversation that followed, Roper reiterated what Vern had already read in the newspaper. The Moores moved there in 1987. They'd lived there eight years. He was an engineer, she a nurse. They kept to themselves. Roper heard no gunfire that night. She saw no people or cars. She was "shocked" to hear what had happened.

But he did garner a few new items of interest from "Gina," who by the end of the interview had seemed to warm to him a few degrees and insisted he call her by her nickname. First: her brother, one Gerald Delmonico, worked closely with Donald at Couch Industries. Second: during the interview she never called the victims, her former next-door-neighbors, by their first names. Third: both Irene and "him" were private people and, although "she was very friendly," "he" could be standoffish, almost to the point of rudeness. Fourth: she once or twice saw "strange Asians" enter their home. Fifth: she was adamant that Donald and Irene were murdered by the Chinese-

American mafia due to gambling debts Donald had accrued while on business in San Francisco—though she had no proof of that. And sixth: "he" was meticulous about upkeep of his lawn, to the point of being almost anal about its maintenance, and Regina, who was opposed to herbicide use and had numerous dandelions in her grass, felt like he lorded his beautiful yard over the other neighbors.

Vern felt ill at ease the entire time. When he left, she gave him one small smile, the only one she bestowed. She told him not to bother going to the Chins, they weren't home, that Lee was away on business and Jane always stayed with relatives when alone "due to fear." She also advised him to "watch out for Manny" when interviewing the man who lived on the opposite side of the Moore house.

***

Even before Vern rang the next doorbell, he had his guard up. Not only from Regina's word of warning, but from the sight of Henderlong lurking in his doorway when he and Nick had earlier walked up Beryl's drive. His apprehension increased when he saw Henderlong's flagpole. It had an American flag streaming from the top, but the flag was upside down. And underneath the stars and stripes was another flag with some type of design Vern had never seen before. The background was red and there were eight white semi-triangle designs arranged in a circle.

Vern assumed it was some new right-wing political design along the lines of the Gadsden flag ("Don't Tread on Me"), or visual code for the platitude "Make America Great Again."

He rang the doorbell. No answer. He rang again. No answer. Then, as he turned to leave, he flinched. A man stood at the corner of the house, staring at him. He was wearing a baseball cap and red plaid shirt tucked into a pair of stiff, dark-blue jeans. Vern walked down the front walk toward him and introduced himself. Henderlong waited a few seconds before replying.

"Ah'm Henderlong. Yeah, saw you and your friend earlier," he drawled in an odd accent. It was rural, but with more precise pronunciation and more musicality, less flatness, than most country people. "I like yer friend's vehicle." He pronounced the last word like most rural Ohioans, with the accent on the second syllable: "vee-HICKle."

Vern studied Henderlong's dour face. He had high cheekbones and dark eyebrows, with tufts of gray-black hair pushing outward from the sides of his cap. He had a long face with a tanned complexion, and soft, sad eyes that contrasted with a wide, frowning mouth. His most notable feature were several vertical, parallel creases etched into his cheek flesh, as if someone had placed a penknife there and dragged it downward.

Vern explained his mission. Unlike at Regina's, he didn't ask Henderlong if he should wear a facemask, figuring it would've fallen on deaf ears. Henderlong listened quietly, never removing his eyes from Vern's.

"Been through all o' this before. Least ya got no canine this time."

Henderlong didn't invite Vern inside his house, and the entire interview, which was more of a "feeling out" than anything—like two dogs sniffing each other's rear ends—took place in the driveway. As with Regina Roper, Henderlong's remembrance of the night of April 15, 1995 matched the newspaper account. His manner with Vern was polite, but reserved. He chose his words carefully, using basic language with little emotion and never exaggerating or offering anything that might overplay his hand. *Your base model of a human being*, thought Vern. Still, Vern felt "something simmering underneath." He couldn't place his finger on what it might be.

Vern did get two nuggets he could later deliver to Nick. Very small, but nuggets nonetheless. First: Henderlong disliked dogs. He made several disparaging comments about Lisa and her propensity to poop in his yard. Second: like Regina Roper, he had very little positive to say about Donald Moore, even venturing to call him "yer basic white-liberal hypocrite"...although he "barely knew the Moores." Third: he, too, had seen Asians visiting the Moores. Fourth: he was adamant that Donald and Irene were murdered by agents of the federal government, "prob'ly the CIA"—though he had no proof of that.

Henderlong's parting words to Vern concerned an interesting coincidence, which was news to Vern's ears. "Murders happened four days 'fore the Oklahoma City bombin'. And first newspaper coverage came out day o' the bombin'. Kinda spooky, huh? Not a good week. I ain't defendin' what McVeigh done—he and those other gun nuts are terrorists, pure and simple. The idea's to hit the bullseye. You pull back too far on the bow, you miss the entire target—but I'll tell ya, government's got too big fer its own good."

***

Vern left Manny Henderlong with a feeling in his innards like a partially digested chunk of ham had lodged there. He crossed Morning Glory to the home of Whitney and Linda Black, Whitney being descended from an old, wealthy, and distinguished Springbrook family. The Black house was one of the largest homes on the street, a two-story brick and vinyl edifice with extra-wide driveway winding up to a side garage, and a large playground on one side of the house. All of the houses on this side of the street were on slightly higher ground. When Vern reached the front door, he turned and looked downward at the homes of Henderlong, Roper, and Beryl and Arthur. Had he been a suburban Ohioan and had he the money, Vern could easily see himself living in Turnham Green on this side of Morning Glory. The south side of the street appeared solidly upper-middle class. But this side felt upper-upper-middle class.

Before he even had a chance to ring the Blacks' doorbell, their front door swung open, as if they'd been observing him. In front of him stood a cheerful-looking couple, roughly the same age as the other neighbors. The man was short, with thinning silver hair and glasses, and he was dressed casually. The woman, much taller, was plump with bright, sloping eyes, rosy and rounded cheeks, and a perky, impish mouth. She looked very Irish to Vern.

Vern went through his spiel and they invited him in, introducing themselves and ridiculing with polite laughter his offer to don a facemask.

"We both encourage social distancing and protection in public venues," said Linda, "as much for ourselves as for others' safety. But the fact you even offered tells us we can trust you!"

After Henderlong, the Blacks were like a whiff of spring honeysuckle. The threesome spent a solid twenty minutes exchanging pleasantries. The Blacks told them they were original Turnham Green residents, Whitney moving to this house with his parents in 1962, then inheriting the house after he married Linda. They'd witnessed both the rise and fall of Springbrook, and had considered moving but "our roots are here, and we just can't leave." They shared anecdotes about their grandchildren, who lived in nearby Grantchester Meadows, "on the south end of Springbrook, of course." Vern told them about Sharon and the kids, especially Frankie's difficult adjustment to Tulane, the school which Whitney had also graduated from "way back in the day."

Again, the Blacks just regurgitated what the paper had said about the Moore murders. They nodded at Roper's words about Donald's meticulous landscape maintenance, adding that he built one of the most beautiful decks in Turnham Green. Unlike Roper and Henderlong, however, they claimed both Irene and Donald were "good people."

When Vern mentioned he got the impression both Roper and Henderlong didn't like Donald, they rolled their eyes. The only thing they offered him was an observation that "even if someone had seen a stranger hanging around the neighborhood, this would not have been unusual." Vern asked why.

"Because that was during the annual Planter Relays," explained Linda. "Every year in the spring, high-school teams from all over Ohio and the Midwest gather in Springbrook for a two-week track and field relay tournament. It's been going on for, oh god, hundreds of years," she added for exaggeration. "They hold the event at the middle school—just behind us, other side of Dahlia. Whitney and I used to enjoy walking up there to see the sprints and relays…what event was it that Tom did, honey?" she asked her husband.

"The hundred-meter dash," offered Whitney. "He was a fast little bugger. Tommy was short, but fast. His pals called him 'Wheels.'"

Linda nodded enthusiastically. "Oh yes, he was like greased lightning. Earned a track scholarship to Williams College and—oh, here I go again, getting carried away, ha-ha! Anyway, so this thing went on all week, still does. And…let's see, where was I? Oh, yes, anyway, many of the out-of-town parents stay with the neighbors here, who open up their houses to the visitors. It's really kind of them. Why didn't we ever do that, dear?"

Whitney closed his eyes and waved his hand, as if in dismissal. "Yes, so what Linda's trying to say is that we here become used to seeing strange faces in the neighborhood around this time of year. The point being, if a murderer was stalking the streets, he'd nary raise an eyebrow. If I remember correctly, the murders happened on a Saturday, the day before Easter. Relay action would have been suspended on Sunday, but not Saturday."

Vern listened intently. He wore his patented cross-eyed buffalo-in-headlights look.

"Wow," he spurted out. He felt lucky he'd made contact with the Blacks, who were a goldmine of information.

"But that's not the only thing, uh, Vern" continued Whitney. "There's another little item, and it bothers the residents here to no end. Only this item isn't visual, it's *audio*."

"What do you mean, Mr. Black?"

"Well, track events have a lot of noise. There's the crowd, of course. There are endless announcements over the loudspeaker. And there are also the starting guns. So, these events sometimes continue into the evening, especially Saturday evening. Coupla gunshots in the early evening? No big deal. We here get used to it."

"But...but," began Vern, "all of the Moores' neighbors—all the others—claim they didn't hear any gunshots that night."

"Right. They *claim*," he emphasized. "Nothing against our good neighbors, but how can they in good conscience make that claim? There was only one household that told the police 'We don't know.' Guess which household?"

"You guys?"

The couple nodded. "We were just being honest, that's all. You get so used to hearing gunshots from the track, it's like music in the dentist office. Just background noise. You get accustomed to it. During the Planter Relays, no one can *honestly* claim they did not hear gunshots in the evening. In the dead of night? Yes, certainly. But not at, say, seven or eight, which is when the murders occurred, and when the Planter events may still have been going on.

"One other thought," Whitney continued, as Vern held in midair a fresh-baked Tollhouse cookie Linda had offered him.

"What's that?"

"Well, please don't think I'm being presumptuous, Vern. You're the expert."

"No, not at all, Mr. Black. Please, what's your thought?"

"Do you perhaps think the killer may have known in advance about starting guns and strangers during the Planter Relays?"

Chapter Six

By the time Vern said a hearty farewell to Whitney and Linda Black, the sun was turning a brilliant late-March burnt orange and his stomach was beginning to grumble—several Tollhouse cookies notwithstanding. He still had some time before Nick was to pick him up at the tennis courts, so he strolled toward the other end of Morning Glory to Jonquil Street, then made a left until arriving at the Planter running track, on the opposite side of the middle school from the courts. It only took him ten minutes to walk the distance. It struck him that, yeah, starting guns from the track would echo through much of Turnham Green, including the homes surrounding the Moore house. But how would those gunshots compare to muffled gunshots from a suppressed 9mm or .45 caliber semi-automatic from inside that same house? Would the sound have been different? Would it have been louder or softer? Would neighbors have known a difference in sound? Since nobody claimed to have heard any gunfire, including the Blacks, who said they "may have or may not have" heard noises that night, and since the killer or killers got away without being detected, did such questions even *matter*?

Vern wanted to get inside the killer's head. He knew Nick would want him to. Vern worked bunko in Philly as a cop for sixteen years and was used to shakedowns, musclemen, and guns—without being an expert on the latter—but he'd been with Nick long enough to understand that, although the type of weaponry used was important in solving a crime, *psychology* was just as if not more important. He and Nick were fairly certain by now that the killer was a professional. Someone who knew the proper equipment to use, when to use it, how to use it. A professional knew how to get to his victims surreptitiously, without breaking a door, window, or lock, activity that would not only alarm his "targets," but also possibly alarm neighbors. He knew how to obtain certain information from a computer while at the same time keeping his two victims a convenient distance apart. And he knew where to place the barrel of his gun, and how to correctly angle it, to make strategic hits that were fatal using only two bullets.

And in the case of the murders of Donald and Irene Moore—assuming the Blacks were correct about the Planter Relays—he evidently also knew how to minimize suspicion by timing his presence in the neighborhood *and* minimize any sound caused by rapidly expanding gasses inside one steel muzzle and two sonic booms issued by two steel-cased projectiles exiting one steel gun barrel.

He looked forward to sharing all of this with Nick.

Although it had only been a short walk from the little enclave of houses surrounding 157 Morning Glory, Vern decided to complete a full circuit and make another left, walking a short grassy section that separated Springbrook Middle School from the football field below. He reached his starting point at tennis court number one just as Nick's Porsche rolled into view. Nick pulled onto the gravel, Vern jumped in, the two fist-bumped, and Vern related everything he'd just gathered from Regina Roper, Manny Henderlong, and Whitney and Linda Black. Nick took special interest in Vern's relating that Roper was related to a co-worker of Donald Moore's, and slightly milder interest that two of the four neighbors believed the Central Intelligence Agency (CIA) or the Chinese mafia had assassinated the couple.

"These unsolved mysteries seem to drag out every kind of theory imaginable," Nick replied when Vern had finished his summation, "conspiracy theories included. It's really funny, and sometimes disturbing, what some people will believe. Did I ever tell you about the lonely hermit at the boarding school I attended after my folks divorced?

"No, but I have a feeling you're about to."

"Yeah, well, this school was way out in the sticks, right? Lots of woods surrounding it. And off into the woods, about a half-mile from the edge of the golf course, was this ugly, flat, concrete structure. Vines growing all over it. It looked like a place where farm hogs might be housed. But a man actually lived in it."

"Who was he?" inquired Vern.

"That's the funny part. Although no one knew what he did, and in the entire history of that school only a few people ever saw him, there was a theory that he was a serial killer who was hiding out. A Ted Kaczynski type. Just because of his house and his shyness."

"What was he in reality?"

"He was the night watchman. He checked on all the dorms at, like, three in the morning when everyone was asleep. The headmaster knew he was real shy, so he put the guy's paycheck in a hidden spot outside Old Main. I only saw him a few times, one week, when I got depressed about Mom and Dad's split-up and was having trouble sleeping, and I heard him coming up the steps. I peeked out at him through a crack in the dorm room door."

"What did he look like?"

"Like a little troll. Short, bowlegged, huge moustache, bottle-nose glasses. Carried a bunch of keys and a gigantic flashlight."

"Okay. Well. What's the moral of this story, Nick?"

"The moral is that he was just the opposite of a mass murderer. He liked people and kept us students safe. Also, I later learned from the headmaster that he had friends and relatives that often visited him in his concrete 'dwelling' in the woods. He wasn't as lonely as most of us thought.

"After my parents' split-up, maybe it was just me who was lonely."

***

On the way back to the motel they gabbed, then grabbed takeout Chinese from Jong Mei Buffet in honor of the absent Chin couple and Xi Lao Bing. Vern shared the Black's information about the Planter Relays occurring the same time as the murders, and about his and Whitney's theory that the killer may have used the relays for cover. Vern told Nick he thought Whitney was "really smart" and had "attended Tulane, Frankie's school" which amused Nick.

But Nick's amusement changed to concern after Vern let slip that the murders occurred "at seven or eight o'clock."

"Where did you hear this?" asked Nick.

"Uh…well, I think it was Whitney."

"How did Whitney know the shots were fired at that time?"

"Gee, Nick, I don't know. I guess he read the newspaper article."

"But estimated time of death was not *in* the newspaper article. Did you ask him from where he got that info? The police just thought Saturday night. Saturday night could be any time between five pm Saturday and sunrise on Sunday."

"Well, Nick. I realize we don't yet know how they were dressed. But if Irene Moore was sitting or standing at the dining room table, it was probably Saturday evening, not Sunday morning, because otherwise she'd have been killed in the bedroom wearing her pajamas. Right?"

"That's correct, Vern. Then my question to you is, how would Whitney Black have known she was sitting or standing in the dining room? We got that detail from Beryl only. The article just said Donald was 'at the computer,' and the two were in 'separate rooms.' Back at Gilly's I told you to remember that detail."

Vern's face dropped noticeably and his forehead scrunched, as if trying to justify why Whitney would have given him such precise information. Nick noticed.

"Don't worry, partner. You did good work. Beryl or Arthur could have spread the gossip, or maybe Whitney is related to the coroner or one of the cops. Anyway, I'm pretty certain the neighbors are in the clear. Cops surely got their alibis and weeded out neighbors and relatives from any 'persons of interest.' But, damn. That unlocked front door really bothers me."

Nick suddenly swerved to avoid a chipmunk that had darted toward his wheels.

"It's like a phantom popped up out of nowhere and shot them simultaneously, without warning. I'm convinced there was more drama in that house than anyone thinks."

The familiar blue, sun-logoed Comfort Inn sign appeared. Montaigne noticed—just under "FREE WI FI" and "HOT BREAKFAST" on the smaller marquee sign underneath—someone had added "JOIN US FOR PLANTER RELAYS!"

"Anyway," he continued, "right now I've got a date with Roy Turlock from the *Springbrook Daily* whatever. This should be interesting, he sounds like a character."

He dropped off Vern and the Chinese chow, spun a smokeless donut in the Comfort Inn gravel, and headed back to where he'd just left. It was only five seconds after his donut that he saw in the rearview mirror a car doing a U-turn. He drove north on Oak through several stoplights, his Porsche pulling the car along as if on a leash. It was dark enough now that he couldn't see the make or model, only that it was a white SUV. Nick had eluded cars in the past, and could have easily done so now, but he wanted to see just how far the car would follow.

He turned right onto Chamomile. The SUV followed. Nick pulled out his cell and dialed Vern.

"Vern, I think I'm being followed. It's a white SUV. License plate…let me see…H…U…something, can't make out the rest—no, don't bother, I can easily lose him. Wanna get to the courts, see what he does. Think we should look into a rental for you tomorrow, though—yeah— okay…bye."

The Porsche continued down Chamomile a good mile, through several stop signs. The school and gravel lot came into view, then the tennis courts. One car sat in the lot. Nick hit the gravel, slowed down, and drove toward the courts, close to the other car. The SUV followed.

What? What kinda tail is this?

Nick parked, got out, and walked to the rear of the other car, where a man was leaning against the trunk, one hand in his pants pocket and the other holding a can of Yuengling lager. The SUV stopped behind both cars.

"Roy Turlock? Nick Montaigne, nice to meet you," Nick said while extending his hand. The man shook it. "I don't know why this SUV is here. Followed me from the motel. Just a second…"

The SUV driver's door slammed. Walking around the front of the SUV was a short, matronly woman about seventy-five wearing a tight-fitting, print dress that came to her knees. She had a wide-brimmed, straw hat with a pink ribbon. Her thick, lipstick lips were stretched into a smile and her eyes were open wide.

"Hello!" she addressed Nick. "Are you Mr. Montaigne?"

"Yes I am." Nick recognized her. She was the woman at the church who scoped him and Vern when they first arrived in town. She smelled like she'd just bathed in lilac water.

"Oh, good, I thought you might be! I followed you from the Comfort Inn. I knew that you drove a hot rod. I hope you don't mind me barging in like this."

Montaigne felt a mix of both irritation and curiosity. He had a significant meeting with Turlock that was suddenly interrupted by a strange woman who had just tailed him. But he was also curious about her identity and her reasons for intruding.

"How did you...?" he sputtered. "I mean, why do you—?"

"I'm sorry to surprise you, let me explain. My name is Dorothy Claunch. I'm a friend of Beryl Henshall's. She told me you and your partner were in town to investigate the Moore murders. And, oh my…Beryl was right, you do look like John Gavin!" she tittered. "Springbrook is honored to have a handsome movie star in its midst!"

Montaigne shot a side glance at Turlock, who was scrunching his face and shifting position uncomfortably.

"All I wanted to do was welcome you to Springbrook. We're so happy that you're here to, maybe, finally, find out what happened. All our thoughts and prayers are with you. That was such an awful, awful tragedy. I actually knew Irene. I was her supervisor at the hospital. You couldn't imagine a more wonderful person. Anyway…" She glanced at Turlock, who was propping his jaw with one hand, the other arm folded across his chest and gripping his beer can.

"Hi Roy, how are you?" she asked frostily.

"I'm fine, Dotty" he muttered, halfway turning his mouth from his palm.

"Anyway," she turned back to Nick, "I know you're busy and I won't take up your time. If there is anything you need, or want, please feel free to contact me. Here's my card." She handed him a lavender business card, at which point Turlock, who was now halfway through sucking in some beer, became seized with coughing fits that spewed out much of the liquid.

"I will certainly do that, Missus, uh…" He glanced at the card. "Claunch."

"Thank you. So happy to have you here, and again, our thoughts and prayers are with you. Have a blessed day and...well...as my dear mother used to say, 'Take it away, Rosedale!'"

She waddled back to her SUV, her chubby white calves jiggling like Jell-O. Suddenly, she turned and took two steps toward Nick.

"Oh, I almost forgot! We would love to see you at Sabbath this Sunday. At Central Congregational Church. We are a very loving and accepting congregation."

"Thank you, Mrs. Claunch, but I'm actually not much of—"

"In fact," Claunch cut him off, "we even have a family of former *Episcopalians*. Imagine that! Of course, it took some time for our parishioners to adapt to the new faces. But now the family are one of our most ardent worshippers!"

She continued to her car and started the engine and left the lot.

Nick turned to Turlock, who was wiping the beer off his whiskered chin.

"Welcome to Springbrook. The red carpet has been unfurled, and by none other than Dorothy Claunch. She's matron and evangelist to the entire town. Just make sure you watch your 'p's and 'q's while you're here, or you'll get furled up and sent packing before you can say 'The butler did it.'"

"Yeah, I knew someone was following me here, but it didn't seem like a world-class tail."

"She's harmless—usually—but she thinks she runs the town because she's headed the Congregational Church Board of Deacons, Board of Trustees, and Board of

Endowment Fund Trustees for a hundred years. And her rubbery lips are really loose, so anything you do or say here will soon be public knowledge. Spreads everyone else's private business, which keeps people entertained. She serves a valuable purpose. The town gossip. And I'm the town drunk."

Nick laughed. He liked Turlock immediately. Short and wiry, he wore scruffy jeans, sneakers, and a ratty brown tweed sport coat over a plain, faded-black tee shirt. He had a skinny, double-twined, leather-cord bracelet on one wrist and a small gold earring in one ear. Hair was black and greasy and hung slightly over his ears. He had a wide, protruding brow. His skin had a dark-yellow tint, whiskers like medium-grit sandpaper, and he had red-rimmed eyes that squinted, especially when he laughed, which wasn't often. He had a gravelly voice. Nick thought he smelled like a tobacco factory. He appeared to be in his mid-forties.

"Should I wear a facemask?" asked Nick, holding up a wrinkled blue cloth.

"Fuck that shit," retorted Turlock. "Draggin' on Marlboros will kill me before any virus. As far as bein' a carrier, I'm single, my gal walked out on me, and if anyone else in this backwater town dies from what I might have, it's a few less Nazis here."

Nick laughed. "Well, the human species does have a few mistakes!"

"Yeah, 'mistakes' is an understatement," said Turlock with a disgusted look. "Sounds like the politicians I cover."

Before Nick even had a chance to pump Turlock, the reporter began snapping off gen like a typewriter on amphetamines.

"Okay, Montaigne is it? Nice name. Yeah, hate to tell you, but Marty Franes died years ago. Biggest loss this paper ever had. I was a cub reporter, fresh out of OU. He taught me most of what I know, gettin' leads, diggin' stories, seein' bullshit for what it was, you name it. Then he got promoted to managing editor, then he died…mysteriously. Prob'ly murdered, related to Moore case." Turlock took a slug of Yuengling and wiped his mouth with the back of his hand.

"Murdered?" asked Nick with surprise. "Really? How did he die?"

"He was found in his apartment in bed and the coroner ruled a heart attack. That's a lotta bull. Marty had a healthy heart. Hell, he jogged every day fer chrissakes! I'm convinced he was strangled, or smothered. Bottom line, he was sniffin' too close to the truth. I know it, I just know it." He took another swig then lit a cigarette.

"Death stick?" he asked Nick while holding out the pack.

"No thanks, I don't smoke tobacco. So…how close was he getting, I mean, what intel did he have?"

"Aye, there's the rub, Montaigne. He called me just before his supposed heart attack to have a tête á tête. Never happened. I felt like shit and wanted to pick up where he dropped off but, hate to say it, I got spooked."

Turlock glanced across the tennis courts in the direction of the former Moore home.

"The cops here acted really weird. Almost like someone was leanin' on 'em. Marty got sick o' writin' *police remain guarded* and *no new leads* and police *unable to confirm*. For Marty's original piece, all he got was basic shit, like gunshots to head, separate rooms, Saturday night, nothing taken, door unlocked. He did a follow-up 'n' got a reporter's equivalent of 'no comment,' which was *no new leads*. Assistant coroner was quoted as saying it was a professional job, that whoever went in there knew what he was doing, but cops refused to comment or elaborate, then the coroner went quiet, too. Then Marty died. I came on the scene here in '96, just after the Moore murders, did a couple anniversary stories 'n' got more from neighbors and relatives than the cops. They all saw Chinese hangin' around the Moore house. All were scared shitless and insisted on anonymity.

"You do know that Donald Moore made a lot of visits to Harban, China for business, right?"

"*Harban?*" asked a startled Nick. He remembered that Xi Lao Bing was from Harban.

"Yeah. He was a design engineer out at Couch and went there for a couple of industrial projects. That's why he and Irene hosted Chinese in their home. Guess it was sort of an exchange program thing."

Montaigne's brain began turning, clicking and chinking like the gears of a clock. He now, suddenly, clearly, connected everything. Almost everything, anyway. *Ramsey is brother-in-law to Moore and Ramsey kills Bing. Ramsey, Moore, and Bing all engineers. Bing from Harban, Moore visits Harban. Bing visits Imperial Inc., contractor to Moore's employer, Couch Industries.* He wondered if there was a fourth player in this game of connect-the-dots, someone associated with all of these men who might view assassination as a way to protect his or herself, or keep something quiet. He looked forward to paying a visit to Couch Industries.

Turlock continued filling in Nick with what he knew.

"So the Ropers, Blacks, Henderlongs, Steens, Schamadans, Blubaughs, and god knows who else in Turnham Green collectively determined Donald Moore got mixed up in some type of seedy Chinese business." Turlock took a big swig, a long drag, and stomped his empty can into the loose gravel. "Montaigne, if you took a poll of this town right now, about half would claim Donald Moore was a CIA agent and was killed by Chinese counterintelligence or the CIA itself. The other half thinks—based on lack of evidence of a break-in or struggle—the killer knew the Moores and was friendly with 'em. Now…" he continued, Nick getting an impression that Turlock was having fun and very satisfied with himself…"given what I've told you and what you've already deciphered from research…what do you think, Montaigne?"

Nick smiled wanly. He wasn't a card player, but he knew when to shield his hand. He needed a few more aces before displaying his cards, even with a guy he trusted, like Turlock.

"Lemme talk to a few more people here, Roy. Then I'll give you my thoughts."

"Spoken like a true chickenshit weasel," Turlock jested.

"I can tell you what my partner and I *do* have, though."

"Shoot."

"Probably one person. Probably male, unless a male hired by a female. Either professional or someone good with a gun. He had to get data from Donald's computer. He went in the den first, forced Donald at gunpoint to get or expunge files. Then shot him at point blank range. He used a silencer, with the door shut, so Irene, who was in the dining room, couldn't hear anything. Killer then left the den, entered dining room, pointed gun at back of Irene's head…two people now dead. Left the house, probably by front door, which he left unlocked, checked around quickly for passersby. Then hopped in his car that was parked in the street and drove off into history."

"Yeah, that's pretty good. I like it. I have him killing her first, then dragging a pleading Donald into the den. But your scenario makes sense, too. Montaigne, you should talk with Joy Dickson, the lead detective, who I think is retired. The bigshot police lieutenant in town is John Augustus 'Augie' Moriarty, scion of one of Springbrook's original families…though he's still working, and he's arrogant as hell, so you won't get jack from him. There are a few others, I forget their names. Gone is Jerry Delmonico. He worked with Donald at Couch, and scuttlebutt was his wife, Monica, and Don had an affair."

"That so? But he's dead, you say?"

"Yep. He was an alcoholic…worse 'n me. Cirrhosis of the liver killed 'im."

"Interesting. Roy, I'd like to stay in touch." He handed Turlock his business card—which, unlike Claunch's, wasn't lavender. "If you get anything, let me or my partner know. Also, we're staying at the Discomfort Inn, south of town."

"Shit, that dump? Whatever. Yeah, I'll dig into Marty's old files. There may be somethin' there. Like I said, I fagged out after Marty was murdered—I mean, after he was killed. But since you came along, I'm as elated as Dotty Claunch. We'll work together. I'll be your Deep Throat."

"Thanks Roy. Stay safe."

"Yeah, I'll try to avoid having a pillow attached to my face. Hey, speaking of Springbrook history…uh, do you know the history of this town?" Nick shook his head. "You have heard of 'Historic Uptown Springbrook,' right?" Montaigne nodded. "Well, it's historic, but not like the town patriarchs want it to be. Springbrook is like a little Peyton Place. For starters, everyone here seems to be related. So be careful what you say in public. Anyway, while the Moore murders take precedence in the crime annals here, there's been a lot of hanky-panky in Springbrook, goin' back to the 1962 tearoom sting. Know what a 'tearoom' is?"

Nick shook his head again.

"Tearooming is also called 'cottaging.' A tearoom is a public place where gay men meet to have anonymous sex. It's usually a restroom. Back in 1962 the town of Springbrook earned a dubious place in history. Cops set up closed-circuit cameras to monitor the sex, then busted every man they caught on camera. Almost a hundred of 'em. A big 'Clean Up America' campaign. The guilty got draconian jail sentences and earned scarlet letters for the rest of their lives. Most later left town or went into hiding. 'Member, this was in the Dark Ages when homosexual sex was sodomy and a crime. So, this campaign of the cops destroyed lives, families, but it was very democratic. It affected white, black, young, old, white-collar, blue-collar. Even a prominent alderman was busted."

"Isn't spying in a restroom, like, a violation of civil rights?" asked Nick rhetorically.

"Duh-uh! You'd think so! What's the saying, 'It can't happen here'? Well, it happened here in Springbrook. And no cop was ever called to task. Fortunately, times have changed. Well, maybe a little.

"The other incident happened in the seventies. Springbrook had a sheriff, Dick Moriarty, who ran the county like it was his own fiefdom. Half the people hated him, but the other half absolutely loved him. He was a big cult figure with the type of people who are unable to critically think…like happens with certain politicians today. The *Ob-Trib* fawned over him, he got re-elected time after time. Then an ambitious reporter—he was Marty Franes' mentor, like Marty's a mentor to me—exposed all this corruption, graft, bribery, suspect intimidation and brutality…and exposed how the paper had looked the other way the whole time. 'Cause Moriarty had connections there. This exposé was huge, even made *Time* magazine. The article heading was 'All-American Nightmare.'

"Anyway," he continued, "just a heads up. These are the kinda law enforcers we got in this county. They're not all bad, mind you. Just mostly." Turlock glanced at his watch. "Fuck, I just remembered, I gotta file another COVID story before deadline. Be a change o' pace, though, from writin' 'bout ministers gettin' rode outta town on a rail by crones like Dorothy Claunch."

"Ha! Just one other question, Roy…you may have heard about that Chinese businessman recently murdered in my hometown of Atlanta. Do you have any clues about the killer's last words? He said 'maraschino cherry' just before shooting the guy in the face."

"Hmm. The only connection I make is *Maraschino Cherry* was the name of a seventies hardcore porn flick. Similar to *Deep Throat* but better. Not as good as *The Ribald Tales of Canterbury*, though. O' course, I never saw those movies. Just heard about 'em."

"Oh, of course," said Nick.

"By the way, nice wheels," Turlock remarked, nodding at Montaigne's green-and-black baby. "Anyway, I stay away from fruit-type cocktails. I'm a beer drinker, so the movie's the only maraschino cherry I'm familiar with."

Turlock's forehead wrinkled. "Aren't maraschino cherries made from Bings?"

Chapter Seven

As Turlock sped out of the Springbrook Middle School tennis court lot, Nick hesitated a few moments before returning to Vern and cold chop suey at the motel. He looked toward the houses two streets beyond the courts and debated stopping by Beryl's. Not that he wanted to discuss Charlotte Brontë over tea and crumpets.

The best PIs understood the value of standing in a criminal's shoes. Montaigne was curious about the circumstances on the night of April 15, 1995, a spring equinox evening probably not unlike the present moment. Had the killer smelled the same faint honeysuckle he now smelled? Were the trees only just starting to bud? What were the chances of a murderer bumping into a passerby on the streets at this hour? Where might the murderer have parked his or her car…if, indeed, he or she even required transport? What might the lighting be outside the Moore home? Bright, only slightly luminous, or murky black?

Would he or she be able to view his victims through that rectangular slot of a kitchen window?

He slid into his Porsche, turned the key, and left the lot, the teenager in him unable to resist spinning another "Jim Rockford" before hitting solid pavement. He turned left, cruised down Forsythia, then made a left on Morning Glory. A single yellow light illuminated the front porch of 157 Morning Glory, but the small section by the door was shadowed by an eave. *A killer could have stood there all night without being seen from the kitchen. Plotting his next moves.*

He continued down Morning Glory, made a left on Jonquil, left on Dahlia, right on Forsythia, then took Chamomile back to the main drag on Oak. It was after the left on Jonquil that he saw the car behind him. Same car as was parked on the side of Chamomile during his interview with Roy Turlock. This one was black instead of white.

Montaigne let up on the accelerator. Without turning his head, his eyes rolled toward rearview and sideview mirrors. *Too dark to see the driver or plate.* He took the stop signs one by one. He arrived at Oak. Turned left. The tail did the same. But this time the street was practically empty.

Nick slowed. Suddenly, he pushed the clutch, shifted, slammed his foot against the accelerator, and spun the steering wheel a hard left, the rubber wheels of the Porsche scraping hard against the pavement and making a sick shrieking sound. The car whipped around a full hundred-eighty degrees. It looped around behind the tail, then repeated the process: clutch, shift, accelerate, spin.

Montaigne was now directly behind the black car. As he accelerated to close the distance, the black car sped up, flying down Oak at a high rate of speed, through a red light, and off down a long hill into the night.

Like a good boy, Nick had halted at the stoplight. There wasn't much he could do as far as identifying the driver. But he wanted to at least send Mister or Missus X a message: *Whoever you are, stay off my back.*

He pulled out of the intersection and upshifted. Then—thinking there was really no reason to rush to an unfamiliar sleep space—he downshifted. He sucked oxygen deep into his diaphragm, slid down into his bucket seat, slid a favorite CD deep into the console, and downshifted his mind to the Hammond organ swirl and sophisticated rhythms of "I Will Be Absorbed" by the band Egg.

***

At the motel, Vern had been busy. He'd gone out to Staples and bought a white magnetic dry-erase board plus four different colored markers. By the time Nick returned, he'd sketched out a large diagram. He'd made a large circle of notations. In the middle of the circle he'd written "Donald Moore." The circumference of the ring had notations for "Bertram Ramsey," "Xi Lao Bing," "Imperial Incorporated," and "Couch Industries." He'd drawn lines among all the names indicating relationships, with various comments scribbled here and there. Off to the left side, floating in space, he'd written the names of all the neighbors he'd met with that day. The right side of the board was blank, but featured a heading titled "Co-Workers."

Nick walked in Room 115 and was overcome by an odd mixture of odors: fried Chinese food, magic marker ink, perspiration, and damp athletic socks. Vern was standing next to the board, holding a long pointer, a proud smile on his red face.

"Whaddya think, boss?"

Nick deliberately delayed before offering any comments, wanting to milk Vern's anticipation. He nodded while pursing his lips in mock concentration.

"Yeah. Yeah, I like it. A few misspellings, but otherwise…I would've used a different color for the headings, but…yeah. Very nice, Vern. But we're going to have to edit that a little. I learned a few things from Roy Turlock."

"Oh?" said Vern. "Hey, that's great! What about Martin Franes?"

"Dead, I'm afraid. And according to Roy, under cloudy circumstances."

Nick removed his coat and tie, sat on one of the two beds—the one that Vern hadn't yet messed up—then slowly slipped off his Forzieri shoes. He went over to the Chinese grub sitting on top of the dresser next to the TV, poked through the plastic and Styrofoam with tired indifference, and decided against eating. Instead, he excavated a bottled water from the mini-fridge, then sat on the bed and gazed at the board.

"You're going to need to add another notation."

"What's that?"

"Harban, China."

"Really? That's where Bing was from. Why add that?"

Nick sighed heavily. "Bing was an agent of the Chinese government. He was here in the states to spy. Or do whatever it is those ferrets do. Roy just confirmed what was already percolating in my head. Donald Moore, as an employee of Couch, made numerous visits to Harban. Undoubtedly it was under the umbrella of his engineering work, and that may indeed be the case. There's no reason at this point to think Moore was in any way tied up in espionage. But the fact that an NSA agent, Bertram Ramsey, murdered Bing at a company whose work Couch Industries had contracted out, which sent its employees to Harban and even had them host Chinese in their homes…the evidence is just too great not to take seriously." Montaigne paused. "Especially since Roy, almost by accident, shed light on Ramsey's last words."

"'Maraschino cherry'?"

"Yes. 'Maraschino Cherry.' Capital 'M,' capital 'C.' It was evidently Bing's code name, and I'm disappointed in myself that I didn't recognize it long ago. Ramsey already knew the name. That's why Bing, quote unquote, 'spun around' after Ramsey uttered it, just before shooting him in the face. He was probably shocked as hell that someone at Imperial knew his secret moniker."

Vern listened in quiet contemplation. "That explains a few things," he said.

"And agent Frank Hardy was down there to stifle Kwiatkowski's investigation. Keep things in the NSA family, so to speak. So, anyway, you may wanna add Harban, China. And also draw another line, only a dotted line that connects Bing with Donald Moore. And probably Couch, too."

Vern picked up a black marker and did just that. He stared hard at his board, to see if there was anything else he might need to add, or may have missed.

"One other thing Roy told me," Nick continued. "By the way, he's a great guy, he'll be a tremendous help to us."

"What's the other thing?"

"Well, not that it's important, but Donald worked closely with a guy named Jerry Delmonico, who is now deceased. Turns out that his wife, one Monica Delmonico, may have been having an affair with Donald. And I think you told me Regina Roper had a brother, one Gerald, who worked with Moore? I'm guessing Regina's maiden name is Delmonico, and Gerald and Jerry are one and the same. We'll need to verify that, though."

"Gotcha. Anything else you wanna tell me, or think is important?"

"No, don't think so. Other than I met an interesting woman named Dorothy Clanch—maybe it's Claunch, I forget—who worked with Irene Moore at the hospital. And I was followed by a malevolent black vehicle—vee-HICKle—on the way back. Man, I'm bushed. It's been a long day."

"I hear you. You need to hit the sack. It might enliven you to hear I've set up meetings for tomorrow with some folks at the hospital, where Irene worked."

"Great, Vern. That interesting Claunch woman will be pleased. And I plan to call on the coroner and lead investigator tomorrow. Also got an appointment at Couch Industries."

"Cool. Just got one question. Why a dotted line between Bing and Moore? Why not a solid line?"

"We're not definite yet that Bing and Donald Moore knew each other. Bing, aka Maraschino Cherry, was an agent, yes, and undoubtedly had dealings with Couch Industries. But he still could have been outside the sphere of Donald Moore. That's why I want you to keep tabs on the Chin house across the street. Lee and Jane Chin. Whenever they get back, talk to them. Since they're Chinese-American, they probably speak and understand Chinese, and I'll bet they had some associations with whomever it was stayed as visitors in the Moore home. Maybe a neighborly visit, or meeting in the street. If they can confirm that, yes, one of the Moores' houseguests was a man named Xi Lao Bing…then we can make that dotted line a solid line.

"And if we can do that, we may be able to place Bing in that house the night of April 15, 1995." His face became pensive. "And assuming certain drivers of certain black cars don't succeed in altering our plans."

Chapter Eight

The north end of the town of Springbrook, Ohio looked very different from the south end. A steep hill descended abruptly from the town square. At either side of the hill were two streets, Maple and Main. Along each of these streets, small businesses were scattered like connecting Lego blocks, the storefronts all narrow, the brick dark and stained, some with faded, smoky lettering high up that dated to the late nineteenth and early twentieth centuries. Maple had a shoe store, jewelry store, lawyer office, café, two bars, pawnshop, loan office, hobby shop, soup kitchen, and the Democratic Party headquarters. Main had two cafés, three bars, a thrift store, nail clinic, Subway, rival pawnshop, rival loan office, and gun shop. Farther north on Maple was the courthouse and several small public parking lots surrounded by tall fences. Main had the county jail. On both streets the concrete was cracked and the sidewalks uneven. Drunks and panhandlers lounged around dirty doorsteps and alleyways. Empty beer and whisky bottles and overflowing metal trash containers added additional ambience to the depressing scene.

Springbrook south-siders seldom ventured into this den of wrecked dreams and shattered lives, which seemed to have a permanent odor—just a few stumbles beyond the smell of stale beer—of a slow, lingering death. South-sider field trips to the vicinity took place on Sundays only and halted at big, beautiful Central Congregational Church. Here, no matter what sermon was being served up, God was always benevolent and loving, and worshippers weren't obligated to view, much less think about, how the other half lived. They ventured beyond the church only if they arrived from out of town, like Nick and Vern, or if desiring the most direct route to Buffalo, Cleveland, Sandusky, Toledo, or Detroit. In fact, many of the youngest south-siders had never even *visited* the north end.

But this was where Roy Turlock lived. He had a second-floor apartment on Main above the gun shop. After leaving Nick at the tennis courts at Springbrook Middle School—*Home of the Planters*—he came here.

Turlock had lived at this address for nine years. Before that he was at a similar apartment over on Marion Street, just a few streets west of Maple. Before that he lived with his parents on the south side, although a brief shack-up with his news mentor, Marty Franes, had separated north from south. Turlock had never envisioned the economic straits that he now found himself in. He'd graduated from Ohio University's Scripps College of Communication in 1996 in the top third of his class, and had even briefly managed the editorial staff at that school's illustrious publication, *The Post*, a well-regarded training ground for successful writers, editors, and broadcasters worldwide. He'd wolfed beer and listened to live music in Swanky's and Bojangles with former television anchor Matt Lauer, a fellow journalism alumnus. Back in those halcyon days of drunken carousels on Court Street and late-night keyboard pounding in the basement of Baker Center to make news deadlines, Turlock had his future set in cobblestone: an entry-level reporting spot at a small Midwestern paper; then a more respectable gig at the *Cleveland Plain Dealer* or *Columbus Dispatch*; then off to New York City with, if he was lucky, a wire service job where he could travel internationally, see the world, and deliver truth to the folks back home.

Somehow things didn't work out. The internet happened, for one. In the wake of this explosion of digital media, newspapers struggled to stay afloat. Many were sucked up by media conglomerates, or went bust, like the venerable *Rocky Mountain News*, where Turlock interned one semester. Others had to severely cut back on staff. There was also the advent of "alternative" or "fringe" news, which Turlock derisively referred to as "propaganda." People suddenly didn't want that most beautiful of things—truth—but only wanted brain candy, to affirm their well-entrenched politics. *Hell, most folks can't even spell "propaganda" much less differentiate it from hard, factual reporting.* Somewhere along the line "mainstream news" became a dirty term, as big a curse word as "racist" was to liberals and "liberal" was to conservatives. Despite the fact that many of Turlock's university friends risked their lives overseas bringing truth to a skeptical public—like Frank Rapp, a college friend of Turlock's who was tortured and killed in Syria—they were now held in low regard, part of a nebulous mainstream media that placed profit and political correctness above substance and objectivity. *Maybe the criticism is deserved*, thought Turlock many times. *We all wanted to be Woodward and Bernstein. Maybe we lost sight of what's most important: hard, factual news delivered with sobriety...ratings and the Pulitzer Prize be damned.*

Oh, if Benjamin Franklin could only see the state of news and politics today.

But—and speaking of sobriety—there was one other thing contributing to Turlock's present-day circumstances.

It had less to do with the state of journalism and more to do with state of intoxication. The problem started while he was an undergrad. Drinking was just part of the scene, it was what you did after classes. It was the social lifeblood of Ohio University, top party school in the nation, where drunken student revelers made every Halloween the "Mardi Gras of the Midwest" and Spring Festival was a bacchanal that had to be seen to be believed. Turlock discovered a love affair with the bottle that eclipsed any other relationship. It was why he couldn't hang onto a girlfriend, let alone a marriage. It was also why he still slogged away as a beat reporter on a half-rate fishwrap like *Springbrook Daily News Journal Observer-Tribune*, which on good days was the "*Ob-Trib*," and on bad days was the "*SNOT*." His parents had tried to intervene, and he'd done the AA thing, but it was all for naught. Turlock was hopelessly hooked on booze. He was a lifer. A dissolute drunk, barely able to bang out a two-paragraph obituary.

After splitting from Montaigne, Turlock swung onto Cook Road then north on Oak. He stopped at the Seven-Eleven north of the square and snatched a twelve-pack, then returned to his hovel above Candy's Guns. Entering the one-bedroom apartment, his calico cat, Squirrel, pranced over with his tail stiff and high, and began rubbing against Turlock's leg.

"Hey Squirrel. What's cookin'?"

Turlock went to the kitchen that was cluttered with crusty plates and pans and ripped open a small can of Purina tuna, scooping the meat into Squirrel's plastic bowl that had "Property of Squirrel" scribbled in marker on the outside. The calico continued to purr and rub as he placed the bowl on the dirt-caked linoleum floor.

As Squirrel chomped away, Turlock stuck a few Yuenglings in the fridge and popped one open for himself, poured it in a glass, and added a drizzle of tequila from the half-empty bottle standing on a small shelf behind the sink. He drifted to a threadbare green couch covered partially by a dirty, cream-colored blanket, set his drink on a standing lamp table, opened up his laptop, and whipped off in twenty minutes his COVID story. He glanced at the wall clock: a quarter till ten. Good. *Four more hours till bedtime. 'Nuff time to call her and dig through the pile.*

He slumped back on the couch, propping one leg on the seat cushions. Squirrel jumped on him, purring, tail spiked. He turned on his cell and dialed.

Babe? It's me—not much. Just need to talk. It's getting' real bad with me—okay—okay—alright, next week. Listen...one other thing...

I need a favor—no, not like that...I need you to dig up some stuff...if you can. Listen, this guy's in town from Atlanta. He's a private eye, and he's diggin' into those Moore murders. You guys have history files, right? Pull the files from, like, early 1995. I need to find out what project Donald Moore was working on. I'll pay you back, baby, I promise—right, whatever project...aerospace, light-rail, marine, crane, dump truck—huh? Look, so they slap your wrist with a misdemeanor! Use your charm, hide it inside a Redbook magazine, I don't know...and keep this shit mum. I'm still convinced it was no accident with Marty—cool, you're a peach. Bye.

Turlock's arm dropped, still holding his phone. He draped his other arm over his forehead. Squirrel was now curled up in the corner of the couch, at Turlock's feet, his motor going. Turlock lay there a few minutes, thinking. He then sat upright and took a long swig of his Yuengling. He set it back down on the table, then got up and walked with a swaying motion into the bedroom. His bed was unmade. Several empty beer cans lay on stained carpet on either side of the bed. Above his bed was a black-and-white poster of a muscular, sleeveless tee-shirted Marlon Brando, a still from the movie *A Streetcar Named Desire*. Another wall had a black-and-white poster of a mug shot of a young Frank

Sinatra. A third wall had a colorful illustration of a bunch of multi-colored flowers. The poster caption read "Earth Laughs in Flowers." There was one dresser in the room. The only item on the dresser was a framed photo of Turlock's parents. The room had a putrid odor of spilled beer, semen, and cat urine.

Turlock opened up the closet door. On the floor was a stack of old newspapers. He sat on the floor, cross-legged, and began sifting through the papers. Occasionally he smiled and stopped sifting, long enough to gloss over a front-page story he'd written long ago. He dug deep into the stack, flinging papers right and left, until he reached an early byline of his, dated April 15, 1997. He tossed this paper on the bed. He dug a little further. When he reached the April 15, 1996 edition, he tossed this on the bed, also. Then he stood up and walked to the bed and lay down, crossing his legs and propping his head against a pillow that he pushed against the wall at the head of the bed. He unfolded the '96 copy of the *SNOT* and began reading:

Who killed the Moores?
By Roy Turlock
Observer-Tribune

One year has passed and local police are still stymied as to who murdered Donald Allen Moore and wife Irene Marie (Ramsey) Moore in their suburban south Springbrook home.

"I don't know why this case is so difficult," said Blanche Ramsey, mother of Irene. "You would think they would have something by now. It's as if a spaceship landed outside that house, an alien came through the walls, shot them, then the spaceship took off. My husband and I so much want closure to this nightmare."

Mrs. Ramsey said she thinks police aren't questioning the right people. "The killer is close to home. Someone they knew. Otherwise, why would the front door be unlocked? They always locked their doors."

Irene Moore's brother, Bertram Cabot Ramsey, believes he has an idea who killed his sister.

"I think I know who did it."

When Mr. Ramsey was asked to elaborate who that person might be, he declined to comment.

Neighbors of the Moores', all of whom choose to remain anonymous, believe the murders are somehow related to Donald Moore's business trips to China.

"He was always going off to Harban, China on business," said one. "The couple also hosted lots of Chinese in their home. I'll bet there's a bad egg somewhere in that basket."

All of the neighbors say the Moores were quiet, low-key people who kept to themselves. "Donald was very meticulous about his yard," said one. "It was common in the neighborhood to joke that, if one leaf fell on his grass, Don would be out there within minutes to pick it up!"

Only one neighbor had anything bad to say about the Moores, claiming that their dog, Lisa, was frequently left unmonitored outside. "Don't know why they never got no invisible fence. Everyone else does it."

Lisa was the only witness to the crimes. She was found by police several days later, wandering inside the house from room to room. She has since been adopted by Dorothy Claunch, a hospital co-worker of Irene Moore's.

Police Lieutenant John Moriarty was asked about the China connection.

"That's always a possibility. However, we don't yet have enough proof to pursue that line of inquiry."

When asked if government representatives had contacted his department, perhaps to steer the investigation, Moriarty responded "That's ridiculous. There's no reason why the federal government should be involved here."

Moriarty was asked to elaborate on the scene of the crime, but thus far has merely reiterated his original statement that "both victims were shot in the back of the head in separate rooms, Mrs. Moore in the dining room, and Mr. Moore at his computer in the den."

Police Detective Joy Dickson, lead investigator on the case, said they know what type of weapon was used.

"We got the bullets and know the type of gun. However, I'm not going to elaborate on that information."

Irene Moore worked as a nurse in the pediatric unit at Springbrook General Hospital. Donald Moore was a design engineer at Couch Industries in nearby Hernan, Ohio.

Turlock reached over to the night table next to his bed. He opened the drawer and removed a yellow highlighter. He snapped the cap off and highlighted the paragraph that discussed the dog. Then he highlighted Moriarty's words, "federal investigation." Then he highlighted Dickson's quote.

He folded the paper and set it on the side of the bed. Then he grabbed the other paper, unfolded it, and began to read:

Police remain baffled on 'professional, clean' Moore killings
By Roy Turlock
Observer-Tribune

In the crime annals of Springbrook, Ohio, few crimes have been as brutal, shocking, and mysterious as the murders of Donald A. and Irene M. Moore at their suburban Turnham Green home.

The middle-aged professional couple was gunned down on a quiet Saturday night exactly two years ago. To this day police remain baffled as to the identity of the killer or killers.

They remain guarded in their comments.

"It frustrates us to no end," said Police Lieutenant John Moriarty, who is supervising detectives in the investigation.

Assistant Coroner Jeannie Butler remembers the case well.

"It was shocking," she said. "Absolutely shocking. I have no doubt in my mind that these were professional killings. Whoever entered that house that night had singular intentions and knew exactly what to do. Professional and clean."

When told what Butler had said, Moriarty refused to comment, insisting Butler's statement was "her view and hers alone."

Lead investigator Joy Dickson said she is working on several leads.

"No killer, whether professional or not, is perfect," she said. "There's always something they will have missed. It would be great if someone could come forward with information, but that hasn't happened."

Police have interviewed dozens of people who knew the couple, including relatives, neighbors, and co-workers at Irene Moore's employer, Springbrook General Hospital.

"Irene was just a lovely person, and a devout Christian," said Dorothy Claunch, who worked with Irene Moore. "Everyone at the hospital loved her. She had the biggest, brightest blue eyes and just lit up the room whenever she entered. We're all still so sad, but we trust in the grace of our lord, Jesus Christ."

Only one neighbor of the Moores', Manny Henderlong, has agreed to reveal his identity. "Everyone else is scared," Henderlong claimed. "Afraid some bogie man going to come and get them. You can guarantee it's the (deletion) federal government done this."

Police have requested that anyone who has information on the Moore killings to contact them immediately.

NOTE: in an earlier story, the paper mistakenly printed Manny Henderlong's first name as "Fanny." The Springbrook Daily News Journal Observer-Tribune regrets the error.

Turlock took the yellow highlighter and slowly slid the ink end across the names of Jeannie Butler and Joy Dickson. He also highlighted Dickson's quote about people coming forward. He also highlighted the words "co-workers" and "Springbrook General Hospital."

Turlock rolled off the bed, snatching both newspapers, then shuffled back to the kitchen. He placed the newspapers on one of the few empty areas on the kitchen counter. He opened the refrigerator door and pulled out another Yuengling, again pouring it into a glass and dousing with a small stream of tequila, immediately taking a long chug.

He returned to the couch and lay down. Squirrel was fast asleep in the corner. He checked the clock again then flicked on the TV.

His head now warmed from the alcohol, his bloodshot eyes half-closed, he drifted into that fuzzy, half-conscious state just before sleep.

Then his weary eyelids cracked open a few millimeters. The name came back to him. *Joy Dickson. Yeah, she was the one. Just before Marty was killed.*

Chapter Nine

Hernan, Ohio is in corn country roughly sixteen miles west of Springbrook. It's not much of a town. Most of the residents are farmers, although a few managed to procure low-paying jobs at Couch Industries as mechanics. The majority of Couch's employees live in Springbrook or Palmersburg, although some make long daily commutes from the larger Ohio cities.

Nick's appointment was at nine o'clock. He was to first meet with President of Product Development Karl Haslett. After him, it was anyone's guess.

Just before leaving for Hernan, Nick and Vern swung into Avis Rentals-Springbrook and rented a nice Honda Accord for Vern. While Nick was out at Hernan, Vern planned to see if the Chins had arrived home yet, then meet several hospital co-workers of Irene Moore's at Sharkey's. Nick had already briefed his partner on Dorothy Claunch, so Vern was clued in to the town matriarch.

Montaigne was surprised at the size of Couch Industries. A three-story brick structure, it extended into the surrounding cornfields for at least a quarter-mile. A large sign was erected at the turnoff from Springbrook-Palmersburg Road. The sign read "COUCH INDUSTRIES: Building American Interests Worldwide"

Manifest Destiny is still alive and well, thought Nick.

He turned into the visitor area just adjacent to a massive parking lot that was half full. Exiting the Porsche, he saw a gigantic flagpole in the middle of a lush, green lawn fronting the facility. Uppermost on the pole was a large American flag. Underneath was the triangular swallowtail state flag of Ohio. Underneath that was a yellow-and-black flag that read "Couch Industries" and which appeared to have the company logo, which was a caricature of a sinister-looking, tusked rhinoceros. Underneath the company flag was a black-and-white POW/MIA flag. And below that was yet another banner: a black and blue "Thin Blue Line" flag in support of police. In the past few years—in the wake of the killings of unarmed blacks by cops and the rise of various groups demanding justice—Montaigne had seen more than a few of what he termed "politically-driven backlashes" down in Georgia. He tried to avoid politics, as well as the opinion-editorial page of the *Atlanta Journal-Constitution*—and as a private investigator whose partner was an ex-cop, he supported law enforcement entities, and even donated to police fundraisers—but he also knew such overt, tribalistic displays to be controversial. So he questioned the wisdom of a high-profile business displaying such a flag.

On the day that Nick arrived to meet with employees who had worked with Donald Moore, the five flags were flying at half-mast due to a recent mass shooting.

He opened the entrance door, which had a sign prohibiting the carrying of firearms, and checked in at the visitor desk. The receptionist—who, other than the Comfort Inn desk clerk, was the only person in Springbrook he'd seen so far who was wearing a facemask—asked to see his identification, and Nick displayed both his driver's license and private investigator license. He filled out a questionnaire that required he divulge his name, address, phone number, age, nationality, height, weight, profession, purpose of visit, time of arrival, estimated time of visit, who he was visiting, and whether or not he'd left the country in the previous six weeks. After completing the questionnaire, the receptionist carried the form into another room. She returned and handed Nick a yellow badge, informing him he "must wear it at all times while in the facility, and must not go anywhere unless accompanied by a blue-badger." Nick asked her to define "blue-badger," and she told him a "blue-badger" is a Couch employee, a "yellow-badger" is a visitor, and a "red-badger" is a visiting foreign national.

Nick jokingly asked her if they might have any purple badges. She looked at him, but with the mask he didn't know if she was smiling or not. She then told him to take a seat, that she would alert Mr. Haslett to his arrival. He unwrapped a half-stick of cinnamon gum, chewed it uncomfortably a few seconds under his mask, withdrew and wrapped it, and flicked it into a nearby trashcan.

Five minutes later a man stepped into the waiting area. He appeared to be in his late sixties or early seventies, though Nick couldn't be sure due to his mask.

"Mr. Montaigne?"

"Yes. Mr. Haslett?"

"The one and only! Please call me 'Champ.' It's an old Army nickname. I won a Golden Gloves tournament and the guys won't let me forget it!"

"Okay…Champ. Feel free to call me Nick."

Haslett led Nick out of the waiting area. Immediately outside, at the end of a long hallway, was a full body scanner. Two uniformed security guards, a man and a woman, stood on either side. Haslett instructed Nick to remove everything from his pockets. Nick removed his cell, car keys, wallet, gum, and a few coins, placed them on a tray, and stepped into the scanner. Cleared, the attendants waved him on. He retrieved the items.

Haslett apologized, "Sorry we have to do this, and I realize it's a pain."

"No, I understand completely."

"Many former employees left Couch under, shall we say, hostile circumstances. So we try to minimize any possible reprisals against the company. Also, and I'm sure you know, some of our work here is quite sensitive. A lot of DoD contracts that involve top-secret information. Many of our employees have to undergo robust background checks, from Controlled Unclassified all the way up to Top Secret with an SSBI."

"Sounds all very arcane," remarked Nick, without knowing what an SSBI was.

"Then again, we have more mundane projects, too. Don was working on a crane project, I think, before his unfortunate demise."

Haslett and Montaigne walked down several long hallways flanked by windowless doors. Nick noticed Haslett's distinct military stride: quick, forceful steps, rigid neck, arms held outward from his body as if he was trying to air his armpits. He noticed the walls were all cinder block painted a bland cream shade. The cracks where the walls met the hall floor were filled with an ugly rust-orange substance. Certain sections of this orange substance were so old they appeared to have black mold spots. The walls were adorned with old photographs of early-model airplanes, trains, tractors, earth-moving equipment, oil pipelines, and military vehicles. Everywhere he looked he saw American flags. Passing through one long section, he picked up a strange odor, an unnatural chemical smell, like mothballs overlaid with sugary orange.

He also noticed small black devices at sporadic locations at the top of the outer wall. He assumed these to be security cameras.

Eventually they entered a large room completely filled with gray, chest-high cubicles. Nick heard the murmur of voices and saw a few heads pop up over the cubicle walls. Almost every one of the cubes had a miniature American flag poised atop. At the far end of the room on the wall was a single large flag about three by five feet. Underneath this flag, someone had Scotch-taped big black letters that read "Support the Troops!"

Haslett told Nick the facility was only half-occupied due to the virus, but normally it was buzzing. The two entered a substantial office just outside the flag. Haslett offered him a seat, then took a chair behind a large oak desk. He told Nick to feel free to remove his mask, which both men did. Nick glanced around. The office was sparsely furnished. He saw a small row of hardbound books on one table. On another table were several framed, colored photos: Haslett and an attractive woman who appeared to be his wife; and several smaller photos of middle-aged and young people who appeared to be his children and grandchildren.

Haslett saw him looking at the photos.

"My reason for being," he said. "Sometimes I sit here for ten minutes staring at those photos.

"That's a very good-looking family. I'm sure you're proud."

"I am. Bobby and his wife Lindsay have three daughters. They're on the left. And Cindy and Chuck have a boy and girl. Nothing like being a grandparent."

Nick liked Haslett, who had a warm manner despite the austerity of the surroundings. He spoke softly and with precision. He was tall, about six-three. Looked like he ran or worked out regularly, which gave him a fit physique that belied a small jowl under his chin and eye wrinkles whenever he smiled. He wore black, semi-rimless eyeglasses that set off a thin face with high cheekbones, narrow nose, thin lips, and a small cleft in his chin. He had a full head of dark-brown hair streaked lightly with gray, parted on the side, whisked high to one side with a small comb of hair over his forehead.

"I'm always curious about surnames," said Nick, testing the waters as he liked to do with interviewees. "Is 'Haslett' English or Welsh?"

"Actually, neither, but nice try. It's Hungarian. It was originally 'Halaleset,' but old Domokos, our immigrant ancestor, anglicized it to make it easier for people. And like so many immigrants, head off bigotry."

Haslett began picking his teeth with a toothpick. With businesslike precision, he shifted to the subject of Montaigne's visit. "So…you're trying to solve a twenty-five-year-old double homicide? Why so late to the ballgame?"

Nick smiled. "Well, Mr. Haslett…Champ…not sure if you heard of that murder-suicide in Atlanta recently. But my partner and I have determined that the killer—one Bertram Cabot Ramsey—has connections to Springbrook. We were hired by his daughter to investigate those connections."

"Roger that. But how does that relate to Don Moore?"

"Ramsey was the brother-in-law of Donald Moore. Additionally, we think the man he killed—one Xi Lao Bing—was a Chinese agent who somehow was involved with your company."

Haslett's eyes widened. "Holy moo goo gai pan, Batman! Well, I can tell you, Nick, that we've had a lot of foreign nationals walk down these halls over the years, including Chinese. They're all here on business, either consulting about product or collaborating with our engineers on non-government projects."

"Sure, I understand." Nick waited a few seconds until his first question, wanting to gauge Haslett's reaction. "Does the name 'Maraschino Cherry' mean anything to you?"

Haslett appeared to concentrate. "Well, I've had a few tropical drinks on various cruises my wife invariably forces me to undergo. They usually have maraschino cherries. But I'm guessing that's not what you mean."

Nick chuckled. "No, not exactly."

"Well…maybe Marv can help you on that…but I never really knew Don Moore. This is only a part-time office for me, I'm closer to upper-level executive dealings, unfortunately. We call it 'Mahogany Row,' the luxurious, wood-paneled offices upstairs, second floor, closer to President Lomax. Don was down here, part of a small group of engineers who specialized in industrial-related projects, some of which took him to China. His closest associate was Jerry Delmonico, someone I did have dealings with. He was VPPD—I'm sorry, Vice President of Product Development—but he's since passed away. Also Marv Goosebill, head of Design Engineering. There's also Melody-Clair Fitzpatrick, who worked with Don a bit, although she started here only just before Don's murder.

"Anyway, I've asked Marv to stop by, give you a company history, show you around, and discuss Don's role. Don't let him put you off. He's…well…let's just say every company has its own culture, including Couch, and Marv is immersed in that culture. I'm actually one of the few left-leaners in this whole joint! Although the facility is only half-filled these days due to the virus."

Nick couldn't help bringing up Haslett's book collection and asked about his small library.

"Ahh, a reader! Are you perhaps a Goodreads member?"

"I certainly am."

"Well, we'll have to friend each other. A lot of my lunch breaks I'm curled up with a book! I'm in the middle of a fascinating book about a nineteenth-century sailing ship, a whaler turned Civil War storage hulk. Very esoteric reading. Anyway, one can learn a lot about someone by their book collection."

"I say the same thing myself."

Suddenly, a shadow passed across the room. Haslett looked up. "Ah, speak of the devil! Right on time, Marv."

Montaigne turned around. Standing in the doorway, his hands dangling at his sides, was a man who looked to be in his sixties. He was partially bald, with dirty black and gray whiskers begging for a shave. His legs were skinny like matchsticks, accentuated by a prominent paunch, his gut even more pronounced than Vern's. He had large ears, the kind whose lobes are thick and droopy, and he wore thick glasses. His singular facial feature was a pair of large, red, wet lips. As he stood in the doorway staring at Nick, the lips were pursed.

Goosebill looked to Nick like someone whose life had been dedicated to a prone rather than mobile position, a large bowl of Doritos within arm's length.

Nick stood up, shook hands with Haslett, agreeing to "hook up on Goodreads," then followed Goosebill down the hall to a room on the other side of the cubicle farm. On the way he passed several casually dressed young men who noticed his three-piece Napoletano suit and two-toned Forzieri shoes—or perhaps saw that he was a "yellow-badger"—and who nodded with a polite "Hello, sir" and "Good morning, sir."

Goosebill and Montaigne took chairs. Unlike Haslett's part-time office, Goosebill's was filled with junk. Papers were stacked everywhere. On the wall behind him was a large framing of a five-dollar bill, but instead of a photo of Abraham Lincoln there was a photo of a smiling and confident Ronald Reagan. A side wall was covered with a gold, snake-adorned "Don't Tread on Me" flag. At the edge of his desk, pushed so that visitors could easily see it, sat a red, pocket-sized copy of the U.S. Constitution.

"Thank you for meeting with me, Mr. Goosebill." Nick debated whether or not to pursue his next comment, then determined the best way to pull information was to get Goosebill warmed. "You have a very interesting name."

"I've been told it's Scottish," Goosebill replied, his thick wet lips glistening. "Supposedly there're a lot of geese in Scotland."

"Lots of sheep, too. I'm a Scotch whiskey man and visited Glengoyne Distillery when I was there years ago. There were sheep all over those beautiful highlands."

"Why do Scotsmen wear kilts?" asked Goosebill. Then without waiting for Nick to answer, he gave the punch line. "To get to the sheep easier."

"Ha-ha," Nick laughed, more out of politeness than humor. Goosebill's delivery seemed as dry to Montaigne as one of Vern's hybrid martinis.

"Anyway, Mr. Goosebill, thanks for meeting with me."

"No problem, sir," bluntly responded Goosebill.

"Mr. Haslett said you worked closely with Donald Moore. As he may have told you, I'm here to investigate his murder. A bit late perhaps, but…"

"Yep, I knew Don. He was under me as a design engineer. Guess Champ wants me to give you some company background first."

"Uh, yes, that would be nice. Thanks."

Goosebill then launched into Couch's history, at times sounding like a programmed robot.

"Couch was started in 1911 when Elias Couch invented a special lugnut that had a rubber reinforcer. A few years later, Couch's lugnuts helped our boys win the Great War, Mr. Montaigne.

"After the war, Elias Couch died, and his family sold the company to a Wall Street investment-banking firm that issued 250,000 shares of stock, converting Couch into a public company. New president H. Uriah Blackman began robust acquisitions. Anything to do with the heavy transport industry: pumps, compressors, brake pads, and especially earth-moving equipment. Later, gaskets used to connect underground oil pipe segments. The oil business brought Couch Industries to Houston, and in 1943 Couch merged with Norgran Thompson and expanded into Army tanks just before the second big war. After that conflict, Thompson broke off and aligned with Granger. A lot of Eisenhower's interstate system is the result of the

Thompson-Granger 'Big Cat' digger. The Big Cat was maybe the sharpest crane ever made, until Bucyrus-Erie's 'Big Muskie' came along."

Nick's eyes drifted toward the walls of Goosebill's office, vainly seeking a window to gaze out of.

"After the Gulf of Tonkin incident in 1964, there was a huge need for tanks again, for our boys in 'Nam. 'Nam was good money."

Duckbill paused as if recalling something. Then he continued.

"Some time during all this," Goosebill drawled on, "Couch Norgran got sucked up by the multi-national Japanese firm Yanaka, whose specialty was surface mining. Yanaka Couch Norgran did robust business, albeit maintaining separate product lines. It also acquired the operating assets of Davis Moeller Manufacturing, which produced mining tractors."

Nick felt an urge to check his Rolex Submariner, but refrained. Instead, he took in Ronald Reagan's smiling face on the framed five-dollar bill behind Goosebill's head. This elicited thoughts of a political cartoon he'd seen as a child. It showed Mount Rushmore with Reagan's head sandwiched between the other four presidents, all of whom were frowning and glaring at him. Nick smiled at the remembrance.

Goosebill halted his monologue. "Something funny, sir?" he asked. Nick held up his hand and shook his head with a "Nah, nothing" expression. Goosebill continued.

"Anyway...as I was saying...culture and communication with Yanaka proved to be a problem, and there was too much intra-competition due to the overlapping markets, so Couch bailed from Yanaka, Norgran, Davis and Moeller in the early 1980s. By then Granger had split from Thompson, since the market was really down after 'Nam, unfortunately. They re-aligned with Couch in the mid-eighties and began doing a lot of DoD work, including aerospace. Don Moore was here during the CG years. CG then merged with oil and industrial giant Hardison out of Texas, becoming HCG. After the Iraq War, Hardison and Granger jettisoned Couch. Till just recently. Last I heard, there was a rumor we may be re-joining Hardison, which is doing a lot of aerospace stuff, including Mars exploration. Couch today, like I said, specializes in heavy industrial. But it's not like the old days. We need a good war again."

Montaigne's mouth hung open like an airplane hangar. He thought he detected froths of spittle leaking from the corners of Goosebill's lips.

"Interesting," was all he said, his eyeballs returning to life.

Goosebill led Nick on a short tour of the first floor, where most of the engineering work was accomplished, the senior engineering staff occupying rooms that surrounded the cube farm. He pointed out Donald Moore's old office, left vacant as a sort-of memorial. Next door to this was an office with the nameplate "Melody-Clair Fitzpatrick." Goosebill tapped on the door, then stepped inside.

"Mel, this is Nick Montaigne. He's here investigating the Moore murders."

A middle-aged woman stood up from behind her desk, her eyes widening. She removed her glasses and stepped around the desk, holding out a tiny, pale hand for Nick to shake. Nick was taken aback. He didn't expect such a beautiful female to be working at, from what he'd gathered so far, a largely male-dominated firm that specialized in hard manufacturing and industrial work. She was very thin with semi-long, pastel-pink fingernails. Her blonde hair was long and wavy and streaked with mocha-brown, framing a small face. Her eye sockets were deep, and she wore baby-blue eyeshadow that painted her eyes with a luminous glow. She wore white slacks and a loose-fitting, reddish-orange, silk blouse that revealed a pair of ample breasts.

"Nice to meet you…Mr. Montaigne," she said in a high-pitched, little-girl voice.

"Nice meeting you, uh, Melody-Clair is it?"

"Just Melody is fine. Or Mel."

Goosebill explained the purpose of Nick's visit, after which Melody told Nick, "Anything I can do to help, please let me know. Don was a very nice man, though we worked together only briefly." She handed him her business card, and Nick did the same.

Goosebill led Nick into the break room, which had a coffee machine on the counter and two banks of vending machines along the walls. They each poured cups of coffee.

Suddenly, the overhead intercom began crackling. Goosebill put a finger to his lips and whispered, "Our president, Byron Lomax. His morning address." A voice boomed over the loudspeaker.

Good morning fellow Couchians! I trust everyone is well. Congratulations to Theresa Ames, who is still leading the Step-Up to Health fitness initiative! Keep taking those literal steps toward fitness so we can reduce obesity, hospital visits, and costs. We will be observing you, and encouraging you, as you do this.

Nick glanced at Goosebill's outrageous belly, and at the two floor-to-ceiling vending machines, filled with chips, cookies, candy bars, and soda pop.

Please remember that Active Shooter Training will be held tomorrow at ten o'clock in Bay Number Two. Let's all show up and welcome our instructors, who are kind enough to share their timely knowledge with us. Additionally, the company picnic will be held Saturday at Richelieu Park. We look forward to seeing all families for a fun day of food and frolic. Lastly, make sure to lock your computers at all times when leaving your offices, even if it's only for a snack or cup of coffee. And let me remind you, if you see any strange behaviors by anyone in the building, immediately report such behaviors to your supervisor. If you observe strangers lurking outside company premises, report it immediately. If you see former co-workers lurking outside, report them immediately. And do not hesitate to report anybody who is not wearing either a blue, yellow, or red badge. We need to protect Couch and those freedoms which our great nation holds dear. Oh yes…and try to wear a facemask and practice social distancing. Thank you, fellow Couchians. And God Bless America!

The intercom crackled and went silent.

"Active Shooter Training?" immediately asked Nick, as he and Goosebill returned to Goosebill's office.

"Yes. We contracted a local company to train Couch employees on how to react in case someone in here goes postal. You never know. I'm looking forward to it."

Nick remained silent.

"What's the matter?" Goosebill asked. "You got a sour look."

"Nothing," said Nick. "Just think it's sad that private businesses—not to mention schools and churches—have to prepare for that kind of mayhem when the government takes such little action."

"Sounds like yer one o' them nanny-staters," said Goosebill in a tone of contempt. Nick ignored the remark.

They returned to Goosebill's office. Nick was just getting ready to ask about Donald Moore's last assignments, and his relationships with both Goosebill and Jerry Delmonico, when Goosebill asked him what kind of "piece" he carried.

Nick answered "I don't carry a piece. I believe psychology is a stronger weapon."

"Wow. I would bet in yer profession yer in the minority."

"Probably. But I'm fine with that. Mark Twain said any time he found himself in the majority he started getting worried. Ha!" He crossed his legs and smiled cordially.

Goosebill's eyelids lowered and he pursed his fat lips, as if studying some new marine creature just hauled from the depths. He continued with guns.

"I'm a firm supporter of the Second Amendment."

Nick glanced at the shiny red book on the edge of Goosebill's desk. He predicted the conversation would sooner or later detour here. He assumed Goosebill owned guns and wondered what kind they were. And if his collection might include silencers.

"You don't think that the Second Amendment's words have been misconstrued?" Montaigne asked.

"Nope. I'm a strict constructionist. 'The right to keep and bear arms shall *not* be infringed,' he quoted part of the amendment's words. "As Chuck Heston once said, those old white guys knew what they were doing."

"No exceptions for 'arms'? Like, assault-style weapons, bazookas, tanks? Not being facetious, just asking."

"Ha! Nice try, but you know what I mean. 'The right to keep and bear arms shall not be infringed,'" he repeated, quoting word for word from the Second Amendment in an imperious voice.

"Okay. That's somewhat problematic, though."

"Oh? How is it problematic?"

"It's a problem because the gun lobby consistently refuses to consider restrictions and exceptions for public health. Take the First Amendment. You can speak in public, right? You can criticize the government all you want. And that's a good thing. But you can't yell 'Fire!' in a crowded theater. It's illegal. Why? Because if you do this, public safety is threatened. Also with the *written* word. You can publish pornography...if you want. But *child* pornography is illegal. So, even though freedom of speech is protected by the Constitution, there are limits. Shouldn't there also be limits with gun sales and ownership?"

Goosebill's upper lip curled into a sneer. "What about my right to protect myself? Huh? Like from whoever killed Don Moore? Did you think about that?"

"No one says you don't have the right to protect yourself. *Within limits*. As far as I know, gun control organizations have never tried to ban handgun, shotgun, or rifle ownership.

"Then, Mr. Goosebill, there's that pesky part about 'well-regulated militia,' which the NRA and gun lobby never mention. 'Militia' is a plural term. It means more than one person, such as a standing army. So you think an *individual* with an AK-47 is a well-regulated militia? Again, just asking."

"Well, that's just the way they talked back then. You know, the language. Times have changed."

"But I thought you were a strict constructionist?"

"They talked that way but they meant an individual," Goosebill retorted, his voice raising a half-decibel. Nick remembered Haslett's words about Goosebill. He thought it wise to gently steer the subject elsewhere.

"Do you own any guns, Mr. Goosebill?"

"Whaddaya think," came the deadpan reply. "I got 'em and I'm licensed."

"How about Donald Moore? Do you remember—"

Goosebill cut him off. "Don Moore had no guns as far as I recall. He was yer classic snowflake do-gooder liberal. I didn't like the guy and most folks 'round here didn't either. 'Mr. China' we called him, always practicing his limited Chinese in the office. But that doesn't mean I killed him and his wife, if that's what yer drivin' at."

"No, I wouldn't dare," Nick replied, his face assuming a mock-serious expression. "Let me ask you this, though— and only because others have rumored such—was there any office chatter about CIA involvement?"

Goosebill's large wet lips spread into a grin. "I'm assuming you mean Don. A few around here brought up that rumor. He had high-security clearance, Tier 5 screening I think, which is why he got a lot of the robust government contract work. That allowed him to go to China. But, no, there's never been any proof of CIA involvement. Can I give you some advice, Mr. Montaigne?"

"Yes, please."

"Don't pursue that CIA angle. It's a dead end. Others already tried."

The two stared at each other several seconds. Nick heard footsteps outside the open door.

Goosebill continued. "You may want to look into Jerry Delmonico. Course, he's dead now. But his wife and Don had an affair. It was all over the office. Someone, I forget who, found them together one evening at Richelieu Park, lips and hands all over each other. His wife—her name's Monica Delmonico—is still around. Talk to her. Just a suggestion, though."

"Yeah, I appreciate that. Thanks. Just a couple other questions."

"Yessir."

"Does the name 'Maraschino Cherry' mean anything to you?"

"Nope. Should it?"

He carefully studied Goosebill's reaction. "No. Just wondered. How about the name Xi Lao Bing?"

Goosebill shook his head. "I'm not real good with Chinese names. There were a lotta red badgers 'round here back in the day, and Don was in the middle of it. I may have met someone by that name but, hell, I can't remember."

"Sure. Sure. Okay sir. Let's see…oh, yeah. Do you remember the last project Donald was working on here?"

"Well…he died in, what…early '95? Okay, I'm guessing that would have been the MaxxDig 60 dragline excavator."

"Dragline excavator? Pardon my ignorance, but what exactly is that?"

"A dragline excavator is a large industrial crane. Used for open-pit mining, mainly. You know, like the Big Muskie that I mentioned earlier. We designed 'em here.

The MaxxDig 60 was the biggest we ever tackled. Woulda been commercial work, not government. Before that he was on a big aerospace project. Think it was a Lockheed Martin contract, Sikorsky helicopters maybe, though not positive."

"Okay. Thanks, this is good stuff."

"Yep."

Nick sat forward in his chair as if to stand up, then stopped. "Oh yes, one other question…this president, uh, I think you said his name is Byron Lomax?"

"That's right."

"How long has he been here?"

"Long before me and everyone else. 'Cept maybe Crashcup, who's been here forever. But Lomax had nothing to do with Don Moore, if that's what yer drivin' at."

"No, I was just curious."

"He came on board after the previous president shot his head off in his office one morning."

"What?" blurted a shocked Nick. "Seriously?"

"Yeah. He evidently had severe depression that no one knew about. Anyway, President Lomax has been controlling things since."

"Is it possible I could meet with President Lomax?"

"Lomax? Ha-ha-ha-ha! You might as well try to change direction of the Mississippi River. Nobody sees Byron Lomax. He sees us, but we never see him."

"Why not?"

"Well, he gets here early, before anyone else, and leaves later than anyone else. That's only when he's in town. He's also really reclusive, like a Howard Hughes. I think only one person's ever seen him. That would be Crashcup."

"Crashcup? That's really his name?"

"No, it's a nickname. His real name is Clyde, but someone a long time ago gave him that name after an old television cartoon."

"Can I talk to, uh, Crashcup?"

"He's working remotely. But I can call him."

Goosebill reached to his desk phone and banged some numbers. After a few rings, a voice on the speaker said, "Hello?"

"Hello, Crashcup? Marv Goosebill here, what's happenin'."

"What's happening? Nobody knows! Many people think they do, but they really don't. It's all a big guessing game!"

Goosebill shot a weary glance in Nick's direction. "Ha, funny, Crashcup. Look, there's a yellow-badger here—a private investigator researchin' the Moore murders—and he was wonderin' about President Lomax. You met him once, didn't you?"

"Who, me? Lomax? I never met him. Who told you that, Delmonico? And Moore murders? He's a bit late to the party."

"I thought you met Lomax years ago. Didn't you talk to him in the parking lot once?"

"Nope. Never have. And don't spread any rumors, to a yellow-badger or anyone else."

Goosebill puckered his lips. "Okay, Crashcup. Sorry for the bother. I'll let you get back to your game of solitaire. Seeya."

"See me? How can you 'see me'? I'm here and you're there. You can't possibly—"

"Bye, Crashcup." He hung up. "Well, sorry Mr. Montaigne. Could o' sworn he'd met Lomax. Oh well."

"That's alright. Well, I think that about covers it, Mr. Goosebill. For now, anyway. I may need to contact you again."

"You know where to reach me. I'll need to walk you out."

They left Goosebill's office and walked down the several long hallways past the black-and-white framed photos, American flags, and sugar-orange-mothball smell. Nick had a perverse urge to flash the peace sign at one of the security cameras, but knowing he'd probably be making a return visit, he didn't want to alienate himself, so he kept his hand restrained. He turned in his yellow badge at the reception desk and signed out on the register. After stepping outside, he and Goosebill shook hands. Nick turned toward the flagpole with its colorful banners half-mast and jokingly remarked "You folks get any more flags and you'll need a taller pole."

Goosebill lifted his upper lip.

As Nick walked toward his gleaming green Porsche—the gaudiest set of wheels in the entire lot, half of which contained pickup trucks—he reached in his coat pocket for another stick of cinnamon. But instead of pulling out the gum, his fingers touched something else. He withdrew Melody-Clair Fitzpatrick's business card.

Chapter Ten

"Nick, do you really think someone like a Regina Roper or Dorothy Claunch could be involved in a double homicide?" Vern had asked his senior partner the morning of Nick's visit to Couch Industries and Vern's lunch date with Claunch. "I mean, really, hondo. How could an old lady even lift with her dainty hand, let alone pull the trigger of, a Beretta or Glock 17 equipped with a heavy suppressor?"

Nick gave Vern his patented "Vern, you've got a brain, use it!" look. Instead, what came out was "Vern, you're smarter than that. First of all, the murders happened two-and-a-half decades ago. So these 'old ladies' as you call them weren't that old. They certainly could have handled one of the weapons you mentioned, especially if they'd practiced ahead of time. Remember, that front door was unlocked, and the Moores were in different rooms, so their guards were down.

"Secondly, who's to say they didn't hire a hit man, someone who was pulling triggers the exact same moment one of these 'old ladies' might have been washing dishes or folding laundry? Or they show up at the door with said hit man or woman in tow? Maybe to have their pretend 'cousin' pretend to ask Don about landscaping ideas? BOOM, then BOOM…?"

Vern nodded in acknowledgment. "Yeah, but what would be the motive? Lisa pooping in their yard? Jealousy over Don's landscape skills? An argument over politics? I mean, come on!"

"Don't discount those scenarios, Vern, as crazy as they might sound. Remember Wanda Holloway? The Texas mom who hired a hit man to kill the mother of her daughter's cheerleading rival? Those things happen. Truth is stranger than fiction."

***

Vern was hoping to digest some truth while eating at Sharkey's. He liked the club sandwich they served. Didn't hurt that, if the interviews got too sticky, there was an upscale bar close by where he could wet his whistle.

But Dorothy Claunch had suggested The Covenant café, two miles southwest of the square, and Vern wanted to be accommodating, so he acquiesced.

Vern had assured Dorothy that nobody at Springbrook General was considered a suspect—it was the furthest thing from his and Nick's mind. They just wanted to get a feel for Irene's background, whether or not she and Donald had any enemies, if Irene had ever exhibited any depression or tension while at work, et cetera. He didn't mention that he also wanted to scope out the Moores' Morning Glory neighbors whom he'd already dropped in on. If Nick and Roy Turlock's characterization of Dorothy Claunch was to be believed, she undoubtedly had some gossip and notions.

The Covenant specialized in breakfasts and lunches and closed down in late afternoon. Sunday brunch was their busiest day, but weekdays always had at least a dozen cars in the lot, usually safe, conventional models like Vern's recently rented Honda Accord.

As Vern walked toward the front door, he saw three older women gathered there. The one in the middle was substantially larger than the others. *That must be Claunch*, he thought. He walked up and introduced himself. Indeed, Dotty Claunch was the middle woman, wearing sandals, baggy black slacks, and a white blouse decorated with carnations. Her hair was stacked high on her head and her pudgy face was covered liberally with makeup. She introduced the other two women: Siobhan Moriarty and Florida Patton, both of whom worked with Irene Moore in the pediatric wing of the hospital, until Moore was promoted as a nurse supervisor of two entire floors. Claunch herself was Director of Nursing and oversaw all three women.

The foursome found a booth in one corner of the restaurant, which consisted of merely one large, sparsely decorated room. Vern sat by the wall and shared a seat with Claunch, the two of them wedged so closely together that their large thighs touched. Vern thought Patton looked very pretty. She was tall and very thin and had a platinum-blonde pageboy haircut with a bright red carnation stuck in the side. Her most notable feature was an exceptionally small mouth and chin. From the time they met until being seated in the booth, Patton wore a small, close-lipped smile and her large eyes seemed not so much to observe Vern as to absorb him.

Moriarty, on the other hand, appeared nervous, glancing around frequently. She had striking blue eyes and neck-length, Raggedy-Ann-styled hair as black as ink. Her only notable facial features were heavy black eyeliner and the beginnings of bags under her eyes.

Vern told her he'd never heard a name like hers before.

"It's spelled S-I-O-B-H-A-N but pronounced 'Shivan.'"

"Oh, is that Middle-Eastern?"

"No, it's Irish" she said perfunctorily. Vern felt his neck getting warm.

"Siobhan is a Moriarty," said Claunch, as if the name was Springbrook royalty. Vern had seen a dozen signs around town with the name 'Moriarty' displayed. He also recalled Nick relaying Turlock's words about disgraced former Sheriff Dick Moriarty.

They ordered their lunches and talked about trivial things. Vern had learned from Nick to approach things gradually, like a good novel that grows organically.

"Thanks for meeting with me, ladies. Oh, by the way," he addressed Patton, "I love that carnation."

"Really? Why, thank you! Are you a horticulturist?"

"Nah. Well, maybe a little."

He turned away shyly then dug into the matter at hand.

"Ladies, I know it's probably tough to talk about, but that must've been a horrible shock twenty-five years ago."

The three shook their heads in synchronicity. "Such a terrible, terrible thing," volunteered Claunch. "And to think I'd only just talked with Irene that morning."

"Oh? What did you talk about?"

"She had some concerns about work. Nothing serious, mind you. We'd just promoted her and I think she was worried about her job performance. I told her she was doing great work and that I had total confidence in her abilities. The children just adored her. In pediatrics she was like everyone's mom."

"She was older than me and I idolized her," said Patton in a strong voice, her upper lip barely moving, as if numb with Novocain. She then flashed Vern a coy smile. Moriarty stared into space.

"So," Vern continued his questioning, nodding at Moriarty and Patton, "the three of you worked together in pediatrics, then Irene moved, uh, upward? Not to rattle the cage or anything, but was there any resentment? Not necessarily from you, of course, but maybe others?"

"Oh, no!" insisted Patton, still absorbing Vern with her eyes. "I was so happy for her! She was a hard worker!" Claunch and Moriarty appeared slightly rattled.

"Yes, she was a hard worker, Florida," added Moriarty testily. "But remember, we both had seniority. If you remember, Dorothy, I'd been with the hospital eighteen years by that time."

Patton dropped her head. Claunch reached out and patted Moriarty's hand. "Siobhan, dear, that was a long time ago." She turned to Vern. "There was some slight resentment among the nurses, but nothing serious. One sees that in every job, right?"

"That's true," said Vern, noticing Moriarty once more glancing around nervously. "And certainly nothing that would incite a person to murder! Ha-ha-ha!" The others smiled awkwardly at Vern's clumsy attempt at humor.

The waiter brought their food. The table became uncomfortably silent. Suddenly, Vern felt a warmth on the back of his hand, which had been resting on the table. He looked down. Claunch had laid her palm across it.

He was momentarily in a state of shock. This was a public place, after all. Two other people across the table would certainly notice this impertinent action. And Vern was wearing his *marriage* ring! He was at a loss how to react.

Just before pulling his hand from under her grasp. Claunch reached over to also hold Siobhan's hand. All four people were soon gently pressing each other's flesh.

"Lord," Claunch droned lugubriously, her head down, "we thank you for your bounty. Bless this food and those gathered here. And give us strength today, and in the days to come, to resolve this terrible tragedy that has befallen our beloved friends, Irene and Donald."

The three women harmonized a soft "Amen." Vern, still rattled from the hand-holding, tacked on a lame "Amen" just a half-second late.

They started to eat, and Vern was just about to ask if anyone knew the Moores' neighbors, when the restaurant's noise level went up a few notches and Claunch and Moriarty looked toward the front of the room. A tall man in uniform was exchanging greetings with several people at one of the front tables. He laughed, then slowly ambled toward their own table. Vern recognized him as the man in front of Central Congregational Church. He knew cop garb and determined the man was a police lieutenant.

The man was average height and had gray-black hair under his hat. He had a small, Irish-looking face, the forehead with two horizontal, parallel creases, and thick eyebrows a striking black. His cheeks were slightly pockmarked, and he had a pair of long sideburns that dated him. His smile was close-lipped; friendly, but wary at the same time.

"Well, good afternoon ladies," he politely addressed the women. They introduced to Vern Springbrook Police Lieutenant John Augustus "Augie" Moriarty. Claunch added that he and Siobhan were brother and sister.

"Okay, well, I'm not surprised," Vern said, "I've been seeing that name a lot!"

"Augie, this is Vern Wister. He and his partner Nick Montaigne are private eyes working on the Moore case. We're all so grateful for their assistance!"

"Good to hear," remarked Moriarty frostily. He turned to his sister. "Siobhan, I need to see you later. When you get time." Then he turned to Vern.

"I applaud your gusto Mr., uh, Wooster. That case is a tough nut to crack. So I suppose you think you'll succeed where we failed, maybe?"

Vern answered with a friendly but confident, "Nick and I don't *think* we'll succeed, sir, we *expect* to succeed."

"That right? You two licensed?"

"We're a licensed agency and a member of GAPPI. Need to see license?"

"What the hell's the GABBI?" Moriarty asked impudently, ignoring Vern's question.

"Georgia Association of Professional Private Investigators. Those are the letters 'P' and 'B.' The letter 'P' as in 'pester.'"

The three ladies looked increasingly ill at ease. Nick had often advised Vern when his temper got out of control. "Stay cool, take a few deep breaths," he admonished him. It's one of the reasons, along with sporadic periods of excessive drinking, that Vern had taken up Pat McCauley's advice to try Bible classes. Pat hoped the classes might offer Vern a little perspective, which in turn might help keep his blood pressure stable. But, unfortunately, the classes turned out to be just another phase. When his study group began discussing Proverbs 23:13-14, which advocates physical punishment of children by parents, Vern got into a heated argument with the other class members and angrily dropped the class—along with the Bible.

"My, the GABBI. That's impressive," said a sarcastic Moriarty. "But this is Ohio, not Georgia."

"Doesn't matter. Our investigation started in Georgia, where we were hired, so we have state reciprocity."

"Where in Georgia...*Haddock Cove*?"

"Atlanta."

"Atlanta? That's a big town. The only thing I know about Atlanta law enforcement is how you mistakenly targeted Richard Jewell during the Olympics."

"Wrong on two counts," spat out Vern, getting increasingly hot. "First, I was a cop in Philly during Jewell, so it wasn't my targeting. Second, the FBI suspected Jewell, not Atlanta law enforcement. So go shine your tin star, buddy." He turned away from Moriarty.

"Calm down, calm down. Nothin' personal."

"No? I suppose a black car tailing my partner's Porsche is also not personal."

"I know nothin' about that. You shoulda reported it."

"Doubt it would've helped. The cops in this county don't exactly have a sterling track record, Sheriff Dick…I mean Lieutenant Moriarty."

Moriarty looked at the women, whose heads hung low. He then turned and left The Covenant.

A minute passed as the group quietly chewed their food. Then Claunch spoke.

"Well, again, we're so happy to have you here in Springbrook, Vern!" Florida Patton flashed him another sly smile. Siobhan Moriarty's mind seemed elsewhere.

"Thank you, ma'am," muttered a now-recovered Vern. "If it's okay, just want to get an idea of the Moores' neighbors. Nick and I just want to rule out anyone who might have had a serious grudge." His eyes darted to Moriarty. "Have any of you—actually, I'm sure you have—met any of them? I had occasion to speak to Regina Roper, Manny Henderlong, and Whitney and Linda Black."

"Manny's an ass," immediately volunteered Moriarty. "He has a grudge against the entire town. Everyone knows it."

Claunch gently admonished her, "Now, judge not lest ye be judged, Siobhan dear."

"Well it's *true*, Dotty." Then turning to Vern she added "All you have to do is attend a Springbrook town hall meeting, and you'll see what I mean. The others are nice. I played euchre with Linda. She's very sweet. But I don't know Whitney too well."

"Vern," Claunch continued where Moriarty left off, "Turnham Green is one of Springbrook's premier neighborhoods. I'm sure you noticed that. Beryl and Arthur Henshall are dear, dear friends, although recent arrivals in town. While they are not native to the U.S., they love their adopted country and are good Christian people.

"Gina Roper is nice. I don't know the Blacks too well. They're papists," she added while clearing her throat. "Although I remember their son Tommy was a star athlete.

I think he got a scholarship to one of the Ivy League schools."

"Williams College, actually" said Vern. "My son Frankie goes to Tulane." The women lifted their eyebrows as if to say "Oh, how impressive!"

"How about the Chins?" Vern asked. "Lee and Jane? I haven't met them yet, I was told they're out of town."

"I saw Jane at the store this morning," said Patton. "So they must be home now."

Vern waited for Claunch to contribute something about the Chins, but she kept a strange silence. He noticed this and decided to push a button.

"Now, do you think they are perhaps first-generation Chinese?"

"I think so," said Patton in her pinched way, her tiny mouth nibbling birdlike at her food. "Their English is a bit rusty still. From my talks with Jane, Lee visits China quite frequently."

He noticed Claunch chewing her food harder than normal. She continued to remain mute. Vern wondered if the Chins might be Buddhist instead of Christian. The rest of the meal was devoted to routine subjects unrelated to the Moores. When the foursome said their goodbyes in the parking lot, Florida Patton placed a soft palm lightly on Vern's chest to say "how much I enjoyed meeting you."

***

Vern had a lot of time left so he decided to revisit the Chin house, especially after hearing that Florida Patton saw Jane at the grocery store. Once again, though, no one was home. The only thing he saw was the red plaid shirt of Manny Henderlong, undoubtedly observing him again, inside the front door. He left Morning Glory and decided to visit the Springbrook Public Library to poke around in the stacks and on the computer.

As he walked along the sidewalk leading to the series of cement steps that led to the old, gray stone building with thick pillars that comprised the library, he saw a familiar face standing at the foot of the steps. It was Police Lieutenant John "Augie" Moriarty. He was conversing with a short, dark-haired man in a three-piece suit. Vern tried to appear oblivious, but Moriarty saw him, mouthed a few words to his companion, then took several steps toward Vern.

Vern steeled himself.

"Yeah, uh, hey, Mr. Wister was it?"

Vern looked both ways before landing on Moriarty and acting surprised. "Oh. Didn't see you. Yes. Got the name right this time."

Moriarty ambled up alongside Vern. The two men were about the same height, despite having different physiques.

"Hey, look," began Moriarty, "I'm sorry for the minor fireworks earlier. Didn't mean to touch a nerve."

"Nerve?" asked Vern. "No nerves here. Just doin' my job, fella."

"Yeah, well, just wanted to apologize. You gotta understand that we've had folks all over our backs trying to solve this damn case. Not so bad these days, but years ago, you wouldn't believe. Half the town lived in fear. And everyone had pegged their own killer. Neighbors were on us, politicians on us, newspaper on us…so, yeah, we're a little touchy regarding the Moore murders. But I still should o' acted more professional."

"Hey, no problem. I used to pound a beat as a cop so I know the score. No hard feelings."

"Right, thanks. Yeah, uh…well, as I'm sure you and your partner know this case has never been officially closed. So our department can't give you guys any leads. All I can say is…don't rule anyone out. That includes friends and neighbors. Everybody in this town is fair game. And since I see you're headed into the library, you might wanna check out some old copies of the Trib. I don't mean the articles on the murders, I mean the editorial page. 'Specially those from back in '95, '96. There are some letters to the editor that will blow your mind."

Vern scratched his cheek. He hadn't intended to read newspaper letters to the editor, but Moriarty's words made him insanely curious. He thanked the lieutenant and began walking up the long steps, when Moriarty called after him.

"Yeah, another thing. Again, *our* hands are tied. If the D.A. finds out I handed you leads, I'm workin' permanent security at the local roller rink. But you might wanna look up a woman named Joy Dickson. She's retired now but she was lead investigator back then. She might be able to help you."

"Yeah, cool. Joy Dickson. We'll do that, thanks."

He continued up the steps till out of breath, then sauntered into the cool, hushed interior of the library, with its marble flooring and overwhelming odor of ancient paper stock and glue. It brought him back to pre-internet days when libraries had all the answers. He had a fuzzy memory of card catalogs and the Dewey Decimal System, but the fuzziness was strong enough that he opted for the Information Desk.

"Excuse me, ma'am," he asked a young woman with hair the color of orange soda, black tattoos on her arms, black paint instead of eyebrows, a nose ring, and a small sore on her lower lip from what Vern assumed was another metal ring, "I'd like to pull up some old copies of the *Springbrook News Journal Herald Observer*...can you help me?"

She looked at him like he'd just passed gas.

"Do you mean the *Springbrook Daily News Journal Observer-Tribune*?"

"Yeah, sorry. That's the one."

"They're all on microfilm. What issues do you need?"

"Well...let's start with early 1994."

She made what Vern thought was an exaggerated sigh and climbed off the tall stool she was sitting on. Ten minutes later Vern was set up at a table with several rolls of microfilm stretching from the years '94 to '97. He clumsily rolled the first roll into the machine, adjusted the viewer, and began scrolling through the newspapers, spinning the handle until each editorial page came into view.

It didn't take him long to notice a pattern. It wasn't every issue, but at least fifty percent of them had at least one letter to the editor signed by the same person: Manny Henderlong.

Many of the letters dealt with Bill and Hillary Clinton. They were the usual polemical attacks that dabbled with conspiratorial themes: the Clintons had Deputy White House Counsel Vince Foster assassinated because he threatened to reveal compromising Whitewater information; Hillary was close friends with Weather Underground terrorist Bill Ayers and had funneled money to him in the 1960s; Bill Clinton's public approval ratings were so high because he had insiders working for him at the Gallup Poll.

Some of the letters, though, jumped across the aisle: Speaker of the House Newt Gingrich's marital infidelities were far more serious than what was being reported by the press; the Republican Party had hired Paula Jones to try to seduce Bill Clinton in a Little Rock, Arkansas hotel room so they could smear him later; Ronald Reagan's Alzheimer's disease was the result of years of alcoholism that was covered up by "his handlers."

Many of Henderlong's letters consisted of vicious attacks on the NAACP. He didn't restrict himself to the federal government, either, penning numerous letters about state and local politics. Although not all of them, many of the letters ended with the all-caps statement "AND THAT'S THE TRUTH!"

But the letters that most caught Vern's eye could be separated into two categories: a bitter feud between Henderlong and Springbrook City Council, and a theory concerning Bush family ties to the CIA.

In 1990, Henderlong tried to buy some land at public FDIC auction that was adjacent to his tool and die shop at the edge of town on Granby Road. Henderlong ultimately lost a fraught bidding war. He then unsuccessfully tried to get a rezoning so he could establish an easement for a sewer line from his shop. Negotiations dragged on several years. He then unsuccessfully tried to sue city council and neighboring businesses who he felt were trying to push him out, and had to pay steep fines for refusing to connect to the main sewer line.

Vern dug up several articles in the vicinity of Henderlong's editorial rants and learned the identity of the party that outbid him: Donald and Irene Moore...his next-door-neighbors in Turnham Green.

Vern printed out the relevant articles and letters to take back to the Comfort Inn to show Nick.

The second category of letters appeared in the months following the murders of Donald and Irene. Henderlong didn't specifically accuse the CIA of masterminding the Moore assassinations, but Vern saw what he was implicating. And, significantly—despite the ludicrous ravings found in other diatribes by Henderlong—Vern found these implications entirely plausible.

Henderlong cited a number of published sources (which Vern planned to consult before leaving the library) that claimed Couch Industries had for years been rumored to employ CIA agents, dating all the way back to George H.W. Bush, and which paved the way for the future president to become CIA director. Henderlong emphasized in his letters how the Moores were killed: cleanly and professionally, shot once in the back of the head, probably by a gun equipped with a silencer, in separate rooms.

The gist of Henderlong's letters was that Donald Moore's engineering work at Couch was merely a cover. He was in reality an agent of the CIA who had been assassinated because that organization had deemed him a liability based on—according to Henderlong—his cozy relationship with certain shadowy figures in Harban, China. And Irene was dispensed with because she was a witness.

Of course, in these letters Henderlong made no mention of his own antagonistic relationship with the Moores.

Vern printed all of these letters as well. He gathered up all the printouts, but—in his excitement to get back to the Comfort Inn and show Nick—he forgot about verifying the sources which Henderlong cited. He also forgot about returning the rolls of microfilm, which were scattered helter-skelter on top of the table, the last roll still spooled on the machine that he forgot to turn off.

As he briskly shuffled past the young woman with the orange hair, his white shirt tail hanging outside his navy-blue corduroys, he gave her a quick, nervous grin. She sighed, shook her head, and returned to her notes on the 1962 Springbrook tearoom sting for her university thesis on the history of homophobia.

Chapter Eleven

They met at Green-Wood Cemetery. It was on the south end of town just north of the interstate and county line, surrounded by corn and soybean fields and farmhouses still with weather vanes, their dilapidated barns still advertising "Mail Pouch Tobacco." The graveyard was quiet and secluded, and they could see in advance if anyone might have followed. The cemetery grounds were flat, with very few fat tree trunks where a person could conceivably hide. Besides, they would have seen anyone approaching via car long before a tree trunk could even provide cover. The other side of Route 31 was an abandoned dirt lot, now filled with weeds, but where cars had once gathered for an anachronism known as a drive-in movie. Faded skeletal scaffolding was the only remnant of the giant outdoor screen. Turlock remembered Marty telling him about the low-budget pornographic, caged-women, and car chase flicks that he once watched there as a teen. Movies with titles like *Mama's Dirty Girls*,

Macon County Line, *The Big Doll House*, and *House of 1000 Pleasures*. Later in the night, after the Springbrook goody-goodies went home to bed, came the really hardcore flicks. They all lacked plot and character, but that hardly mattered to Franes and his buddies. Yeah, Turlock remembered Marty talking about how flicks like *Mary! Mary!* and *Maraschino Cherry* had assisted with his burgeoning "education."

Maraschino Cherry! Turlock was struck by how the name now had a much different meaning. And right over there, at the back end of Green-Wood, was where poor Marty's remains lay. And Donald and Irene Moore lay toward the back as well, with a larger gravestone, on the opposite side of the cemetery. Yeah. This was a good place to meet. It was poetry. A passion play. A Greek tragedy, with Roy Turlock as a supporting actor. But the dénouement had yet to unfold.

The day was chilly, standard early-April weather for Ohio. He reached Marty's grave and zipped his windbreaker, then pulled his pack of ciggies from the pocket and lit one up. *Gotta make the vape switch, these things are killin' me.* Several cars swished by on Route 31. He squatted by the stone and focused on the granite engraving:

MARTY FRANES
June 16, 1955 – February 19, 1998

Just a name and two dates. Nickname, no less. Simple, no bullshit, just like Marty had lived.

I'm right in your footsteps, chief. But I got time before story deadline. Keep the faith; we'll get to that beautiful thing. He took a long drag and blew smoke toward the stone.

Turlock reflected a few more minutes until hearing the crunch of gravel. He turned and saw a red SUV coming down the main cemetery lane. The car turned right onto a side lane then stopped. After a few seconds a tall woman stepped out of the car and closed the door. She turned her head several times as if looking for someone. Turlock walked toward her. She saw him. She walked toward the rear of the car and glanced several directions as if making sure the coast was clear. Turlock stepped up to her.

"Hey babe. No one else here."

Melody-Clair Fitzpatrick bounced her car keys in her hand. "I got what you wanted. It wasn't easy. I'll be lucky if someone didn't see me."

"Yeah, I know. That place is like a fishbowl. I really appreciate this, hon."

Fitzpatrick glared at him with her deep, blue-shadowed eyes. "You know, you've got a helluva nerve. After the way you treated me, you're lucky I didn't hang up on you. I can't go through that again. And I don't want you following me like last time."

"Look, I told you I was sorry. I'm trying to change, baby. I've got a monkey on my back that I can't shake."

"You mean a monkey between your legs. A twenty-two-year-old cocktail waitress from the Kitten Club? That was the last straw. You had a good thing, Roy, and you blew it. Anyway, I'm tired of arguing. I'll get your stuff." She opened the rear car door and removed a thick manila folder. She thrust it at Turlock.

"It's all here," she said resignedly. "History of Don Moore's last project. The MaxxDig 60. Not sure why this helps. I only did this because I'm a nice person. Anyway…hope you're satisfied."

Turlock began leafing through the pages. "Cool. This is great, Mel. It's not for me, anyway. There's a new detective in town who's—"

"I know, I met him."

"You…how did you meet him?"

"He was out at the plant. Talking with Goosebill."

"Oh. Well, uh, yeah, he seems like he knows his shit. I promised to help him, though god knows why. The case is a fuckin' sinkhole. I'm lucky to still be alive."

"You didn't deserve Marty."

"That's harsh."

"And so? Maybe you need a little harshness, the way you've treated people. Marty, your parents, all the anonymous women before me."

Turlock continued flipping through the papers, only half-listening. "I just…I just thought…I need to know what these mean. Like, what's this thing?" He held up a paper with boxed charts and very small print.

She sighed and craned her neck to look at the paper he held up.

"That's a materials spec. These other pages," she began, impatiently grabbing the folder from Turlock, "these are Couch assembly drawings. And these here…" she continued, holding out several pages with company names printed in color "…are PDFs of company operations manuals."

She shuffled through some more papers. "These are BOMs. That stands for 'Bills of Materials.' These are parts lists." She sighed again. "And these are…goddammit, why am I telling you all this?!"

"I'm sorry, baby, but I gotta know what Moore was into that might've got him killed. For all I know there's something here sensitive. It's a long shot but I gotta take it."

He reached over and gently pulled her hand away. "Okay, now, please tell me…what should I zero in on here? Which of these papers might be compromising? Know what I mean?"

"I'm crazy for doing this, just crazy. But okay. On one condition."

"What's that?"

"You leave me alone after this. I don't wish to see you again. Okay?"

Turlock winced. "Okay. Okay baby. I promise."

"All right. You probably want to look at anything written in Chinese or that has the location 'Harban, China.' Or anything that has the company name 'Kibitsu Consolidated.'"

"Cool. That helps. I'll—"

"Also the materials specs," she added. "That's pretty important. I can't translate chemical formulas for you, but you can find out yourself. But those things are important. They can be game-changers."

She then explained to him what certain engineering print symbols meant, as well as revision histories and rev dates, including sign-off signatures.

"That's about all I can tell you, Roy. Is that good?"

"Yeah, Mel, that's great. Thank you."

"Welcome. I gotta go."

"Sure. Sure, Mel. Thanks again. I'll leave you alone. Promise."

She stared at him hard in silence. Her hardened face became a little smoother. Her blue swimming-pool eyes became a bit softer.

"You take care, now," she said. "And tell Squirrel I said hello."

"Yeah. I'll do that Mel. Bye."

***

Nick was preparing a Glenlivet on the rocks in Room 117 when Vern returned from his busy day. His head was swimming with thoughts of CIA, Byron Lomax, Second Amendment, the ghost of Jerry Delmonico, Active Shooter Training, and Melody-Clair Fitzpatrick. That last thought seemed to cushion all the other bullshit in his head. But as much as he wanted to let his sexual fantasies run wild, he needed to get a grip on factors that might have contributed to two people splayed out at their suburban home in pools of blood.

He heard a knock on the door, set the Scotch bottle down, and went over to open it. Standing in the hall was a disheveled Vern, holding a stack of dog-eared papers, with a big shit-eating grin on his chubby red mug. "Okay, brother, wait'll you see what I got! Been a big day. You wanna go first, or you want me to?"

Nick laughed. "Vern, you're like a big fuzzy blanket on a gray winter day. Since your day was so great, we'll save the best for last."

Vern charged in and plopped the papers on the circular table with a loud THUNK. He flew out briefly to grab his vodka bottle from Room 115, then returned and plopped down on the bed opposite Nick's. "Okay, shoot," he barked, tilting his glass and taking a swig.

"I guess 'shoot' is the operative word, Vern." He proceeded to fill in Vern on meeting Goosebill and Fitzpatrick and experiencing the awe and mystery of the control voice of President Byron Lomax.

"I also met with Karl 'Champ' Haslett, one of the viceroys under Lomax. Nice fellow, and I got the impression he's pegged me as a fellow moderate. Acts like we're in a select club and need to stick together. Maybe he's lonely out there in Flagville—I mean Couch. Should I accept his Goodreads invitation, Vern?"

"Yeah, prob'ly," advised Vern, "just outta the kindness of your heart and to keep your contacts close. Not that it will help solving the case."

"Well, you never know. A friend in need, and all that. When I was at boarding school the last thing I expected was to be a prefect. A sort of student leader. It never dawned on me I might be one. But an outgoing senior, a popular jock, liked me. He thought I should be a prefect and convinced enough people to make me one.

"It was a life lesson for me; no matter how many people dislike you, you just need *one* with sway who does. It can make a huge difference. Not for selfish reasons, but to help you get through life. Anyway, *Champ* could come in handy." Nick paused and smiled. "On the other hand, there's Marv Goosebill. We had an interesting conversation about guns. Let's just say, he's not exactly Noam Chomsky. Undoubtedly slurping his Coors Lite at the altar of FOX News as we speak. He seemed real anxious to steer me away from any notion of CIA involvement by Moore. And this other guy who died, Jerry Delmonico, he was real tight with Moore and Goosebill. There's not only that love triangle, but a work triangle, too. He and the other two worked closely on a sensitive aerospace project…followed by a dragline excavator."

"What the hell's *that*?"

"A mega-sized industrial crane. Earth scraper. They claw up the ground to get to minerals to help us travel faster so we can get to meetings to find new ways to claw up the earth."

"God help us."

"Right, well, I plan to first do a little genealogical research on my laptop, but we need to look closer at the late Mr. Delmonico. Even though he's now under the earth, I plan to drop by and see his widow, Monica Delmonico, the apex of the love triangle. Also plan to meet Roy. He says he dug up some kind of papers for me. Did you have any luck with Lee or Jane Chin? The specter of Bing— *Maraschino Cherry*—continues to hover over everything."

"No, still not home, though Jane's in town, supposedly." Vern told Nick about lunching with the ladies and meeting Augie Moriarty.

"Nick, there's some real resentment by Siobhan Moriarty on a hospital promotion Irene Moore got. I mean, probably not a psycho Wanda Holloway thing…but it's there."

"Interesting. What about the other two?"

"Well, Mother Claunch hovered over everything. Don't think she likes Chinese people, at least, she didn't say much when I brought up the Chins. And Florida Patton…Nick, I think she's hot for me!"

"Really? Well, you still got it, big guy."

"No, I'm serious! She smiled at me the whole time, and tickled my chest when we said goodbye!"

"What does she look like?"

"Not bad. Tall, platinum blonde. A little lean, but still attractive. Talks kinda mousy though."

"Hmm. Okay, I won't tell Sharon, but anyway, what I want you to do tomorrow is get hold of Amber Ramsey. Give her a status report, and also see if she can conjure up autopsy findings for her Aunt Irene. They didn't have kids, but Bertram Ramsey certainly got a copy of the report, and Amber may be able to locate it."

"Autopsy reports are public knowledge, Nick. All we gotta do is contact the county coroner."

"Which we'll do if Amber can't find a copy. But if her dad, Bertram, got a copy himself, he may have jotted notes on it, which we can use."

"Good thinking."

"Also, swing by the Chins again. Maybe one or both will be home. After that, I want both of us to meet with Detective Joy Dickson. Roy gave me her name. She's retired now, but she was the lead investigator back in '95. She'll know—"

"Yeah! Moriarty told me about her! Let me guess…type of wounds, weapon, ballistics…right?"

"Exactly. The more dabs of paint we can add to that canvas that was the interior of that house on April 18, 1995—the day they were found—the better. I'd see her myself, but you were a cop and I'd feel more comfortable with you around. Don't wanna put my foot in my mouth."

Vern pursed his lips and nodded. "Just don't bring up your old boarding school." Nick pointed his finger as if to say "point taken."

The two investigators then shared their news of the day as Nick poured more Glenlivet and Vern added more vodka to his melting "rocks." Comfortable and slightly giddy, Vern spread out some of the printouts he'd made in the library. He directed his boss's attention to Henderlong's letters to the editor, as well as news articles, mostly written by Martin Franes, which concerned the Henderlong-Moore bidding war and property sewer line. He knew Nick would be pleased, but didn't anticipate just how much.

"Vern, you just landed on Boardwalk. This is actual motive, much bigger than Lisa pooping in Henderlong's yard. This makes him a person of interest, and I can only guess how this guy was grilled by Dickson and Moriarty back in ninety-whatever."

"Yeah, but they musta not got anything tangible. The guy's still peering out his front door, not a jail cell."

"Sure. You gotta get something that's going to hold up in court that will convince a jury. This is circumstantial, definitely. But at least it gives us something to chew on. Nice work."

Vern leaned back smiling and crossed his heavy legs, looking very pleased with himself.

"You know, Nick, we make a good team. Not only that, but we're good friends. Even though we might be very different as people."

Nick quelled his urge to laugh. "We are that, Vern. Kind of like the famous friendship between Marlon Brando and Wally Cox." He stayed quiet for a few seconds, allowing Vern to process the anomaly.

Vern then showed him Henderlong's letter speculating about Donald Moore using Couch Industries as a front for CIA activity.

"Henderlong sounds like your classic conspiracy kook, I'll admit," said Nick. "But unlike most of them who parrot a standard narrative, he actually cites sources, and they look reputable. Vern, after touching base with Amber and the Chins, I'd like you to jump on the 'net and see how solid these sources are. Take your laptop to Starbucks or the library if you want. We know Moore visited Harban, China. We know he hosted Chinese in his home, maybe even Xi Lao Bing, a known agent. We also know he had high-level security clearance and worked on sensitive government aerospace projects. Somebody like Moore would be a perfect candidate for CIA employment.

"Goosebill seemed to want me to steer clear of the CIA angle," Nick continued. "Why, I don't know. But so far all road signs lead there. Let's just hope the destination isn't a dead end. In more ways than one."

"Gotcha," said Vern.

Suddenly, just after another Glenlivet gulp, the muffled notes of "Town Without Pity" emerged from Nick's sport coat pocket. He fished out his cell.

"Montaigne here," he answered, phone in one hand, glass in the other.

"Mr. Montaigne? Hi, this is Melody. Melody-Clair Fitzpatrick. We met out at Couch earlier today."

Hearing Fitzpatrick's little-girl voice, Nick almost spilled his drink. He rose from the bed and walked toward the door, to distance himself from Vern's ears.

"Yes. Yes, hi Melody. How are you?"

"I'm fine. Say, you gave me your card, and I just wanted to reach out. Could we, uh…could we maybe meet somewhere? You know, outside of Couch? It's difficult to talk there."

"Certainly, Melody. Just name the place and time."

"Okay. Well, do you know Sharkey's? Uptown?"

"Yes, I do. We've already eaten there. Superb broiled walleye with capers, but I'd like to sample one of their filet mignons."

Nick heard a derisive laugh coming from the bed behind him.

"Right," replied Fitzpatrick, "yes, they do have good food. Well, how about tomorrow evening? Say, seven-thirty?"

"Perfect. I'll see you there."

"Okay. Bye."

"Bye."

Nick sucked in a load of air and exhaled with a loud whistle. He slipped his phone back in his coat pocket. He turned around, a satisfied smile creasing his jaw, and returned to the bed area, where Vern sat. Vern was shaking his head and smirking.

"Shit, here we go again," he muttered.

<u>PART TWO</u>

Chapter One

April 15, 1995...

It was a Saturday on Easter weekend. Weather for Springbrook, Ohio was partly cloudy with minimal precipitation. A low temperature of forty degrees Fahrenheit had hit in the wee hours of the morning, rising to a *high* of fifty-three degrees by mid-afternoon. The white pines in the neighborhood of Turnham Green were just beginning to get fat with new growth, the needles burgeoning with dark green chlorophyll, and the deciduous trees had colorful buds, some of which were spreading their tiny petals. Forsythias and redbuds were already in full yellow and pink glory, the crocuses had sprouted, and several of the most proactive homeowners in the neighborhood had already pushed or ridden mowers across their lawns, the grass clumpy and still littered with leaves that had fallen the previous autumn and twigs and slivers of tree bark that the winter winds had blown down.

One of the most industrious neighbors on Morning Glory lived at house number one-five-seven: Donald Moore. His driveway had a leftover pile of hardwood bark mulch from the previous weekend. Moore enjoyed doing his own landscaping. He took pride in his home's appearance, but he also enjoyed the invigoration of exerting his muscles in chilly spring air. Working with dirt, fescue, shrubs, and trees was soul-satisfying. Such labor connected him in a different way than his engineering work out at Couch Industries. Brain work five days in the week; body work for two days. Combined with the spiritual fulfillment he received from church, the routine he'd set for himself since he and Irene purchased their beautiful home eight years earlier was a perfect recipe for a healthy and fulfilling life. Like most Springbrookers, and most Americans in general, Donald was smitten with the idea of the "American Dream."

In fact, Donald and Irene had been so conscientious and frugal with their money, their mortgage on 157 Morning Glory was paid off. They had that small piece of business-zoned property out on Granby Road—coincidentally next door to the tool and die business owned by their residential next-door-neighbor—but they'd kept peace with the bank through regular payments, and all the while that property was accruing value. Life was good.

Donald's plan was to knock off the rest of that mulch pile before it left too grotesque a stain on the cement. After that, another mowing, then some weed-pulling in the pachysandra bed along the walkway, then some shearing of the yew bushes along the house front. If time permitted, hit the backyard with some pruning and weeding. Hopefully Gina wouldn't step outside. Hopefully Henderlong wouldn't, either.

Donald stretched his arms high and yawned loudly. Lisa lay curled up at the foot of the bed between him and Irene, on top of the bedspread, a warm, furry lump of love that helped keep their toes toasty.

"Hey girl!" he beckoned to her. "C'mere!" Lisa unraveled her long wiener body and took a few steps toward the couple's heads, then plopped down at waist level, curling up again. He reached down and gently stroked her soft golden-and-black fur.

"Has she had a bath recently?" he asked his wife, lying on her side, her face turned toward the window that looked out on the deck.

"I told you yesterday! You never listen to me!" she rebuked him playfully. "Yes, I gave her a bath earlier this week!"

"Okay, sorry! Gee!" He yawned loudly again.

"You did your arm thing again last night," she said. "Up goes the arm, waving in the air like a flimsy tree bough. I felt a breeze on my face all night long."

"Yeah, I don't know why I do that. Some strange subconscious thing. Or maybe the polio. Who knows."

The couple had had this same conversation numerous times over their nineteen-year marriage. It was a playful repartee that required no real thought or exertion. It was a pleasant domestic ritual. The rituals disappeared for a while, but had returned in the last few months.

"Did you see the Easter card Bertie and Joan sent us?" Irene asked.

"No. Where is it?"

"Right next to you, dummy! On the night table!"

"Oh." Donald opened the card and read aloud. "*Hope you both have a wonderful Easter. Come on down if you want to escape that Ohio cold. Would love to have you! Love, Joan and Bertie. P.S. Amber says hi. She's a sophomore already. How time flies!*"

"Wow," Donald remarked, "she's already in high school?"

"Yes. And still a lovely girl, from what I hear. Has her father's looks and her mother's brains. But don't ever tell my brother I said that."

Donald grunted in recognition. He rolled out of bed, his loose-fitting pajamas rolled up high on one leg. He bent over and stretched his arms downward toward his bare feet and bounced up and down fifteen times until his fingertips grazed his toes. He began to change into his Saturday uniform of jeans, old sweatshirt, and white socks while Irene disappeared into the master bath. Lisa was still curled up on the bed.

"What's on the agenda today?" hollered Irene from behind the closed bathroom door.

"Spring cleanup!" yelled Donald. "Mulching, weeding, yadda-yadda!"

"Watch out for you-know-who! Old cranky pants! Behave yourself! Don't get into any arguments! Planter Relays later today…wanna go?"

Donald wasn't yet decided about that, so he feigned like he didn't hear and strolled out the bedroom door, down the hall, then through the living and dining areas. He glanced at the roll of scarlet-red fabric on the dining room table. *Wonder how long that will be there. Hrumph.* He stepped into the kitchen. Lisa had jumped off the bed and trotted after him. He fixed a small pot of coffee and a bowl of Cheerios. Then he opened a small plastic container and pulled out a miniature Milk-Bone biscuit which he allowed Lisa to steal from his outstretched hand. After the coffee was ready, he sat down at the circular kitchen table in front of the fireplace, slipped on his Asics sneakers, and began crunching the oat rings while sipping his coffee from the mug with the word "COUCH" printed on it above the company's rhinoceros logo. He could hear Irene singing while taking her morning shower in the master bath. Lisa snuggled close to his mulch-smudged sneakers. *She knows I'm going outside*, he thought.

After finishing his breakfast and just before heading out the door, Donald remembered something. He went into the den and sat down in front of the bulky Packard-Bell computer that the couple had purchased only a year earlier at Best Buy and were still getting acquainted with. He wanted to see if he had any replies yet on the message board of the AOL Civil War forum, especially from that unreconstructed rebel who claimed Abraham Lincoln was treasonous for suspending the writ of habeas corpus during what the man called a "War of Northern Aggression." Donald smiled. *Takes all kinds. Wonder if 'JEB_S' is in reality Henderlong. Wouldn't that be something? My next-door-neighbor and town hall rival is also my rival on AOL. Can't escape the guy!*

Donald also looked forward to hearing that familiar robotic voice sounding out "You've Got Mail!" He also wanted to polish up the formal letter he'd been writing. It was a letter which he'd been thinking about writing for a long time but had been putting off. He was almost finished with it. All it needed was a final run-through. One final proofread before printout and delivery. That would be early this week. He wondered if he still had the guts. He hadn't yet told Irene. About *anything*. After all, their marriage was still in repair mode and he didn't want to upset her. He wanted to wait until after the deed was done, otherwise it may never happen. *Better to ask forgiveness than beg permission.*

He spruced up the letter a bit, checked his mail (empty in-box), and dropped into the forum. JEB_S had submitted an uncharacteristically short response: "Jeff Davis never suspended no writ of habeas corpus! That's a fact!"

Donald figured discretion might be the better part of valor and logged off without replying to Jeb. He went to the hall closet, donned his green work jacket, and he and Lisa stepped outside the front door, where the pile of mulch, pitchfork, and wheelbarrow awaited. It was still chilly, but the sun was rising, and Donald Moore looked forward to a glorious spring day.

***

Irene Moore stepped gingerly from the shower and carefully dressed. She put on her new jeans and her proud "Springbrook High School Plant 'n' Run 10K" race t-shirt that she'd earned last year after running—rather, jogging—in the town's big road race held each autumn, for which her employer was a principal sponsor. She secretly hoped Dorothy Claunch would make one of her impromptu house visits, just so Dotty could see her wearing this shirt. *Maybe I'll wear it to the Planter Relays. Dotty will certainly be there. Maybe Florida and Siobhan. Hopefully not Carol. God, what a little gossip! I'll never get over what she told Gina. Never. Oh well. These things too shall pass. It would be nice to see Florida. She has such good taste in clothes! And she designed her house impeccably. I wish I could design as—oh no, I left the faucet running!*

Irene turned off the bathroom faucet then headed into the kitchen, walking barefoot and passing the roll of fabric on the dining room table and letting out a groan. She fixed an English muffin with apricot preserve jelly and poured a small cup of coffee that Donald had left her, flavoring it heavily with zero-sugar sweet-cream. While munching and sipping she thought about dinner. *Easter weekend? Let's see, smoked ham tomorrow. But tonight? Something simple. Don loves my Mexican casserole, but that's too much bother, and better for a winter meal. Hmm. I've got that angel-hair pasta in the cabinet. Leftover Prego as well. Great, will make spaghetti—oops, forgot about the Silver Queen! Strip steak and corn, then.*

Finishing her muffin, she walked to the kitchen window and gazed out at Donald, who was dumping a wheelbarrow of mulch on the bed ringing the large oak tree in the front yard. Lisa stood near his feet, watching the action.

"His shadow," she whispered to herself. "That dog thinks the world of him."

She glanced across the street at the Chin house. She lifted the receiver of the wall phone and dialed.

"Hello, Jane? Irene here. Nĭ hăo! How are you?—good, I just want to thank you for the Easter flowers, they're absolutely beautiful! How is Lee?—wonderful—he's outside with his best companion—yes, I hope that man doesn't make an appearance, I mean show up. Speaking of which, have you talked to Gina at all?—yes, well, I'm guessing it has to do with Donny's work, Donny works closely with her brother, Jerry—right, there's always some tension—well, truth be told, Donny hasn't been himself lately, and that company is just so odd…on another note, are you going to the relays today?—yes, we hope to, and happy Easter, and thank you again for the gorgeous flowers—oh, why thank you, Jane!—well, I was honored, but it just means more work!—right, okay Jane…bye-bye."

Irene hung up the phone. She washed the dishes then walked into the dining room, groaning again after eyeing the rolled curtain fabric on the table, then sat on the loveseat in the small living room, crossed her pale legs, and flicked on the television. She landed on the morning news program *Saturday Today*. The host, Matt Lauer, was interviewing film actor Samuel L. Jackson. Jackson was one of the stars of a Miramax film that had been released the previous October and was, according to Lauer—who in Irene's view seemed to almost be swooning over the movie's success—now grossing over a hundred million dollars. Irene had overheard Dotty Claunch discussing this film with Siobhan in the pediatric ward the previous week. Dotty deplored the film's "gratuitous violence" (though she hadn't yet seen it.) The film was called *Pulp Fiction*.

Irene turned off the television and returned to the curtain fabric.

***

"Hey, girl," Donald called to Lisa. "Wanna go for a ride?"

The poogle wagged her tail. Donald lifted Lisa and placed her gently in the bed of the wheelbarrow. He pushed the barrow slowly while balancing his little cargo and returned to the mulch pile. Then he picked her up and set her on the concrete. Lisa ran back and forth excitedly.

"Ahoy there!" Donald heard a voice. He looked up and saw Whitney Black approaching him along the curb. Black was wearing a red-and-yellow "Planter Relays 1994" sweatshirt.

"Hey, Whit," Donald greeted his neighbor.

"So, who are your Browns gonna take in the draft?"

Donald let out a sigh of exasperation. "Hell, probably another quarterback. Need a linebacker, though. Not that it will matter. Best player in the world can't do squat without coaching."

"Got that right. Yeah, Bengals need a running back. I'm hoping we get that Penn State guy, Carter, but Carolina or Jacksonville will probably scoop him up."

"Clowns and Bungles, Whit. Things never change."

"You read my mind. You guys going to the relays today?"

"Well, if I ever finish this yardwork."

"Aw, you love it, and you've got a little helper there," Black nodded at Lisa.

"Yeah, she's a slave driver. Aren't you, Lisa? Yes, you are! Yes, you are!" The dog wagged her tail.

"Your yard looks good as ever."

"Hey, thanks Whit. Nice of you to say."

"Need to ask a favor. We're thinking of putting in a new deck."

"Yeah? That's great."

"Yeah, but I'm not much good at carpentry. We'll probably get a contractor. Anyway, you did such a nice job on your own deck, you mind if I come over some time and pick your brain?"

"No, not at all. Ask away, whenever."

"'Kay. Uh…how 'bout tonight? You be around after the relays?

"We'll be here, all night. We're homebodies."

"Cool. Maybe I'll stop by. How's your new computer doing?"

"Still getting used to it. Especially moving that 'mouse' thing. But it's a lot of fun. Has practical value, too. I can bring work home. Some of it, anyway. Not that I want to."

"I hear you. We're thinking of getting one, just haven't gotten around to it. Anyway," Black abruptly shifted gears, "if I don't see you guys at the relays, maybe…uh…tonight or tomorrow. Tell Irene I said hello."

"Will do. You do the same with Linda."

Whitney Black stepped down the street and crossed over to his house. Donald's eyes followed him. Then the eyes turned to the house next door. A man stood motionless inside the front door.

***

"THE NEXT EVENT, LADIES AND GENTLEMEN, WILL BE THE FOUR-BY-FOUR-HUNDRED-METER RELAY," the announcer boomed over the loudspeaker at the sixty-eighth annual Planter Relays being held at Planter Field at Springbrook Middle School.

Donald and Irene Moore sat next to the aisle in the tenth row on the left side of the bleachers, their normal position for the annual relays. It was 4 p.m. and they'd only just arrived. They were looking forward to the four-forty because their neighbor, Tommy Black, was anchoring the Springbrook team, which was favored to win. Being a Saturday afternoon on a holiday weekend, the stands were packed with spectators. Small groups huddled about outside the circumference of the track. Other groups were gathered in the grass farther away, where the field events were taking place. It was easy to pick out the Springbrook parents and boosters: they wore the school colors of dark red and canary yellow.

Although Donald waited stoically for the boys to line up on the track, Irene was restless to mingle with someone she might know. Her head swiveled right, left, and behind, and her eyes darted here and there. Although Whitney and Linda Black usually sat on the left side of the bleachers, they were nowhere to be seen. Irene assumed they were on the right side, or perhaps huddled alongside the track— somewhere where they could get a good view of Tommy. However, she did see two familiar faces from the hospital: Dorothy Claunch and Siobhan Moriarty. They were by themselves, away from the track, near the parking lot. They appeared to be in the middle of a deep conversation. Siobhan, who Irene knew to be animated and high-strung, was gesturing forcefully with her hands. Dorothy at one point reached out and placed her hand on Siobhan's upper arm, as if to calm her.

Irene knew that her recent promotion to floor supervisor had not sat well with Siobhan. She wondered if this was what the two were discussing. It bothered Irene and cast a pall on her enjoyment of the relays.

She nudged Donald. "Look," she pointed, "do you see those two?"

Donald peered where she was pointing.

"No...which two? Oh, you mean Dotty and Siobhan? Don't let it bother you. You deserved that promotion, not her. Couple o' harpies, those two, if you ask me."

"Dotty's okay. She's just nosy. It's the other one."

"Forget about it. Enjoy the events."

The gun fired. The four boys took off down the track, Springbrook red and yellow in the lead. After the first lap, the Palmersburg runner had taken over, and this lasted until halfway through Tommy Black's anchor lap, when he pulled ahead to nip Palmersburg at the finish. The crowd cheered wildly, chanting "BLACK, BLACK, BLACK, BLACK" in rhythmic unison.

After the cheering subsided, Irene turned to her left and looked upward, toward the top row. "Oh, look, Donny. I think I see Jerry." Donald turned and stared for several seconds.

"Yep. That's him." Donald held up his hand in a half-hearted wave. Jerry Delmonico nodded in recognition.

"You think Monica's with him? I don't see her up there."

"Maybe."

"How about Marv? Does he ever come to the relays?"

"Are you kidding? He's about as boosterish as a troll under a bridge. Probably at the shooting range right now, blasting his heart out."

"How is that project you three are working on? What is it...the MaxxDigger 50 crane?"

"MaxxDig 60," Donald corrected her. "It's going okay. I've got some stuff to do when I get home. Assuming that mouse doesn't give me fits."

Donald and Irene stayed for one more track event then headed home. He had some final tidying-up in the yard, then computer work. Also, Irene wanted to stop at Kroger to pick up some Merlot for dinner, which she always liked with corn-on-the-cob.

They walked back to their beloved bungalow on Morning Glory, passing several strangers—undoubtedly out-of-towners temporarily visiting Turnham Green to cheer on their favorite athletes—and arrived at a freshly-mulched and lush, dark-green lawn. Donald finished his yard chores and Irene made a quick trip to Kroger for her groceries, then prepared a hearty dinner of steak and hybrid Silver Queen sweet corn, one of Donald's favorites.

Later...after dinner and a short-lived rain shower...Donald retired to the den to finish his computer work. Irene cleared the dishes from the kitchen table—the dining room table was still cluttered with curtain fabric and aluminum rods—and began her much-dreaded evening chore of rinsing, dishwasher stacking, and storage and refrigeration of leftovers.

It was while she was standing at the kitchen sink, her right hand holding a plastic scrub brush, when the doorbell rang. Lisa galloped to the door, yapping with excitement, her stringy tail flailing back and forth.

Now, who could that be? Irene wondered.

Chapter Two

Twenty-five years later…

Grantchester Meadows, popularly known as "GM" in Springbrook, was a south-end neighborhood much like Turnham Green, only a notch higher, more upper than upper-middle class. Most of the Moriartys lived in GM, they being one of the town's oldest and most respectable families (though both Augie and sister Siobhan lived elsewhere). The streets were more serpentine, the trees were taller and fuller, the plots had more green space, and the houses were of greater variety, with many of them mansion-caliber. A few had private tennis courts and swimming pools. In the 1950s Mayor Hamilton had a large Tudor house in GM, with both a horse grazing pasture and large woods adjacent, and this is where Jimmy Stewart bunked during his famous stayover. Legend has it that Stewart and Hamilton went fox hunting on the grounds.

Though the hunt was unsuccessful, it nevertheless raised the ire of the local SPCA.

Monica Delmonico lived on Brae Burn Road in Grantchester Meadows. She and late husband Jerry had inherited their house from Monica's parents, who were Mayhews, yet another old family (even more respectable than the Blacks and Moriartys), a branch of which had immigrated to the town from Martha's Vineyard not long after Ezekiel Eastabrook pitched camp against his rock. Monica's spread was less ostentatious than others in GM— it had a straight instead of a half-moon driveway. But unlike in Turnham Green, Nick Montaigne's Porsche 911 GT2 RS didn't look out of place here. Not that there were many pedestrians along the wide sidewalks to gawk. The brick and stone mausoleum-like homes seemed as silent as a cemetery. Other than one middle-aged woman walking her black lab, the only signs of life in the neighborhood came from lawn chemists and HVAC contractors.

Nick always made sure to wet his skin with Lacoste Blue before meetings—especially if his interviewees were the fairer sex—and today was no exception. He checked his Rolex, removed his cinnamon, clicked up the sidewalk to the Delmonico landing, and knocked the large brass door knocker shaped like a horseshoe, luck side upward.

He was greeted by a woman he judged to be in her early sixties. She was short with a reddish-brown, layered haircut and black eye liner. Her face was pretty, but it had a cold, hard look, with penetrating eyes. Normally, the women Nick met for the first time offered at least a hint of a smile. Not this one. She reminded Nick of the actress Lee Grant (pre-facial reconstruction). And if she was anything like what he knew of Grant—a film director as well as actor and famous for her defiance after being blacklisted by the House Un-American Activities Committee—he would have to tiptoe around the well-established rumor of an affair with Donald Moore.

"Hello, Mrs. Delmonico? I'm Nick Montaigne."

"Come in," she said in a flat, world-weary tone. "You don't resemble your voice."

"No? Well, not sure if that's good or bad."

"Does it have to be either?"

"I guess not!"

She led him into a large living area with floor-to-ceiling windows on one side of the room that framed a natural amphitheater outside. Nick noticed two young landscapers, one who was weeding and the other pruning a bed of rose bushes. Delmonico sat in a gold wingback chair and Nick took the couch. His attention was immediately drawn to a domed birdcage in the corner of the room near the window. It held a large, black, hill myna bird. Over the course of the half-hour interview, the bird periodically squawked, "Take the cannoli!"

"That's Carlo," Delmonico remarked when she noticed Nick staring at the bird.

"Ah. Named after the wine, Carlo Rossi?"

"I couldn't tell you. He was my father's bird. Came with the house."

She asked him if he wanted a drink, but Nick declined, it being before his official drinking time of noon. She poured herself a gin and tonic. After returning to the chair, she cut to the quick.

"My late husband and I went through the whole interview deal twenty-five years ago. What was her name...Detective Nixon?"

"Dickson, I believe."

"Yes. Dickson. Jerry was at the relays, got home about six. We were together at home the rest of that night, and vouched for each other. He wasn't feeling well and went to bed early. Visited relatives the next day, Easter Sunday, in Cleveland. Next thing we heard, they'd found the bodies. So our alibis are foolproof. So, as you can imagine Mr. Montaigne, I'm a little surprised I'm being interrogated again at this late date."

Nick clasped his hands and dropped his head. "Well, I can certainly understand your feelings, Mrs. Delmonico. We're here only because we were hired by a Moore relative, and the case, as you know, is still officially open. Jerry worked closely with Donald Moore, and we have reason to believe the murders were work-related. So we're meeting with anyone even remotely associated with Donald or Irene, both work associates and neighbors."

She smiled for the first time, although "smile" might be an overstatement. "Aren't you forgetting something? That my husband may have had a motive other than work? I know that you've heard the town chin-wag. Nothing remains secretive long in Springbrook. Of course, other than 'who killed the Moores.' And to spare you any discomfort, yes, Don Moore and I did have an affair. But it ended long before the murders. *His* decision. The usual reason. He loved his wife and didn't want to hurt her. I went back to my daytime fantasies and..." She glanced at her gin glass.

Nick shifted uncomfortably. "Come to think of it, maybe I'll join you. Scotch on the rocks, please. Glenlivet, if you have it."

Her smile broadened. She got up and fixed him the drink, remarking on his good taste in whiskey. Nick went into his patented spiel.

"Yes, I like the taste of Speyside single malt, and Glenlivet eighteen-year is one of the purest single malt Scotch whiskies in the world. Their distillery is also the oldest continuous distillery in Scotland. I like old things. They have class."

"It sounds like you enjoy living in the past."

"No offense," retorted Nick with a slight chuckle, "but I've always found those words to be a slight put-down. I don't live there. I just enjoy visiting. The past is comforting and secure. Womblike. It's filled with people, places, and events. I hear a lot of people saying it's all about the future. They chant 'future' almost like a mantra. Right, okay, we all need to plan for tomorrow. But tomorrow is empty space, a void, and voids don't interest me.

"I'm a private investigator who solves mysteries. But I don't do it to fill a void necessarily. I do it because I believe in justice."

"Well said. Then if you indeed like 'old things,' Mr. Montaigne, I'm sure you're enjoying Springbrook. All the young people have left. I can't say I blame them. Nothing here after college, unless working out at that toxic, moldy facility in Hernan fits into your plans. Jerry was trying to get out. So was Don."

"Really?"

"If you've been out there, you know the feeling of paranoia. Eyes on you the entire time. That creepy Lomax. Most people think it was the affair and the Moore murders that drove Jerry to alcohol. It was that place that killed him. Killed his spirit, then killed *him*. Jerry was just a skin too few for this world. He was definitely *not* a murderer. I say that as one married to him for twenty-three years. Not always happily—we were married way too young—but I did know him."

Nick sipped his Scotch. He had intended to somehow work in his theory that the trigger finger may have been hired, and that whoever did the hiring must have had money. Instead, he chose to press the Couch angle.

"Yes, I did sense a sort of oppressiveness out at that place. So...were you privy to the last project that Jerry and Don worked? Some type of industrial crane?"

"No, I never talked to Jerry about his work. Nor to Don the short time we were together. The only thing I know is that there was a lot of stress at that time. I could feel it. Something was happening out there. But Jerry never said anything to me."

"Right. Yeah, I never talk to my girlfriend about my work...at least, until the case is wrapped. So...I won't detain you too much longer, Mrs. Delmonico."

"You're not detaining me. I have little to do these days except pine for what once was. Besides, I like talking to you."

Nick chuckled. It crossed his mind that, despite showing signs of Father Time, Monica Delmonico was still a desirable woman. A bit hard, her corners a bit sharp, somewhat pickled from the alcohol...but still attractive.

"Thank you, and I enjoy talking with you. I'm curious about the name 'Delmonico'. That's Italian, isn't it?"

"Italian-Swiss, I think."

"Where have I heard that name before?"

"It's the name of some famous restauranteurs. They were immigrant brothers, I think."

"Ah, that's right. They opened a famous restaurant in New York City, I believe."

"Right. There or maybe New Orleans? I forget which. Their famous creation was a really thick steak. The Delmonico."

Nick nodded. An amateur epicure, normally he would pursue the food topic. But there was something else on his mind. He was glad he waited until the end of their interview before dropping the bomb he had in store for this Lee Grant lookalike. "Your ex-husband's full first name was 'Gerald,' is that correct?"

"Yes."

"Born in the year 1949, in Youngstown, Ohio? The third son of Salvatore and Maria Delmonico?"

"Correct. Why? What does that have to do with anything?"

"I'm trying to think of a way to phrase this delicately, Mrs. Delmonico. Both my partner and I, as well as numerous people in town—including the assistant coroner—believe the murders of the Moores were professional. Contract killings. This is based on circumstances surrounding manner of death and location of the corpses in the house. Might it not be within the realm of possibility that your husband had connections—"

"Get out," Delmonico spat at Nick. "Get out of here. Get out of my house."

"Look, I'm sorry—"

"No you're not. I know what your veiled game is. I guess it was only a matter of time before my late husband's surname came into the picture. I suggest you spend less time watching Italian mobster dramas and more time learning your craft. Get out."

Nick set his glass gently on the glass table in front of him and stood up. "Mrs. Delmonico, I'm sorry if I touched a nerve." He paused. "You know, it's amazing the things one can learn from the internet. Yes, much of it is garbage, but not everything. I've always enjoyed the hobby of genealogy. In the past few years I've learned a lot about my Alsace-Lorraine Montaigne ancestors from a genealogical database called RootsWeb. It's quite useful, especially if reliable sources are listed, and one takes the time to consult them.

"It's a known fact that one Joseph Delmonico was an associate of the Gambino crime family in New York City. Also, the city of Cleveland, not far from Springbrook, had in the early 1990s a very powerful La Cosa Nostra, with Domenico "Three Fingers" Delmonico acting as consigliere for Cleveland-Youngstown mob boss Carmen Provenzano. I've learned through my research that your late husband— Gerald Delmonico—is a third cousin to Domenico. Now, I *don't* know how often you and your late husband visited Cleveland in early 1995, and you know him much better than I. But from my angle, it's perfectly within reason that Jerry might have reached out to Domenico or another family member. Either to shut Don Moore up due to some shady operations at his work, or in a fit of passion over the affair you and he had."

"I-told-you-to-leave-my-house," she repeated in staccato fashion in no uncertain terms. She stood up and turned her back to him.

After several seconds of awkward silence, Nick muttered "Goodbye, Mrs. Delmonico, and thank you for your time."

She swung around to face him, her black-rimmed eyes like daggers. "This poor excuse of a town has had a vendetta against me and my husband for twenty-five years. For *twenty-five years* I haven't been able to visit the grocery store without getting sideways glances and hearing whispers. It's bad enough that my private life was fodder for the town's gossip-mongers. Now you come along like Sir Lancelot and start digging up trash about my husband hiring a hit man. If you like trash talk, go talk to that bitch of a sister-in-law of mine. Her name's Gina Roper. She turned her back on the family years ago. Or talk to that Bible-banger Claunch. They'll fill your head with all sorts of sordid scenarios. But I live in the real world and don't cotton to hearsay.

"Yes," she railed, her voice becoming shaky, "my late husband and I fell out of love. But I won't stand to have his memory besmirched. By you or anyone else."

Nick left the house, his underarms damper than they'd been in a long time, the smell of Lacoste Blue thick inside his nostrils. The last sound he heard before gently shutting the front door was Carlo, squawking about cannoli.

***

About the same time as Nick was taking his first sip of Glenlivet in the Delmonico home, Vern Wister was rounding the corner of Morning Glory Lane in his rented Honda Accord. He'd already called Amber Ramsey and asked her to sift through her father's papers to see if there was a copy of her aunt's autopsy report. She promised to look, and send or text him or Nick photos if successful, but didn't sound too optimistic. Regardless, later that day the two investigators would be meeting with retired Detective Joy Dickson, and both hoped Dickson could fill them in on ballistics and forensics data, as she surely would remember details of one of Springbrook's most infamous crimes.

The team of Montaigne-Wister had now been in Springbrook several days. Neither of them had been looking forward to vacating their familiar digs of Atlanta for an unfamiliar corn town in Ohio. Vern, especially, missed his wife's home cooking and the soft king-size bed with the Beautyrest mattress he was accustomed to. He was substantially older than his partner, so routine and familiarity were much more important. Today, he was beginning to feel the effects of the Comfort Inn. At breakfast he made a sarcastic remark at the kitchen helper because the eggs were those uniform pre-fab deals that looked like they'd "popped out of a toaster." He also scolded the morning desk clerk because the lobby coffee was "weaker than an old lady with a blood condition." And the previous night he'd had trouble sleeping because a select little-league baseball team was in town for a pre-season tournament and the "sons of Cain" in room 113 made a racket all night.

So he wasn't in the best of moods as the Accord turned into the sedate environs of Turnham Green.

Vern cruised down Morning Glory, parked in front of the Chin home, and approached their front door—for the third time—waving at Beryl, who was clipping stray pachysandra vines from her front walk. And once again, nobody was home. This time, however—soon after hissing an obscenity—Vern stuck a handwritten note on the door, explaining his mission and leaving his cell number. He was halfway through the note when he suddenly heard loud voices. He strained his ears. The voices weren't coming from inside the Chin house. Nor were they coming from across the street, where Henderlong, Beryl, and Gina Roper lived. They were coming from next door. The home of Whitney and Linda Black.

Vern hurriedly finished writing. He wanted to get a little closer to the Black home, in hopes of picking up what was being said. He had a fleeting memory of when he was ten years old and he and his friends used to eavesdrop on a childless married couple with the last name of Parks who lived on his street. They frequently argued, loudly, the result usually being that Wally Parks would fly out of the house, fling his jacket over his shoulder, then hop in his car to burn down to the nearest bar, returning much later...much quieter...but completely soused.

The little boy in Vern had never totally left the building. So he was curious.

After slipping the note inside a crack in the door window pane of the Chin house, Vern shuttled quickly toward the side of the driveway closest to the Black home, his blubber belly shaking like jelly. Once there, he pretended—in case any prying Morning Glory eyes might be watching—to be searching in his pants pocket for something. As he had a hearing problem, he turned his good ear toward the Black house.

The voices started up again. Whitney's was the loudest. He caught snippets of what sounded like an argument.

... (indecipherable) OVER TWO DECADES AGO LINDA! (indecipherable) GODDAMMIT, WHADDAYA WANT ME TO DO! (indecipherable) THEY ALREADY DID! (indecipherable) AND HOW IS THAT GONNA LOOK! (indecipherable) THAT INVESTIGATOR (indecipherable) DICKSON AND MORIARTY (indecipherable) FUCKING BING! (indecipherable) MURDERS! (indecipherable) LEAVE ME ALONE, DAMMIT! FORGET IT, I'M OUTTA HERE!

Vern took two steps into the grass, but as soon as he did so the front door of the Black house flew open and Whitney Black came barreling down the walkway toward his driveway. Vern straightened and scuttled back onto the Chin driveway, acting as if he hadn't heard anything, but Black saw him and did a double take just before rounding the front of his car, whipping open the door, starting the engine, then flying down the driveway and revving down Morning Glory, out of sight.

Vern took a deep breath. Perfect timing, he thought. *Wish he hadn't o' seen me, though.*

He hopped in his Accord. Beryl was now inside her front door and gave him another friendly wave. Then he glanced toward the Henderlong home, which was directly across from the Black house. The red plaid shirt was also inside its front door. But Henderlong didn't wave. Instead, Vern thought he could make out some white teeth. As if Henderlong was smiling.

***

After leaving Morning Glory, Vern made a beeline to the library. His mission was twofold: like Nick instructed, he wanted to check on those sources that Henderlong had cited in his letter to the editor, to gauge the veracity of Couch Industries providing cover for CIA agents; secondly, he wanted to examine flight records from 1994 and 1995. Back in Philly he'd helped expose a "sugar sale"—a street con game using small-businesses—by getting airline passenger data that linked a convicted Baltimore swindler with a Philly suspect that cops had been unable to pin down. Doing the same thing here was a long shot. But if he could link Xi Lao Bing with someone at Couch, including Donald Moore (whom he and Nick had not ruled out as covertly working for the CIA—a Bing nemesis) they would be that much closer to finding closure for Amber Ramsey.

Vern climbed the familiar cement steps of the Springbrook Public Library and entered the still, church-like interior. He passed a table that featured a carefully arranged display of books—*Ulysses, 1984, Fahrenheit 451, The Adventures of Huckleberry Finn, Alice's Adventures in Wonderland,* and *Anne Frank's Diary*—carefully arranged around a stark placard reading CHECK OUT A BANNED BOOK. He passed the information desk and was privately pleased to see that the rough-looking girl with the orange hair, arm tattoos, and metal in her face wasn't working today. Instead, there was a pale-skinned girl with pink and purple streaks in her hair.

He found a table in the corner, opened his laptop and began researching.

He learned that in 2009 a book was published that detailed the Bush dynasty in America extending back to family patriarch Prescott Bush. The book revealed that both Prescott (known as "Pressy") and son George H.W. Bush ("Poppy") were members of Skull and Bones, the oldest secret society at Yale University, which after World War II had numerous faculty members employed by the Office of Strategic Services (OSS), which was the spy organization that preceded the Central Intelligence Agency (CIA). The book implied that Poppy, due to his naval intelligence work and membership in Skull and Bones—and his family's cushy social connections—would have been viewed as a prime candidate for CIA membership. The CIA was also known to recruit heavily from Ivy League schools immediately after the war.

Vern checked the footnotes for this information. They led him to magazine articles and a book detailing the history of Skull and Bones, as well as personal interviews with Pressy, Poppy, and friends, former friends, and associates of theirs.

The Bush dynasty book also revealed that, upon graduating from Yale, Poppy immersed himself in what Dwight D. Eisenhower would in 1961 warn was "misplaced power" due to a growing "military-industrial complex." Bush worked for several companies whose principal assets were in oil and heavy industry and which were closely tied to defense contracts and sub-contracts. *One of these companies was Couch Industries*, where Bush got his start in the petroleum industry, eventually leading him to Texas.

Vern checked the footnotes again. The source was a biography of Couch Industries written in the late 1970s, which he then located in the Springbrook Public Library stacks. The footnotes for *this* book, which cited original sources, confirmed that high-level employees of Couch were *routinely recruited to work for the CIA.*

He then located a second book, written in 2008 by a Villanova University professor, covering CIA activities in the Caribbean, and which revealed that Couch employed salesmen and engineers who were covert CIA agents and were "sent overseas to negotiate sales contracts and observe and advise on engineering and manufacturing operations." The footnotes for this work cited none other than testimony contained in Volume IX of the Warren Commission report on the assassination of President John F. Kennedy.

Vern made photocopies and printouts of the information and stacked the papers in his frayed laptop case. *Henderlong really did his homework*, he thought.

Thrilled at his discoveries and totally forgetting about checking airline records, but satisfied he had enough information to confirm a mutual relationship between Couch and the nation's highest, most shadowy, and most controversial spy organization, he shifted to his second task: revisit Manny Henderlong and press him on his city council fight over the sewer line and bidding war with the Moores.

Vern backtracked down Oak Avenue, turned onto Chamomile then Forsythia, then left onto Morning Glory. He glanced right: *Beryl must be preparing blood pudding.* He glanced left: *Whitney must still be at the bar.* Then, almost as an afterthought, he swung a glance at the Chin house, next to the Blacks.

A car was in the driveway.

Chapter Three

Nick thought it odd that Roy Turlock had designated Green-Wood Cemetery for their rendezvous. He knew that Turlock didn't have the most opulent digs, and was probably embarrassed to bring anyone home. *But why not Sharkey's? It's got a nice bar. Good place to talk business.* Nick surmised that Turlock's mentor's "suspicious" death had something to do with it. Nick well knew that doors and eavesdroppers have a way of finding each other, and an open outdoor setting would minimize intrusions. He could tell that Turlock had never completely gotten over the death of Marty Franes. Or maybe he wanted to meet at the graveyard because it was appropriate for a Sunday. Turlock had told him over the phone that he had "good stuff," as news types often say, to show him. Maybe "good" means dangerous. *Yeah. Cemetery will work.*

He couldn't help wondering, though, that a cloud of morbidity seemed to perpetually hang over Turlock like wet mist on a lake.

***

Nick drove under the gated arch of Green-Wood just as the sun dipped under the clouds. He saw a green, older-model Buick Verano at the back end of the graveyard, a man leaning against the driver's door. Nick eased his GT2 RS behind it and got out.

Turlock watched Nick approach. "Follow the honey," he called out.

"What?"

"'Follow the honey.' That's what he always used to say." Turlock nodded toward the stone with the unambiguous letters and numbers that represented Franes' brief time on earth. "He took it from that famous line in *All the President's Men*. You know, where Deep Throat advises Woodward and Bernstein to 'follow the money.' Marty was a bit of a ladies' man and always believed a beautiful woman was lurking around the heart of every sleazy activity. Maybe he's right."

"Yeah," said Nick, casting a side glance at Turlock and recalling his most recent case. "Yeah, you know, he may have had something there."

Turlock continued musing. "I often wonder what he's thinking, watching all of this."

"*Watching?*"

"C'mon Montaigne. Just 'cause I'm a base agnostic and misanthrope doesn't mean I don't believe in spirits. That motherfucker's up there somewhere, smiling. Watching us make chopped liver of a deed from two-and-a-half decades ago. Sometimes I wonder, 'does it matter'? We'll all be dead in a few years, and nobody will care about Donald or Irene Moore."

They stared at the stone in silence for a full minute. Turlock was the one to break the hush.

"How's your partner?"

"Vern? Yeah, he's fine. I guess. You'll meet him soon. That Comfort Inn is getting to him a little."

"Hell, I'd let him stay at my place, but I don't wanna depress him even more. Anyway, I'd have to get permission from Squirrel."

"Huh?"

Turlock laughed. "Don't worry, just yankin' yer chain. 'Squirrel' is the name of my cat. Can't remember why I saddled him with that name. He probably hates me for it. Don't know if I was drunk at the time."

They stood in front of the stone a long while, Turlock sharing anecdotes of his years at the paper and reminiscing about his association and friendship with Franes. Nick thought he seemed less exuberant than during their meeting at the tennis courts. He didn't have his trademark rushed, clipped manner of speaking. He didn't have the same caustic humor. The skin under Turlock's eyes appeared darker. Nick's impression was that Turlock might be taking the Moore case too personally. As if he might have felt obligated to finish the work that his news mentor had begun. Maybe as some kind of payback for Franes' training of Turlock? Had Franes forced some kind of promise out of Turlock, a "When I'm gone, I hope you..." kind of guarantee? That sort of burden might pressure anyone. Then again, maybe it was something in Turlock's personal life. He did mention something about his gal walking out on him.

Then again, maybe it was the general pandemic blues that everyone else seemed to be experiencing.

"Roy, how did the coronavirus story pan out?" Nick asked in an attempt to pull Turlock away from the tombstone.

"Huh? Oh, yeah. Sure, I filed it under the deadline. No biggie. Not that it will amount to anything. Nobody seems to care. Except my editor, of course."

"Yeah, Vern and I have noticed people here don't seem too concerned. Not a lot of facemasks, except on service personnel. We've stopped asking if we should wear ours."

"Right, well, for some people their silly ideology is more important than life and death. You're in Springbrook, Ohio, brother, heartland of 'Merica! Lotta folks here despise any and all forms of government. Forget mandate, even a government *recommendation* gets them worked up. Wait, I take it back...they do love the Pentagon. Springbrook jumped from the Eisenhower fifties to the Reagan eighties and missed those other two pesky decades."

Nick smiled. "Speaking of which, I was out in Hernan at Couch Industries recently."

Turlock guffawed loudly. "You bastard, why didn't you take me with you! I love that place. Did you notice all those flags flying out front? I call that place 'The Compound.'"

"Yeah, I did notice. Hard not to."

"I can give you all sorts of stories about The Compound, and all of them would make your hair curl. The former president who couldn't take it anymore and blew the top of his head off. The current president whom nobody ever sees. The rumors of Agent Orange. The—"

"Wait," interrupted Nick. "Agent *Orange*? You don't mean to tell me they made Agent Orange out there."

"Montaigne, I said 'rumors.' I'm a journalist, remember? And I'm not cable news, I'm old school, I deal in *facts*. They didn't *make* the chemical, they stored and used it. Back in the day Marty did a whole series on Couch Industries, and it didn't go over well with the brass there. All his sources were anonymous, but a number of lower-level employees went on record claiming Couch manufactured the MC-1 hourglass pumps that sprayed Agent Orange for Operation Ranch Hand during the Vietnam War. They used barrels of the chemical itself when testing the pumps. Why they didn't just use water, I have no clue. Anyway, god knows how many ex-employees of Couch began having grapefruits start to grow inside them."

Nick flashed back to his brief time with Haslett and Goosebill. He recalled the funny smell, and the dried, orange residue along the baseboards of the hallways. He mentioned this to Turlock.

"Ha! Well, it's called Agent 'Orange,' but I don't think it has that color. I wouldn't worry too much, Montaigne. Probably another chemical caused that. Maybe they're still making DDT there. Some firms have a tough time with progress. Profit is everything to them."

Shafts of sun began to pierce the limpid clouds overhead and Turlock got down to business. He opened the door of his car, reached in, and pulled out an attaché case. He opened the case and withdrew a stack of papers, which he began to lay across the hood of his vehicle. One by one he explained to Montaigne what each sheet represented, based partially on what Melody had told him. Nick scoured the papers as if looking for something ominous that might jump at him. But all he could do was shake his head in bewilderment.

"Roy, this is pretty complex. I have no idea what I'm looking at. I mean, I see Harban, China here," he pointed to the bottom right corner of one of the sheets. "And over...here," he pointed at another sheet, "it says Kibitsu Consolidated. Okay, we know Maraschino Cherry was from Harban, and Don Moore visited there. And Kibitsu is the name of the company where Bing worked. But I don't understand anything else. I mean, what are these lines here, and what do these symbols mean?"

Turlock laughed. "Yeah, right, I'm not an engineer either, Montaigne. But my gal—my ex-gal—said there were certain areas to concentrate on. So, like, you see where I highlighted?"

Nick saw the yellow highlighted areas. "Yeah," he responded.

"Okay, those are what's important. This shit is the last project Moore worked on. It's, as you can see, diagrams for manufacture of the MaxxDig 60 excavator. They use these to scrape away mountaintops in Kentucky and West Virginia. You see?"

"Right, I get that. But like here...this chemical formula for, what...the brake pads? You highlighted this. Why?"

"Well, Mel told me that—"

"Did you say *Mel*?"

"Yeah, Mel. My old girlfriend. Why, you know her?" Turlock asked, knowing full well they'd met.

"Uh," Nick stalled, thinking of a quick response, "no, but that's an unusual name for a woman."

"Sure, well, that's her nickname. Her full name is Melody-Clair."

"Ah, I see," said Nick.

"Okay, well, she works at The Compound and got me these prints. Risky business, there, so I owe her one."

"She must still like you to risk her neck."

"I don't know about that. She was always out of my league, so no surprise I lost her. I don't know what she ever saw in me, I sure as hell wouldn't want me. She's smart as a whip, though. Not to mention she has a pair of headlights that would light up a Siberian mine shaft."

Nick cracked a wicked grin. He looked forward to dinner at Sharkey's later.

"So, anyway—hey, you still with me Montaigne?"

"Yeah, Roy," Nick snapped out of his reverie. "I, uh, was asking about this headlight. I mean *highlight*. This chemical formula." He pointed at a materials specification for the brake pads that read $Na_2(Fe^{2+}{}_3Fe^{3+}{}_2)Si_8O_{22}(OH)_2$.

Turlock leaned over the car hood and stared at it. After a few seconds, he pulled back, shaking his head.

"You got me, Montaigne. I'm no engineer, and I'm certainly not a chemist. Flunked quantitative analysis chemistry while a marine bio major at Ohio University, and that's when I switched to journalism. But she said it might be important. That's all I know, dude."

Nick bit his lower lip. The cemetery was completely quiet, no cars on Route 31, not even a bird whistling. Nick reached into his coat pocket and removed his cellphone.

"Well, that's what this little device is good for. Can't hurt to plug this gibberish into Google."

He punched some buttons with Turlock leaning over. Nick ignored the overwhelming odor of booze, but subconsciously nudged a few inches away from Turlock.

The two men looked at the Google results. Nick clicked on the Wikipedia link. He slowly scrolled down the Wikipedia article for *riebeckite*.

"Holy shit," said Turlock. "Also called *crocodilite*. That's fucking *blue asbestos*."

Nick began to read the article out loud from the top. His voice became louder when he got to key terms like "asbestos" and "most hazardous" and "mesothelioma."

"Sheesh," he gasped. "They once used this shit in *gas masks*." Turlock for once remained silent. He merely turned his head, his lips pressed tightly together. Finally, he offered "Gas masks, and obviously brake pads used by Couch Industries."

Nick left the Wikipedia article and clicked on several other links, all of which confirmed that the highlighted chemical formula was blue asbestos. He then inserted the words "asbestos outlawed" in the search engine and clicked. The majority of the results were articles and papers that dealt with the lung disease known as mesothelioma. He clicked on the link leading to The Mesothelioma Center and, again, read aloud.

"On July 12, 1989, the U.S. Environmental Protection Agency issued a final rule to ban the majority of asbestos products."

He looked at Turlock. Turlock stared back, his mouth hanging open.

"Roy, if I'm not mistaken, our friends out at The Compound were using asbestos long after it was banned by the EPA. Yet still at the time Donald Moore was alive and employed there."

"What do you think that means, Montaigne?" asked Turlock.

"It means that I and just about everyone else may have been barking up the wrong tree. The Moore murders may have had nothing to do with either Bing or the CIA. This looks like a possible case of 'kill the whistleblower.'"

Montaigne and Turlock were silent for a long time. Nick mused how the case had suddenly swiveled its wheels under him. Yeah, now he had a motive. Not entirely solid, but a motive nonetheless. But after all the mind cartwheels over China, the CIA, Bing, Ramsey, Henderlong, love triangles, and god-knows what else, this sudden shift in direction threw him for a loop. He needed to rest his brain.

He turned to face the front of the cemetery and Route 31. He heard a cow moo in the distance. He took a long, deep breath and gazed at the green, tree-covered mounds in the distance, then at the scaffolding that represented the remnants of the old drive-in. *Opening Day*, he mused. *Would o' been right about now. Lots of changes. Time don't stand still. Wonder if the Moores were Indians or Reds fans. Maybe neither. Wonder how Vern is doing. He's probably talking to the Chins now. Hopefully. Not that it matters. Case has taken a sharp turn. Par for the course.* He smiled. *He sure hated being inside the Henshall home. The* Moore *home. Lovable lout.*

Then he thought of Annie. *Need to call her. Haven't been too good. But she gave me this time away. A last fling for her Nicky? Then what happens. She wants marriage. Can't blame her. "Annette McBain Montaigne." Hell, if I hear that one more time.*

"What are you thinkin'?" asked Turlock.

Nick took another deep breath and snapped back. "Time. Just that."

"Huh?"

"If you could go back in time, what's the one thing you would do?"

"Hell, I don't know. Maybe treat folks better."

"That's noble. Know what I'd do, Roy?"

"Let's see. Never come to Springbrook?"

"Ha! You read my mind. Actually, I think I'd visit my ancestor. He lived in the sixteenth century, in France. His name was Michel de Montaigne. He was a thinker and writer. A very smart guy. I'd like to go back and have him advise me. You know, whenever you come to a crossroads, it always helps to have a sounding board. Too much time is wasted banging one's head against dead ends."

"Very philosophical," said Turlock, while vaping his Mr. Fog Switch Bubblegum Gang Wild Strawberry Ice. "Though I'm sure Michel would have said it better."

"Or maybe I'd go back and study to be a jazz musician."

"Now you're talking, Montaigne. That's more up my alley."

Nick's phone began to vibrate and Ronnie Montrose's "Town Without Pity" blasted across the cemetery. He quickly hit the green button, then put it on speaker mode.

"Montaigne here...Vern?"

"Nick, guess what."

"What?"

"I'm on Morning Glory and guess what vehicle I'm staring at."

"Uh, I don't know, Vern...a Good Humor Man truck?"

"No! The Chins' car! It's parked in their driveway!"

"Okay. Well, what are you going to do?"

"Whaddya think, hondo. Talk to them! Finally!"

"Okay, Vern, you do that. Let me know how it goes."

"Sure thing, boss. Seeya."

Montaigne and Turlock laughed. "He sounds like a fun guy," said Turlock.

"Yeah, he's a great guy. Most of the time. And keeps me grounded.

"Okay," he continued, "where were we? Asbestos at Couch. Mesothelioma. Got an idea. May not go anywhere but worth a try."

Nick pulled up Google again. This time, he punched in "asbestos" and "Couch Industries." The results list gave him dozens of articles, and many of them originating from law firms. Turlock, observing what he was doing, did the same thing on his phone. For the next ten minutes each man silently read about how Texas-based oil and industrial giant Hardison Incorporated, after buying out Couch and Granger in 1998, inherited over three-hundred-thousand asbestos-caused mesothelioma lawsuits that had originated at both Couch and Granger. Hardison had to set up an asbestos trust to compensate all those victims diagnosed with mesothelioma and other asbestos-related diseases. Lawyers for the victims claimed Couch and Granger were aware of the dangers from asbestos but chose to continue using the material as a cost-saving measure. Hardison eventually declared bankruptcy.

"Can you *believe* this?" gasped Turlock. "All from those brake pads in the MaxxDig 60?"

"Well, there may have been other parts, too," said Nick. "But the MaxxDig 60 was what Moore was working on at the time. So were a few others." He thought of Goosebill and Delmonico.

"Roy, where's that sheet that has the chemical on it?" Turlock pointed at the sheet with the brake pads. They scanned everything around the highlighted chemical formula for asbestos.

"Didn't think so," said Nick in a disappointed tone.

"What?"

"There are no signatures. I was hoping there would be some kind of signoff signature for these brake pads. Somebody who gave the go-ahead for use of asbestos. If we can determine that, then we get closer to a motive for murder. Do you think your ex-girlfriend can go back into the Couch vaults and find some kind of...what do they call them...*piece* drawing?"

"You mean 'piece-part' drawing?"

"Right. This print here," he pointed at the sheet, "is good, but we need some kind of a link."

"I don't know. She was really reluctant to get these. But I'll try."

"Wait," jumped in Nick. "What's her last name? I can dig her up and ask her myself. Save you the trouble, and anyway, I've got some experience with this kind of thing."

"Sure, I don't mind," he agreed, aware that Nick probably knew it. "Her last name is Fitzpatrick. Full name is Melody-Clair Fitzpatrick." Turlock then gave Nick her phone number—unaware that he already had it.

"Thanks, Roy."

"No problem-o, signor."

As Turlock and Montaigne started to tuck their cellphones back in their pockets, a car turned off Route 31 and began to slowly cruise along the main lane that circled the cemetery grounds. When the men saw this, they quickly scooped up the engineering prints and Turlock stuffed them back in his attaché case. They then turned to face the tombstone of Marty Franes, bowing their heads.

The car continued to ease along the lane. Then it stopped. It was toward the back, where Nick and Roy stood, but at the opposite end. A man got out. He walked over to a large headstone, then crouched in front.

Nick studied the man for a few moments. "I think I know that guy," he said. "That looks like...Karl 'Champ' Haslett, from Couch. I guess he's paying respects to his parents, or something."

"I doubt that," said Turlock. "Unless his parents were Donald and Irene Moore. That's their tombstone."

Chapter Four

He had planned to see Henderlong first, but seeing the car in the Chin driveway convinced Vern he'd better visit them first, in case they evaporated again. He backed his Accord up and parked along the curb directly in front of the house and huffed up the moderately steep drive that led to their door. His heart raced from the exertion, as well as the anticipation of finally meeting them. Heck, thus far they'd managed to evade him. But now he had them cornered. He knew exactly how the conversation would go. Late at night, while tossing and turning in Room 115, he'd worked out an entire fictitious dialogue once he eventually had them face-to-face. His inner Mandarin assumed the Chins spoke broken English—a blatant ethnic stereotype, but which Vern's subconscious had innocently absorbed through Charlie Chan movies and episodes of the TV western *Kung Fu*:

"Hello, Mr. and Mrs. Chin? Hi, I'm Vern Wister. I'm investigating the murders of your old neighbors, Donald and Irene Moore. Do you have a few moments?"

"Yes, please enter!"

"Thank you. So, did you ever see any Chinese visitors at the Moore home while they were alive?"

"Why, yes we do. Many time."

"Did you happen to meet any of them?"

"We do. We become good friend with one of them."

"And what was his name?"

"Mr. Xi Lao Bing."

"Ah. Mr. Xi Lao Bing. And did Mr. Bing stay with the Moores often?"

"Yes, many time."

"And did he stay there around the time of the murders?"

"Yes. He stay previous night."

"Really? He stayed there the night before their murders? And did you know Mr. Bing to ever carry a gun?"

"Yes, he do. He carry a (blankety blank) with a (blankety blank) suppressor."

"Ah. And do you have reason to believe he worked with Red Chinese counterintelligence?"

"Yes, he tell us. We do not mind."

"Ah. So do you also have reason to believe he killed the Moores?"

"Yes, he tell us he do so. He tell us is necessary to eliminate to protect safety of homeland. He tell us 'We are Chinese!' He say we Chinese must stick together."

"Ah, I see. And did you give the police this information?"

"Yes we do. But they do not believe us. We wait for man like you to come along...we make tea now. You like?"

Vern looked forward to wrapping the case up this neatly, and presenting everything to his boss in hopes of a healthy salary increase.

But after ringing the Chin doorbell, things didn't turn out as he'd hoped.

"Hello, may I help you?" asked a pink-complexioned Caucasian girl who looked like she couldn't have been more than fourteen years old.

"Uh...hello...are either Mr. Chin or Mrs. Chin home?"

"No, I'm sorry, they're away on vacation. They just left early this morning. I'm here to feed their cats and clean their litter box."

"*Fuck!*"

The girl's eyes became big as dinner plates.

"Hey, I'm sorry," he quickly apologized. "I shouldn't have said that."

"That's okay."

"It's just that...well, I've been trying to talk to them for a while, and they never seem to be around."

"Sure, I understand. They stay pretty busy. Do you want me to give them a message?"

"I already left a note, but what the—" he began before catching himself. "Yeah, sure, that's fine." He dolefully gave the girl the same information he'd left in the note.

Vern thought it best if he decompressed a few moments before confronting Manny Henderlong, so he sat behind the Accord steering wheel long enough to allow his heart to return to a reasonable rate. While sitting, Whitney Black returned from his angry dash to wherever and entered his house. Vern opened his car window, but there were no more loud voices.

Just before getting out and crossing over to Henderlong's house, a police cruiser came gliding down the street. The car slowed and pulled next to Vern's Accord. Vern turned his head. Augie Moriarty was staring right at him.

Vern rolled down the driver's window the same time as Moriarty rolled down his passenger's window. Vern tried to think of a quick explanation why he was sitting alone in the car, knowing from experience that cops are innately suspicious of even the slightest behavior that was out of the ordinary. He nervously cleared his throat.

"Hello, Officer Moriarty. How are you?"

Moriarty continued staring.

"I'm, uh, sitting here collecting my, uh, thoughts a little."

"Yeah, I can see that."

"I, uh, plan to speak with one of the neighbors concerning the Moore murders. Just making some last-minute notes."

Moriarty stared at him a few more moments, in Vern's mind to heighten Vern's embarrassment. Then he told Vern "Fine. You do that. But you might want to reposition your vee-HICKle. The back tire is partway on the curb."

"Oh, I'm sorry, I didn't know that. Sure, I'll reposition it. Thanks."

"No problem. Wouldn't be here to talk to Henderlong, would you?"

"Why, yes, as a matter of fact, I did have some questions for him."

"You're probably wasting your time."

"Oh? Why is that?"

"We already dealt with him. Long ago. Like tryin' to tackle a greased pig."

"Right, I kinda got that impression. But I've had some experience with his types, so I'm hopeful."

Just then a car came down Morning Glory, behind them. "Just a minute," said Moriarty. He pulled his car in front of Vern's and parked and walked to Vern's open window.

"Anyway...you say you got experience, eh? That's right, I forgot, you were a cop in Philadelphia. What kinda cop?"

"Bunko."

"Bunko? Don't know much about that other than it's a card game. Okay, bunko-boy, have at Henderlong. Maybe you can do more than we could. Did you have a chance to read those letters to the editor?"

"I sure did. That's what I plan to ask him about."

"Fine." Moriarty glanced up and down the street. "Okay...what did you say your name was?"

"Wister. Vern Wister. And my partner's Nick Montaigne. Say, uh...Lieutenant Moriarty...your sister worked at the hospital with Irene Moore, correct?"

"Yes. Why?"

"Oh, just checking. I'm sure she was questioned at one time."

"*Everyone* was questioned who knew the couple." Moriarty's forehead wrinkled. "What are you getting at? You suspect her or something?"

"*Everyone* who knew the couple is a suspect, Lieutenant Moriarty. 'Specially if there was a motive. Now, I know the name 'Moriarty' means something around here. But from what I've learned there was some work-related friction between Siobhan and Irene Moore."

"Yeah?" said Moriarty mockingly. "Enough for her to commit homicide? Or hire a hit man?"

"Ever hear of Wanda Holloway, Lieutenant? The Arizona mom who hired a hit man to kill her daughter's cheerleading rival?"

"Yeah, I know about her. 'Cept she was from Texas, not Arizona, and it wasn't the rival daughter, it was the daughter's mother."

Vern's crossed eyes became uncrossed.

"Mr. Wister," the lieutenant continued, "you seem like a decent fellow. And I know you're only doin' your job. But don't go walkin' in the jungle where there's no trail. I'd hate to see you get lost."

Moriarty slapped his palm hard on the roof of Vern's car and returned to his car and drove down Morning Glory out of sight.

Vern pulled the Accord off the curb, then got out and walked to the front door of Manny Henderlong's home. This time there was no plaid shirt gazing out the door, nor was Vern startled by Henderlong's sudden appearance outside. The window blinds were drawn and the house interior appeared dark. *This guy better be home or my next visit's gonna be to Sharkey's.*

A sign was on the door: SOLICITORS STAY AWAY! Vern pushed the doorbell but heard no sound, so he knocked on the storm door. He breathed a sigh of relief when, a few seconds later, the door opened. Henderlong stood before him, wearing jeans and a plain white t-shirt.

"Help ya?" Henderlong said curtly.

"Hello, Mr. Henderlong, it's me, Vern, again. Just wondered if I could talk to you. We're still asking questions about the Moore murders."

"Sure. Got nuthin' to hide. Meet me out back. On the patio."

Vern looped around the house to a half-moon-shaped cement patio. He saw a single bird feeder in the middle of the yard and a small rectangular garden plot in one of the corners. The patio had a black Weber grill, a square glass table with a faded pea-green umbrella extending out the center, four patio chairs, a single pot of dirt that looked like it contained a stunted clump of chives, and what appeared to be a large storage box pushed against the house. There was nothing fancy about Henderlong's backyard. No flowers, nothing decorative. It was obvious there were no women in the Henderlong household. It was a scene of pragmatism and practicality. Unambiguousness. It was perfectly in keeping with what Vern had gleaned was the man's personality.

Henderlong came out of the back door and the two men took seats.

Vern started the conversation. He knew that Henderlong was one of those with a congenital wariness of everything, including near-strangers like himself, and he figured this caution was probably multiplied by the fact Vern represented a form of authority. And also by the subject of their pending discussion. So he wanted to dip into that discussion carefully and—to paraphrase Augie Moriarty's jungle analogy—stick to the path as much as possible. One thing he had learned since leaving the force and teaming with Nick was to start things off with a few hors d'oeuvres. That way, when the main entree came later, the vegetables might not be too "icky."

"Got a nice backyard here. What kind of birds you get?" Vern thought placement of a bird-feeder pole smack-dab in the middle of the yard was unusual, and not exactly artistic.

"Get all kinds. Sparrows. Wrens. Blackbirds. Red-headed woodpecker once in a while."

"Woodpeckers love those suet cake things. You put them on a tree trunk, in a little cage thing, and they can perch vertically and peck."

Like Moriarty, Henderlong just stared at him.

"Uh, you live alone here, Mr. Henderlong?"

"Fer 'bout seven years. Wife died."

"Oh, I'm sorry."

"Why?"

"Oh, uh, well, I'm sure that was difficult. I'll be at a loss if my wife goes first."

"Ain't easy. But life goes on. Saw you over at Chins earlier today." Vern was taken aback by how quickly Henderlong switched gears. *Probably to head off any emotional display*, he thought.

"Yes, I've been hoping to meet with them but they're never around."

"What you wanna ask? I'll ask for ya if ya want."

"Really? You, uh...you know them that well?"

"Better 'n' I know anyone else on this street. Play mah-jongg with 'em all the time."

Vern was startled. *Mah-jongg with the Chins?* Friendship between Henderlong and Lee and Jane Chin was the last thing he would have imagined. He'd pegged Henderlong as a committed loner, someone who might have a few contacts through political outlets. Certainly not friendship with a married couple across the street, least of all a Chinese-American couple. He had a hard time picturing Henderlong sitting at a table with three other people, smiling, throwing dice, and arranging small tiles with colored flowers and dragons and Chinese characters.

He wondered if there was a fourth person in these casual games of mah-jongg.

"So...tell me...is mah-jongg a three-way game?"

"Nope. 'Nother friend o' theirs usually joins us."

"I see. So, how long have you been playing?"

"Long time. Before the Moore murders. If that's what you wanna know. And I think it is. Yep, sometimes played with one of their visitors. He and the Chins became friendly 'cause of the Chinese connection. But if you want me to say his name, I won't."

"Why not?"

"Simple. I don't remember it. Not real good with Chinese names."

Vern's tightened shoulders relaxed. *Reached a dead end on that one.*

"Chins might 'member it."

"Right. Chins might. Maybe when they get home...if you don't mind...could—"

"Yeah, I'll ask 'em. Saw you listenin' in on the Blacks, too."

He doesn't miss a beat, thought Vern. Henderlong continued, as if warming up to something.

"I've had a front row seat for nigh on forty years. Sure, they come on like the perfect all-American family. Scholar-athlete boy, Optimist Club, loyal Roman Catholics, all John Wayne and apple pie. But there's dirty little secrets all up and down this street, and in this whole town. Don't let Springbrook fool ya, Mr. Investigator. If you wanna find out who killed the Moores, ya need to peel back the layers a bit.

"I tell ya," he continued, "it's the government. You need to find out who here's workin' for 'em. Then you'll have yer killer."

"Thanks for the advice. Speaking of which, I read some of your old letters to the editor in the *Springbrook Daily*

News Journal Observer-Tribune. I thought they were really good."

Henderlong's eye glared at Vern like an angry raptor. "Why was you readin' *those*?"

"Well, I was in the library and wanted to get a picture of the town immediately before and after their deaths. It was hard not to recognize—"

"Tryin' to make me out a suspect, huh?" Henderlong cut him off. "I went through that with Dickson and Moriarty ages ago and I ain't doin' it again. I paid my ticket! You...you come 'round with accusations, innuendoes, sniffin' dogs and stuff. I...I done passed the test. You got no proof of *nuthin'*. That Granby Road fight we had got nuthin' to do with what happened to 'em. They won the FDIC auction and I walked away but they never got over it. Acted like I was some kinda monster or somethin' only 'cause I wanted a piece o' land. They was total assholes, cuttin' into my yard with their mower, lettin' their damn dog crap in my yard...

"Course, Dick Thompson on town council was their good buddy so then I couldn't get a re-zone for that sewer line easement and then the whole council, prob'ly the whole town, paints yours truly as Simon Legree. Only folks with any decency here is the Chins. Everyone else, 'cause of their tongue-wagging, wants to run me outta town."

Henderlong appeared to run out of gas and, gripping the arms of the porch chair tightly, sagged his body back.

"Mr. Henderlong," Vern began, "those Granby Road altercations were all over the newspaper. You kind of earned a reputation there, so when the Moores were killed, you were a ready-made 'person of interest.' It's well known you and the Moores never got along after the Granby fight, right? I believe the FDIC auction was in 1990? Secondly, why did you lie to me when I first met with you? You claimed you barely knew the Moores. But you were in a well-documented battle with the Moores over that Granby property. That doesn't sound like 'barely knew.'"

Henderlong cleared his throat. "Listen! Listen! I got me an alibi! I was playin' mah-jongg with the Chins that night! Then came home to my wife! You don't believe me, go check it out!"

"Yeah, I'll do that, if I can ever get hold of them. But why should I think you're not lying to me again? You already lied once."

"Okay, I lied. I'll admit it. I knew what you were here fer and I didn't want that dirt dug up agin. But I'm tellin' you the truth now. I didn't kill 'em, and I got an alibi!"

Vern knew it was time to back off. He got as much out of Henderlong as he was going to get. But he had a feeling Nick would want to visit Henderlong himself. Maybe after they got more details from Joy Dickson—such as forensics data. So he shifted gears.

"I noticed your one flag out front. What does it represent?"

Henderlong said gravely, "That's my heritage. Those designs are tipis. A red flag for Red Nation, eight white tipis for Sweat Lodge. It is an Oglala Lah-ko-tah flag. Pine Ridge Reservation. Mother was half-blood Oglala. We're descended from Crazy Horse."

"*Really?* Wow. Wasn't he a chief at Little Big Horn?"

"Not a chief, a war leader. But he was there. Helped kill Custer."

Unlike Nick, Vern didn't know much history, but he did know about how the government had treated America's indigenous population, and he knew it wasn't pretty.

"So...you've got a pretty good reason for hating the U.S. government."

"Reason enough. Tunkasila mitawa—'my grandfather'—was forced to leave res as a kid for school in Carlisle. Got beat any time he tried to speak Lakota. Forced to wear wasi'chu clothes. Forced to chop his hair off. Forced to pledge allegiance to flag, after flag destroyed us. Forced into Christian church. The idea was 'kill the Indian, save the man.' We couldn't practice our own religion till

1978. Government denied us. Had to be white man's faith. Think of that. *Two-hundred years* after this country's founding and its supposed 'freedom of religion.'

"But, o' course, they don't teach much Indian history in public schools. Too embarassin' for the established narrative, I guess. Yeah...I got reason enough."

Vern felt like he should say something like "Sorry," but knew it would be awkward and inappropriate and probably fall on deaf ears anyway. He thanked Henderlong for meeting him and rose to leave.

Henderlong followed him around the house to the front. On the way, Henderlong pointed at an area of parched, patchy grass and told Vern, "This is where that dog kept pissin' and crappin'. I've tried seed and sod, but for some reason can't get it back to what it was."

Vern shook Manny Henderlong's hand in the drive and walked toward his car. Halfway down the drive, Henderlong called out to him.

"Hey Mr. Investigator."

"Yes?"

"When you meet the Chins, ask them about how the *Chinese* were treated."

"I'll do that."

"One other thing."

"What's that?"

"Remember: Custer died for your sins."

Chapter Five

Nick debated whether or not to stroll through the
gravestones to Haslett. The next day he hoped to
be at Couch to question Goosebill about this newly
discovered asbestos business, so he knew he would then be
seeing Haslett, who would have to escort Nick down the
long halls.

He also didn't want to disturb the man. Haslett's head
was bowed. Out of politeness, it might be best to leave him
alone.

At the same time, he thought it odd that Haslett would
be paying respects to a lower-level employee who had been
dead for twenty-five years. He was under the impression
that the design engineers—which included Moore,
Goosebill, Delmonico, and Fitzpatrick—worked
independently from the product development president and
were essentially given free reign. From his brief meeting
with Haslett, he'd formed an opinion of the man: family
guy, liked to read, probably politically neutral, easygoing,

good sense of humor, and though he obviously had a military background, lacked the rigid esprit de corps that many veterans exhibited throughout their lives.

Nick flipped the proverbial coin in his head. The coin landed on "stroll on over." So he said goodbye to Turlock—who promised to continue digging around the office archives for anything on the Moore case that Franes might have left behind—and he walked over to Haslett.

"Mr. Haslett!" called out Nick. Haslett's head jerked up. He seemed shocked to see Montaigne.

"What?! Hey! I know you! How are you, sir!"

"I'm fine, and I'll be doing even better once I wrap this case up and can return to Atlanta."

"Sure you don't want to remain in Springbrook? We got a really robust night life. Ha, just kidding! By the way, please call me 'Champ.'"

"Right, sorry, I forgot. Anyway...I couldn't help but notice you visiting the Moore gravesite and didn't want to drive off without saying hello."

"That's really kind, Mr. Montaigne. I'm sure you're wondering why I'm here."

"Well, kind of. But don't feel obligated to tell me."

"No, no, no. There's nothing mysterious about my being here. Fact is, even my wife thinks it's funny why I do this. I'm not here out of any obligation to Don or his wife. I come out here every year on the anniversary of...well, you know...as a representative of Couch. No one else does, that I'm aware. I don't bring flowers or anything. I'm a softie, yeah, but not *that* sentimental. And I'm not religious. No, I just want to pay my respects to a guy who gave himself unselfishly to our company. I do this with a few other Couch potatoes, too. Sort of an idiosyncrasy of mine. Am I weird, Montaigne, or what?"

Nick laughed. "No, not at all, Champ. I admire you for taking the time. Not many company executives would go out of their way for a deceased employee. But you said 'anniversary.' They died on April 15, I believe. That's not until later this week."

"You are correct sir! My reason for being here today— now, you'll probably laugh at this—but the last day I saw Don was on the *twelfth* of April. I passed him in the first floor hall after asking Melody—a fellow design engineer of Don's—about an HR issue. I barely knew the guy. Met him and his lovely wife at a company picnic, saw him a few times in the hall, but that was the extent of it. All we did that day was exchange hellos.

"But, you know how it is. After getting the tragic news, my mind shot back to that moment in the hallway. Still can't get my head around..."

Haslett dropped his head and his voice caught in his throat. Nick felt stuck. He was halfway between hugging Haslett with a "Dude, it's okay, I understand" and gripping his shoulders and shaking him with a "Pull yourself together, man!" But he figured an ex-Army guy had certain reserves of strength and would soon recover. He was right. Haslett looked up and shook his head as if disgusted with himself. His cheeks were dry.

"There you go, Montaigne!" he said. "Major Champ Haslett, just an old softie!"

"Naw, I totally get it. Hopefully Vern and I can get to the bottom of this damn thing and it'll take the edge off a little. That reminds me, mind if I head out to Hernan tomorrow some time? I'd like to ask Marv Goosebill a few things. My friend, who just drove off—name's Roy, works for the newspaper—discovered a couple things. So I've got a fresh round of inquiries."

"Hey, no problem sir. What time you thinkin'?"

"Well, let's see...is 10 a.m. all right?"

"Perfect sir. See you at the reception desk at ten tomorrow."

The two men shook hands. Nick started to walk back to his Porsche. Haslett hollered after him, "By the way, what did you think of Marv?"

Nick scrunched his face. "Let's just say you were right about him. There are some folks in this world that, no matter how hard you might try..." He swept both arms in front of him making sure they didn't touch.

"Ha! You are correct sir!"

***

Nick checked his Rolex. He and Vern had planned to rendezvous at The Covenant Café, close to Joy Dickson's home in the sparsely populated area southwest of Springbrook. There, they wanted to nab a late lunch then head over to the retired detective's house for what Nick hoped would be a long discussion. Nick looked forward to this meeting. Dickson had been out of town since he and Vern had first arrived in Springbrook. But now he would finally get the lowdown on what exactly happened inside 157 Morning Glory on the night of April 15, 1995.

Well, not all the lowdown. Just a few more puzzle pieces dealing with forensics. Dickson had sounded pleasant on the phone. Almost eager, as if she wanted to unload. Nick knew the feeling. He had Vern to confide in and bounce ideas off and empathize with. Dickson had nobody. Augie Moriarty? Forget it. A supervisor on the force and part of the checkered Moriarty dynasty would probably avoid snuggling up to a now-retired detective, one whom he had undoubtedly butted heads with, especially when leads began freezing up back in ninety-five. And—at least until Montaigne-Wister appeared in Springbrook—the Moore case was as cold as a Popsicle in permafrost. Nick hoped to parry ideas with a fellow investigator who might be sympathetic to the vexations of cracking such a rock-hard crime case.

Nick and Vern shared their individual tales since parting at the Comfort Inn, as they chowed down at the most happening place in Springbrook on a Sunday afternoon. Nick ordered the Noah Burger and Vern had the Sunday

Solomon Special, which was a pork cutlet smothered in onions and mushroom gravy. Vern told Nick about his discoveries at the library; Whitney Black's loud outburst and mad dash from home; and his success in confronting Manny Henderlong about his relationship with the Moores. Nick described his confrontational meeting with Monica Delmonico; the revelation about asbestos brake pads in the MaxxDig 60; and Champ Haslett's timely visit to the Moore gravesite.

"You know, Nick, that's mighty strange how Haslett showed up right when you and Turlock were scouring those prints. You got any suspicions about him?"

"Certainly, Vern. Those could've been crocodile tears he was attempting. But I've got suspicions about everyone we've met in town so far, and some we haven't met—and some who are dead. It's still a giant crap shoot. I'll tell you what, though."

"What?" asked Vern, a speck of mushroom resting on his upper lip.

"That asbestos is a game-changer. We and everyone else may have been digging down the wrong gopher hole with this CIA theory. I'm looking forward to my second discussion with Goosebill. And if we can just get some kind of signoff for those brake pad prints, we'll have a face that might lead us to another face with a whistle in his mouth."

Vern also got a kick out of Nick's getting thrown out of Monica Delmonico's house for accusing her late husband of having mafia connections. His boss's stature, in Vern's eyes anyway, dropped just a few centimeters.

"Workin' bunko in Philly, yeah, I met a few of those types," said Vern. "But you gotta be careful, Nicky. You need solid proof, or you'll get a plate of pasta in your face."

Nick defended his suggestion of a mafia connection by observing she used the word "vendetta" and had a bird named Carlo who quoted lines from *The Godfather*.

The detectives finished their meals and paid the bill and left the restaurant. Soon after stepping off the sidewalk and into the parking lot, Nick hurriedly said "Go this way," hustling Vern away from their cars. Before Vern could ask why, Dorothy Claunch called out to them from twenty feet away while waddling briskly toward them.

"Hello, Detective Montaigne! Detective Wister! So nice to see you at The Covenant!"

They turned to face her. "Oh...hi Mrs. Claunch, we didn't see you!" Nick lied.

"Come now! How could you not notice this large waddling form! Ha-ha! I just wanted to say we missed you in church this morning."

Vern's chin dropped slightly as Nick rushed to think of a response.

"Yes, uh, we're so sorry Mrs. Claunch. We actually had pressing business and were unable to make it. Maybe next Sunday, though."

"Oh yes, I'm sure you're both very busy with your private eye-ing work. Shall I call you Napoleon Solo and Illya Kuriakin? Ha!" But even Nick, who liked old things, was unfamiliar with the sixties television show *The Man from U.N.C.L.E.*

"Well," Claunch continued, "we do hope you'll join us next Sunday. We have a lovely new interim pastor. He's very knowledgeable and respectful of church tradition. And easy on the eyes, I might add! Next week's sermon should be a good one. It's entitled, 'The Value of the Rod of Correction.' We do hope you'll join us!"

"Oh, we'll make every effort, Mrs. Claunch," gushed Vern sardonically, recalling his unfortunate Bible class experience.

"Wonderful! Oh one more thing...I spoke with Beryl Henshall, and she said...and I quote...'The offer still stands.' I don't know what that means, but perhaps you do. Anyway...ta-ta!"

The men turned and looped around to their cars, Vern making several disparaging comments that brought a mild reprimand from Nick.

They drove separately down Route 31, past the gas stations and fast-food joints and into thick corn and soybean country. They almost missed the dirt road with the five or six mailboxes that indicated the lane to Dickson's house. Nick slammed on his brakes, followed by Vern, whose rental car came within a few feet of the Porsche rear bumper. Then they turned left down a long gravel lane that wound between tall pines, maneuvering around several potholes, until they came to a wooden A-frame house buried in shadows and shade. In front of the house was a flagpole with the stars and stripes on top and a rainbow flag just beneath. *Couch is winning by three flags*, thought Nick.

Soon after parking, a large golden retriever came flying around the corner of the house.

"River, stop it!" yelled a woman who was standing on the front porch. "Don't mind River," she called out to the men. "He thinks he's a guard dog but he's actually a big sissie, River, leave those men alone!"

Nick and Vern climbed a short hill on slate-stone steps and introduced themselves to Joy Dickson. Like many other greater Springbrookers, she appeared in her late sixties or early seventies. She was dressed casually, in sandals, jeans, and a t-shirt that had a cartoon of the Peanuts cartoon character Peppermint Patty, with the caption "Charm School Dropout." Her hair was yellowish-blonde and cut very short, especially on the sides. Her eyes slanted downward and were slightly hooded at the corners. She had thin lips with no lipstick, and her face had no other makeup. *Looks like a female ex-cop*, thought Nick. Her most noteworthy feature was a mild Tourette's syndrome tick: her eyes periodically squinted involuntarily.

She welcomed Nick and Vern to her "humble abode" and apologized for being gone so long.

"Had to visit my parents. One of the nice things about being retired," she remarked cheerfully, "is you can pull up stakes and *go*, whenever you want."

"I'll bet," said Vern, as they stepped into the cool, dark interior of the home. "Maybe one day we can do it too. Eh, Nick?" But Montaigne was in the middle of scanning the bookcase along one wall...getting a "feel" for the kind of person he would soon be speaking with. As his eyes absorbed the titles of several rows of books, he nodded subconsciously, as if approving Dickson's library.

"I like that one car out there," Dickson enthused about Nick's garish green "chick magnet."

"Hey, thanks," responded Nick. "She's a Porsche 911 GT2 RS. Always gets a lot of attention. Should o' seen the kids in Turnham Green."

"You boys and your toys," said Dickson in good-natured condescension. "You just love big, shiny, metallic things that make lots of noise."

Vern piggybacked with, "Nick's in a state of perpetual adolescence."

"Okay, guilty as charged," Nick said, raising his hands in resignation.

They took seats in three cushioned chairs in the large living area and River plopped down contentedly on the faded, square Oriental rug in the center of the triangle, breathing heavily and smiling with his big red tongue hanging out. Dickson asked if they wanted coffee, saying she'd "just brewed a fresh pot of sustainable Fairtrade," and Nick and Vern accepted the offer. Their coffee arrived in red-and-gold mugs with "Planter Pride" written below a cartoon of a man puffing out his large chest, wearing a floppy hat, and balancing on one shoulder a long implement that could have been a rifle, but was actually a garden hoe.

"Mmm! That's good coffee!" raved Vern. Nick thought he seemed exceptionally upbeat...maybe due to his success at Henderlong's house and the library...or maybe it was the afterglow of his Solomon Special.

"Thank you so much for meeting with us, Ms. Dickson," said Nick. "The Springbrook force is prevented from sharing anything with us—understandably—so we're lucky to find a retired detective like yourself. And someone willing to open up."

"Please, call me Joy. Yeah, this case has been bottled up in me for a while. It's good to be able to purge. I *really* wanted to solve it, but whoever did this made darn sure all his or her tracks were covered. I've sort of been waiting for someone like you to come along.

"So you're...Nick...and Vern?" she asked, pointing at each man respectively.

"Yes," they both said, with Nick adding that they usually do interviews separately, but Nick wanted Vern along for his expertise as a cop.

"Nice to meet another brother in blue," said Dickson. "It's a good time for the three of us to meet, since my partner and I are between vacations. So..." she started, reaching for a manila folder that lay on the TV table next to her chair, "I've written a few notes from what I remember about the case. It was so long ago, and there are certain things I have trouble recalling. There are also things I'll never forget. Such is the world of the cop. Right Vern?" Vern nodded in agreement. "Why don't you shoot me with your—oops, sorry, bad choice of words—direct to me your questions, and I'll answer them as best I can."

River groaned loudly and closed his droopy eyes. A grandfather clock ticked loudly behind them.

"Actually, Joy," replied Nick, "if it's okay with you—sure, yeah, that's a great idea—but I was hoping maybe you could walk us through the day of discovery. Like, when you first heard about the murders, your arrival at the house, what you saw, then maybe fill us in on forensic pathology. Then maybe Vern and I could ping some random questions at you. Just so we can get the most accurate picture of what happened."

"Sure," said Dickson, "that's a great idea. Okay, here goes. Time machine...here we go."

Dickson began. Vern scribbled in a notepad and Nick recorded the conversation on his phone.

"I received the call around eleven hundred hours on Tuesday, April 18, 1995. Neither Mr. nor Mrs. Moore had shown up for work Monday or Tuesday, and a co-worker from Couch Industries in Hernan had called to report Mr. Moore's absence, as well as a nurse from the hospital—pretty sure it was Dorothy Claunch—had called concerning Mrs. Moore's absence."

"So, do you know who it was from Couch that called?"

"No, I'm sorry, not with certainty. Dispatch got a name, but I forget who it was. I'm guessing it was Marvin Goosebill, because he was Mr. Moore's immediate supervisor. But not totally sure."

"Gotcha, thanks."

"Anyway, dispatch sent out a patrol because neither of the victims had appeared at work. Patrolman Paul Kelton was the first officer to enter the house. The front door was unlocked, so he entered the premises unobstructed. Patrolman Kelton surveyed the crime scene. He searched the premises for any other individuals besides the two victims, and for any weapons, but saw nothing—other than a canine. Immediately after searching the premises Officer Kelton called requesting the presence of a supervisor."

Nick interrupted again. "Did the patrolman—" but Vern stopped him.

"Nick, let her continue! The patrolman on a crime scene doesn't do anything. He surveys, then calls for a super. That's it."

"Yeah, okay, thanks Vern. Sorry Joy. See why I brought him along?" he smiled.

"That's okay. Anyway, after Patrolman Kelton contacted dispatch, they contacted the shift supervisor—

who on that day happened to be Sergeant Herbert Streicher—and also Coroner Annette Robinson, Public Information Officer Thomas Taliaferro, a forensic photographer, and myself. The five of us converged on the crime scene—I'm sorry, four of us, since Coroner Robinson arrived later—at approximately twelve hundred hours. We immediately strung police tape around the property of the victims. Once I surveyed the crime scene I commenced work on a search warrant. The warrant was obtained very quickly, Judge John Estes signing it. Once our warrant was obtained, we began processing the crime scene. This is where things got interesting."

Dickson paused in her monologue. River licked his lips and blinked a few times. Vern finished scribbling. Nick took a sip of coffee. The grandfather clock ticked.

Dickson continued. "We proceeded to take photos, video, measurements, and make sketches of the scene—the scene being the dining room, where Mrs. Moore was found, and the computer room or den, where Mr. Moore was found. Coroner Robinson then arrived and bagged the hands of the victims then dusted for fingerprints. Oh, I almost forgot. Officer Kay Parker of the Canine Unit also arrived and took control of the canine."

"How was the canine...dog—I believe her name was Lisa—behaving?" asked Nick.

"She was very subdued. I was surprised, since she hadn't eaten for several days. Perhaps it was due to her breed? I don't know. Officer Parker just scooped her up out of the den and brought her back to headquarters. She didn't make a sound or seem panicky at all. If River had been there, he'd be climbing the walls!"

The three looked at River, fast asleep, his long strands of hair splayed out on the Oriental rug like the mythical Golden Fleece.

"So Lisa was in the *den*?"

"Yes. Laying near the body of Mr. Moore. They must have been close."

The three processed these last words of Dickson's while gazing at sleeping River. Then Nick broke the silence. "So, let me ask you, Joy. By the way, this is very, very helpful. You say their hands were 'bagged.' Why is that?"

Vern interrupted. "Police will bag a victim's hands to preserve 'em for the autopsy later. They'll do the fingerprinting there, and also check under the fingernails for DNA evidence. If not, the DNA could be compromised."

"Vern's right," affirmed Dickson. "Even though these appeared to be hit-man-style murders, with no signs of struggle, it's a matter of course to bag the hands."

"You two make me feel like I'm back in Cub Scouts," joked Nick. "Okay, so what did the autopsies reveal?"

"Right, well, hold your horses and I'll get to that. You probably want to hear more about the crime scene, don't you?" she smiled. Both men nodded.

"Well...the dining room scene was not pretty. It appeared that Mrs. Moore had been sitting at the dining room table. Across the table lay some drapery material and several aluminum rods. My hunch is that she was measuring, since also on the table were sheets of paper with figures, as well as one of those flexible tape measures. And Sergeant Streicher found a pencil on the carpet, located under the table.

"The force of the projectile had knocked Mrs. Moore entirely off the chair. She was found crumpled next to one of the legs of the table. The back of her head was entirely matted with dried blood. There was also blood on the table, on the paper notes, the curtain material, and of course on the carpet where her head lay.

"One thing I noticed—and this is one of the things I won't forget—were her eyes. The one eye was completely obliterated from the projectile, and the other was a terrible black-and-blue. This struck me—I guess—because in photos she has extremely beautiful eyes. Large, blue, and a tinge of sadness to them. They were very pretty.

"Based on the position of her body—having been seated in the dining room chair with her back to the den, where Mr. Moore was killed—I determined that someone had surprised her from behind. Until the moment that projectile fractured her skull, she had no idea what was in store. I guess if you have to go..."

"...better to go at once than to have to suffer," Nick finished her sentence.

"Yeah," added Vern, "Nick figured that was how she got it, too. Surprised from behind."

"Oh? How did you two arrive at that?"

Nick fessed up that he and Vern had visited Beryl Henshall's house after first arriving in town, and Beryl had given them a guided tour.

"Ah, I see. Not a bad idea. Nice that the current resident was so accommodating."

Dickson continued. "As for Mr. Moore, his case was a little different."

"In what way?" asked Nick.

"Well, he was found on the floor in a pool of blood, same as Mrs. Moore. But the entry and exit points of the missile—the bullet—were different. Similar to Mrs. Moore, it entered the top and back of the head, right side. But exit point was different. Upper left cheek instead of eyeball socket. This meant the killer was standing above Mr. Moore—who was fairly short, only about five-seven or five-eight—and off to the right. Perhaps to view the computer screen.

"An important detail now: the computer was powered on."

Vern looked up from writing. "We wondered if that was the case. Not that the computer was on or off, but if, maybe, the killer wanted to get at a file or files on the computer. Something incriminatory. Something he needed Donald to delete."

"Sure," replied Dickson. "That was our theory."

"You say that was your theory," said Nick. "Did this theory change?"

Dickson got quiet and dropped her head, as if seeking the right words. She started back slowly.

"Yes. It did change. Okay...on the surface, yes, this crime looks like it was professional. No struggles, backs of heads, no one heard anything, no evidence. But at the same time, if it was a professional killer, someone contracted, why was the house not broken into? Who would allow entry of a stranger into their home late on a Saturday night? Why was Mrs. Moore caught completely unawares? Mr. Moore, too. If it was a stranger, this couple would have been clinging together in possible fear of their lives. At least Mrs. Moore, if not Mr. Moore, would have been *facing* the killer. 'Please, don't shoot! We'll do anything you ask!'

"It is quite possible that the reason Mr. Moore was on the computer was that he was showing somebody something totally innocuous. Nothing to do with work. Theirs was an almost brand-new Packard Bell. Remember, this was 1995, before internet phones, when homeowners were just starting to get big, bulky personal computers for their dens. Could he have been showing someone how to play, I don't know...*Rollercoaster Tycoon* or something? Maybe just showing him or her how to use a mouse, or a scroll bar?

"And if this is the case, the killer wouldn't have to be a hit man. He or she could be a neighbor or co-worker who had a grudge. A closet psycho, maybe, who knew them and lived in town and who owned a gun. That way, they could have been let in the front door, no questions asked. Mrs. Moore could have returned to her drapery work without any concerns.

"And ultimately, they would have been completely unaware that they only had a few minutes remaining to live."

Chapter Six

Nick had, indeed, wondered about someone local who might have known the Moores and wanted to kill them. But he figured if that was the case, they would have had to hire someone. Even if that hired "someone" was a friend or relative tagging after a neighbor or co-worker.

He also hadn't thought about there being another reason Donald Moore was found seated at the computer. Montaigne had assumed someone had forced him there to either retrieve or expunge critical information. Dickson's theory about Moore sharing a computer game or discussing PC basics made good sense.

But he still had a nagging question: the weapon. The gun must have had a sound suppressor mechanism, popularly known as a "silencer." Otherwise, neighbors would have been alerted to something happening inside the house. Or, at least, the killer or killers would have been concerned about such an alert and taken pains to prevent it.

He didn't want to interrupt again, but Montaigne felt he needed to settle the gun question.

"Joy, sorry to intrude again, but this gun thing really bothers me. I'm not much of a gun guy—my partner will attest to that," he said, smiling at Vern, who seemed preoccupied with a picture on the fireplace mantelpiece. "But if it was a neighbor or co-worker, why would they have one of those silencers? That's hit-man stuff, isn't it?"

Dickson laughed, then shook her head. "I'm sorry, Mr. Montaigne," she said, trying to stifle her laughter, "I don't mean to be rude, but you're like many others. You've seen too many Hollywood movies. Maybe *Pulp Fiction*? Maybe that poster of the two hit actors pointing their gigantic silencer-equipped guns?" She laughed again, setting her coffee mug on the table so as not to spill the liquid. Nick didn't normally blush, but his face became slightly warm. Vern's crossed eyes still seemed preoccupied.

"I'll get to the gun in a bit. Okay, we've done the house. Morning Glory Lane, number one-five-seven. Now I'll jump to the autopsy and maybe I can clear things up a little.

"After the victims' bodies were removed, and a fairly large crowd of onlookers had gathered around the police tape, we awaited the autopsy results. This took approximately sixteen hours. I don't know if you know this, but the Oklahoma City terrorist bombing happened the day after we arrived at the crime scene. April the nineteenth. The autopsy results arrived that same day. Needless to say, the *Springbrook Daily News Journal Observer-Tribune* was running out of paper pulp and ink for all the stuff in the news. They weren't used to all this violent excitement."

At Dickson's mention of the newspaper, Montaigne thought of Roy Turlock, whom he knew hadn't yet been hired. He grinned slightly thinking of Turlock stumbling around a college campus, notepad in one hand and beer in the other. But Dickson's next words snapped him out of his reverie.

"It comes as no surprise, I'm sure," Dickson continued, "that the victims died of massive trauma to their brains caused by metallic projectiles fired at point-blank range," said Dickson, deliberately trying to sound like a coroner. "As I said, the trajectory of both bullets, according to the autopsy report, was right to left. And downward. Just slightly different entry and exit locations."

"Sounds like the killer was right-handed," Montaigne remarked. "Him standing, both of them sitting."

"That was our thinking."

"Vern, when you interviewed those neighbors, did you notice whether they were right or left-handed?"

"I did, Nick. All were righties except Regina Roper."

"Not a prime suspect, but can't rule her out if the killer was hired. Right or left-handed does us no good."

"As far as the bullets themselves," Dickson continued, "we did manage to retrieve them. They tore a wide swath on the inside of the skulls then exited the cranium. Neither wound had what is known as a 'stellate pattern' on the scalps. It's a star-shaped injury caused by the gases ejecting below the skin and causing an outward rupture, which is a pattern that resembles a star."

"What does that imply?" inquired Nick.

"It means the gun barrel was not against the backs of their skulls. There was probably a gap of at least several inches." Dickson waited for the two detectives to process this before adding "We already determined that Mrs. Moore was unaware of what was about to happen. Mr. Moore...slightly different. And I'll get to that in a moment."

Nick tried to play the scene out in his mind. While in Beryl's house, after first arriving in town, he came to a supposition that Donald had been killed first. He bounced it off Dickson.

She confirmed it. "Yes, we're fairly confident the murderer targeted Mr. Moore first. Whether or not he needed to access computer files is irrelevant as far as timing. It was just more convenient for him—or her—or even *them*, since we haven't ruled out a slaying by *team*, although unlikely—to isolate Mr. Moore in one room so as not to panic Mrs. Moore. The killer probably waited a few minutes to see if Mrs. Moore heard anything, in which case she would have called out or entered the room. Then the killer quietly vacated the den, tiptoed through the kitchen eating area, approached Mrs. Moore while she was seated and immersed in her work...and pulled the trigger a second time. Since there was no stellate pattern, and the wound indicates a right-to-left bullet trajectory, he or she had the gun in his or her right hand, several inches from the skull.

"Mission completed, he then disappeared into the night. And he's remained disappeared for the last twenty-five years.

"There's really only one bright spot to this sordid crime," Dickson added.

"What would that be?" asked Nick.

"Mrs. Moore was not sexually assaulted. I've dealt with those. They add another layer of horror."

By now beads of sweat had formed on Vern's forehead, as he continued scribbling in his notepad. Nick steadily sipped his coffee, which was now lukewarm.

"Would you like some more coffee?" asked Dickson. The investigators declined the offer. Nick remembered he would soon be meeting Melody-Clair Fitzpatrick at Sharkey's for dinner.

Vern spoke up. "Ms. Dickson—I mean Joy—this is great autopsy stuff. Angle of bullets, stellate pattern...but you say you retrieved the bullets. Were you able to trace them to type of firearm?"

"Good question, and I was just getting to that. You're going to be surprised at what I tell you."

A blue jay shrieked outside the window. River's body began twitching as if he was dreaming. The grandfather clock continued to tick. Nick wanted to turn toward the clock, or check his watch, but knew that would be rude.

"Okay...okay..." Dickson continued. Nick could tell she seemed to relish her role as storyteller and was grateful to be able to release. *She's probably had all this bottled up for years, and being able to finally pop a cork gives her some personal closure.*

"Right, bullets. We found both bullets near the victims. Our lab of course did a ballistics examination. I won't go into all the technical characteristics—not necessary for our purposes—but they were subsonic hyper-velocity hollow-point. They were fired from a snub revolver. And the lands and grooves of the bullets led us to the actual *type* of gun. Cops aren't always able to do this, so we were lucky. Are you ready? The gun used was a High Standard Sentinel. It's a nine-shot, twenty-two weapon that was made between 1955 through the 1980s. Cheap gun, weak cartridge. But 'cheap' doesn't necessarily mean 'junk.' The Sentinel does the trick close range. There are no spent casings. No need to scurry around picking up evidence afterwards. No suppressor required. In fact—"

"There was no suppressor used?" interrupted a surprised Nick.

"No. This is why I laughed earlier. A lot of people think murderers, especially professional contract killers, use these mega-guns with silencers. Moviemakers like them because they're sexy and look badass. 'Oooh, scaaary!' Dickson mocked. "They pull in large crowds who want to see the ultra-violence. It's all about image. But in reality, murderers don't need all that equipment. A nine-shot snub revolver, aimed close, fired at the head, is sufficient to kill. Wanna know another interesting thing?"

"Of course," said Nick and Vern simultaneously.

"The killer used a pillow. On Mr. Moore."

Nick and Vern appeared in shock. Dickson grinned.

"Eureka! Yes, we found the blood-stained pillow on the computer-room floor, at Mr. Moore's feet, a hole right through the center. The canine was actually resting her head on it. Although the Sentinel would have been quiet enough—doubtful a neighbor would have heard anything, especially with two walls and yard space separating—the killer stuck a pillow between the gun barrel and Mr. Moore's head. Just to make sure. And probably so Mrs. Moore wouldn't hear, either. We don't know if the television or radio were on or not. One of them may have been on, with the killer turning it off before leaving. But if so, that would have further drowned out any noise.

"This killer knew what he was doing."

"Yeah," began Nick, taking a deep breath, "he certainly did. Now...about this High Sentinel gun...can you, uh, tell us—?"

"Sure I can," Dickson eagerly jumped in. "Now, remember I said it was manufactured between 1950 and the 1980s? Okay, older gun, which may mean older killer, though not necessarily...a lot of murder weapons are stolen. But here's something interesting—and take this as you may—that specific gun was at one time easily obtainable. You could even buy it at *Sears Roebuck*. Also...the manufacturer wanted this gun to appeal to females as well as males. So the grips came in not only standard black, but also pink, turquoise, and gold colors. And the Sentinel snub, being a revolver, easily tucks into a person's clothes."

"Holy crap," said Vern.

"Complicates things even more, right? *Might* the killer have been a woman?"

Nick thought about some of the women he and Vern had spoken to: Dorothy Claunch, Regina Roper, Linda Black, Siobhan Moriarty, Monica Delmonico...minor suspects, but suspects nonetheless.

"Yes, Joy, I think I will take another cup of coffee," he said. Dickson poured both him and Vern a fresh mug, careful not to disturb the slumbering dog.

"Joy," Nick resumed, "earlier you mentioned bagging the victims' hands to preserve DNA evidence. I think I can anticipate your answer, but what were the results of the DNA tests? It's my understanding that, ninety-nine percent of the time, cold cases are solved through forensics, and mainly DNA."

"If you anticipated my answer about DNA tests to be a big fat zero, you would be correct. Forensic DNA testing was still in its infancy in '95. The first prosecution of a criminal in the U.S. based on DNA evidence was only eight years earlier. Remember the O.J. Simpson trial? Never mind, of course you do. That trial was in '95, the same year as the Moore murders. L.A. cops retrieved blood samples from a rear gate at the murder scene. They also retrieved blood from socks—Simpson's socks—found at his residence. DNA tests showed that Simpson's blood was on the gate, and the victim's blood was on his socks. Despite these positive DNA results—which one would *think* was enough to convict him—his defense team successfully convinced the jury that the samples were tampered with and compromised—or maybe manufactured, I forget which—by the police. One of whom they convinced the jury had a history of racism.

"So in 1995 there was still a lot of skepticism about using DNA in criminal trials. And this is li'l ole Springbrook, not Los Angeles. But we did gather evidence, and test. What evidence we *could* gather.

"That's another reason we believe the killer was either a contracted professional, or someone who was very shrewd regarding evidence. We tested all hairs. We tested the bloody pillow, we tested the front doorknob...you name it. Nothing. The hairs were mainly from the dog. Those that weren't matched the victims' hair. And he or she had to have been wearing gloves. Probably wearing a hat, too, to prevent any hairs from drifting to the floor. This person had either killed before, or studied up."

"And the gun?" Nick asked. "Was it possible for Springbrook police to trace ownership of this High Sentinel gun?"

"Unfortunately, no. And you can thank successful lobbying of Congress by pro-gun groups. The ATF still has no national registry containing records of firearm sales. Even with a gun serial number—which, of course, we don't have. And despite this unholy escalation of firearm deaths and mass shootings. As far as the state of Ohio? Still no law requiring retention of sales and background check records. You're required to register your car, but not your firearm."

She halted, her last words ringing in the air. "Wonderful priorities, right?"

Nick swiveled his head toward Vern. The ex-cop's head was down, his pen raised several inches above his writing pad.

"To make matters worse," she continued, "Ohio has one of the most inconceivable open-carry laws in the country. If Dorothy Claunch wants to carry a loaded AR-15 into Central Congregational for Sunday services—not that she would do so, mind you—she can legally do it."

Loud shrieks sounded from outside the den window, as if two jays might be battling over a scrap of food. Dickson rose, walked to the window, and scanned the wooded outside. She returned to her chair with a remark about bird droppings and the "pros and cons" of living so close to wildlife.

"Anyway, without the actual gun, or its serial number, there's no way for ATF to trace the gun's owner. Could have been purchased anywhere, at any time. If not stolen. And an older gun, which only expands the question marks.

"Even if we had a severe 'person of interest,'" Dickson continued, "the Fourth Amendment to the Constitution prevents a search and seizure, for a gun or anything else, unless there is probable cause. In the case of the Moores...who had compelling cause to kill them? To this day we have no legitimate suspect. An argument at work or an angry neighbor doesn't make for a legitimate suspect in a double homicide in the eyes of the law. And I know you've already talked to a few people and have a few suspicions. Sorry, gents. This is what we're up against."

Nick thought about some of the recent revelations of his and Vern's that Dickson wasn't privy to. He debated sharing them with her, but was more interested in learning how Springbrook police had conducted their investigation. Foremost on his mind were whom *they* considered to be suspects, and why the investigation (according to Amber Ramsey and Roy Turlock) seemed to peter out after only a short time. He asked her.

She replied, "We covered the gamut of anyone who remotely knew the victims. Neighbors, relatives, and co-workers, of course. For a while, Mr. Henderlong was high on the radar due to a property dispute. But we could never find any solid evidence of a crime, and I think he had an alibi for the night of the murders. Of course, you probably know about the CIA rumors. Again, even though we established Mr. Moore had made business trips to Harban, China, we could never confirm he was employed in espionage and, thus, may have been a target of counter-espionage. Like I said, that old Packard Bell may have just housed video games. We found no CDs or floppy discs in that room. We know he had Chinese business associates staying at his home, but Couch would not reveal their identities—it was their legal right not to divulge them—and they've remained anonymous."

Nick saw Vern's head turn toward him. *Does she not know about Maraschino Cherry?* Nick wondered.

"We were successful," Dickson continued, "in obtaining clearance to view Airline Manifest reports for area flights. We wanted to see if any Chinese may have flown out of Ohio immediately after the murders."

"Did you find any?" asked Vern, recalling his intention to do this while at the library.

"We did. There was one individual...excuse me, I'm not very good with Asian names. I'll have to dig it up again."

Dickson rose from her chair and walked to a cabinet behind her. She pulled a box of papers from a lower shelf.

"These aren't official," she mumbled while digging, "they're just personal notes I've kept from all my cases." She began flipping through the papers. "Let's see...1995...okay, here it is. His name was...Bing. Xi Lao Bing."

Vern slapped his knee. "Is it acceptable to say 'Bingo,' Nick?" he asked.

"You just did."

Dickson then said "I see you're already familiar with that name. Yes, unfortunately we could never do anything about him. Never had an opportunity to interrogate. He flew to San Francisco then immediately to Beijing. After that he just fell off the map. Lieutenant Moriarty informed the FBI, and they said they would take it from there.

"And that's when our investigation, for all intents and purposes, ended. Lieutenant Moriarty instructed all officers to concentrate on more pressing business. He said the feds were now handling the Moore murders. About once a year, usually near the anniversary of the homicides, we would contact a neighbor or relative or visit Couch or Springbrook Hospital. Talk to someone, you know. But it was more for show than anything else, more to appease the local citizenry and the *Ob-Trib*. There was one reporter there who was very persistent and kept at us. But then he died.

"That bothered me to no end," she added.

"Why, that the reporter died?" asked Nick.

"No. What I meant was that it bothered me that Lieutenant Moriarty curtailed investigations. I just wasn't convinced this Bing was the murderer."

"Why not?"

"Well, I know this sounds funny. But because of the weapon. I can't see a Chinese using an older High Standard Sentinel .22 caliber revolver. It's like...well, it would be like Pat Garrett killing Billy the Kid with a Japanese samurai sword.

"I don't think they even *have* Sears Roebuck in China."

Chapter Seven

The sky began turning a warm springtime violet when Montaigne and Wister said goodbye to retired Springbrook Police Detective Joy Dickson. She promised to sift through her "notes" for any other material that might be of use. One tantalizing morsel was "something" about "another person" associated with Bing, but she couldn't then place the name. Nick left his card in case she came across what that *something* was.

River trotted gaily alongside as the two detectives slowly headed toward their cars, Dickson again taking note of Nick's flamboyant vee-HICKle. When out of earshot, Vern grabbed Nick's arm.

"Nick, did you see those photos on her mantel? The eight-by-eleven of her and another woman? Her partner?"

"I did. So what? It's the twenty-first century, Vern."

"No, not that. I know that woman. I met her at The Covenant when I met Dorothy Claunch for lunch. It's

Siobhan Moriarty. She's the lieutenant's sister, who worked with Irene Moore at the hospital."

"You sure?"

"Yeah! You know what that means? Dickson would o' had a conflict of interest. She must've interviewed all of Irene's hospital co-workers. And we know Moriarty was pissed off at being passed over for that promotion."

"Right. Okay, we need to put that with our other index cards. Not a great motive for murder, losing out on a promotion, but you never know."

"Exactly. Wanda Holloway. It also means we need to take whatever Dickson says with a couple grains o' salt. If a potential suspect is a love interest..."

"My thoughts too, Vern. Let's wait and see if Joy gets back to us with that 'another person' stuff. Last thing we need is her tossing us a red herring to lead us away from the real killer."

Vern nodded. "One other thing. I noticed you didn't ask her about your murder-suicide theory. You know, Donald wasting his wife, then himself, with an accessory who later confiscates the gun. Any reason why not?"

"Yes. I figured if there was credence to the theory, she'd offer that up herself. Plus, learning about that pillow squashed things and I didn't want to sound foolish." He looked away with a mischievous smile. "In other words, I was expecting *you* to ask it."

They traded several more ideas before getting in their cars. As the time approached for Nick to head to Sharkey's to meet Melody-Clair Fitzpatrick, and Vern to return to the Comfort Inn, Nick noticed Vern's mood seemed to take a sudden downturn. He wondered if the Solomon Special was struggling to gain traction in Vern's intestines, or if maybe Room 115 was becoming too oppressive. In an effort to cheer his partner, he promised Vern a day of rest and relaxation. But it only seemed to make Vern more sour.

"Look, just don't worry about me, okay?" Vern snapped. "You go off and have fun with what's-her-name. I'll find a good show on the tube or something. Maybe I'll head to the indoor pool."

"Okay partner, I shouldn't be out too long. Need anything from Sharkey's? A carry-out burger or something?"

"Naw, that pork thing for lunch was enough for two meals. I'll prob'ly just get some coffee in the lobby. Just hope that damn desk clerk passed the word to the manager. Shittiest brew I ever drank. More like coffee-flavored *pool* water."

Vern maneuvered his car down Dickson's shady drive, Nick following. Gravel under Nick's wheels was an invitation, but he restrained himself out of regard for Dickson and River. After hitting Route 31 he inserted a Bill Evans CD. Then he remembered Evans was Annie's favorite jazz musician, which didn't feel right on the evening he was meeting Melody, so instead he inserted Grover Washington Jr.'s *Mister Magic*. He also slipped in, not his usual half-stick, but a full stick of cinnamon gum, and donned his Persol sunglasses. Nick always tried to separate business from pleasure, but tonight felt more like a date than a business meeting. It bothered him more than a little. It wasn't just that he had a steady gal back in Atlanta—albeit one now pining for marriage. But he knew his partner had to return, alone, to a dismal motel room.

But any guilt feelings he had he placed on the bottom shelf once he recalled Melody's soft hand and voice after meeting her at Couch. He pulled into Sharkey's parking lot at 7:40, hoping she wouldn't be upset at his late arrival.

"Welcome!" said a casually dressed man wearing a facemask, as Nick let the heavy oak "speakeasy" door close behind him. "I'm Rick."

"The same 'Rick' from *Casublanca*?" asked Nick. "You don't look like Humphrey Bogart."

"Ha! You know your old movies! I'm the manager. Can I get you a table?"

"Actually, I'm meeting someone...ah, there she is," said Nick after recognizing Melody's cascading blonde locks. "Thanks anyway."

He walked to the booth along the wall and squeezed into the seat facing Melody. The restaurant was even darker than at lunch, the table's only light provided by two small electric candles near the wall. Unlike Gilly's, there was no music being piped in. The only sound was muffled conversation from the dinner guests.

Nick thought Melody looked even prettier than when he first met her. She still had the light-blue eyeshadow setting off her deep-set eyes, but she'd added a thin layer of ruby lipstick, which Nick was always a sucker for. Nick also picked up the scent of lilac perfume—though the odor was more subtle than Dorothy Claunch's.

"Sorry I'm late," he breathed heavily.

"Oh, no problem. I'm sure you're very busy."

"Today, especially. But we managed to knock off some important items."

The waitress arrived and took their drink orders. Melody ordered a martini and Nick opted for his favorite.

"Glenlivet, eh?" Melody asked. "Is that special for you?"

Nick went into his spiel about "Speyside single malt" and "oldest distillery," which cracked a cool, tantalizing smile from Melody.

"You're a man who knows his cocktails."

"And you're a woman who has fantastic taste in perfume. I love that smell."

"It's lilac. Eclat d'Arpege. Nothing special. Actually, I liked the way the bottle looked!"

"You're too modest, Mel. It's 'Mel,' right?"

"Yes. And is it 'Nick' or 'Nicholas'?"

"Nick. 'Nicholas' is for formal occasions. I like to keep things simple."

"Well...then we already have something in common."

The waitress returned and they ordered their meals—Montaigne honored his promise to try the filet mignon and talked Fitzpatrick into the broiled walleye with capers. Nick was curious how Fitzpatrick got her start at Couch Industries. He told her she seemed out of place there.

"Yeah, I know, I'm the rare female who doesn't spend half her day in admin or HR meetings. As you probably know by now, Couch is pretty conservative and somewhat stuck in the past. 'Progress' for them means a designated smoking area. When I heard the company had switched to an ecological lawn company, I had to poke myself with my precision compass.

"I keep waiting to work on something like commercial light rail, or solar, or wind turbine. That would be so exciting. Instead, it's always fossil-fuel-related industries. Gas turbine engines, dragline excavators, oil piping specialties, mining products, earthmoving equipment. And lots of military.

"You're okay with that?" Nick asked. "Military-related work, I mean?"

"No," she said with a sigh. "Don't get me wrong, I believe a country needs to defend itself. But war profiteering has always made me queasy. I envy people who have never been forced to make compromises. Unfortunately, I'm not one of them, and at this late stage, if I left Couch, I wouldn't know where else to go."

"How did you start there?" Nick inquired.

"I began straight out of college in 1993. I had an engineering degree from Purdue. I really wanted to get out of the Midwest, but my father's health was bad, and I felt I should stay in the region, since I grew up around here. Champ was really the one who got me on at Couch. Had my second interview with him, and he convinced HR to bring me on."

"Yeah," Nick followed up, "other than his military background, he seems out of place there, too."

"Right. Well, to tell the truth, I think he saw a kindred spirit in me. He's a nice guy, and well-regarded in the industry."

"Funny, I saw him this morning out at Green-Wood Cemetery. He was actually visiting the Moores' gravestones."

"Yep, that's Champ. He's got a heart as big as Lake Erie." She gave Nick an inquisitive look. "If you don't mind my asking, what were you doing out there?"

"I was meeting someone to discuss some papers." He looked at her sideways. "And I think you know about those papers, and whom I met. Correct?" He said it with a mischievous grin.

Fitzpatrick's cheeks flushed. In the middle of taking a bite, she set her fork down and gave Nick a demure smile.

"Yeah," she said sweetly, stretching out the word. "I got those papers for Roy. We used to go steady."

"That was nice of you to do that. It really helped us."

"Oh? In what way?"

"Well...I can't go into too much detail. You know, professional discretion and all. But one of the prints had some things that kind of shifted the slant of this investigation."

"And do you have any suspects?" she asked, then quickly followed with, "And I understand you can't mention names."

Nick took a sip of his Glenlivet. He thought for several seconds about how to best answer.

"Our prime suspect is dead. He was murdered before we even arrived in Springbrook. Our second person of interest is much closer to Springbrook but also very deceased. Now, just because they're now dead doesn't mean they didn't kill the Moores. But we have a whole slew of...less-promising suspects, shall we say. And as far as this recent turn in the case, you might be able to help."

"In what way?"

Rick then stopped by their table and asked if everything was okay.

"Fantastic," said Nick. "The filet is superb, cooked to perfection." Melody chimed in about her walleye.

"Wonderful!" gushed Rick. "We here in Casablanca aim to please. Just watch out for those Nazis after you leave," he kidded, then left.

Fitzpatrick gave Nick a horrified look. "Nazis?"

"It's an in-joke," he assured her. "This place is as dark as a speakeasy, and when I came in I told him it looks straight out of the movie *Casablanca*." Nick got the impression Mel hadn't seen the movie."

"Can you maybe dig up another print?" he asked.

"Like, what kind?"

"Well, that MaxxDig 60 project. Specifically, the brake pads. You know more about assembly prints than me, but would there be some kind of signoff document for those? You know, something where the engineers approved those pads?"

"Certainly. Everything that we either manufacture or purchase gets a final approval. But for me to find it means some serious rummaging. Most of that old stuff is piled up in Iron Mountain boxes stacked in the archives room. I was lucky to get what little I got."

"Yeah, I realize that. And, again, what you got was great. But we're looking at a possible whistleblower thing. It's possible it got Moore and his wife killed." He halted. "Mel, did you have anything to do with the MaxxDig 60?"

"No, I'd only been at Couch just over a year. I was still doing a lot of cataloging and engineer admin work. And like everyone else at that time, trying to wrap my brain around Microsoft Word."

"I understand. Let me ask you: after the murders, who all was questioned by the police? Can you remember?"

"That's easy. *All* of us. At least, anyone who even remotely had any dealings with Don."

"So…how about this fellow, Crashcup? Mr. Goosebill rang him up from his office. Was he questioned, too?"

"Ha!" she closed her eyes and shot her head back. "Yeah, Crashcup too! But he could hardly be guilty of murder. He's just too weird for that. He analyzes everything and is way too honest. In fact, if I remember, a small group of us hid outside his office to see Dickson's face when she emerged after questioning. She came out looking like a ghost, white as a sheet. I think Crashcup analyzed every question she shot at him. Probably analyzed her, too."

"Sounds like a character. What type of work does he do?"

"He's part of a small tech doc group. Most of our writing and illustrating we farm out to Imperial, down in Georgia. But we do keep a small staff of writers and illustrators here. They mainly work on IPBs and BOMs— sorry, those refer to illustrated parts breakdowns and bills of materials. Crashcup's one of the writers."

"Hmm. Too strange, huh? Okay. Well, how about yourself, Goosebill, and Delmonico. And your big cheese, this Byron Lomax. You all were questioned, I'm sure."

"I can vouch for the three of us…and also Champ…but not Lomax. He's upstairs. Third floor, practically by himself. I don't know if he's got Asperger's syndrome or what. Nobody ever sees him."

"So I've heard. He sounds like something out of a science-fiction story."

"Exactly. But even though we don't see *him*, he definitely sees *us*. At Couch, the walls have eyes."

Montaigne had been ignoring his filet, engrossed in all that Fitzpatrick was telling him. He took several quick bites, washing it down with some Scotch.

"Mel, I have to apologize."

"Why, what do you mean?"

"Well, you asked me out, and here all I've been doing is grilling you. I'm really sorry."

"Oh, you're sweet...Nick. Look, I enjoy talking with you. Actually—even though I like you—I did have a reason for our date. I wanted to fill you in."

"On what?"

"Just what you've been leading up to. Goosebill, Delmonico, and Moore."

Nick's ears perked. "Yes? And what about them?"

"Well...like I said, we all were questioned by the cops. Detective Dickson, I think. But nobody ever said anything about this. And I'm sure it was out of regard for Jerry...Delmonico...because he was having a rough time. Not only with Don's tragic death, but also his marriage. He was drinking a lot."

"Said anything about *what*?"

"Well...just before the murders some things happened at the office. Nothing solid, but...well...the tension level seemed to be really high. I don't know if you've ever worked in close quarters in an office environment. But there's a lot of body language, voice inflections, comments. I've never said this...again, out of sympathy for Jerry...but there seemed to be a battle with him and Goosebill on one side, and Don on the other. Don got real morose over it, for a while. It was so bad at one point, they weren't even speaking.

"And I remember one time, passing Jerry's office, shouting coming from inside. And it was Don's voice."

"Do you know what they were arguing about?"

"I don't know the exact reason, but I'm sure it had to do with MaxxDig 60. All of our nerves were frazzled with that project. The customer was pressing really hard for us to get it done. A couple lower-level employees, and one tech writer had quit over it. They just got fed up. So...I believe there were some accusations going back and forth. Maybe passing the buck, that sort of thing."

"Interesting. Can you recall any violence?"

"No, nothing...wait, yeah, I do recall one thing. Not sure if you could call it 'violent,' but I do remember Don flinging his slide rule across his office right when I walked by. There's probably still a dent in the drywall. Do you think this has anything to do with those brake pads?"

"I don't know yet," said Nick, now thoughtfully holding his chin. "Might. Just might."

"Does it help you any?" she asked in her pixie voice.

"Mel, it helps a *lot*. And I know it's a big imposition on you...but if you are able to find a print with approval signatures, well, that would help even more." He dabbed the corner of his mouth with his napkin and felt a familiar warmth surge through him. "You know what else helps?" he asked mischievously.

"What?"

"This dinner with you. It's been a long day. I really enjoy your company." She smiled at this, batted her swimming-pool eyes, and dabbed her lips with her napkin.

They finished their meals, Nick insisting on paying the bill, then said farewell to Rick and walked leisurely to Melody's car. Each of them, shyly, thanked the other for the "wonderful evening." They shook hands, Nick holding her tiny hand a few seconds longer than necessary.

On the drive back to the Comfort Inn he analyzed their restaurant conversation. He considered arranging a meet-up with Crashcup, then dismissed the idea. He wanted more to meet President Byron Lomax...if it was even possible. *I'll ask Haslett tomorrow.*

His prevailing thought concerned what Fitzpatrick had said about the tension between Moore, Goosebill, and Delmonico. Also Moore's angry flinging of the slide rule. *Gotta be about those asbestos-coated brake pads. He challenged those two. I know it.*

Montaigne had entered the motel and was halfway down the hallway to Room 117 when "Town Without Pity" chimed from his phone. He removed it and looked at the caller ID. It was Melody. *She's probably calling to tell me how much she enjoyed the dinner date.*

But when he answered, her voice sounded panicky.

"Nick? Thank god I got you. I don't know what to do."

"Mel, what happened? You all right?"

"I was followed home. I *know* I was." She began to whimper.

"It's okay, Mel. Where are you now?"

"I'm at home."

"Is the car at your house?"

"No. No, he turned off somewhere. But I'm nervous."

"I realize it's dark, but did you see the type of car?"

"All I know is it was black. A black car. And it tailed me. Nick, I don't know what to do."

"It's okay, don't panic. Did you lock up the house?"

"Yes, of course! But I'm still scared. Nick, I don't want to stay here. I'm afraid he'll try to break in. This has never happened to me before. I keep thinking of Donald Moore and his wife."

"Okay, okay. Uh...can you stay with a friend maybe?"

"No, I don't have any friends close by. Just Roy. There's no way I can stay *there*."

"Yeah, yeah. I understand. Okay, tell you what. I'll get you a room here. Sunday night, not crowded...hell, it's fricking *Springbrook*, right?" She laughed. "Are you okay with driving here?"

"Yes. I think so."

"Good. Okay, I'm heading to the front desk now. I'll get you a room. They'll have a key waiting. When you get here, I'm in Room 117. Just tap on the door. Okay?"

"Yes, I understand. Room 117. Gawd, I feel like such a fool."

"No, don't. You've every right to be scared. I'll see you soon. Remember, Room 117. *Not* Room 115, or I won't hear the end of it."

He heard her take a deep breath. "Okay. Okay. Thanks Nick."

"Welcome. Bye."

Fifteen minutes later Nick heard a soft tap on his door. He let Fitzpatrick in, held her hand and pulled her gently inside, then shut the door and locked it. She had a small duffel bag with clothing protruding from the partially closed top. They walked together to one of the two beds and sat next to each other. The smell of her lilac perfume was intoxicating.

"Would you like a drink?" asked Nick.

"Sure." He stood, walked to the dresser next to the TV, and fixed two Scotches. When he returned, he handed her the drink and put his left arm over her shoulders.

"Are you okay now?"

"Yes. Thank you for understanding."

Nick quizzed her about the car. When did she first notice it, how close did it follow, did she speed up, had she ever seen the car before, when did it turn off...Her answers were halting and confused, and she apologized. He changed the subject, thinking this would further help steady her nerves.

"So...Roy Turlock. Pardon me for saying this, but—and don't get me wrong, I think he's a lot of fun and a great guy. In fact, right now he's probably trying to dig up Marty Franes' old notes on the Moore case—but, um...you two seem an unlikely pair."

She dropped her head and nodded. "That's nice of you to say, I guess. Roy hasn't always been like this. Like you said, he's a wonderful man, but he has a lot of issues. He never seemed to get over Marty's death. Roy was convinced Marty was murdered. And when nobody else believed it, he became bitter. He's always had a strong sense of justice, which is why he's a reporter. But too many brick walls can take a toll on a man. Even before Marty passed, he was a drinker. And he feels like he's in a permanent rut here in Springbrook, career-wise. I probably stayed with him longer than I should have. But he needed me. I just can't deal with it all anymore, though.

"How about you?" she asked Nick. "I'm sure you have someone down in Atlanta."

"I have a special woman. She's smart, like you. And pretty...like you. She comes in colors. You can actually tell her by the clothes she wears."

"One of *those* women, huh?"

Nick smiled. "Lately we've had some...turbulence, let's say. She's older than me and feels time running out. You probably get the picture."

"Yeah. I know that picture well."

"Sorry, I didn't mean that!" he blurted, as she patted his arm. "Anyway, we had a discussion before I left. I consider this trip a sort of 'spring fling.' And she seems okay with it. It's like John Lennon's 'long weekend' away from Yoko. At least, that's how I choose to look at it."

A few seconds of silence followed. The comforting, assuring pat on his arm Montaigne viewed as a minor cue. His feeling was exacerbated by a single, kittenish glance from Fitzpatrick, and he felt that familiar warmth inside.

"Another drink?" he asked, seeing her Scotch level had lowered.

"Sure."

He fixed another. They traded light banter, she poking fun at Couch Industries, he sharing humorous anecdotes about Vern, and both of them poking fun at Springbrook. Then she turned to him, and with a demure smile.

"I really should go."

"Right."

She set her glass down and stood up. She picked up her clothes satchel, and walked slowly toward the door, Nick following her lithe form from close behind.

"Is that lilac smell only for spring, or do you wear it year-round?" he asked.

She turned. Their smiles dropped. Suddenly, he pushed up against her, her back pressing against the wall. The duffel bag fell to the floor, and their mouths hungrily came together. Their hands gripped and grasped each other's body in a frenzy of desire. Her eyes rolled back in her head. His knee slipped between her legs; her crotch pressed down. Their mouths, lips, and tongues merged seamlessly as he pulled her back into the room between the two beds and they frantically flung off each other's clothes.

They made hard, frenzied love before climaxing together. When their breathing returned to normal, she turned her warm, milky back and buttocks to him with a beatific smile, allowing him to wrap his arms around her and sink his face into her soft mound of tousled hair. They spooned for a long time until falling asleep.

In the morning—as the low-lying eastern sun began to chink through the cracks of the closed curtains of their room—they made love again. Only now it was much slower, more exploratory, though no less intense. It was more like a tender yet profound ballet.

Chapter Eight

The bar at Sharkey's was separated by a long wall about four feet high. The top of the wall was decorated by planter boxes filled with dark-green parlor palms, maidenhair ferns, and English ivy. This privacy barrier, combined with the dim lighting, effectively obscured the restaurant tables from the barstools. It also acted as a modest sound barrier. If one was to enjoy a drink at the bar, there would be no way of seeing who was eating, except to take a long stroll around the wall of plants.

Seated at the bar enjoying a series of Lageritas—Modelo Especial beer bolstered by tequila, Cointreau liqueur, and lime juice—Roy Turlock had no idea his ex-girlfriend was eating dinner with Nick Montaigne.

Turlock was in no rush. Hell, it was Sunday evening, the slowest point of the week for a newspaperman. The big, fat Sunday paper loaded with ads had been delivered...on time. His stories had all been filed, including the one about parents protesting outside City Hall because Springbrook

School System was requiring their children to wear facemasks to protect everyone's health.

The rest of the weekend's news was lame. One reported burglary, at Mac's Sporting Goods. A charity raffle at Florida Patton's Flower Parlor. And the seemingly daily, COVID-era, national wire stories dealing with crackpot conspiracy theories, race baiting by white supremacists, and petty tirades in the White House.

For Roy Turlock, it was time to relax and unwind with some John Barleycorn.

But Turlock could not have imagined it would be his last time communing with Mr. Barleycorn. Nor that Tuesday's issue of the *Springbrook Daily News Journal Observer-Tribune* would display the name "Roy Turlock"—but this time, it wouldn't be as a byline.

Long after Montaigne and Fitzpatrick had left for the evening, Turlock dragged himself away from his favorite barstool.

"Adios, Rick," he croaked to the bartender.

"Okay buddy. Need a cab?"

"Nope. Need a sugar mama."

He managed to find his Buick Verano in the corner of Sharkey's lot. He slipped behind the wheel and checked the passenger seat to make sure his papers were still there. *As if they wouldn't be.* He patted them. It had taken two hours of scouring the SNOT offices after hours to get them. Marty's crib notes, stuck in a file drawer in a folder of Virgil Grossman's old clippings related to his popular "Pets 'n' Such" series from the eighties and nineties. They were like ink rimmed with gold. *Montaigne will flip. Should bust the case wide open. Too bad his phone's shut off. He'll get the voicemail, though.*

Turlock turned the key. The engine groaned, then died. He turned the key again. Rumble...silence. *Shit, not again!*

He reached in the back seat and grabbed his hammer. He got out, squatted down under the front of the Buick, and aimed his cellphone flashlight up into the machinery. He located the starter. He positioned himself for a well-angled swing, then tapped the starter several times. He then slowly pulled himself from under the car, stood up shakily with a loud moan, and stumbled into the driver's seat. He turned the key a third time. The engine turned over. He dropped his throbbing head on the steering wheel. *Thank god.*

North Main was usually dusky and drab, and especially so on Sunday night. All the businesses were shuttered, locked up, cages on the windows. Candy's Guns, above which Turlock lived, had cleared out at 6 p.m. As Turlock climbed the narrow stairs to what he not-so-affectionately called his "pod," his mind flashed back to the good times. When he and Mel were squeezed together on these same stairs, his arm wrapped around her dainty waist, her head resting on his shoulder with her beautiful blonde strands tickling his cheek. Now he was totally alone. Just his dreary job, his cat, the endless bills, and what few moments of escape he could wrest from booze and weed. His throat tightened at the thought.

"Squirrel, how the hell are ya," he droned anemically at the calico after closing his door. He scraped some tuna out of a tin and set the crusty, meat-caked plate on the kitchen floor. He dropped the precious papers he'd surreptitiously lifted from Virgil Grossman's old files onto the coffee table by the sofa. He powered up his Hewlett-Packard PC to check his email.

He had two items in his in-box. Both were rejection letters from publishing houses he'd recently queried about the book he'd spent four years writing. They had reviewed the sample chapters he'd submitted concerning a fictionalized version of Springbrook's infamous 1962 "tearoom" sting of gay men in public restrooms.

"Although our editors feel that you possess talent," the first letter read, "and we are always interested in stories sympathetic to the LGBTQIA community, we also seek stories with a strong action/adventure hook at the beginning. Our readers like books that start off with a bang."

Turlock angrily began typing a venomous reply that his book had all sorts of "banging" at the beginning, but ultimately decided to delete the letter while muttering "Screw you."

The second rejection letter also praised his writing, noting it had a "riveting storyline" and a "deep understanding of character." But it also told him that, despite the homosexual subject matter, it "wasn't woke enough" and that their editors liked to see "a strong woman character." Something his book definitely lacked.

"Woke *this*!" Turlock shouted, slamming his fist against the keyboard and sending a frightened Squirrel under the sofa.

In an effort to chill, he pulled out a CD of *Spirit of Eden* by Mark Hollis and Talk Talk and slipped it into his CD player. Then he lit some choice *C. indica* and collapsed onto the sofa...coughing up phlegm on the first two drags.

"Mell-lowww," he murmured while exhaling the third drag, smooth and sweet, from deep in his lungs. His head was cushioned by the soft, beer-stained pillow at the end of the sofa. His feet were propped and crossed on the arm of the opposite end. The steady, throbbing notes of the music lulled him into temporary, stoned oblivion.

He took one final suck of his joint, blew the smoke toward Squirrel, who was now purring contentedly on his stomach, then quashed the roach into an ashtray, kicked off his shoes, and nodded off.

But in his zeal to visit the lush marijuana groves that graced the fields of Eden, he'd forgotten to put the latch on his apartment door.

Chapter Nine

By the time Nick rolled out of bed, Melody had already left for work. He found a note on the dresser that read "Thank you for your understanding...and our wonderful evening."

He started to dress, and while slipping on his Forzieris he powered up his cell to see a text message from Roy Turlock. With only one shoe on, he tapped the link:

"Montane, turn yer fuckin phone on. Big news. Found Franes papers. Stuck way back in SNOT file. We're talkin DOGS here! The Moores mutt! Will stop by Comfort 2nite. Roy."

Nick immediately tried calling Turlock but got no answer. He was now so excited, so "chuffed," as Beryl might say, that he forgot onc cufflink. He found Vern in the lobby, who noticed the missing cufflink while they gnawed their stale bagels and discussed the day's agenda.

"The Moore *mutt*? Lisa?" asked Vern dubiously. "You can't be serious. What, did she tell Franes who the killer was?"

"You're asking the wrong person, partner. We need to hook up with Roy. Here's the plan: you and I will head out to Couch together. I want some backup for this Goosebill character. Maybe his buddy Crashcup will be there, too. We gotta get a handle on these asbestos-laced brake pads, I want you there to gauge Goosebill's reactions. If he claims he doesn't know anything about them—which he'll probably do—I want to make him sweat. If he gets nervous, he might do something stupid.

"Next item is to visit the Black family. Something happening there with Whitney. I know your hearing's not the greatest, but if he indeed yelled out Bing's name like you said, he knows more than he's letting on. I'd like to make *him* sweat, too."

"Gotcha," replied Vern. "How 'bout the Chins? Oh yeah, they're on vacation. Where the hell do you think they go, Nick?"

"Don't know. Maybe they're hanging out with Byron Lomax. Anyway, after Black we're back here to wait for Roy's arrival. By the way...Melody's staying at the Comfort Inn for a while."

"I know. I heard you two. These damn walls are like rice paper."

"Oh," said Nick sheepishly. "Well, won't be for long. She was followed home after leaving Sharkey's. And I don't think it was Dorothy Claunch."

***

The green-and-black turbo-charge crawled through corn country, past the sign with a smiley face and the words "Hernan, Ohio, Capitol of Nice People" with the third word misspelled. Then past a gas station, convenience store, ice cream shop, barber shop, and roughly a dozen plain,

Carpenter-Gothic-styled houses. Then turned onto Springbrook-Palmersburg Road and the expansive grounds of Couch Industries. Vern's jaw dropped when he saw the titanic flagpole with the five flags, now back to flying full staff, rippling in the wind.

"Lordy! Does this place manufacture flags, too?"

"That's why I call it 'Flagville,'" said Nick. Then Vern made out the "Thin Blue Line" flag at the bottom.

"I see that pro-cop flag. No Black Lives Matter flag, though." Nick flashed him a look as if to say "Are you kidding?"

Nick parked in the same visitor parking spot as before and the investigators signed in with the same aloof receptionist and received their yellow badges. Then they waited for Haslett to arrive and escort them to Goosebill's office.

"Anything I should know about this place you haven't already told me?" asked Vern.

Nick reflected a moment. "Make sure you smile for the candid cameras."

Several minutes later Haslett arrived. He was wearing a bluish-green, tight-fitting sweater, tight slacks, and shoes that resembled Nick's Italian Forzieris but were entirely black instead of brown and white.

"Hello kemosabe!" he greeted Nick cheerfully. "And you must be Vern. Nice to meet you."

The three shook hands, Haslett pumping them vigorously.

"Marv's in a meeting but should be in his office by the time we negotiate the scanners and the long halls. If not, we'll tell stories in *my* office."

Nick and Vern unloaded their pockets and successfully penetrated the metal scanners. Instead of two guards there was only one, a pasty-looking thirty-something man with a double chin. Haslett gave Vern the same apologetic he'd previously given Nick.

"Vern, as I'm sure Nick told you, some of our work here is quite sensitive. A lot of DoD contracts that involve top-secret information. Many of our employees have to undergo robust background checks, from Controlled Unclassified all the way to Top Secret with an SSBI."

"I know what DoD is. What's an SSBI?" asked Vern.

"Vern, that stands for 'Single Scope Background Investigation.' It is governed by U.S. Intelligence Community Policy Guidance Number 704.1. Robust professional and personal checks that may even include an NLCLC.

"We try to leverage these as painlessly as possible, but they can be burdensome to the recipients."

"Champ, pardon my ignorance," Nick said as he exited the body scanner, the chubby guard waving him onward, "but I've never figured out what that word 'leverage' means. Seems to be used a lot in business."

Haslett's eyes brightened. "You know Nick, I'm glad I'm not the only one, because I don't know either! But it sure sounds impressive, doesn't it?"

The three men walked down the halls, Vern glancing at the thin line of orange substance along the baseboards, then lifting his head to the security cameras. They passed the displays of early twentieth-century photographs and the bevy of American flags. Both Nick and Vern had to scurry to keep up with Haslett, who walked briskly and forcefully, his arms held stiffly outward, military-style.

"What's that smell?" brazenly asked Vern.

"Smell?" replied Haslett. "Did I toot or something?"

"Ha, no! It's a kind of chemical smell. Kind of...fruity."

"Hmm. Maybe I've been here too long, 'cause I don't smell it."

Suddenly, a crackling sound was heard.

"Good morning, fellow Couchians!" came the voice of Byron Lomax. Haslett stopped in his tracks and held his arm out to halt his companions. Nick and Vern abruptly stopped behind him, Vern almost tripping over Nick's

heels. As Lomax began to speak, Nick noticed Haslett's head tilt back slightly and his eyes took on a glassy look. The three men stood in the hallway as if frozen.

I trust everyone is doing well. Congratulations to Theresa Ames, who is still leading the Step-Up-to-Health fitness initiative! Keep striding toward fitness so we can eliminate obesity and hospital visits and reduce costs. We will be observing you, and encouraging you...

It was practically the same address Lomax had given before. As if it was a recording. The only change Nick could discern was the part about Active Shooter Training. Lomax thanked everyone for "welcoming our AST guests" and made what Nick thought was a veiled threat.

Those few of you who did not sign in at the door we will soon be visiting. Although this training was purely voluntary, Couch Industries wants to make sure all employees are prepared in case of an emergency.

As soon as the morning address was over, Haslett spun on his heels and continued his stiff stride down the hall as if nothing had happened. Nick and Vern exchanged perplexed glances.

"Uh, Champ?" asked Nick after several steps.

"Yes?"

"Before we get to Marv Goosebill's office, I was wondering if I could ask you a couple questions."

"Certainly!" Haslett turned down a side hallway and entered the break room. "They removed the furniture from my downstairs office, as we've had some layoffs due to the virus. And Mahogany Row, upstairs, always gets cleaned Monday morning. But we can talk in here. Please, help yourself to coffee."

They removed three mugs from the overhead cupboard and Haslett poured three cups, Vern lifting his mug close to his crossed eyes and scanning the rim for residue.

"Fire away, sir," Haslett said, peering at Montaigne.

"Yes, well, I'll keep it brief, Champ. But—and I know you spend the majority of your time up in Mahogany Row, so maybe you're unaware—how closely did you work with the MaxxDig 60 contract?"

"Sure, Nick. My only involvement with that, and with most of our non-government projects, was strictly contracts and sales. I believe I did the initial proposal, and the SOWs and SOPs. If you really want the nitty-gritty on the MaxxDig, talk to the SMEs—the subject matter experts. Those still around, anyway. That would of course be Marv and Melody. Mainly Marv, since Mel was still new in ninety-five."

"Right. We'll definitely do that. So, you wouldn't know anything about material specs? Like, for the brake pads?"

"No, sorry sir. Although..." He paused in deep thought. "Gosh, it's coming back to me. Yeah. Yeah."

"Something, uh, you remember?" coaxed Nick.

"Yes. I do remember a lot of, I guess the word would be 'tension.' And I remember mentioning this to the detective. What's her name...escapes me now..."

"Dickson. Joy Dickson."

"Right, that's it. I don't know if you know this. Maybe you do, as it's now a matter of public record. But Couch Industries was bought out by Hardison in ninety-eight and inherited some asbestos issues. There was a huge class-action suit against Hardison by mesothelioma victims. And it was rumored—mind you, nothing was ever proven—that the brake pads in some of our products might have been tainted with asbestos.

"I'm sure our people were completely unaware of this. Many of our designs incorporate structures which are intermediary and proprietary to other contractors. I'm sure this was the case with those that, unfortunately, used asbestos."

"Yes, I'm...sure that was the, uh...case," responded Nick slowly. "Thank you for your candor, Champ."

"Roger that. But Goosebill can probably help you more. Ready?"

They carried their coffee mugs down the hall to the office of Marv Goosebill, Vern spilling some of liquid on the floor due to the fast stride. On the way, Nick glanced into Melody's office. She was behind her desk and wearing reading glasses. She raised her head and flashed Nick a smile.

Haslett, ever the banterer, swung his stiff body around and asked Vern if he liked to read books.

"Uh, no sir, I'm not much of a reader. Except newspapers. Nick's the reader."

"Yes, I do know that. Monsieur Montaigne, who are some of your favorite authors?"

Nick smiled. "Oh, I don't know. Anyone whose name on the cover isn't printed bigger than the title. I don't like feeling like I'm buying a brand."

"Ha, roger that! You must like the old books, then. Literary stuff."

"Yep. Old white guys, I guess. Not because of those adjectives; I just figure life is short, so might as well read books that have proven staying power."

"Roger that. Yeah, I've heard that 'old white guys' expression more than a few times from Goosebill...and he always intends it *favorably*! Speaking of which, I'm reading *Hillbilly Elegy* by Vance. Pretty good, though I don't agree with *everything* he says." Nick smiled out of politeness.

They arrived at Goosebill's office.

"Wake up, Marv!" barked Haslett. Nick and Vern said goodbye to Haslett and stepped into Goosebill's office. Nick introduced Vern to Goosebill.

"I hear yer a former cop," said Goosebill to Vern in his monotone voice.

"Bunko," responded Vern. "Sixteen years. Up in Philly."

"Almost went into that work. What kinda piece did ya carry?" He shot a glance at Nick when he said this.

"Carried a Glock 19. Never used it though. Fortunately."

"Glock 19? Never used it? Sorry to hear that."

"Mr. Goosebill," Montaigne interrupted, "I brought Vern along as backup because we have a few pointed questions to ask you. Hopefully we won't take up too much of your time."

"It is what it is. What questions you got?"

"They concern the MaxxDig 60 project. Please take a look at this. It's a print used in the assembly of the MaxxDig 60 crane, which you, Jerry Delmonico, and Donald Moore helped design." Nick handed him a copy of the brake pad print. The one with the chemical formula $Na_2(Fe^{2+}_3Fe^{3+}_2)Si_8O_{22}(OH)_2$.

"Okay," Goosebill muttered indifferently. "Brake pads. What about them?"

"Do you see that chemical formula? Right here?" he pointed to the formula for blue asbestos. "Do you know what that is?"

"It looks like a chemical formula. An 'N' and a—"

"Yes, we can read the letters. Together, they stand for asbestos. Blue asbestos, also known as *riebeckite* or *crocodilite*."

"Crocodile light? Sounds like an Aussie beer," said Goosebill with a mocking grin.

Nick glared at him. He felt his blood rising, but Vern came to the rescue.

"This is pretty serious stuff, Mr. Goosebill. Asbestos was an illegal product in 1995, at the time of the murder of Donald Moore, whom you worked closely with. Anything you'd like to say?"

"I got nuthin' to say. Did we use those brake pads in the MaxxDig? Yes. Did we know what was in 'em? No. You got no proof of anything here."

"So you mean to say," Nick jumped in, "that as a design engineer you helped design the MaxxDig 60 dragline excavator without knowing what materials went into it? That seems pretty sloppy, and I find it hard to believe."

"Unless you can prove that I approved that...whatever you call it, that *asbestos*...you got nuthin'. Besides, what does this have to do with Don Moore's death? Tell me that."

"We just spoke with your superior, Champ Haslett, who admitted there was tension during the MaxxDig 60 development. We also have that information from another source. Willful approval of carcinogenic products for use in the public sector carries a heavy penalty, as I'm sure you know. It's within reason that Donald Moore may have tried to blow a whistle about such illegal activity. And that may have gotten him killed."

Goosebill lifted his thick upper lip in a sneer. He glanced between Nick and Vern.

"I already answered questions twenty-five years ago. I don't need to go through all this again. I didn't approve *nuthin'*. And I'm no murderer. You try accusin' me, Detective Montaigne, I'll get my lawyer."

Nick sat back in his chair. He gazed at the "Don't Tread on Me" snake on Goosebill's wall.

"That's fine, Mr. Goosebill. That's fine. But if I find out you lied, and that you did indeed approve use of blue asbestos in those brake pads, you're officially what we in the business call a 'person of interest.' And I'm gonna be back in here like Grant took Richmond."

He stood, and so did Vern, and the two whisked out of the office.

"Wait!" yelled Goosebill. "You gotta have an escort!" But they ignored him and continued walking. When they passed Melody's office, Nick stopped and looked in. She

saw him, waved a sheet of paper at him and mouthed the
word "Tonight."

***

They dropped their yellow badges and coffee mugs at
the receptionist desk and stepped out into a warm, sunny
day, Nick feeling relieved that he could once again breathe
clean air, away from things like peculiar chemical odors,
earth-scraping machines, polemical flags, and mysterious
orange crud lining cold brick hallways. He'd wanted to
duck into Mel's office, but with Vern along that was
difficult. Plus, he knew that, without a blue-badge escort,
Couch security would be descending on them any minute.

They took the Porsche down Springbrook-Palmersburg
Road then westward toward Springbrook town and
Turnham Green, where Nick hoped to talk with Whitney
Black. On the way, Vern reviewed with Nick his
impressions of Couch Industries.

"There's no way you could get me to work in a place
like that. I'd rather commit suicide."

Montaigne laughed. "It has an oppressive atmosphere,
doesn't it?"

"Oppressive and *de*-pressive. I feel like I need a hot
shower. Haslett seems okay. A little weird, but he's a
bookworm, which explains it. Goosebill's a jackass. And
you were right about Byron Lomax. Sheesh, could you
imagine having to hear that dictator every morning? Yeah,
I'd commit suicide, no doubt about it. Or murder
someone."

"You may be closer to the truth than you think. I guess
Mel's learned to deal with it."

"I guess so. So was she on that MaxxDig 60 too?"

"Supposedly just admin stuff. She'd only just started
employment at Couch."

"I know Delmonico and Moore were on it. I can see
Goosebill or Delmonico doing in Moore. They pushed the

asbestos, then Moore pushed back, they got scared of repercussions, then one or both got stupid and committed murder. Two murders. Hard to believe."

"I'm pretty convinced our killer isn't Delmonico," said Nick. "That love triangle bothered me for a while, but not anymore."

"Why'd you rule him out? The alibi his wife gave of him being in Cleveland?"

"No."

"Because he seemed too soft to be a killer?"

"No, that's not it either."

"Why then?"

"It's actually because he died of natural causes. Liver cirrhosis, caused by his drinking."

"Come again? He died of liver disease, so what? What's that got to do with anything?"

"Vern, readers don't want a killer who died before the story started. They want to see the killer brought to justice by the hero—which is us—either by conviction or gruesome death. Readers want solid vengeance. If Delmonico turned out to be the killer, readers would feel cheated."

"You've got a point. That means Bing isn't the killer either, right?"

"Well, he makes more sense than Delmonico, because he died violently, by Ramsey, who was one of the good guys. At least, the reader is supposed to *think* he's a good guy. But Bing's probably not the killer, either."

"Gotcha. Bottom line: you, me, and everyone else in this story are pawns in the hands of the author."

"Sadly, that's true. All we can do is hope he makes good decisions for us. And the reader doesn't object to our flirting with the literary 'fourth wall' like we're doing now."

***

Montaigne and Wister had just passed the entry road to the Comfort Inn, on their way to Turnham Green, when Nick's cellphone rang.

"You need to get a new song, that guitar thing is getting old," mumbled Vern.

"Hello, Nick Montaigne here." He hit the speaker button.

"Hi, Mr. Montaigne? This is Joy Dickson."

"Oh, yes, hi Joy. How are you? And how's River?"

"We're fine, ha-ha, thanks. I had a chance to dig through my old notes, as promised. And I found something. Not sure it will help much, but it concerns one of the Moore neighbors."

Vern raised his eyebrows.

"Okay...which one?"

"Whitney Black."

"Quite a coincidence, we're headed to his house right now. What about him?"

"Well, remember I said that we discovered, immediately after the homicides, that Xi Lao Bing flew to San Francisco on his way to Beijing?"

"Yes, I remember."

"Well, I apologize for not remembering earlier. I wanted to question him, but he was out of town when we got the manifest report, and by the time he returned, Lieutenant Moriarty had pulled the plug on the investigation. Prompted by the feds, like I said."

"Who was out of town that you wanted to question but couldn't?"

"Mr. Black. Whitney Black. He was on that same flight as Xi Lao Bing."

Chapter Ten

At Dickson's words, Montaigne and Wister exchanged looks. *Timing couldn't be better,* thought Nick. But it further complicated what was starting to look like an endless string of "persons of interest." Even with several of them now eliminated from Nick's radar.

"What was this guy like?" he asked Vern.

"Sheesh. Typical family man. Nice house, a scholar-athlete son. Regular churchgoer. In the interview him and his wife seemed to be real lovey-dovey. Course, the morning when he blew his top at her and bolted sort of changed my thinking.

"Henderlong made some kind of comment about him, now that I remember. Like maybe we should be lookin' closer at him. Then again, maybe he was tryin' to divert attention from himself. Or maybe he just didn't like him. Who knows."

Nick's mind rolled over the best way to interrogate Whitney Black. Coming on too soft would produce nothing, but too strong could alienate the guy and cause him to totally clam up. He needed to find a comfortable middle ground that might catch Black in a lie, or get him to make a mistake. If, indeed, he caught Black in a lie, he then had to think about forcing a murder confession. Tying him to Maraschino Cherry was a huge coup. But as Montaigne knew, coups meant merely a transfer of power. The big picture often didn't change.

"You say he saw you when he made his mad dash to the car?" he asked Vern.

"Yeah. Unfortunately. Want me to come along?"

"I don't think that's a problem. I'm guessing he thinks you didn't hear anything, you just witnessed his anger. He'll probably have some innocuous excuse for what happened. Then he and his wife—assuming they're both home—will probably put on an Ozzie and Harriet routine to show there's nothing wrong. I'm not going to bring up Dickson's airline manifest report till later—after he denies flying to San Francisco. Then after exposing that lie, I want you to hone in. They've already met you, and like you, so his guard will be down.

"How do you want me to hone in? Charm him somehow?" asked Vern, a touch of nervousness in his voice.

"No, if Black's the murderer he's had a quarter century to fine-tune his alibis. Just do your bunko act. Make him feel like his back is up against the wall. Make him feel like his best option is to confess, that a judge might be more lenient, especially with someone of advanced age.

Vern cracked a half-smile. "Yeah. Okay. This should be fun."

***

Vern rang the doorbell as Nick glanced around the neighborhood. Regina Roper, whom he'd yet to meet, was outside pruning shrubs. The Chin house once again appeared dead. No sign of Beryl or Arthur. He saw a flash of red behind Henderlong's front-door window. *He's another one I want to meet.*

The Black entry door swung open. Linda Black was wearing a gray sweatshirt over black yoga tights. Her long black hair was piled on her head. She opened the storm door.

"Hello! Vern! What a nice surprise!"

"Hi Mrs. Black, how are you? This is my partner Nick Montaigne. Just have a few more questions for Whitney, if you don't mind."

"Of course not! I was just heading to the Y for Pilates classes. You've got Whit all to yourselves. He's in the den doing the crossword puzzle."

She led them through a porcelain-tiled hallway into a large brown-carpeted family room with a massive wide-screen television mounted on one wall and a built-in bookcase filled with hardbound books on another wall. A third wall contained a country-style red-brick fireplace with andirons on one side and a stuffed wolverine on the other. The mantel above the fireplace had a half-dozen framed photos of people. Centered above the photos was a large painting of a rocky seacoast. A floor-to-ceiling window was at the rear of the den and looked out onto a patio of multi-colored paver stones, a huge rectangular patio table with umbrella, and beyond that a lush green hedge of boxwood plants. Off to the right of the patio was an attractive, redwood-stained wood deck.

Montaigne's first thought was how this lovely upscale home resembled that of Monica Delmonico's Grantchester Meadows estate. He was also itching to get over to the bookcase.

Whitney Black sat in a rickety-looking, black rocking chair, a folded newspaper sitting on his crossed legs. He wore a red-and-yellow "Planter Relays 2005" sweatshirt over avocado-green corduroys and white athletic socks—a dress ensemble that Nick, ever the stylish clothes hound, found rather dreadful. He also wore a pair of bifocals. When the three entered the room, he lifted his head and his mouth opened as if in surprise. He pushed his glasses up and set the newspaper on a small table next to the rocker.

"Whit," Linda announced, "Vern's back, and he brought his partner, Nick...Nick..."

"Montaigne," volunteered Nick. "Thank you, Mrs. Black," he nodded toward her.

She offered them some pound cake, which they declined, then said goodbye. Whitney offered them the chenille sectional couch to "relax in" and asked, with a concerned expression, how he could help.

"Sorry to bother you, Mr. Black," began Vern. "Oh, hey...I like the taxidermy," he said, pointing at the wolverine.

Black smiled. "I'm glad someone does. I hate it. We inherited it from Linda's folks years ago, after they passed. Unfortunately, Linda insists on having it in the same location her parents did in *their* house!"

"Well, nothing wrong with a little sentimentality," said Nick. "Actually, I like your nice bookcase. What kinds of books do you read?"

"Quite a bit of history and geography, actually. I'm fascinated by different places, people, cultures. The more exotic, the better."

"That sort of ties in with why we're here, Mr. Black."

"Oh?"

"Yes. As you can probably guess, we're still putting puzzle pieces together regarding the Moore murders. I realize you and Mrs. Black had solid alibis when you were questioned—"

"*Foolproof,*" quickly interjected Black.

"Right. I think you told Vern that you and Mrs. Black were...where was it...either at home or at the Planter Relays?"

"Well," started Black, lines creasing his forehead, "it was both. We were at the relays for much of that afternoon. Till early evening, I guess."

"Did you happen to see the Moores there?"

"No. I expected to, though. I'd spoken to Don earlier in the day and—"

"You saw him that day? That Saturday?"

"Yes. He was out working in his yard, spreading mulch. Their dog, Lisa, was with him. I remember because I thought it was cute how he rode Lisa around in the wheelbarrow."

Nick and Vern smiled. "Yeah, that's cute," said Vern.

"All right. So what did you two talk about?"

"I can't remember everything. I think mainly about decks. I wanted some ideas, since he'd done a nice job on his deck. He said I could stop by some time and we'd go around back. But, sadly, that never happened."

"Okay. Now, you say you expected to see him at the relays. Right?"

"Yeah. Like Linda and I told Vern, the relays are a big deal around here. Most everyone goes. And I said maybe we'd see you guys, and he said something like 'yeah, maybe,' but we never saw them. I just assumed they were at the other end of the bleachers."

"So, what time was this? I mean, what time did you leave the relays?"

"I *told* you," Black responded testily. "Early evening."

"Early evening," repeated Nick. "Say, five or six or seven or eight—"

"I don't know. It was a long time ago. Six or seven I guess."

"All right, all right. No sweat. Just trying to—"

"Look," Black interjected after a long swallow, "am I on trial here? Am I a suspect? Vern? Because if I am, I know some good attorneys. I've got my rights, after all."

Black rose from his rocker and began to pace.

"Hey, sir, it's okay," assured Nick. "We're not accusing you of anything. We're just trying to establish some times." He paused while Black continued to pace. "May I continue?"

Black grunted.

"Now, you say six or seven o'clock you left the relays. Now, when you met with Vern a few days ago, you mentioned the murders occurred about, quote, 'seven or eight.' How did you know this?"

"Hell, I don't know. Maybe because it was in the papers."

"It wasn't. The paper said 'Saturday evening' but never gave the specific time."

"Well...maybe I heard it somewhere. You know, like from someone else who maybe knew. You're from Atlanta, right? Springbrook is a small town, and stuff gets around."

"Right," said Nick. "That's probably it." Nick was getting Black worked up to where he wanted him. Black returned to his rocker.

"So, Mr. Black, I think you told Vern you didn't hear any gunshots. Right?"

"Right. And if I remember, I very helpfully explained to him about noises coming from the track. Which might obscure the sounds of gunfire. Didn't I, Vern?"

Vern nodded.

"So...so...if I was guilty of murder, why would I assist him like this? Why wouldn't I say that I *did* hear gunfire? That would show that it was someone *other* than me!"

"Yeah-uhhh," began Nick. "But—"

"And also, also...also" stammered Black, "what would be my motive. Huh? Why would I want to kill my neighbors? Huh? Tell me that."

Nick was feeling confident.

"Well, that kind of brings me to my next questions. I know you're retired now, but what kind of work did you do?"

"I was an insurance adjustor. I handled losses for a number of Fortune 500 companies."

"And so you did a lot of traveling, I assume?"

"Yes I did."

"Uh-huh. Now, how often did you visit the city of San Francisco?"

Black stared hard at Nick. He reached over and picked up the pencil he'd been using for his puzzle and began tapping the rubber end on the table.

"Hardly ever. Most losses were east of the Mississippi. I think we had one convention in Frisco, back in the, oh, late nineties, I think. But I can't remember exactly when."

"Hmm. So you never made any trips to Frisco—that you're aware of—in 1995?"

Black made an exaggerated frown and shook his head.

"I think you're lying," said Nick. His knee almost imperceptibly pressed against Vern's knee.

Black glowered at Nick and Vern open-mouthed. "What do you mean I'm *lying*? What does flying to San Francisco have to do with anything, anyway?"

Vern took over. "Nick, cool it, okay? Just because he doesn't remember taking that flight doesn't mean he's lying. Okay? Jeez."

He feigned a dirty look toward his partner. Then he turned to Black while rolling his eyes.

"Sorry, Mr. Black. Nick doesn't mean it. Bottom line, we do know you flew to San Francisco immediately after the Moore murders. As a matter of fact, we just received that information from Joy Dickson, who was lead detective for the initial investigation. We also know that on that very same flight was a man we now know was a Chinese intelligence agent. His real name was Xi Lao Bing. His code name was Maschino Cherry."

"*Maraschino*," gently corrected Nick.

"Right. Now," he continued, "your being on the same flight out of Springbrook immediately after the Moores were murdered looks very suspicious. And to share the flight with a Chinese agent and potential suspect? Even *more* suspicious. Whether you pulled the trigger, or Bing did and you were merely in league with him. So why don't you come clean with us. It will go a lot easier for you if you confess. We can vouch for your cooperation, you'll probably get a more sympathetic judge or jury, and at your advanced age...well, you get the picture."

Black shifted his head back and forth between the two men, still open-mouthed. Then he dropped it and flapped his hands in his lap in resignation.

"I knew you'd find out sooner or later."

Nick and Vern's hearts raced.

"Find out what, Mr. Black?" asked Nick.

"You know. Find out about me and Bing being on that same flight. BUT I DIDN'T KILL ANYONE!"

"Would you like to explain it to us, Mr. Black?" asked Vern.

Black took a deep breath. He stood up and began pacing again. He closed his eyes and pinched the bridge of his nose. Then he began talking, slower and calmer now that the flurry of incriminating questions seemed to have stopped.

"I knew Bing. He stayed with the Moores several times. It was hard not to know him. He was a friendly, ingratiating man. As a matter of fact, we were becoming pretty good friends. Lisa liked him, too. She'd come flying out the front door with her tail wagging whenever he pulled into the driveway. He's the last person you would think would be a Red Chinese agent. We all thought he was just here on business with Don's company. You know, a buyer or representative from Kibitsu Consolidated. I think that's the name. Yeah, he seemed like a good fellow."

"You say 'We all thought.' Who do you mean by 'we'?" asked Nick.

"All of us on Morning Glory. The Chins, Henderlongs, Ropers, Robertsons, Steens...all of us in the general area. We all knew him. Course, other than Don and Irene, the Chins knew him best. Then probably me. I like geography so I peppered him with lots of questions about China, which he liked. He knew all the dynasties. Talked about Chinese cuisine, which Linda and I enjoy. I tried to get him to talk about Mao and the Cultural Revolution, but he clammed up on that. Guess that makes sense.

"Anyway, yeah, we were on that same flight. I did have business in Frisco. He was heading back to Beijing, then Harban. I was surprised the cops never asked me about it. As time went on, I was so glad they didn't, 'cause I knew it would be suspicious. But deep down I knew it would come back to haunt me."

"Is that why you and Mrs. Black were arguing the other day?" asked Vern.

"Yes. She knew about our being on the same flight and wanted me to fess up to you. She figured you'd find out eventually. Wife is always right. So...so we got into a shouting match and I got angry and flew out the door and headed to Park Lanes—it's a bowling alley. I like to fling the balls whenever I'm mad. Takes some of the steam off."

Vern coaxed him further. "Are you saying, Mr. Black, that it was a *coincidence* you two were on the same flight?"

"That's what I'm saying, Vern. I'm *not* a murderer. And I wasn't 'in league' as you put it. Me working for the Chinese? That's not my bag. I'm an ex-insurance adjustor with corns on his feet and a bald spot who's an enthusiastic chorister at Our Gracious Lady of Immaculate Assumption Church. How could I kill anyone, especially a woman like Irene Moore, one of the sweetest ladies I've ever met? I can't even tolerate stuffed mammals."

He returned to his rocker. He began rocking back and forth, his head lowered, his hands gripping the arms. Vern looked at Nick and raised his palms as if to say "Now what, boss?"

"Okay, Mr. Black," said Nick. "Thanks for coming clean with us. One or two other questions and we'll let you get back to your crossword puzzle."

"Sure."

"You said you got to know Bing pretty well. Other than immediate neighbors, did you see anyone else talking with him?"

"No, I can't say I did."

"'Kay. How about any, oh, non-Asian visitors to the Moore home? Perhaps work associates of Donald or Irene?"

"Well, yeah, once in a while I saw visitors. I think I met his brother-in-law. He had a Southern accent. But they pretty much kept to themselves, those two. I wasn't like, you know, one of those nosy neighbors who has to know everything. That would be Henderlong."

Nick and Vern smiled. "Yeah," agreed Nick as he stood, "he likes communing with that window in the front door, doesn't he?" Black also stood and wiped his hands down the legs of his corduroys, to smooth the pants and to dry his sweaty palms.

"So...you do believe me, don't you? It was just coincidence. That flight, I mean."

"Yes, we believe you," said Nick, after which Black released a sigh of relief. "Thanks again for your time, Mr. Black."

"You're welcome. Whew...that's a relief! Oh, yes. I wanted to ask you. About Xi Lao. Is he a suspect? Is it possible he killed Don and Irene?"

Nick looked toward Vern.

"Well," Vern answered, "for quite some time we did. Although it's still a possibility, we're now exploring a different avenue."

"That's good to hear. I mean, I realize he may have been a Chinese agent. But still...he was a nice guy. That's all I can say. I'm not much for politics."

"Yeah, neither are we," said Nick. "Unless it involves murder."

"So is he still around? Bing, I mean. Have you talked with him?"

"Mr. Bing is no longer with us, sadly," said Vern. "He died recently while in Atlanta, Georgia."

"Oh, no," said Black, his face dropping. "I'm so sorry to hear that. How did it happen?"

"Uh..." slowly replied Nick, "our understanding is that it was...um...an extreme type of cerebral hemorrhage."

Chapter Eleven

The investigation until now had been making inroads, but it was a slow, incremental progression at best. The prime focus had shifted from assassinations tied to espionage (with Donald Moore having furtive connections to the CIA or other federal agency, his employment at Couch Industries being simply a convenient cover) to the possibility of crimes of passion committed by either a cuckolded husband (Jerry Delmonico) or a disgruntled neighbor and rival (Manny Henderlong) to the now very real possibility of the silencing of a whistleblower (Moore's perceived discovery and outrage over illegal use of blue asbestos in the MaxxDig 60 brake pads). Hovering on the fringes were several ancillary figures who were still question marks.

Other than shady vehicles that had followed Nick, then Melody, under the cloak of darkness, and several blowups by individuals whom Nick had pressed hard, the drama of this twenty-five-year-old cold case had kept a low simmer.

But this simmer was soon to heat up until it reached boiling point. The first real indication occurred once Nick and Vern left the Black home. It was a bombardment, and it would blow the lid off the case.

***

They left the Black house and had a late lunch at Sharkey's. Afterwards, on the way to Richelieu Park, which was recommended to them by Dickson and where they hoped for a short nature break, Vern received a text. It was from Amber Ramsey.

"Nick, it's Amber Ramsey! She...she says 'I looked everywhere for the report.' I'm guessing she means the autopsy report of her aunt. 'And I found it in an old briefcase of Dad's. Here it is. I hope it helps. Thank you for doing this. It means a lot to me.'

"Wow," he said.

"Cool," murmured Nick. "What does the report say?"

"Just a second, let me enlarge it. Yeah...okay...hmm."

"Well?"

"Yeah, it says basically the same stuff Joy Dickson told us." Vern then proceeded to describe to Nick in detail County Coroner Annette Robinson's autopsy report.

"At the top it gives her name, address, age, gender, and date of death. But for time of death it has 'Unknown.' Guess the time came from the cops. Maybe from her clothes, or dirty dishes or something?

"Entry wound was 'right posteriorly in the occiput one-and-a-half inches from midline. It measures point seven centimeters in diameter and shows some brown discoloration of the edges.'

"Nick," Vern paused, "the discoloration means the shot was fired at very close range. It causes what's known as 'stippling,' which is a kind of gunpowder tattooing."

Nick nodded in affirmation. "But Dickson said no stellate pattern. So shot was evidently very close, but gun barrel didn't contact the head."

"Right. Then it says, 'The wound of exit is in the left eye and shows marked laceration of the upper and lower eyelids. The underlying eyeball is completely collapsed...fractures radiating from bullet hole both left and right...'

"Sheesh, do I gotta read this?"

"No, that's okay, just give me a summing up."

"Okay. Well, it says 'ecchymosis' of the eyes, whatever that is. Gives her height as five-foot-three and weight at a hundred forty. She had some 'nevi,' whatever that is."

"Moles."

"Oh. Okay, let's see...gives a bunch of stuff about her organs, but...uh...nothing unusual. Says her liver had a 'slightly yellow tinge.' Probably a casual drinker. Looks like she had corn for dinner. They found that plus, quote, 'some meat material' in her G.I. tract.

"Then, uh...further down is a section about microscopic examination. It, uh...looks like it repeats what was said earlier. Man, that bullet did a number. Says here 'mid brain shows complete separation from the remaining portion of the brain above.' Holy cow.

"Then there's a 'Final Summary' at the end. Same stuff. Bullet fired close range, right side of back of head, exited the left eyeball... 'extensive destruction and hemorrhage, entire brain base including mid brain and pons.' Signed by Annette Robinson, M.D."

"Anything unusual on the report? Anything that looks like it doesn't fit? Strange handwriting?"

"Lemme see," said Vern. "As a matter of fact, yeah. Top of the very first page. Different handwriting. On the left is...wow..."

"What?"

"The name 'Marty Franes.' And a phone number. I'll bet her dad Bertram wrote that in."

"Could be. What else?"

"On the right side, at the top is...I don't know what this might mean."

"What's it say?" asked Nick impatiently.

"It says '2HB.' And it's underlined a bunch of times. Like someone wanted to emphasize it. *2HB*," Vern repeated. "Isn't that a type of pencil?"

"I think so, though who uses pencils these days? It's also the title of a song by Bryan Ferry and the British glam band, Roxy Music. The song is an ode to Humphrey Bogart. But I can't imagine Bertram Cabot Ramsey being familiar with Roxy Music."

"He's not the only one," deadpanned Vern.

"That's pretty interesting. Ramsey must've gotten that from Franes. It sounds like a code name. Ramsey got Bing's code name. He may have gotten a second name from Franes."

The Porsche entered a peaceful, tree-lined section of town then turned into the entrance to Richelieu Park. The men left the car and walked over to a pretty white gazebo with a blue-green cupola, the structure smelling like it had recently been painted. Nick sat on the gazebo bench and polished up his notes on the case, while Vern wandered off to "get a little exercise." While Vern was gone, Nick managed a somewhat lukewarm conversation with his steady flame, Annie McBain.

Nick looked up from his notes to see Vern—who had strolled down Richelieu Park path to the pond to feed the ducks with a bun—frantically waving his arms and pointing. Nick turned his head.

Dorothy Claunch was toddling along the sidewalk toward the gazebo. Nick hurriedly stuffed his notes into his attaché case in hopes of making a quick exit without her seeing him. But he was too late.

"Mr. Montaigne!" she called out from thirty feet away. "Mr. Montaigne!"

"Oh, hello Mrs. Claunch. I didn't see you!" He took a deep breath as she approached the gazebo, herself breathing heavily.

"Oh, Mr. Montaigne, I'm so sorry. It's so shocking."

"Huh? What do you mean?"

"Roy Turlock. I know you and he were friends."

"Roy? What about him, what happened?" Nick's eyes widened.

"He died last night. In his apartment. Not far from Central Congregational."

Nick froze, speechless. He stared in disbelief at Claunch.

"Evidently he didn't show up for work this morning and didn't call in. Didn't call his editor. Now, it was not uncommon for Roy to miss work, mind you. Most Springbrookers understand that for a long time he has had a substance abuse problem. How *many* times I saw him being helped into a cab outside that den of iniquity where he...anyway, John and I—Lieutenant Moriarty, I mean— had so often tried to coax him into church, but he was steadfast in pursuit of worldly things and turning his back on—"

"What was the cause of death?" hastily interrupted Montaigne.

"They don't know yet. But they think it was a heart attack. I can only imagine with all the chemicals he—"

She turned toward Vern, who was struggling for wind while negotiating the gazebo steps. "Helluva climb from that water hole," he gasped. Vern locked onto Nick's face. Nick knew he knew something was up.

"Vern, they found Roy Turlock today. Dead."

"Holy...how'd he *die*?"

Claunch jumped in. "They think it was heart-related. Found him on his couch in that ratty apartment of his. Drugs galore. Shocking. Just shocking."

"The *drugs*?" asked Nick "Or his death?"

"Both! I don't know why people can't just say 'no.' His poor cat was crying outside the door."

Vern wanted to say something to Nick but didn't know what. He put his hand on Nick's shoulder.

"Nick, I know how much you liked him. I'm sorry."

Montaigne took a deep breath. The emotional wallop of Turlock's death spun him a little, but he quickly recovered. Foremost in his mind, now, was Roy's last phone message. About the dog. That was a lead. Roy's *final* lead, though one absent a byline. Montaigne was determined to pursue it.

"Thank you, Mrs. Claunch, for informing us."

"I'm so sorry, gentlemen. I always hate being the bearer of bad news. Rest assured, I will request interim Pastor Higginbotham to offer a special prayer for Roy this coming Sunday. And the Board of Endowment Fund Trustees will make a generous bequeath to whatever cause his family requests. Although I don't know if Roy has any family left...or if he has many friends, for that matter."

"*We* were his friends," insisted Vern, "regardless if anyone else wasn't."

"Yes. Yes, Vern, that's so noble of you. Anyway, again, I'm sorry, and I'll let you both get back to your private detecting work. Until Sunday, if you find yourselves struggling a little, I highly recommend Springbrook's Living Bible Museum. People come from all over to visit— the wax exhibits alone are worth the price of admission— and it is a wonderful balm to the troubled soul.

"In fact, if I'm not mistaken, the Hall of Christian Martyrs is offering a two-for-one deal this month. Only ten dollars admittance fee."

She steadied herself against the gazebo stair rails and hoisted her large form down the steps and waddled away, leaving Nick and Vern to absorb the shock of Turlock's death. Nick called the newspaper offices, which confirmed what Claunch had said and added the police were ruling it a heart attack "pending autopsy." *How the heck did that woman find out?* thought Nick. *Wonder if Mel knows yet. Heart attack my ass. He was murdered, just like Franes.*

Probably asphyxiated while stoned and asleep. He got too close to the fire.

They walked solemnly back to Nick's car, climbed in and cruised slowly and contemplatively back to the motel. Once entering the lobby, and the caffeinated and decaffeinated coffee carafes caught his eye, Vern's mood took a downturn.

"Turlock was murdered. I'm going to Sharkey's," he firmly announced, "to pound vodkas."

"Hold on, we gotta discuss this '2HB' thing, and Roy's death. Did you hear what Claunch said? They found the cat *outside* the door. Why would his cat be outside?"

"I don't know. Maybe it was an outside cat. We got one. Damn thing's always draggin' mice to the front porch."

"He lived in an upstairs apartment, middle of town. I doubt it was an outside cat. If somebody snuck *in* there, like when he was asleep, the cat might've snuck *out*. And how convenient. Right after Roy calls me about the Moores' *dog*. This surreptitious 'sneak-in, sneak-out' with animals around is eerily familiar to the Moore murders.

"Anyway, I wanted you to meet Mel. She's coming over after work with some papers, and I think it's the silver bullet we've been waiting for."

"Yeah, fine, sure, whatever. I'll meet her and *then* go to Sharkey's to pound vodka. My way of honoring Roy. He would approve, I'm sure."

"I don't think you met him, did you?" Nick asked, as they entered Room 117 together.

"No, but I feel like I've known him for years."

Nick had Vern forward him the text that Amber had sent, then Vern threw himself on one of the two double beds.

"Gee, I hope I don't rough the covers up too much for you two," he said sarcastically. Nick ignored the remark. He studied the autopsy report while Vern scratched his right sock. "Think I got poison ivy," he mumbled to himself.

"This '2HB.' Vern, I'd like you to contact your brother-in-law again. The one with the purple Speedo who worked for the NSA. See if he has any idea what this might mean."

"Okay. But what do you think it means? You know, besides being a song by Roxie's Music."

"*Roxy*," corrected Nick. "You know what I think it means? I think it's a sort of cryptonym."

"What's that? Another code name?"

"Yep. Less creative than 'Maraschino Cherry' though. There are these code names the CIA used called 'digraphs.' Two-letter prefixes for a specific geographic area. This one's a little different, though. God knows what the '2,' the 'H,' and the 'B' stand for. But I'll bet they stand for something. Ramsey probably got it from Marty Franes, and maybe that's what got Franes killed. Despite Springbrook police claiming it wasn't murder. Like I bet they do with Roy.

"Anyway, give your brother-in-law a call. I'd *love* to get a contact for Frank Hardy, but we'll take what we can get. I also want you to call every veterinarian in the county. Roy obviously thought the Moore dog, Lisa, holds some kind of hot information. I can't imagine what it would be. I mean, it's not like a dog can point a paw and say 'He did it.' Anyway, I want to know who treated the dog. A cockapoo, I think our dog whisperer, Beryl, said she was."

"I think she was something like a cavapoo," said Vern.

"You sure? Whatever. Dorothy Claunch adopted the pooch after the Moores were killed, so I'll get hold of her. Shouldn't be too hard, she's everywhere. Not the dog. Claunch, I mean."

Vern swung his legs off the bed and started toward the door.

"Yeah, I'll call them all. Right now I'm thirsty."

"Partner, you gotta stay sober. We're *this* close to cracking the case, but we can't do it if you're half-crocked."

"So what am I supposed to do?" Vern angrily shot back. "Sit here in this fleabag motel like a wooden cigar-store Indian while you bang Melody Milky-Breasts every night?"

"Look Vern, she's going through a lot. Tailed home by a strange vehicle. Her ex died, probably murdered. She needs comforting."

"Yeah, right. She needs comforting like I need a hole in the head. The only thing that wants to be comforted is your plonker, don't try to kid me. I've a good mind to call Annie."

"You wouldn't."

"Well...least I can do is get this Discomfort Inn washed out of my system at Sharkey's."

After hearing from Dorothy Claunch about Roy's untimely death, not to mention having earlier waged a verbal war with Goosebill and been excommunicated from Monica Delmonico's house, Montaigne was getting antsy as well. He didn't like backwoods Springbrook and the Comfort Inn any more than Vern. But until now he'd managed to hold his mud. After Vern's insistence on getting drunk at Sharkey's, however, he reacted uncharacteristically.

"Vern, you had the opportunity to stay at Beryl and Arthur's but you turned it down. Like a little boy, you were afraid of ghosts. Go ahead, drop into Sharkey's, I don't care. But two Vodka Vernons only. That's it."

Vern glared at Nick, his eyes like burning coals. He grabbed his shirttails and pushed them under his paunch into his pants. Then he angrily raised a fat index finger.

"*One* Montaigne orgasm and that's *it*!"

He spun, left the room, and slammed the door.

***

Fitzpatrick got to the motel about seven o'clock. She'd already heard about Turlock's untimely death. Despite their romance being dead and buried, she was still distraught, telling Nick she was "confused," that Roy had his issues but was deep-down a "good man," that she knew he'd die young although "not this young." Nick asked her if he had a history of heart issues, and she told him he once had a severe case of heartburn after going to a Detroit Tigers game, but figured the five hot dogs and six D-Light beers at Comerica Park were the culprit.

She and Nick talked for a half hour in Nick's room, working out their grief, then excused herself to go to her own room and go to sleep early. Montaigne said he understood. Turlock's death was so traumatic it temporarily displaced what both of them had been looking forward to— and not just a night of physical affection. It was the paper that she had waved in the air while mouthing the word "Tonight." Nick only remembered it when she was halfway out the door.

"Mel, wait! What about that paper you waved in your office?"

She put her hand to her forehead and apologized. "I'm so stupid. Yes...I've got it here," she said while lifting her briefcase. "I think you'll be pleased."

She returned to the bed. She opened the case. She picked up the first sheet of paper and handed it to Nick.

"It's a Couch assembly print. The other one—the one with the formula for asbestos—was a Kibitsu manufacturer's print for brake pads only. This one is called a 'next higher assembly' print and has the brake pads as part of the dragline excavator. And has Couch approval signatures."

She pointed to the upper right corner of the print. Nick focused on the information. Most of it he didn't understand. But he did understand the two signatures in the horizontal box. They had dates of "12 January, 1995" next to them.

The signature of "Gerald Delmonico" was on top. And "Marvin Goosebill" was just below it.

Chapter Twelve

Montaigne stared at the two signatures and broke into a smile. He ran his fingers through his thick black hair.

"This is it," he said. "Our smoking gun. Mel, I love you!"

"Would that were true," she replied.

"All we need to do is wave this in Goosebill's face and watch him melt."

"Do you think he'll unfold? I mean, confess to murdering the Moores, or hiring someone?"

"There's still some work ahead," Nick admitted. "But we've at least pegged him guilty of illegally approving the use of asbestos in Couch's products. There's no way he can now dispute that. If it comes to it, would you be willing to testify about Moore and Delmonico's heated argument? And until then let me use the power of suggestion on Goosebill?"

"Sure, anything, if it will help."

"I hate to go back there again—no offense, Mel, but I don't know how you stand that place. Hopefully this will be my last time. Just hope Vern is up to the task."

"Where *is* Vern? I wanted to meet him."

"He's grieving over Roy. In his own way. Among other things."

***

The next morning Nick took his shower, donned his gray suit, checked his phone for messages, and scribbled some notes to add to Vern's eraser board, which was now as marked up with names, dates, notations, connector lines, arrows, and asterisks as an atomic energy government presentation. Room 115 had been noticeably quiet during the night—normally Montaigne began hearing loud snores soon after midnight—so Nick debated whether or not he should grab a quick bagel and coffee downstairs before tapping at Vern's door. He was anxious to share the news of the "next higher assembly" print, though. So he walked over to Vern's door and tapped. No answer. He tapped louder. Still no answer.

"Hey Vern!" he called out. "Get up, you lazy butt! Got pressing business out at Couch today!"

But Vern still didn't open the door.

Nick tried calling his cell number. But even that failed.

Either he closed up Sharkey's last night and is sleeping it off, or he's in a higher-class motel. Does Springbrook even have *another motel?*

He left a text message with Vern to meet for lunch, after which they'd visit Couch together. In the meantime, he took it upon himself to investigate Turlock's last, cryptic message about the Moore dog. He first called the precinct to ask Augie Moriarty if the cops had recovered any papers from Turlock's apartment—papers that might have watermarks or letterheads with "Springbrook Daily News Journal Observer-Tribune," or that might have something related to dogs. But Moriarty was out of the office, and the receptionist told him they were not permitted to share details of what might be an ongoing investigation.

So as an expedient to calling every veterinarian in the county to ask about a dog who may have died anywhere from twelve to twenty-five years earlier, he reluctantly called the person whom Beryl had said had adopted Lisa after the Moores were murdered: Dorothy Claunch.

"Hello, Mrs. Claunch? Hi, this is Nick Montaigne—I'm fine, how are you?—right, it was terrible news, which is why—yes, drugs are extremely dangerous, but—Mrs. Claunch, you adopted the Moores' dog, Lisa—well my question concerns Lisa's veterinarian—he's still around and practicing?—great, and how do you spell it?—K, R, A, Y, B, I, L, L—Dr. Henry Kraybill. Wonderful, you've been so helpful, Mrs. Claunch—thank you, Mrs. Claunch and— yes, you have a blessed day, too. Goodbye."

Nick immediately did an internet search for veterinarian "Henry Kraybill." He discovered Kraybill's office was located on the seedy north end of Springbrook, on Maple Street, very close to the county jail...just a stone's throw from Roy's apartment. He called the office to make an appointment, explaining to the vet technician he didn't have a pet but wanted to talk to Dr. Kraybill about someone else's pet that had a peripheral association with a crime.

"Oh," she said with a surprised tone. "Did the dog, like, attack someone?"

"Well, I'm not at liberty to discuss the details. It's a matter of some urgency, though. It's...it's related to an investigation."

"Oh. I see," she politely replied, "Well, Dr. Kraybill has, like, a full plate today, but he can probably talk to you late in the day, like around 5 p.m."

"Sure, that would be great. Thanks a lot. Oh yeah, my name's Nick. Thanks. Bye."

Montaigne hung up. *What the hell could Turlock have had that's so important? The dog's dead, for one. When she was alive, it's not like she could have spoken or pointed her paw. Did she maybe bite the killer? Did they trace any hairs? If so, why wasn't the killer ever apprehended? Only one way to find out. Talk to Henry Kraybill and hope he has a good memory.*

Having time to kill before lunch with Vern, another pilgrimage to Couch, and his meeting with Kraybill, Nick drove to Richelieu Park and strolled along the crushed gravel path that wound through the hills above the lake. Only a few people were there, all young mothers and their children, playing on the playground swing sets, slides, and giant plastic tunnels. The joyful domestic scene clashed harshly with what was then sifting through his brain: the bodies of Donald and Irene Moore...Donald slumped at the foot of his computer table, Irene crumpled on the dining room floor, their dog Lisa perhaps frantically running back and forth from one corpse to the other until bedding down against the bloody pillow near Donald. He wondered whether or not canines could become permanently traumatized by such violence. In his eagerness to get the vet's identity from Claunch, he didn't ask her.

"She was the only witness" were Beryl's words. Well, at least there was one, even if she wasn't human. This Kraybill meeting should be interesting. May not even need it, if Goosebill breaks down completely. Not likely though. Probably get more outrage about his "rights." Maybe he can find another amendment to twist that permits him to murder two people in cold blood.

Suddenly, just as he reached the gazebo, Ronnie Montrose's guitar screamed from Nick's coat pocket. He pulled his phone out. He didn't recognize the number.

"Hello, Montaigne here, can I help you?—Beryl!—what?—yes, he didn't return last night, so I assumed he was at another motel—okay—the Blue Room?—okay, so is

he available to speak?—okay, well, please have him call me when he's no longer 'peckish,' and tell him we have another visit to Couch, then we're seeing a man about a dog—right—and thank you for retrieving him, and please tell Arthur I'm very grateful—okay—okay, Beryl, have a good day—bye."

Vern reunited with Nick back at the motel in the early afternoon, after Beryl had dropped him off at the Sharkey's parking lot, where his Accord had sat since the previous evening. He sheepishly handed to Nick a care package of blood pudding while struggling to explain himself to his boss, that he'd had a "few too many" and called Beryl for a ride because he was too embarrassed to call Nick. Nick pretended like it was no big deal. He merely mentioned the two appointments that day, telling him that Florida Patton wanted him to contact her, and asking if Vern had had a chance to get with his brother-in-law about that '2HB' notation at the top of the autopsy report.

"Nick, I apologize, I just haven't had a chance. I'll get with him, though, I promise."

"No problem. No need now to dig up Lisa's vet, I already did that. We gotta be out of Couch by half past four to make our appointment with Kraybill. Just keep your eye on the time."

On the way to Hernan, Nick discussed with Vern how he wanted to handle Goosebill. He also wanted to get some "alone" time away from any Couch "handlers." Vern asked him what he meant, but Nick wouldn't go into detail. He emphasized he didn't plan to use "kid gloves" on Goosebill, that the man lied once already, and he wanted to make sure he didn't have opportunity to spew any more untruths. He was adamant that "that sonofabitch" come clean on anything and everything.

"Nick," Vern turned to him as they left the few buildings that comprised the town of Hernan, "please don't take this the wrong way."

"What?" asked Nick.

"Well, I know you don't like Goosebill. I don't like the guy, either. But you always taught me to remain professional. Do you think maybe you're letting your personal feelings about him influence the investigation?"

Nick thought for a few moments, his brows furrowed.

"Well...I've asked myself that a few times. Sure, you're right, he's not my favorite person. But after all, he did *lie* about not knowing about asbestos."

"You sure he lied? It was a long time ago. Maybe even though he signed off, he didn't know what that chemical formula was. You know, like, it was an oversight. Or..."

"Or what?" asked Nick.

"Or maybe he *did* know it was asbestos but didn't think it was illegal. Back then there was still a lot being learned about the stuff, and how it causes meso...meso..."

"Mesothelioma," assisted Nick.

"Yeah. Maybe he or Delmonico didn't know about the health hazards."

"Then why was Donald Moore so rattled? He argued with Delmonico at least once. He also angrily flung his slide rule against the wall."

"Okay. And where did you get that from?"

"Melody."

Vern stared at him.

"Wait a second," said an irritated Nick. "There's no way she would've made that shit up. Hell, she'd only been working at Couch a couple years. And what would be her motive? She was just an admin on that crane project. Are you saying she's trying to divert attention from herself?"

"No. Why would I say something like that?" he replied with a sarcastic grin.

The Porsche turned into the parking lot. The five flags were half-mast again after another mass shooting the day before.

The men left the car and signed in with the same surly receptionist.

"You'll have to be escorted again," she said sullenly.

"Yes, we know...Mr. Haslett," replied Nick.

"He's usually not around."

"Oh?" asked a curious Nick. "Why do you say that?"

"He travels a lot. Often with President Lomax. But the pandemic has kept both of them in town. So you're *lucky*."

Halfway through signing in, Nick's pen stopped moving. *Haslett never mentioned his traveling with Lomax. Though...I guess he would have no reason to.*

Haslett arrived and again escorted them through the security gate and down the smelly hallways, quizzing Nick the entire time about books. When they arrived at Goosebill's office, Haslett pivoted and disappeared down the corridor. Goosebill looked at them with as much shock as his whiskered, thick-lipped, ill-disposed countenance had thus far managed...meaning his lips parted. He invited them in.

"Thought you two would o' given up and gone back to 'Lanta by now. What's it about *this* time?"

"Hello to you, too, Mr. Goosebill," spat out Nick. "We were just in the neighborhood and wanted to drop by to discuss mesothelioma."

Goosebill stared at Montaigne, his large lips in a familiar pucker. "I have no clue what yer talkin' about."

"Well," volunteered Vern, "maybe we can jog your memory. Last time we were here you denied knowing anything about the use of asbestos in the MaxxDig 60 crane project."

"It ain't a crane. We call it a dragline excavator."

"Whatever," said Vern. "The point is, you said you had no knowledge of blue asbestos being used in the excavator brake pads. Correct?"

"That's right."

Nick placed a copy of the print that Melody had obtained in the middle of Goosebill's desk. "I give you Exhibit A," he said.

Goosebill pushed his glasses up and leaned forward, his chair creaking, to look at the print.

"Hmm...hmm. Okay. I can see this is a Couch Industries print."

"I believe it's a 'next higher assembly,' as you people call it," remarked Nick.

"Where did you get it?"

"None of your business. We got it, and it proves you signed off on—"

"Now wait," Goosebill interrupted, appearing distressed. "This print we signed says nothing about asbestos. Where on here is the chemical formula?"

"Mr. Goosebill, we're not engineers, but we're not totally clueless either," said Nick. "This symbol here," he pointed to a geometric shape where the crane brake pads were located, "indicates reference to a manufacturer's print. The manufacturer is Kibitsu Consolidated of China. Now, we do have the Kibitsu print as well, which we showed you last time we visited." He presented the brake pad drawing. "And you can clearly see the chemical formula $Na2(Fe2+3Fe3+2)Si8O22(OH)2$. Asbestos was not illegal in China in 1995. But it was illegal in the United States. Hardison inherited over three hundred thousand asbestos-caused mesothelioma lawsuits that had originated at both Couch and Granger.

"I told you that if I found out you lied about knowledge of asbestos, I'd be back. And that's what has happened. You lied to us, Mr. Goosebill. Either that, or you're the most pathetic design engineer on the planet. Which is it? Sir?"

Goosebill let out a long groan and collapsed back in his chair. The office was as quiet as an ice cave in Antarctica.

"You caught me," he finally said.

Nick and Vern looked at each other in disbelief.

"You got me," he repeated. "Yeah, we knew."

"Who did?" asked Vern.

"Me and Jerry."

"You want to tell us all about it?" asked Nick. "And, please, no games this time. Tell us the truth. Everything. We'll find out the truth sooner or later anyway. It will go easier if you fess up now."

"Yeah, okay." He took a deep sigh. "It was a profit-savin' measure. We had solid brake pads from a company we were used to dealing with. Kibitsu. Been usin' their products for years. So, what did a few brake pads matter? Who's gonna find out? The alternative was NAO pads with organic insulation. Palm slag, groundnut shell, cow bone, maize husk, PKS. You know how much that shit *costs*? Everyone uses it now, but back then it was pricey as hell.

"Jerry and I made a decision. We thought we were doin' right for Couch. That MaxxDig 60 project was a royal bitch. Customers crawlin' all over us to 'git r done.' So we went with the Kibitsu pads. Didn't think anythin' of it. I don't see a big deal. All these workplace rules and EPA bans. If you've enjoyed a good life working with asbestos products, why not die from it? Huh? See my point?"

Nick stared at him open-mouthed. "Did you just say 'why not die from it'?"

"Yeah! Why not have a good, easy time of it and save some money, rather than bend over backwards with all this foo-foo natural shit? Anyway, that was my thinkin'. Not sure if it was Jerry's or not."

Nick just shook his head. "Aside from the fact that thousands of people have had to suffer and perhaps die from a vicious lung disease, I find your cavalier attitude stunning. But please...continue."

"Yeah, well, then you-know-who found out about it. Don Moore, aka 'Mr. China.' Raised a royal ruckus. Said he was gonna go to Lomax.

"But we didn't kill him! This all happened right before he and his wife died. Yeah, there was lotsa tension on this floor. Jerry started drinkin' again. After Don and his wife got killed, it only got worse for him. Poor Jerry."

"But..." Goosebill continued, "I'm not sure if there wasn't somethin' else goin' on. The asbestos conflict—I can't imagine that causing Jerry so much grief. I mean, it wasn't that bad. But Jerry just seemed to go downhill."

Goosebill seemed to arrive at a kind of finality. Vern finished jotting in his notepad and cleared his throat. Nick was staring holes through Goosebill.

"You realize, Mr. Goosebill, that the timing of the Moore murders with this asbestos imbroglio is more than coincidental. Especially after Don Moore's threat to go to Lomax."

"I know. But I didn't kill nobody! I'm not a murderer. You gotta believe me."

"You lied to us once already. How do we know you're not lying again?"

Goosebill sat like a wilted shrub scorched by a mid-July sun.

"I guess you don't. But I ain't lyin'!"

"Do you have any idea, then, who else might have killed them?"

"No. Maybe it did have somethin' to do with Don bein' in the CIA. Maybe somethin' happened on one of his trips to Harban. I don't know."

Montaigne heard shuffling footsteps in the hall outside. For a moment he worried someone might have been eavesdropping. Then he thought about Melody, who was only a few doors down. *She went to a lot of trouble to get these drawings. It's looking like asbestos may not be the smoking gun we need.*

"Is it possible you could do us a favor, Mr. Goosebill?"

"Depends. What is it?"

"Just for our records, could we maybe have a photo of the final product? The MaxxDig 60 crane? I mean dragline excavator?"

"Yeah. Easily done." He tapped his computer keyboard several times. "There. On its way to the printer. Um..."

"Yes?" Nick asked.

"This illegal asbestos. You won't report it, will you?"

Nick gave Goosebill a jaded look. "We probably should. Yours was a pretty flagrant environmental violation, Mr. Goosebill. But considering it was a quarter-century ago, and Hardison-Granger paid a stiff penalty, and Couch Industries no longer uses asbestos...I think Vern and I can stay mum.

"The folks who have suffered and died due to asbestos are a profound tragedy. But our immediate concern is finding the killers of Donald and Irene Moore."

Goosebill lifted his corpulent frame from the chair. "Hang on, and I'll get that MaxxDig print from the printer." He slipped between Nick and Vern and out the door.

"Come on," said Nick, quickly standing up.

"Huh? Come on *where*? We need an escort!"

"Screw the escort. Let's go." He put his head outside the doorway and glanced in both directions. Vern rushed to pack his notepad. Assured that Goosebill was out of sight, Montaigne stepped into the hall and quickly walked to the corner, rounded it, then rounded another corner, then walked past the break room, then down another hallway. Vern scurried to keep up. Several blue-badged employees passed them, walking in the opposite direction and acknowledging them with "Hello, sirs," but Nick ignored them and kept walking.

They came to the long hallway decorated with flags and old framed photographs and walked in the direction of the security guards and body scanner. But when they came to a door on the left—with a small window through which one could see a stairwell—Nick opened it.

"What are you doing!" loudly whispered Vern. "You can't go in there! That leads to Mahogany Row! They'll come after us!"

"What's the worst that can happen?" asked Nick with a smile. "They terminate our yellow badges and kick us out? That's a good thing. Anyway, we're not going to Mahogany Row. That's on the second floor."

"Where are we going then?" implored Vern.

"Third floor. I wanna meet Byron Lomax."

Chapter Thirteen

Two stairwells connect the first floor of Couch Industries—where engineering, information technology, support engineering, and technical documentation employees sit—and the second floor, popularly known as "Mahogany Row" due to the plush mahogany desks and paneled offices occupied by Couch executives, human resources, and sales and marketing staff. Montaigne and Wister entered the stairwell farthest from Marv Goosebill's office. Once inside, surrounded by the cold, painted cinder block walls, Vern felt bold enough to grab Nick's arm and pull him from the first step.

"You're crazy, brother. Those fricking security guards have guns, and these idiots shoot first and ask questions later. 'Specially in a company that flies a blue-line flag. You wanna get us *killed*?"

"Vern, calm down. We won't get killed. Nobody goes up to that floor. For all we know Lomax has the whole place to himself. Most Couchers are working from home now, anyway."

"That don't mean they won't search for us there. You act like you're a Navy SEAL who's hunting Osama Bin Laden."

Nick ignored him. "You don't have to go in. I'll do it. But at least stand guard outside, case someone *does* come along. Then signal me with a knock on the door."

"What if I say 'no'?"

"Then I'll fire you and you can do what you've always wanted to do: sweep the sidewalks at Disney World."

Vern mumbled a few curse words. "Okay, I'll do it. But only because I owe you for last night."

They scurried up the stairs, each glancing through the tiny square window in the second-floor stairwell door. When they got to the third floor, Nick took a deep breath before turning the doorknob. Vern kept close to his partner, his hand on Nick's lower back for security. They opened the door and stepped into the third-floor hallway.

The top floor was just as quiet as the stairwell. The men turned left and walked on carpeted flooring around a large square with offices spaced every thirty feet, all with their doors closed. The walls were decorated with more framed photographs of airplanes, helicopters, U.S. Army trucks, industrial-sized washing machines and kitchen units, HVAC equipment, oil pipelines and derricks, super-sized cranes, and smaller products like joints, couplings, valves, and drill bits. Halfway around, they passed men's and women's restrooms, then what looked like a secretary area decorated with large plants. There was no one seated behind the lone desk.

At the end of the last hallway, they came to a door with a nameplate: BYRON A. LOMAX, President. Nick stopped and turned and whispered to Vern, "Here it is."

He knocked. No one opened the door. He knocked a second time, slightly louder. Still no one came. He turned to Vern.

"Remember. You hear or see anyone, tap on the door."

"Got it. But don't take too long."

Nick turned the knob, stepped inside, and shut the door.

It was a large room, one of the largest offices Montaigne had ever seen. The room seemed to Nick much cooler than anywhere else in the building. The walls had dark wood paneling and the floor was carpeted with chocolate-brown wool fiber carpet. On the right side was a massive oak desk, and a large black, leather executive chair pushed up against it. On the wall behind the chair was a built-in bookcase extending from floor to ceiling, with a mammoth wide-screen monitor in the middle that dwarfed the books. One of the shelves had a rectangular placard with the words "MACHINES ARE EVERYWHERE," the letters all being comprised of slivers of metal with rivets.

On the other three walls were more framed photographs. Almost all featured some type of industrial product. But in addition to "big, shiny, metallic things that make lots of noise"—Nick recalling Joy Dickson's words—these photographs also had a number of people—Couch employees—posing with the products.

Nick drifted left, as if in a daze. As one who liked old things, he felt as he did when he visited an old, abandoned cemetery in rural France one time that held centuries-old graves of his ancestors. He felt a kind of sacredness, mingled with a tingling nervousness.

The photos all had dates and went back to the year 1922. Some of them specified the product that the Couch employees were posing in front of. He saw the Thompson-Granger "Big Cat" digger that Goosebill had mentioned. Several photos from the sixties featured Asian people, and Nick assumed they might be Japan-based Yanaka employees. One photo had employees posing, not in front of any piece of equipment, but at the edge of a gaping hole in the earth. All of them wore placid smiles.

As he circulated the room, the black-and-white photos gave way to color. Most of the people in the photos were male. All were white. He noticed the clothing becoming more florid and the hair longer. When he reached a photo with the caption "Bicentennial," he stopped.

There was no equipment in this photo. Instead, it was a formal group pose. A row of maybe a dozen serious-looking men stood in a perfect line in the back. In front were about the same number, but they were all seated. The man in the exact center of the seated row was wearing tight, straight slacks that were hiked high up on his shins, revealing bare ankles. His hands tightly gripped both his knees. His legs were splayed wide, so wide in fact that the others in the seated row were forced to push *their* knees close together to accommodate the middle man. He looked about thirty-five years old, had thin, parted hair that was plastered across his forehead, and his face wore a defiant-looking scowl.

Montaigne was struck by how closely the photo resembled those which his boarding-school instructors once posed for at the beginning of each school year, with the school headmaster solidly in front and center. He assumed that *this* dominant figure was the president of Couch. But he was unsure if it was Lomax or his predecessor who had committed suicide.

He did recognize one person: Karl "Champ" Haslett. He was first row, second from left. With his seventies-style bushy black hair, sideburns, and thick moustache, he looked very different. He was the only one in the photo smiling.

When he got to the 1980s photographs, Nick began seeing Goosebill. One showed him posing with others in front of what looked like a Chinook helicopter. He looked much the same: thick-lipped with patchy whiskers, but he lacked the protruding belly. He recognized Donald Moore, having seen Moore's photo in one of either Franes' or Turlock's news pieces. He was struck by how short Moore was. He had a blank expression. And like most of the 1980s engineers pictured, he had short hair and wore a button-down, collared shirt and business-casual pants.

Several photos showed another short-statured man near Moore and Goosebill. He was pale-skinned with receding black hair and a woebegone look. Montaigne assumed this might be Delmonico. And a strange-looking red-haired man whose eyes never looked at the camera and who wore a complacent smile, as if amusing himself with a private joke. Based on the odd phone conversation in Goosebill's office, and Melody's characterization of him as being "analytical" and "weird," he wondered if this red-haired man might be Crashcup.

Melody-Clair Fitzpatrick didn't appear until 1994. The employees were standing in front of a UH-60L Black Hawk helicopter. She appeared again in a 1995 photograph displaying the MaxxDig 60 dragline excavator. In Nick's eyes she looked as pretty then as now. She was standing between Goosebill and Delmonico.

In the lower right of this last photograph, someone had handwritten in red ink: *Not Pictured: Donald Moore*.

Montaigne hoped to see more images of the man from the Bicentennial photo, the one whose knees were spread wide. He wanted to see what Byron Lomax looked like...assuming this was Lomax.

When he reached Lomax's monstrous desk, he was struck by how organized it appeared. Everything was perfectly ordered and geometrically positioned: pens lined up parallel; sticky-notes stacked uniformly; computer propped neatly in center of desk with wires stretching out neatly. He had hoped to see some type of personal items. Maybe photos of Lomax's family, or memorandums scribbled in his handwriting. But there was nothing. Not one item that would put a face or personality to this mysterious figure.

The book collection, too, revealed nothing. Just dry volumes relating to systems and logistical engineering, user manuals, parts catalogues, IT books, office leadership guides, and maybe a dozen books on different world cultures, including Chinese culture.

Until this point of his clandestine, one-man office tour, Nick had gained no knowledge about Byron Lomax, other than that one photo from 1976. And even *that* photo offered no guarantee the "man in the middle" was Lomax.

The oak desk had seven drawers: three small drawers on each side, and one large horizontal drawer that was top, center. Nick wrapped his fingers around the brass handle of the large drawer and slowly pulled it open.

Inside was a stack of white papers. His heart quickening, he put his hand in and lifted out a chunk of about a dozen sheets. He looked at the writing.

All of the sheets have Chinese characters!

He rummaged in the drawer to try to locate something written in English. At the very bottom of the drawer was something colored and shiny. He grabbed the corner of the sheet and withdrew it. It was a photograph of the head of a beautiful Asian woman. She had snowy-white skin, red lipstick, and classic Asian, almond-shaped eyes with heavy, dusky, lower eyelids. She wore a subdued smile and was gazing sideways and upwards with her twinkling eyes. She had reddish-brown hair pulled back behind her ears and a large, white, parasol umbrella decorated with orange and turquoise flowers that was tilted upward over the back of her head.

Lomax scored well on one of his China trips, thought Nick.

Then he turned the photo over. On the back, in delicate handwriting toward the top, Nick read: "To HB. With Love."

Suddenly, Nick heard the tapping on the door and Vern's muffled voice. He quickly stuffed the photo in his coat pocket, shut the drawer, and scurried around the desk, positioning himself behind the office door, his ear up against the wood.

"What are you doing here?" Nick recognized the voice of the unfriendly receptionist. "Where's your escort? This is Mr. Lomax's floor, you're not allowed up here!"

"Sorry, ma'am," he heard Vern say, "but I was looking for the bathroom."

"Up here? There are several restrooms on the first floor!"

"Uh, okay, I'll go down there."

"We have rules! You're not obeying the rules! You need to—where's your friend? Is he in—?"

Nick grabbed the inside handle of the door just in time. He felt it turn, but his grip prevented it from turning completely.

"I'm getting the security guards!" he heard her yell. "Right now!"

Nick waited a few seconds then cautiously opened the door and put his head out. "She gone?" he asked a startled-looking Vern.

"Good, let's go!" he barked.

The investigators whisked down the same hallway the receptionist had. At the top of the stairwell, through the window, Nick saw her reach the second-floor landing, then continue down the steps. He opened the third-floor door and urged Vern into the stairwell. They tiptoed down the topmost stairs. When they heard the bottom door shut, they rushed to the first floor, then opened the bottom door. Nick saw the receptionist midway down the hall getting very close to the guards. He knew that that direction was the only way to the entrance/exit door, then the parking lot and his car. But that meant risking physical altercation with the guards...or worse.

He ducked back into the stairwell and climbed up, Vern in tow, to the second floor landing, then through the door and into the second-floor Mahogany Row offices. By this time, both men were breathing and perspiring heavily. Vern reclined against the wall, shutting his eyes and mumbling about a drink at Sharkey's. Nick peered through the window, then quickly pulled his head back. He waited until the sound of footsteps faded, then pulled Vern through the door and into the stairwell.

At the last second, Nick saw Karl Haslett swoop around a second-floor cubicle and head toward them—as usual, arms held wide as if ventilating his armpits, and strong legs moving purposefully. But his head was down and he was whistling to himself. Nick yanked Vern into the stairwell just in time.

Finally, the coast being clear, they flew through the first-floor stairwell door, jogged down the long hallway, through the body scanner, into the reception area (where a well-dressed young woman, legs crossed, appeared to be waiting, and whose head jerked up in fright when the investigators ran out the door), then into the parking lot and into Nick's Porsche 911 GT2 RS, which was red-hot due to the burning sun.

Just as hot was Nick's exit from the parking lot of Couch Industries. He managed to a lay a thirty-foot patch just behind the row of vehicles that were reserved for Couch's top-tier executives. The rubber stains he left behind didn't disappear for several years.

***

"Oh, by the way Vern, I forgot to mention: you're supposed to call Florida Patton."

The Porsche was now safely west of the "Capitol of Nice People" and on its way back to "Historic Uptown Springbrook," where Nick had a much-anticipated five o'clock appointment with Dr. Henry Kraybill.

"Yeah, I think you already told me," Vern replied. "Who told you this?"

"Mother Claunch."

"Hell, Nick, I can't see *her*! I mean, she's not bad...even though she speaks kinda nasally. But I'm happily married! Well...married, anyway."

"I didn't know you were so righteous. Was it the Bible classes? Ten Commandments?"

"Got nuthin' to do with any *command*," he growled. "It's individual conscience. I made a vow. A promise—even though I was sorta forced into it. So, you know, I feel obligated to honor it."

"I understand," said Nick, momentarily feeling a twinge of guilt about Annie. "That's real admirable, Vern. But listen...I think we should split up. I mean, not permanently. I want you to head back to the Comfort Inn—or wherever you feel comfortable—and get hold of your brother-in-law. Check this out." He pulled the photo from his pocket and handed it to Vern.

"Turn it over," he directed Vern.

"Wow. Yeah, I see why it's so important. 'To HB, With Love.' And no numeral 2, but spelled out."

"Right. And his office drawer had a bunch of Chinese documents. We need to crack that code."

"Yeah, okay. I'll do it. You think this Lomax is our man?"

"The killer of Donald and Irene Moore has evaded the law for a quarter-century. He's a phantom. And here we have a guy who's in a high place and who has a lotta pull and who's a phantom within his own *company*. The problem now is getting to him.

"Vern, remember what I said earlier about having just one friend who has significance?"

"I remember, Nick. You told me that boarding school story about becoming a perfect."

"*Pre*-fect. Yeah, well, I haven't had time to connect with Karl 'Champ' Haslett on Goodreads. But he could very well be the friend we need now. He's a person of significance who has access to Lomax. I plan to get hold of him and see if we can't arrange a little surprise party for Lomax. Maybe bring Springbrook's finest with us."

"You gonna see that veterinarian too, right?"

"That's next. I'm hoping he has something on that dog. I feel Roy's spirit hovering over me. And Lisa's, too."

Montaigne dropped off Vern and the blood pudding at the motel and chugged up Oak, passing Central Congregational Church and entering the seamier side of town. A half-mile down Maple he came in sight of a large brick building with a high fence surrounding the parking lot. This was the county jail. *Kraybill's office should be just south, opposite side of street.* He looked for a lot to park in, and seeing none, he made a U-turn and parallel parked along the curb, parking as close to the vet office as possible and hoping there was a window from which he could keep an eye on his car.

Nick had never owned a pet, but he'd never seen a vet office quite like Kraybill's. It looked like a squalid rowhouse, sandwiched between several other small businesses in a long red-brick building. The sidewalk outside had colored chalk drawings local kids had made, including cryptic expressions Nick didn't understand, and more than a few four-letter words. He saw several unkempt men gathered in small groups on nearby steps.

He walked up the short series of steps to the vet office. A sign outside the door said "Come In!" He opened the door and stepped into a large room with a long table in the middle and chairs arranged along one wall. The room was sparsely decorated. Just photos of dogs and cats on the wall. The room had an antiseptic smell. One elderly woman was seated in the middle of the row of chairs. She held a leash, at the end of which was a black poodle who was panting nervously. He sat several chairs away, pulled out his cellphone, and checked for messages.

After several minutes, he heard a door open. At the far end of the room, a man in a wheelchair came rolling out. He was wearing a facemask and a wrinkled dress shirt with the sleeves rolled up. He had long, greasy hair that extended to his shoulders. His face and body were very thin, and he wore thick, horn-rimmed glasses. Nick thought he looked like a seedy ex-hippie who had literally "gone to pot."

As he pushed hard on his wheelchair wheels, rounding the corner of the long table, he said loudly, "Good afternoon, Mrs. Mecurio! I hear our Totesy isn't feeling well!"

The woman related a few of Totesy's symptoms, and the man bellowed, "Well, sounds like the case I just treated an hour ago. Skin condition on a calico Dorothy Claunch just adopted. Though your pooch looks considerably healthier. Anyway...let's take a look at the little bugger!"

The woman propped the dog on the long wood table which served as the examining platform. Nick thought it unusual the waiting room also served as the examining room, but figured the vet was maybe down on his luck and hard up for decent real estate.

The vet poked around under the poodle's fur, several times exclaiming "Hmm," then sat back in his wheelchair with a smile.

"Nothing serious. Just some minor sebaceous adenitis." He withdrew a notepad from somewhere in his lap and wrote down a few words, tearing off the paper and handing it to the woman.

"Here you go. This shampoo works wonders for SA. Give her lots of vitamins, too."

The woman asked what specific vitamins she should give Totesy.

"Oh, A, E, C...omega supplements...whatever. She should be fine in a few months."

The woman thanked him and led Totesy out the door. The vet turned to Nick.

"My last patient! That woman brings that damn thing in here practically every week. I think she's grooming him for one of those ubiquitous, social media 'poodle-on-skateboard' videos. Anyway, I'm all yours, Mr..."

"Montaigne. Nick Montaigne."

"Right, that's it. I'm Hank Kraybill. Now, I forget...my daughter told me something about a crime involving a *dog*?"

Nick explained about him and Vern traveling from Atlanta to investigate the Moore murders at the behest of Amber.

"That's quite interesting! What brought your attention to our little neck of the woods after all this time?"

Nick let out a long sigh. "My partner saw a newscast on television."

"Ahh. Yeah, I try to stay away from the news. Adversely affects my blood pressure and mental health. Well, you're in luck. I remember the Moore murders well."

"Really?" said Nick. "That's great, we could use a little luck."

"Just a minute." Kraybill rolled to the door, locked it, and turned the sign around, as Nick glanced out a side window to check his Porsche. "Let's go to my office where we can talk in more comfortable surroundings."

Nick followed him into the back room which, with its stained carpet and mess of books and papers, looked hardly comfortable. He saw Kraybill's vet school degree, framed on the wall: Cornell University, Class of 1985. A small, red-white-and-blue, Grateful Dead "Steal Your Face" sticker was pasted on a bottom corner of the glass frame, partially obscuring the print.

"Looks like you're a Deadhead," Nick remarked, nodding at the sticker.

"Oh, a long time ago. Back when Jerry was still around. During high school I was front, center for the Barton Hall '77 show. Unforgettable."

"I'll bet," Nick replied, having a vague familiarity with that popular bootlegged concert.

"These days, with my practice and this contraption," Kraybill smiled and slapped his wheelchair handles, "I can't road-trip anymore. An occasional Jimmy Buffett show is about it."

"So you're now a Parrothead?"

"Not at all. I just like a few songs. There's something disturbing about bourgeois, middle-aged white Americans play-acting like that."

Nick's mind shot to his lime-green baby parked on Maple Street. "I get your drift."

"Anyway, in Springbrook, Parrothead plays better than Deadhead."

Montaigne asked him about his work. Kraybill told him he once had a large office in the country, and worked a lot with large animals like horses, but after his equestrian "accident" he shifted exclusively to small animals. He said he was "hanging on" a few more years in north Springbrook until retirement.

"I never met Mr. Moore," he said. "But Irene was a wonderful person. Always smiling. I'll never understand how heartless some people can be. Maybe that's why I work with animals. They offer unconditional love, and unlike children, never grow out of it."

Kraybill then offered Nick some lemonade, which he accepted. Nick asked about how Lisa fared after her owners were killed.

"Dogs are very adaptable," Kraybill said. "She was always a friendly, playful dog, but after the murders the playfulness seemed to fade. For a while she was in the kennel, until Mrs. Claunch adopted her. Over time she got back to her old self."

"I guess I'll come to the quick, Dr. Kraybill."

"Please, call me 'Hank.'"

"Sure...Hank. We received a lead that Lisa might, shall we say, direct us to some information we could use to identify the killer or killers. I'm not an animal expert, so I don't know how credulous a dog's 'knowledge' of a crime can be. I'm hoping you might shed some light."

Kraybill asked if he could remove his mask, and Nick said "fine." Nick saw he had a very serious expression.

"I can only share the basics with you, Mr. Montaigne. You'll have to make your surmise from those." He then went into a detailed monologue.

"Not long after the murders, I was approached by Augie Moriarty and Joy Dickson. They wanted to know if there was any way a dog—i.e. Lisa—might recognize a person and react a certain way. I told them that, from what research I've read on this subject, dogs don't have specialized areas in their brains to process faces like humans do. They can recognize certain faces they're familiar with, but not to the extent of humans. They actually react more to emotions and vocalizations.

"That being said, the most powerful sense a dog has is its sense of smell. Canine experts claim they have a smell sense a hundred thousand times that of a human. They have up to three hundred million olfactory receptors compared to a measly five million for a human. This is why dogs are used to track missing people and to sniff for hidden drugs.

"I told Moriarty and Dickson this, and they got very excited. They told me they wanted to use Lisa in an experiment. They wanted to see if Lisa might identify the killer by sense of smell."

"How did you react to that?"

"Well, I'd never heard of such a thing. As a veterinarian, I was most concerned about the welfare of the animal. I didn't want Lisa stressed out any more than she already had been. It was my understanding that she was cooped up in that bloody house, no food or water, for several days. When they found her she was lying near the body of Donald. Soaked in blood.

"They told me that, if it made me feel better, I could be with them during the experiment, just to make sure Lisa didn't become too frazzled. So I agreed to it. Uh...more lemonade?" he asked Nick, who declined.

"So," Nick asked with great curiosity, "it sounds like Moriarty and Dickson may have paraded various suspects near Lisa, to observe her reaction? I'm not a legal expert, but I'm not sure law enforcement has the right to do that."

"No, from my understanding, they don't. But at this point they were so desperate to find the killer they threw caution to the wind. Springbrook citizens were becoming very impatient, particularly the families. This was sort of a last ditch effort. Now, obviously they couldn't *force* anyone to come in. It was all strictly voluntary. Which *is* legal. And to further convey an appearance of legality, they merely asked these people to come in for questioning. The idea was to have them show up at the precinct, and have Lisa leashed up outside near the entrance. I would be the one holding the leash. They instructed me to observe how the dog reacted when each person walked past."

"Who were the individuals called in for, quote unquote, 'questioning'?"

"There were about a dozen of them altogether. Friends, neighbors, and co-workers. And everyone who was asked to come in did so. I'm guessing none wanted to appear hesitant, since it might indicate guilt.

"Even though it was strictly voluntary, and everyone agreed to come in, I remember they had a difficult time convincing one man to comply. He was very surly and kept barking about his Constitutional rights. I think they finally lured him in with free tickets to a Cavs game.

"It went very well. I'm not sure if anything like this had ever been attempted before. I was as excited as the police to see if there would be some kind of 'Lassie' moment."

"And was there?" asked Nick while crossing his legs and taking a sip of lemonade.

"Yes. With one person. Problem was, the district attorney found out what we were doing and raised holy hell. We were told that, not only could nothing be used in a courtroom—that a judge and jury would laugh and throw such evidence out the window—but that having a dog parked outside to identify the killer—even only to provide cops with a 'person of interest'—was intimidation of suspects. We were ordered in no uncertain terms to forget about anything that happened, and to keep our mouths shut about the results. Otherwise, if word got out about someone, that person could be scapegoated and possibly targeted by vigilantes. Especially in a small, gossip-prone town like Springbrook.

"This was just before the investigation seemed to come to a halt."

Nick listened, fascinated. *This is why Dickson never said anything about it. They put duct tape on her mouth.* He realized that Springbrook cops had been fairly vigorous in their investigation, despite what he'd pulled from the local grapevine. He also wondered how Franes got this information, which Roy had later uncovered. He asked Kraybill.

"There were no reporters around for this," he assured Nick. "It was just Moriarty, Dickson, and myself. I remember Marty Franes. A fine newsman. We attended school together. Marty had a real talent for uncovering things where no one else could. What may have happened was that he managed to contact someone in the D.A.'s office to get this scoop. Or maybe someone inside the precinct—a woman perhaps, since Marty was somewhat of a ladies' man."

Nick felt the time was approaching to spring his million-dollar question.

"Hank, you say Lisa reacted strangely to one of the volunteers who showed up. How exactly did she react?"

"Well, for all of the others, she reacted warmly. As I'd known her to behave when Irene Moore brought her to the office—my old office—as she was always very docile with people. During the experiments, the individual would approach the door, while Lisa and I and either Moriarty or Dickson were about six feet away. Lisa would see and smell the person, then wag her tail and strut slowly up to the person's legs. Then, most couldn't resist to bend down and pat the cute pooch on her little head.

"The sole exception was when, after this one volunteer showed up...rather than wagging her tail and approaching, she became very shy. Now, she didn't tuck her tail between her legs or anything. But she certainly didn't wag it. And instead of approaching, she hid behind my legs and rested her head on her front paws. And her eyes never left this person's face."

Nick let Kraybill's words linger in the air. He knew that timing and mood were extremely important when pulling information from an interviewee. So he waited a short while. Then he popped the question.

"And can you tell me who this individual was?"

Kraybill let out a long sigh of regret and gripped the wheels of his wheelchair. "Unfortunately, no. Like I said, I made a vow. All three of us did. And I have to honor that vow."

"Even after twenty-five years?" asked Nick.

"Look," Kraybill said, leaning close to Nick. "All I can tell you is this. And, please, listen to me carefully—listen to my emphasis—because I won't repeat it."

Kraybill paused with measured, deliberate effect, his chin on his chest, his silence pregnant with suspense. Then he lifted his head and looked up as if desirous of tunneling into Nick's heart.

"We were instructed by the D.A. not to divulge the identity of this *man*," he said, strongly underscoring the last word and several words that followed. "The D.A. was concerned about repercussions from the populace. And considering the *man* may still be *alive* today, and possibly even *employed* somewhere *close by*...well, as you can see, my hands are shackled.

"Good luck, Mr. Montaigne."

Chapter Fourteen

Nick stepped onto the sidewalk outside Kraybill's office. Two boys, one black and one white, leaned against either side of a streetlamp while admiring his machine. The white kid tossed a dirty basketball up and down. Both stared at Nick as he rounded the front of his car and inserted his key in the lock.

"You boys protect my baby while I was gone?" he asked. They smiled shyly.

"Like chewing gum?" They both nodded enthusiastically. Montaigne reached into the car and pulled out a large pack of cinnamon gum and tossed it to them. The black kid caught it with one hand.

"Enjoy!"

"Hey, thanks mister!" they said, tearing into the pack greedily.

On the way back to the Comfort Inn, Nick stopped at an Outback Steakhouse and grabbed some take-out steak to go with a blood pudding care package Beryl had entrusted with Vern. Melody had called to say she was there and waiting anxiously for him. Vern had left a text that he couldn't reach his NSA brother-in-law about the "2HB" notation and suspected cryptonym, but that he'd contacted Pat McCauley, and McCauley promised to "pry some kind of intel about Frank Hardy from Lurch Kwiatkowski."

Montaigne chomped hard on his cinnamon while mulling over Hank Kraybill's obvious hints regarding the identity of the man whom Lisa seemed so wary of.

A man. Still alive. Still employed. Works close by.

Then he added the ingredient of *right-handed*. He added the ingredient of the weapon being a *High Standard Sentinel* pistol, probably old. He supplemented this with the determination that either Donald or Irene, possibly both, knew the man. He considered the possibility the killer was someone local, who knew about the Planter Relays being a diversion. He thought about who might have a motive to kill them. Finally, he weighed in this strange "2HB"—or "To HB"—and some kind of connection to East Asia— Nick almost certain it was the one-party, communist dictatorship and economic powerhouse known as People's Republic of China.

But none of the "persons of interest" on our graph at the motel have names with first initial "H" and last initial "B."

He was so engrossed in concentration he barely remembered parking and walking to his room. Five minutes after loosening his tie and fixing a Glenlivet, there was a knock on the door. It was Vern. He entered Room 117 carrying Beryl's care package for Nick, a roguish grin on his red face. Once inside, he took the liberty of pouring himself his own Glenlivet.

"I deserve this, partner," he informed Nick, who was preparing to chow down on his steak and pudding.

"Oh? Why is that?"

"Hey, you're gonna love that blood pudding! Beryl is a *fantastic* cook. And that Arthur is a cool guy. Real strong

Brit accent, smokes a pipe, wears a cardigan sweater...the works."

"Yeah, and I hear you stayed in the Blue Room. Why not Red?"

"Real funny, Nick. Anyway, listen up. McCauley somehow got Frank Hardy's contact number from Lurch. So I called it and guess what?"

"I think I know," said Nick, devouring his pudding.

"Go ahead," said Vern.

"The '2HB' just refers to the song. Ramsey was a huge Roxy Music fan."

"No! Are you serious? Listen to this: Hardy said he didn't know what the letters stand for, but he thinks one or both might be either someone's initials, or code—a digraph, I guess it's called—for a geographic region."

"Right," agreed Nick. "But we already assumed that, correct?"

"Yeah, we did, but the big news is the number. Hardy asked me if I was sure the number was a two. He asked me if it wasn't a number *one*. And I told him 'Yeah, we're positive, it was on the autopsy report as 'two,' except in numeral form.

"And know what he said? He said a number two before a digraph indicates a *double agent*. A number one is just an agent. You know, like CIA. But *two* is a *double agent*!"

Nick had placed a chunk of steak in his mouth but suddenly stopped chewing. "Ahhhh...jeez. Ahhhh...then I'm guessing that little salutation on the back of the photo of the Asian woman is inside humor. She knows his code identity and did a play on words to joke with her lover. Instead of the numeral '2,' she spelled it out before sending the photo *to* him. A joke. She's inside the People's Republic and probably working for the government. Lomax—or whomever received that photo—is working with her...and *them*."

"Yeah. Nick, it's gotta be Byron Lomax. That's the letter 'B.' The 'H' probably stands for geographic region, you know, like the Midwest. That photo of the Asian beauty links him to Red China and to double-agent espionage, with Couch Industries as his convenient cover. Donald Moore must've been on to him.

"I'm anxious to meet this SOB, Nick."

Montaigne finished eating and the two men mulled silently. Nick told Vern he needed to process all they'd learned and come up with a plan. Somehow they had to accrue enough evidence with which to confront Lomax, and get Haslett, Moriarty, and the D.A. on board. He wasn't concerned about Haslett or the D.A., but Augie Moriarty might be difficult. He told Vern tomorrow morning they would be visiting the Springbrook Police Department. He told him to "get enough sleep," and that "tomorrow will be a big day." Vern gave his senior partner a fist bump and retired to Room 115.

Soon after Vern had left, Melody opened Nick's door and entered, Nick having previously given her a key. *She must've been watching for him to leave*, thought Nick. She sidled close to him, her head lowered. They held each other close while she shed delicate tears over Roy Turlock. Then they undressed, turned off the lights, and slipped into bed together.

***

Nick woke early, the morning darkness not completely faded. He reached across the bed. But Melody had already left for work. He rubbed the sleep out of his eyes, yawned, and staggered into the bathroom to shower. Letting the hot water cascade over his head and body, he firmed up the day's agenda. *Rouse Vern, get with Augie Moriarty...plan the attack...then one final, dramatic visit to Flagville*. He knew that Moriarty was as cautious and recalcitrant as Lurch Kwiatkowski, though, so he didn't hold out hope for immediate action. His trump card was Amber Ramsey. *Worse comes to worst, have a relative of the victims plead for action.* He also knew the power of the press. *The Moriarty family wears a scarlet letter. Even if that newspaper dawdles, the larger Ohio cities can be reminded of disgraced Sheriff Dick Moriarty.* And as a cherry on the top—a maraschino cherry—he had Dorothy Claunch to work on Moriarty, who was a fellow esteemed Congregationalist. *She seems to like me. A snoop and a nuisance, maybe. But she's got more clout than Billy Graham.*

He stepped from the shower, toweled off, shaved, slapped on some Lacoste Blue, and left the bathroom. When he turned the corner toward the beds, he saw a dark form in the morning half-light. It was seated on the edge of the bed—the bed that was still made up—that was closest to the window.

At first he thought Vern had slipped in, uncharacteristically beating him to the day's punch. But when his eyes focused, he realized it wasn't Vern.

"Haslett."

"Nǐ hǎo."

Sitting on the bed, facing Nick, his back to the motel window, sat Karl "Champ" Haslett. His right hand held a large, black, ominous-looking, silencer-equipped gun. The gun's shiny barrel was pointed at Nick.

Nick stood frozen, droplets of shower water still falling from his hair. He was confused. In the whirlwind of considerations his brain conjured over the next few moments, the first crazy thought was that Haslett was a jealous lover who'd learned about him and Melody. His next crazy thought was that Haslett was here to protect his boss, Byron Lomax. It took him another few ticks of his inner clock to realize the truth.

"Let me guess. You're 2HB."

"That's a start," replied Haslett with a sick grin. "Wanna go double or nothing?"

"B—Byron Lomax?"

"I'll answer to that as well. And I wouldn't expect Detective Nick Montaigne to be any less perceptive."

Montaigne's figurative and literal nakedness left him feeling more vulnerable than ever before. His mind flashed back to Haslett's visit to Green-Wood Cemetery while he and Roy Turlock examined the engineering prints.

Haslett casually cross his legs, tilting the gun he was holding from Nick's stomach toward his chest. "I just wanted to drop by for an early-morning book discussion. And if you believe that, I've got a nine-millimeter bullet with your name on it. Hell, even if you don't believe it."

Nick's mind did several more convoluted pirouettes. He'd been backed into corners countless times, but the demon in front of him was something new.

"Oh, don't worry, Melody's fine," Haslett added. "She's working for me, and right now she's undoubtedly reaching for a box of tissues next to her in the car. She grew to like you. I hated to ruin her day by informing her it's time to bring your romance to an end. Hate to ruin yours, too, Montaigne."

"I'm sure you do," Nick replied with seething sarcasm. "Rather, 2HB. You're evidently quite effective with hit-man tactics."

"Early CIA training. Looks great on a résumé. And comes in handy in upper-middle-class suburban homes."

Haslett then held out his non-gun hand and impudently offered the facing bed for Nick to sit on. Montaigne sarcastically thanked him for offering him a seat "in my own room," then sat on the end of the bed, which he and Fitzpatrick had just slept so comfortably in. He had a million questions for the man opposite him.

"First on my mind, Haslett—if that's your name— what's the code mean?"

"It's a digraph with a number tacked on the front. The 'B' designates zone of activity. Which in my case is the U.S. Midwest. 'H' is initial letter of my surname—which, to answer you, is indeed Haslett. And the number two is

what the Chinese MSS, or Ministry of State Security, uses
to designate its double agents. Although I hate that term.
Too banal. I prefer 'creative mole.' With apologies to
writer John le Carré, of course."

"Ever the bookworm, eh *Champ*?" spat out Nick
contemptuously. "And your *nom de guerre*, 'Byron
Lomax'? Merely a convenient wizard behind a curtain?"

"Every corporation needs a Big Brother to watch out for
its employees. After the former president came to some
kind of moral reckoning and blew his brains out, I assured
the rest of the brass I'd find a suitable replacement. Most
were too startled to ask any probing questions. And the
worker bees on the first floor, most of whom are ex-
military, are very good at following orders without asking
questions. Not a lot of critical thinking, let's put it that way.

"I did a little ventriloquism in my army days, just to
entertain the guys, and that came in handy. Most Couch
potatoes seem to like those morning addresses, many of
which I merely recycle. Kind of like when mommy tucked
them in at night. Comforting, loving, reassuring. Humans
have a marvelous capacity for self-deception."

Listening to Haslett's impudent, self-assured ramble,
Montaigne felt a mix of disgust and admiration. *This guy's
smart as a whip*, he thought. *Smart like a fox. So were
Hitler and Stalin.*

"Do you mind if I at least get some clothes on?" he
asked Haslett. "I'd like to look like a gentleman, if
possible."

"No problem. I'm sure Coroner Butler will appreciate
that."

Nick slowly dressed himself—tie included—his eyes
focused on Haslett the whole time. The only thing he didn't
don was his sport coat.

"Feel free to grab your coat, Mr. Nick. I'm not
concerned. I know about your admirable foible regarding
guns."

Montaigne's distress was temporarily displaced by seething anger at Haslett's haughty politeness, and especially his condescending "Mr. Nick" comment. "Thanks...*Mr. Champ*...but no jacket needed. Too much hot air in here." Haslett winced. "So you're not worried I just led Goosebill on about not carrying a gun?"

"Of course not. I have to be a good judge of character in my line of work. I take you for a man of character."

"That's something, anyway. I suppose Melody clued you in that I was on to you?"

"She's a good girl. I saw her qualities immediately after we hired her in '93. Brought her into the agency myself. They paid off her college. I led her along. Then we became lovers. Of course, I'm much too old for her now, but it was fun while it lasted."

"So does she play both sides of the street—is she a *creative mole*—like you?"

"Oh no," answered Haslett haughtily. "She's a loyal U.S. Central Intelligence agent. She has no clue about my, uh, 'other' work. And she'll continue to be uninformed long after you're gone."

Nick's jaw muscles tightened. Haslett jerked the gun slightly in response.

"You seem somewhat chagrined, Montaigne. Maybe confused? How could an intelligent woman condone the assassinations of a married couple and two pesky reporters? Simple. Like many, including Bertram Cabot Ramsey, she's convinced Bing orchestrated them. And Bing was, indeed, a candidate for that role. But he was strictly information gathering and logistics. Penny ante espionage. He didn't have the backbone for 'elimination' work. Whereas I do, from my early CIA years.

"After the Moore murders, Bing laid low. At least until Couch returned to government aerospace work. Then we brought him to Conyers to infiltrate the tech doc work at Imperial. Which, of course ended abruptly when Ramsey came along. The NSA was on to Bing, and Ramsey was their trigger man. For all I know he suspected Bing of his sister's murder. If so, he got that part wrong.

"As far as Melody's betrayal of *you*, it took me a while to convince her to play Midwest Mata Hari. I determined after first meeting you that her looks—and your, uh proclivities—would be very useful for tapping into your information databank. The Montaigne model is single, handsome, personable...and a horndog. So I put Mel to work.

"She eventually signed on after I explained that your meddling would compromise the success of what 'we'— meaning the CIA—were achieving out at Couch and Imperial." Haslett then imitated himself. "'*Mel, years and years of careful scrutiny of Harban and Beijing will go down the drain! Numerous CIA covers will fall like dominoes!*' For added security, I reminded her of who hired and promoted her, and who paid off her college debt. She felt obligated…though it was a reluctant obligation.

"Melody's very valuable to me, and to Beijing, in her current role. I like her. And not just because of her tits…with that little brown mole on her left tit, three inches northwest of that gorgeous nipple that you've undoubtedly become acquainted with."

"You're sick, Haslett."

"The word 'sick' is a clinical term, and I don't think you're a doctor, Montaigne. Bertram Cabot Ramsey was sick. Bullous myringitis, I believe, poor fellow. I'm perfectly healthy."

"That's debatable. But why did you have to kill Roy Turlock?" demanded Nick. "He wasn't any threat to you, Haslett."

"He was feeding you too much information. I never thought he'd find out about that dog experiment. I thought that ended after I put Marty Franes to sleep years ago.

"I figured a pillow over Turlock's cannabis-soaked head would be easy, like with Franes. And it was. I scooped those dog files off his coffee table and left. Other than the

cat sneaking out, no evidence. Everyone in town knows he
was a notorious stoner and alcoholic, including the
Moriarty brigade, and Mel herself, who lived with him for a
while. Only you and your partner suspected it wasn't
accidental."

Nick asked, "So how much did Ramsey know? About
your sideline work with Beijing, I mean."

"Ramsey was NSA and strictly information technologies
down there in the swamps, as you well know. He didn't
come on to Bing until late in the game. Though," he added
parenthetically, "he had suspicions, nurtured by Franes.

"Up here in Ohio," Haslett continued, "Bing and I had a
nice little thing going. Lots of juicy DoD technologies were
we able to feed Beijing. Sikorsky was *huge*. Then Don
Moore had to upset the apple cart on one of his Harban
jaunts—or maybe it was one of Bing's sleepovers at the
Moore home. Regardless, he found out. The Chinese are
wonderful people—humble, ingratiating, smart, spiritual—
but they can't handle alcohol well, and Maraschino Cherry,
as the NSA tagged him, was no exception. Anyway, Bing
opened his mouth too wide one night, and Moore got
suspicious. Moore came back to Couch and shared his
'insights' with Delmonico. Then Delmonico came to me
and tried to get the straight dope. O' course, I vehemently
denied I was a creative mole. We had it out in the office.
He learned that if he pushed his 'false' accusations, I might
soon have him waiting tables at Sharkey's. So he shut up. It
ate at him, though, which undoubtedly contributed to his
early demise.

"Don Moore was a different story. Like I said,
Montaigne, I'm a good judge of character. I knew that he
wouldn't keep quiet long. So I gave him an early pink slip.
A permanent one.

"Was never sure if Goosebill knew. But he's too stupid,
and I don't think Moore or Delmonico ever confided in
him. Even if they had, he's a coward and would never say
anything. I tossed him and Dickson and Moriarty dainty

chunks of red herrings about Moore and the Chinese mafia, Moore and Chinese counterintelligence, and occasionally some sushi about Jerry and a love triangle. It's amazing what some folks will believe."

Nick pressed him, knowing his time was running short. "And asbestos in those crane brake pads? Nothing to do with anything, I'm guessing."

"Exactly," replied Haslett, cockily. "An unintentional albeit convenient red herring that I encouraged—with Mel's help—to shift attention from me. It did have you going for a while, right?"

Nick refused to grant Haslett the privilege of even a nod. Oddly, though, the conversation was making him somewhat relaxed—as relaxed as he could be with a gun barrel leveled at him.

"And Irene Moore? You had to kill her, too?"

"Sadly, yes. She was in the house that night. I didn't want to. She was a sweet woman. She loved world geography, and we talked that subject, especially China, at several company picnics. Very pretty, too. Big, wide-set blue eyes. I really hated to ruin her appearance by blowing her brains through one of the sockets. But…," Haslett smugly sighed, "sacrifices have to be made sometimes."

Nick asked Haslett about the circumstances of what happened inside the Moore home the night of April 15, 1995. The assassin gave him a relaxed narrative of each horrible moment, as if a realtor conducting a mini-tour for a home buyer.

"Don't you have any *compunction*?" Nick asked in disbelief at Haslett's indifference. "All those lives wasted? Donald, Irene, Franes, Turlock, and indirectly Delmonico and Ramsey? And your partner in crime, Bing? And to sell out your own country?"

Haslett let out a belly laugh that actually shook the gun he was holding.

"C'mon, Montaigne, fer chrissakes. You're a reader and certainly understand history. You don't really swallow that

American exceptionalism bit, do you? Of all people, how could you be handcuffed to a nebulous patriotism that crosses into blind nationalism? Those poor kids out at Couch flying their 'Old Glories' all over the place have been totally indoctrinated and have no clue about their country's history.

"Zealous nationalism is a hallmark of fascism. It started early: the greed and imperialism we tried to justify by calling it a 'Manifest Destiny'; our duplicity and ethnic cleansing of indigenous peoples; our land grab of Mexico; our secret funneling of U.S. arms to prop up anti-communist dictatorships at the behest of Wall Street; over eighty foreign election interventions since 1946; *evaporation* of women and children at Dresden, Hiroshima, and Nagasaki.

"Do you know what occurred seventy-five years ago this month? Possibly not. The April 1945 firebombing of Tokyo, known as 'Operation Meetinghouse,' was a U.S. war crime and the single most destructive bombing raid in human history. It killed 100,000 *civilians*—not soldiers—and left over a million homeless. That means women and children, Montaigne. Yet only a few people in this country know about it.

"Then there's the more familiar abomination of the Vietnam War. Its devastation, lies, and ruined lives, where my older brother was fried at Ia Drang for no other reason than to prevent an illusory domino from falling. Which destroyed my parents."

Haslett paused and, for a brief moment, appeared pensive... even sad.

"And those are just appetizers," the murderer droned on. "But schools, churches, politicians, military, Hollywood, advertising—even some historians, anxious to further the cushy narrative—for generation after generation promote the whitewash of America's supreme goodness. It's nothing but a hypocritical hunk of Swiss cheese, riddled with holes.

Montaigne, if you only knew what I know about America's dirty little secrets. It would make your mind reel.

"No, Montaigne, I have absolutely no qualms about what you term the 'selling out' of my country—that 'country' being merely an arbitrary set of boundary lines. Like Jack London wrote in *White Fang*, I realized 'my own meaning in the world…life achieves its summit when it does to the uttermost that which it was equipped to do.' It's either be an eater or that which has been eaten. And my family—who, believe it or not, I love—has eaten very well."

Nick closed his eyes and squeezed the bridge of his nose. He tried to collect himself so his voice wouldn't quiver—difficult to achieve with a nine millimeter pointed at him.

"That's quite a manifesto, Haslett. Ted Kaczynski would be proud. You even managed an undergraduate history lesson, wrapped in a red bow and made to order. Very laudable. Now it's my turn.

"You make some good points," Montaigne began. "I had a cousin wasted in Iraq looking for non-existent 'weapons of mass destruction.' We stole the land from the Indians and Mexicans, and you can't base a democracy on an original sin like that, no matter how hard you pretend. It's like a heavy table balanced on two wobbly legs. Gore Vidal called us the 'United States of Amnesia.'

"But all you've done, Haslett, is trade that for a totalitarian regime whose legs have been entirely sawed off. I've heard a lot about how you hate America, but not much about China. I guess their Cultural Revolution sits well with you? Selling secrets to a repressive dictatorship and placing in harm's way your family, and others—no matter how amnesiac they may be—is no way to fix things. And *murder*? You're willing to stoop that *low*? Your personal morals are no less repugnant than the morals of the country you deem to hate.

"'Old Glory' may not be as glorious as some people make out," Montaigne tacked on, sweat forming on his brow, "and the Constitution and Bill of Rights are probably honored and abused in equal parts. But at least we have something in place. At least the country has something to aspire to."

The two men glared at each other in fraught stillness. Then Haslett, after a deep sigh, retorted "Okay, you can have the last word, Montaigne."

Nick turned his head toward the brown, plastic Comfort Inn tray that held his Glenlivet bottle. "I'd rather have one last Scotch," he said. "Since you're so intent on adding another notch to your gun belt."

Haslett smiled. "Go ahead sir. I may be an assassin, but like you, I'm also a gentleman. Anyway, you deserve it. You've gotten closer than anyone else has. But after Melody told me you were trying to unravel '2HB' and had visited Kraybill—and my security cameras showed you visiting my third-floor office—I felt I had to intervene."

Nick stood and carefully stepped around the bed corner, then poured a Glenlivet—straight. He tried to offer Haslett one, but the killer was too clever. As he lifted his left hand to steady the bottle, he noticed a shadow pass outside the motel window. It moved slowly and was too close to the glass to be a vehicle. It looked more like a human body. A rather large one.

He carried his drink back to the bed. Haslett looked perfectly comfortable, facing him steadily with his weapon, which he steadied by placing his right forearm, his gripping arm, on his thigh; the gun, hand, and wrist extended slightly over his knee. But Nick did not sit directly across from Haslett this time. Instead, he sat at a slight angle, closer to the night table.

"That bed spot was getting a little warm," he casually remarked to Haslett. "Thanks for allowing me a final Glenlivet."

"My pleasure. Don't take too long, though. After dispensing with you I have to wake your sleeping bear of a partner, whose snores I could hear through the—"

Haslett's face changed. His eyes widened, as if suddenly realizing Vern was no longer asleep next door.

Then KKKKSSSSHHHH!!!, the motel window completely shattered.

In an instant Nick's foot flew up, the toe of his Forzieri hitting the scaphoid bone of Haslett's wrist, which sent his gun flying upwards, but behind the killer. He dove toward the killer's head, wresting it toward the bed while Haslett struggled to free himself. The gun was nowhere in sight. Haslett managed to land a hard punch to Montaigne's kidney, which momentarily stunned Nick, giving Haslett the opportunity to escape the grip on his head. He dashed toward the door, as Nick recovered from the gut punch.

Nick staggered off the bed while gasping and holding his stomach, then reeled toward the door, which Haslett had just flown out of. He suddenly remember to grab his car keys, so he turned, rummaged around the night table—*damn, where are they?!* Then he glanced at the floor and saw them lying next to one of the bed legs. He scooped them up and finally dashed out the door. Haslett was gone.

In confusion, Nick turned right, then left, then right again. He figured Haslett was headed for his car, but wasn't sure which door was closest to his Porsche. Then Vern appeared at the end of the hall, farthest from the lobby.

"Nick, this way! He shot out this way!"

Montaigne sprinted down the hall, past Vern, and slammed his body against the motel's metal exit pushbar and entered the parking lot. He heard Vern yell something then got to his 911 GT2 and heard tires squealing, front of the motel. He jumped in, banging his knee against the door, then fired up his engine, slammed the clutch, spun backwards, slammed the clutch again, then WHAM!—the Porsche jerked forward like a rocket, its rear wheels spinning into the gravel and firing pebbles in all directions and sending up a cloud of dust.

When Nick reached the motel entrance he managed to make out a black car bulleting south down Oak Street toward the interstate. He turned left and followed. The car was about two hundred yards ahead and traveling at a furious rate of speed. Nick countered. He rammed his foot down on the clutch and jerked into fourth gear, then stomped the clutch again and shifted up and to the right into fifth gear.

As he shot past Green-Woods Cemetery, his mind perversely recalling the quiet day he and Roy perused engineering prints in front of Marty Franes' tombstone— and when he later came damn near close to bro-hugging Haslett—he realized he was gaining ground on the black car. Suddenly, just after he zoomed past Eastabrook Rock, while squinting in the fiery morning sun, a black shape came between him and Haslett's car, dead center of the road. As he flew up close to it, he saw it was an Amish buggy, a large orange triangle centered on the back of the carriage.

"*Shit!*," he screamed.

He had to make a quick decision. Left or right. Wrong decision meant calamity. He chose left.

Jerking the steering wheel slightly left, his sweaty palms gripping the wheel with all his strength, he whisked past the buggy, the left tires sending up clouds of dirt, with only inches between the Porsche and the carriage. Then he jerked the wheel right and flew onto the entrance ramp of the interstate. Haslett's car had just entered the highway.

Somehow in the fury of the moment Nick managed to call Vern and bark out his whereabouts and the direction Haslett was headed. It was still early enough on a weekday morning that few cars were on the highway, so Montaigne and Haslett practically shared their own private racetrack. And Montaigne was, by this time, burning up much more pavement. He'd narrowed the separation by half...though he wasn't sure what he'd do if and when he caught up.

Fortunately, he needn't have worried. For what happened next was like something out of an Evel Knievel video game.

Every U.S. highway has median barriers on the left that run parallel to the road. Ohio's interstate system is no exception. The barriers are a type of guardrail designed to prevent cars from running off the road, either into a ditch, concrete overpass beam, or into the opposite two lanes. They are made of steel and are typically about three feet high. Most of the time they remain at three feet. But when near an overpass, they often slope toward the ground, even *into* the ground, with what's called a "buried-end treatment." This is to prevent a head-on collision between car and rail.

The downside of a buried-end guardrail is that a car traveling at a high rate of speed that strikes this buried end can actually become airborne.

Haslett must have seen Montaigne inching closer through his rearview mirror. His car, suddenly, began to wobble, most likely from the high rate of speed the make and model were unaccustomed to. As the two cars approached the overpass, Haslett's car suddenly swerved left. Nick couldn't believe what happened next.

Haslett's car hit the buried end of the guardrail perfectly, dead center of the chassis. At a speed well over a hundred miles per hour, the velocity catapulted the car high into the air like a projectile shot from a cannon. It wobbled left-right-left briefly, then smashed into the concrete overpass, shattering into a hundred torn chunks of metal. Nick later recalled that the explosion of machinery resembled a massive nighttime star shower. The two largest chunks of vehicle arced into the air on either side of the highway, with the front end of the car landing in the ditch below the underpass, the back end at the edge of a weed field on the right side.

Nick downshifted as quickly as he could, hoping to avoid the metallic downpour. He shifted into reverse in the gravel on the berm on the left side of the highway and slowed to a halt. The scene in front of him was something from a war zone. Smoke curled up from various piles of metal. Flames erupted from the engine contained in what was left of the front end of Haslett's car. Traffic on the southbound lane had stopped completely. Behind him, also, all cars had stopped, some drivers and passengers leaving their vehicles to view the carnage. Nick stepped out of his Porsche, which itself had smoke rising from the radiator, and walked closer to survey the scene.

Where Karl Haslett's body lay in all this wreckage, he had no idea. *There's no way anyone could have survived this.*

Nick glanced at his watch. It was quarter after eight. The day was April 15.

***

The Ohio State Highway Patrol arrived about ten minutes after the crash. Five minutes after that, Vern came puffing up the berm, completely out of breath. Nick was leaning casually against the driver's door of his Porsche.

"Oh, shit...thank...god...you're alive...Nick."

"Still here, partner. And I thank the cosmos you didn't stay with Beryl last night, or the outcome would be a lot different. Waiting now to see about Haslett."

"What...happened? How'd he—?"

"A long story," Nick halted him. "Wish there was a video. Incredible. But what I want to know is, how'd you find out I was being held at gunpoint?"

Vern took a few moments to catch his breath. "Melody. She...she called me. Must o' been drivin'. In tears. I guess after Haslett...took her place in your room. I...I shot outta bed like a bat outta hell. Snuck...around outside to what I hoped was your window. Couldn't...find a decent rock, though! Finally got one."

"Well, you heaved it just in time. He was a few seconds short of interrupting my morning Glenlivet. I'll tell you the rest later."

The lead trooper then arrived to take down Nick's story. Nick wanted to know about Haslett.

"Whatever's left of him is lyin' over there," the patrolman pointed toward the smoldering engine. "Craziest lookin' corpse I ever saw."

"Why is that?" asked Nick.

"The steering wheel was where his ribcage should have been. But the strangest thing was his face. Not a scratch. And it was almost like he was smiling."

Epilogue

The fifteenth of April the year Montaigne and Wister visited Springbrook, Ohio wasn't unlike that same day in 1995. Sunny and mild with a few clouds. Excitement in the air over the Planter Relays, which kicked off that evening. Morning Glory Lane had not changed much, either. The trees were taller and fuller, and some of the houses had newer coats of paint, and the robins that pranced across the lawns looking for earthworms were more than a few generations removed. But many of the same people lived there. And their memories of what happened inside 157 Morning Glory were indelible. What Montaigne and Wister had accomplished was significant, to be sure. But there's often no *real* justice in life, no matter who lives or dies or what a courtroom verdict might render. And when it comes to homicide, the only guarantee—at least in twenty-first-century America, and which is better than nothing—is an *opportunity* at a tepid sort of *partial* justice. After all, you can't return the dead to life.

Haslett's grisly death didn't change things much in Springbrook. There were no Moore family members remaining in town who might feel liberated knowing Donald and Irene's killer had received his "just due." The Morning Glory residents still locked their doors at night. Nobody felt vindicated, since none were ever considered serious suspects. Gina Roper continued dying her hair and snarling about how her sister-in-law had treated her deceased brother, Gerald. Manny Henderlong continued to fly his upside-down American flag and bitch about the feds. Linda Black kept up with her Pilates at the Y, and Whitney exercised his vocal chords at Our Gracious Lady of Immaculate Assumption Church. The Chins continued their games of mah-jongg—when they were home— occasionally politely inviting the widower across the street to join them. And Beryl and Arthur Henshall periodically renewed mini-tours of their noteworthy home whenever anyone new dropped in for tea.

As for Nick and Vern—after explaining everything to Augie Moriarty down at the precinct and answering innumerable questions thrown at them by the recently promoted cub reporter representing the *Springbrook Daily News Journal Observer-Tribune*—it was finally time for some well-earned rest and relaxation. Fortunately, they'd brought their swimsuits along, and even though the outdoor pool at the Comfort Inn wasn't exactly the water park at Six Flags Over Georgia, the water was at least clean.

"That's a helluva tale, Nick," Vern exclaimed, aghast at his boss's version of what had transpired that morning in Room 117. "The guy had his own little kingdom out there at Couch, feeding who knows how much sensitive information to Red China. Wonder who will replace him— meaning Byron Lomax—as president?"

"Well, knowing Couch Industries, and the corporate world in general—probably Goosebill, I'm sorry to say."

Vern made a face while rubbing oil on his prominent belly. "Tell you what, this sure feels good soaking up the sun. All we need out here now are a couple dancing girls. Speaking of which, you gonna call Melody?"

Nick turned his head away. In a flat voice he said, "No, I don't think so. She's already tried me several times."

"Yeah. Well, least she came through for us in the end. Anyways, you got Annie to come home to. You got somethin' real special there, Nick. Don't ruin it."

He turned and faced Vern. "Words of wisdom, Vern. My loosey-goosey days may be over."

"We'll see," said a dubious Vern. "Good to see you back with your Persols on, though. Montaigne outdoors without his shades, by that burnin' car, was scary-lookin'."

The investigators spent the rest of the day trying to repair their frayed nerves. They squeezed in one last meal at Sharkey's, where Rick congratulated them on solving the case by telling them "no charge, fellas" after their meals, and sharing several memorable stories about Roy Turlock. The following morning they checked out of the Comfort Inn, Vern presenting the desk clerk with a small list of premium coffees they "might want to look into." They dropped off the Accord at the rental agency then made one final visit to Morning Glory Lane. Although the Henshalls and Blacks weren't home, and Manny Henderlong's door blinds were drawn for some reason, they were shocked to see an open garage door at the Chin house. And two cars parked inside the garage.

"Nick, we gotta stop!" shouted Vern. Nick pulled alongside the curb, and Vern jumped out. He scurried up the steep drive as an Asian-looking man wearing a facemask rounded the corner of the house. He was carrying a pair of garden shears half the size of his body.

"Excuse me," said Vern. "But would you be Mr. Chin?"

"Yes."

Vern's mouth began sputtering while his body swayed backwards. The man's eyes widened with fright.

"Uh...hello...uh...my name's Vern Wister. You, uh, don't know me, but—"

"*Vern?* You *Vern?*" The man became wildly excited. "Oh, nice to meet you!" He grabbed Vern's beefy hand and pumped it several times. "We hear much about you! Beryl and Linda talk about you! We want to meet you! Jane...Jane...come here!" he yelled into the garage. A petite woman with wire glasses and facemask stepped out of the garage.

"Jane, this is Vern! We finally see him!"

Jane Chin rushed to Vern and began pumping his arm. "Oh, we so glad to see you! We sorry we away so many time! We hear much about you! We hear you solve case!"

By this time Nick had joined them. Vern introduced his senior partner, but the Chins seemed far more interested in the junior partner. The Chins invited them inside their home for coffee, tea, and vanilla wafers, and the investigators gave them a rundown of their Springbrook experiences. The Chins listened attentively the entire time, interjecting with boisterous exclamations of "So terrible!" and "Manny very nice man," and "We always knew China connection!"

Nick and Vern remained with the Chins longer than Nick wanted, but eventually they said goodbyes in the driveway, promising to stay in touch via email. Just before heading to the Porsche, Nick told them, "You know, other than one or two people in town, you folks are the only ones wearing facemasks. You set a really good example."

"Oh, we try to be responsible," said Lee Chin earnestly. "We love America and want to do right thing. This virus very bad. People should think of freedoms. Wearing facemask, social distance, they not anything to do with lack of freedom. They *responsible*. With freedom come *responsibility*. You need to wear facemask, too!" He shook a finger to chide them good-naturedly.

"You're absolutely right, Mr. Chin," Nick said, then turned to Vern. "Vern! I *told* you we should wear our facemasks!"

They hopped in the Porsche, swerved around to Chamomile, jumped on Oak, passed Central Congregational Church, then cruised slowly down Main through "the other side of town," glancing upwards at the single window on the second floor apartment that graced Roy's old "pod."

Somehow, they managed to exit the city limits of Springbrook without once being accosted by Dorothy Claunch.

***

Gilberto was a firestorm of activity after discovering Nick, Annie, Vern, and a friend were ensconced in the booth at the back of his restaurant. He hadn't seen his favorite female guest in a while, not since before she and Nick had flown off to Telluride for their annual ski vacation. He put his favorite waiter in charge of their table—his nephew, Enzo. And after learning Montaigne and Wister had solved a twenty-five-year-old cold case up in Ohio, he made sure all the drinks were on the house, and double-checked with the bartender that Vern had enough vodka in his White Russian.

"So what do you think of Gilly's so far, Amber?" Nick asked. Amber Ramsey blushed and admitted she hadn't eaten in such a nice restaurant for a long time.

"Gilberto can be a little over-the-top sometimes," said Vern, "but he's a decent guy. Took me a while to understand him, though."

"Nick, you still haven't told us what Haslett said about that night!" scolded Annie, whose hand had rested on Nick's thigh since they first took their seats.

Montaigne smiled and gave her hand a squeeze as Anita O'Day's voice came over the speakers, doing a live version of "Sweet Georgia Brown."

"Well, there's not much that Vern and I and Detective Dickson hadn't already deciphered. I'll go through it—unless you'd rather I not, Amber."

"No, that's fine," she answered, tilting her rounded forehead and batting her wide eyes. "I already saw the autopsy report. If I can handle that, I can handle anything else."

"Okay. Well, here goes."

Nick proceeded to relate what Haslett had told him in the motel room about the night of April 15, 1995.

"Haslett parked at the middle school tennis courts, right where I first met Roy—Roy Turlock, our reporter friend and onetime informant. Walked to the house at twilight, hoping that if anyone saw him they might think he was merely a spectator for the track meet. Rang the doorbell and Irene unlocked the door and let him in. She vaguely knew him, having met him at a Couch company picnic. They made small talk while little Lisa—like dogs will do—sniffed him over well.

"He told Irene he had some crane business to discuss with Donald in anticipation of an important meeting on Monday. She didn't think anything of it and led him to the den. It's where Donald had his new Packard Bell computer. Donald was then sitting in front of it. Haslett set his briefcase down, and as soon as Irene left, he shut the door. He withdrew the gun—a High Standard Sentinel revolver that he'd purchased years ago, and had actually used to assassinate a Russian agent back when he was a legitimate CIA man—and pointed it at Donald's head, quickly ordering him not to make any noise, or he'd, quote, 'blow Irene away.' He told me Donald was so scared that he began trembling and perspiring heavily. This is consistent with police lab findings that his shirt had an unusually high sodium concentration. Donald must've known why Haslett was there.

"Haslett said he wanted to make sure Moore had nothing on his computer that would indicate his status as a double agent—or 'creative mole,' as Haslett perversely called it. So he instructed Moore exactly what to do. He told him to delete every file in his hard drive. Then he instructed him to permanently cleanse his hard drive by overwriting it. Then he forced Moore to give him every disc he owned, either CD or floppy, which he then dumped in his briefcase. After making a quick search of the vicinity for anything else potentially incriminating, he lifted a pillow from a nearby couch. He held the pillow inches from the back of Donald's head, pointed the gun...and fired.

"I forgot to mention that he wore latex gloves his entire time in the house. This is why the cops found no incriminating fingerprints.

"Haslett said he waited at least several minutes, behind the door of the den, in case Irene heard the gunshot or became suspicious. Then—"

"What about the gun?" interrupted Vern. "Did he say why he used that type of gun?"

"Yeah, I asked him that, and he said the Sentinel held sentimental value for him. Which I find pretty sick. He knew that such a weapon wouldn't be as noisy as a forty-four magnum or nine millimeter, but would still penetrate the skull. But for safekeeping he used a pillow to stifle any noise.

"Anyway...where was I? Yeah, okay, so he waited. And Irene didn't show up. Then he carefully opened the door and walked quietly through the kitchen into the dining area, where she was sitting at the table, her back conveniently toward him. He said the TV was on, which may have also helped drown out any noise. He walked up to her, without the pillow—since he no longer needed it—placed the gun inches from her head, and fired. This time the angle was slightly different. The bullet exited the left eye socket—Donald's exit wound was upper cheek."

"My god, this is horrifying, Nick," gasped Annie. "What a monster." Amber, who had given Nick the green light earlier, now looked like she was about to faint.

"I know, Annie. Sorry, Amber. But the worst is over. Anyway, after this, Haslett turned the television off. He had such a good memory, he told me Irene had been watching *Dr. Quinn, Medicine Woman*. Then he casually strolled out the door to the garage, then through the garage and out the door that led to the backyard. Then he looped around in darkness to his car. The man was so cold-blooded, two days later—the day after Easter—he turned up at the Planter Relays."

"What about the cockapoo?" asked Vern. "Lisa?"

"I think it was a cavapoo. Yeah, sorry, I forgot. Hope this isn't too bothersome for you, but...Haslett said that while still inside the house, strolling toward the garage entry door, Lisa was running back and forth between Donald and Irene, panting furiously, as if in complete confusion."

"That poor dog," said Annie, shaking her head.

"Of course," Nick continued, "several days later the cops found her lying near Donald. She had a decent amount of dried blood matted on her fur. Evidently Donald and Lisa were pretty tight."

The foursome picked at their food, each with his or her private thoughts. Nick finally broke the hush with, "He was extremely smart. Haslett, that is. Anyone that can pull off a wizard act like he did has to be. And he fooled a national agency whose middle name is 'Intelligence.' Haslett is proof positive that brains are no indicator of morality."

The grim mood enveloping the table wasn't lifted until Amber raised her wine glass and offered a toast to "Montaigne and Wister...for vindicating my father, and for finally bringing peace to the souls of Aunt Irene and Uncle Don."

Nick then offered a toast to Vern for scooping the case, and especially his "timely interruption of the cocktail party in Room 117" the morning of April 15.

"The key figure in this entire case, though, is Xi Lao Bing. He was the connection, Amber, between your father

and your aunt. That's what got Vern and me up to
Springbrook. And he was also—sadly—the glue between
your uncle and Haslett. Had Bing not imbibed too much
one festive night in Harban, China, seven people might still
be alive, and we wouldn't be sitting here."

Montaigne then read aloud a thank-you card sent by
Dorothy Claunch. In it, she quoted Luke 11:9-13 and
testified that her "fervent prayers" had finally been
answered. To which Vern remarked, "It's a shame her
prayers couldn't have been answered without Roy Turlock
getting murdered."

They finished their meals—Amber insisting on picking
up the check—said goodbye to Enzo, and left Gilly's. But
not before Vern took Gilberto aside to apologize for being
too gruff with Enzo last time he was in the restaurant.

On the way to Annie's apartment, while Annie and a
newly contrite Nick exchanged double entendres and
anticipated an evening of soft jazz and intimacy, "Town
Without Pity" suddenly blasted from Nick's cell.

"Uh-oh," said Nick with exasperation. "It's Vern." He
answered the call.

"Hi Vern. What's up?"

"Hey Nick!" Vern practically yelled. "Guess what?"

"I'm waiting with bated breath, partner."

"Well, remember at the beginning of the investigation,
when I looked into NSA agent Frank Hardy? And we
kicked around the notion that Donald Moore might be in
the CIA? Well, I also contacted an old law enforcement
friend in Philadelphia. This Philly guy had a contact in the
State Department, and he told me he could try to contact an
anonymous State Department employee to see if he or she
could release any declassified information on Donald
Moore—only because Moore was long-deceased—as long
as I promised anonymity and dis...dis..."

"Discretion?"

"Yeah. Discretion. Well, this Philly friend just got back
to me with a declassified, one-page dossier on Moore. The

main part of the dossier is that...get this...while in Harban, China, Donald met after hours with four known CIA operatives on numerous occasions! But all of them are long-deceased—just like Moore!"

"Okay, Vern. But we solved the crimes. The killer was Haslett. This stuff is interesting, strong evidence of a CIA connection for Moore, but meaningless now...Does this dossier indicate confirmation of CIA activity by Donald Moore? Anything that says 'confirmed' or 'unconfirmed' or 'negative'?"

"Well, there's a line at the very bottom of my anonymous friend's anonymous report, which he got secondhand from an anonymous source. In capital letters it says 'STATUS RESOLUTION,' and there's a colon after it."

"So…what comes after the colon?"

"I don't know. It looks like there's a word or words that might confirm something. But...unfortunately...they're blacked out. *Redacted*. Guess we'll never know, huh?"

Annie covered her face with the palm of her hand and shook her head. Nick inhaled deeply and gripped the steering wheel tightly with both hands while his foot involuntarily pushed harder on the gas pedal.

"Goodnight, Vern."

"Yeah, goodnight Nick. Goodnight Annie...oh, wait! One other thing...it came to me just recently...she wasn't a cockapoo *or* a cavapoo. *Lisa*, that is. The dog. I remember what Beryl called her. She was a cross between a poodle and a beagle: a *poogle*!" He chuckled. "Whaddaya think of that, huh, Nick? A *poogle*! What'll they come up with next. Nick? Nick? You still there?"

Finis